GREEN HARVEST

PAMELA OLDFIELD

C

CENTURY PUBLISHING
LONDON

First published in Great Britain in 1983 by
Century Hutchinson Ltd,
Brookmount House, 62–65 Chandos Place, Covent Garden,
London WC2N 4NW

Reprinted 1984
Reprinted 1985

ISBN 0 7126 0077 9

Printed in Great Britain by
Redwood Burn Limited
Trowbridge, Wiltshire

For my Mother and Father

CHAPTER ONE

Vinnie sat under the table with her back against the wall, her short bare legs thrust out in front of her and a small grimy forefinger pressed into each ear. In this way she could block out the sound of her father's mumbling and her mother's shrill reproaches while still observing the phenomenon of passing feet below the red fringe of the tablecloth: her mother's ill-shod feet darting angrily, occasionally landing a blow on her father's defenceless ankles. Vinnie knew he must be drunk or her mother would never have got the better of him. Pa was a big man and dangerous. He had huge meaty fists and cruel fingers with a grip of iron and he wore a broad leather belt which Vinnie had often felt across her back when a particular misdemeanour had inspired him to retaliation. She watched impassively as the knee-high drama continued to unfold, for it was all very familiar. Fights and quarrels were part of the fabric of everyday life and she accepted them with no more than a bemused wonder. Bertie had removed baby Em to the comparative safety of the next room but she knew he would return promptly to try to bring about an end to the hostilities. Bertie, her beloved brother, was eleven. Em was nearly two and sickly. Vinnie was just five. The year was 1887 and the place a dilapidated room in the poorest part of Whitechapel.

Tentatively Vinnie relaxed the pressure on her fingers, allowing a little sound to enter. There was a crash as her father fell against a nearby chair which jerked backwards and disappeared from her sight. She leaned forward and lifted a corner of the tablecloth and was relieved to see that Bertie had returned.

Green Harvest

'Give over, Ma! He's 'ad enough. He 'as, I tell you. Give it a rest, Ma.'

His voice was pleading. Vinnie had no need to see the expression on his face – she could imagine the frightened grey eyes and nervous twitching mouth. Bertie was not strong; he coughed a lot and they said his cheeks burned too brightly. They said too that he was chesty like his grandmother, God rest her soul, for she had gone in her prime and he would go likewise. Vinnie did not want him to go.

'You keep out of it, Bertie, if you know what's good for you.' Her mother's voice was high-pitched with a practised fury born of long and bitter experience. '*I'll* say when he's had enough, the idle, useless sod.'

The last three words were accompanied by three dull thuds and suddenly there was her father, reduced to her level, sprawled across the linoleum, ungainly and horrible. The unshaven, bloated face was only a yard away from the table under which she sheltered and quickly Vinnie tucked her legs under her for fear the heavy-lidded eyes should open and discover her. Her father's breath came thick and rasping and Vinnie hated the sound. She also hated the prostrate figure who shared their home, for he had never shown her a moment's kindness and his presence was always the signal for a disruption of their normal existence. Sometimes he stayed away for days at a time and Vinnie enjoyed his absence. Then, as now, he would return, drunk and penniless, the housekeeping squandered on drink and betting.

'*He's* had enough!' screeched his wife in answer to Bertie's renewed pleas. 'Well, that's as bloody maybe, but what about me? *I've* had enough, I can tell you! More than enough of the lazy, stupid lout and I swear I won't put up with another day of his rotten, no-good ways. I'm sick to death of him coming home, reeking of beer and God-knows-what-else! Sick of it, I tell you, Bertie, so don't you go taking his side against me. D'you hear?'

She landed another kick in the middle of her husband's back and he groaned and rolled over, covering his head with his hands as she knelt to pummel him with flailing fists. Vinnie caught a glimpse of her mother's grim white face and hastily closed her eyes. Her father's cruelty was bearable – her mother's vengeful passion was not. Vinnie's fingers went back into her ears, she closed her eyes and was thus removed from the rest of the fight, sitting there oblivious until at last Bertie reached in and tugged her hands away. She had lost track of time and did not know how long she had sat there, but her arms and legs were stiff and he had to pull her out into what remained of the daylight.

'It's all over and done with,' he told her with a pretended cheerfulness. 'Pa's gone and Ma's next door with old Mrs Batty. It's all over.'

Vinnie surveyed the room cautiously and saw that the damage was worse than usual. The chair had been broken and lay in one corner. Nothing remained on the mantelpiece. The clock was face down in the coal bucket and the two blue vases were scattered in pieces across the floor. There was a pane missing from the lower half of the dirty window. Bertie, following her gaze, grinned.

'I can soon fix that,' he told her, 'and the chair, too. And we didn't like the vases, did we?'

'No,' Vinnie agreed dutifully. 'Where's Em?'

'Ma's taken her round next door. She'll be back.'

'Where's Pa?'

He shrugged and Vinnie thought he avoided her eyes. 'Don't know and don't care,' he said. 'Good riddance, like Ma says.'

Vinnie continued to inspect the room, reassessing the extent of the disorder in the light of Bertie's remark about her father's disappearance. Usually he slept off his drinking sessions, snoring loudly from the depths of the sagging mattress at the far end of the shared bedroom. Vinnie would creep over and watch him as he slept, her face pressed against the brass rails of the bed which her mother cleaned so lovingly. The brass bedstead was her mother's pride and joy, making her a cut above the neighbours who mostly slept on mattresses on the floor, and was shown off to visitors as proudly as any family heirloom. Vinnie frowned as she allowed Bertie to lead her to the table. If her father was not snoring off his drink – if indeed he was not anywhere to be seen – then where was he?

'Where's Pa gone?' she asked again.

Again Bertie averted his gaze. 'I told you, he's gone and he's not coming back and that's all there is to it. So give over asking. Now, d'you want a bit of toast and dripping? Or jam?'

Vinnie's frown lifted as she nodded her head.

'Which then, doll?'

A faint smile touched the corners of Vinnie's small rosebud mouth. She liked it when Bertie called her 'doll' although she did not know why.

'Jam,' she whispered.

She sat at the table and swung her legs, wondering about the jam – it was a luxury only offered in time of trouble. When she had recovered from the whooping-cough there was jam – and when Bertie had fallen down the stairs. Now her father was not snoring in the next room and Bertie was offering jam. If she chose dripping, perhaps her father would come back. She hesitated, struggling with the immensity of the problem while she watched her brother cut the bread – a thick slice which he pushed on to the toasting fork after poking up the fire.

'Here, you do it,' he told her.

As she slid to the floor, footsteps clattered on the bare stairs – the man in the flat upstairs was late for work. She heard him slam the street door and the fat woman downstairs screaming after him in her thick foreign accent. Vinnie toasted the bread, grateful for the fire's comforting warmth, while Bertie righted the broken chair and propped it against the wall. He swept the broken vases into a dustpan and retrieved the clock. Holding it to his ear he nodded, pleased, and replaced it on the mantelpiece.

'I don't want Pa to be gone away,' said Vinnie, her lips trembling slightly. 'Why is he?'

'Because he is, that's all. And you *do* want him to be gone, Vinnie. We all do. Ma says he's no good and we don't want him here. So don't you go saying nothing to upset Ma, d'you hear me? Vinnie? D'you hear what I say?'

She nodded. Smoke began to rise from the toast.

'Watch it!'

He snatched the toasting fork from her and turned the bread, ignoring its blackness. Bread was never thrown away. He glanced at Vinnie and saw the downcast droop of her mouth.

'It'll scrape,' he told her.

Vinnie nodded wordlessly, feeling strangely bereft. How would it be without Pa, she wondered, a knot of anxiety forming somewhere inside her. Already the room looked big and empty without the prospect of his return. Her gaze wandered from the small table still laid with the morning's unwashed crockery to the washing draped along a string which reached from the window to the picture rail. The big armchair with its faded covers dared her to sit in it and the newspapers stuffed behind its cushions belonged to Pa. The grey cloth cap that hung behind the door was his, too. How odd that he was walking the streets without it.

Bertie saw her eyes resting on it and said quickly, 'He didn't want it. He's going to buy another one.'

'Is he?'

He rescued the toast and spread it with raspberry jam. Vinnie watched him with a deepening feeling of guilt: if only she had chosen the dripping perhaps everything would be the same as it was. But she loved jam and now it was too late and everything was going to be different. She accepted the toast and bit into it hungrily. It was warm and sweet and crisp, but hard to swallow because of a certain tightness in her throat. Her father had gone away and each delicious mouthful was an unspoken reproach.

*

Next door Mrs Batty regarded the stranger on her doorstep with suspicion.

'What d'you mean, you're the agent?' she demanded. 'Fred Lees is agent and 'as been for the last six years.'

'Fred Lees is in bed with his leg broke and I'm taking his place.' The man had small ugly eyes like a rat, she decided, and he smelt of stale pee.

'Hmm,' she hesitated. 'Did Fred Lees send you to me?'

'Nope. Colonel Lawrence did. Is that good enough for you?' She wavered visibly. Colonel Lawrence owned Foxearth Farm and half Teesbury with it.

'Prove it,' she said, just to let him know she was not a woman to be easily fooled by any stranger who chanced to knock on her door.

'I've a letter of authorisation—' he began but she raised her eyebrows, mocking him.

'Ooh, a letter of authorisation!'

He scowled. He had a long nose, and thin lips. 'Either you let me in or you come off the list,' he said sourly.

'Suit yourself. It's no skin off my nose.'

With an exaggerated sigh, Mrs Batty held open the door and led the new agent inside.

'Sit yourself down,' she said, 'and make it quick. My old man'll be home in half an hour, wanting his dinner. What d'you say your name is?'

'Harry Samm, and this year you have to have a letter.'

'A letter? What letter?' she cried indignantly. 'I'm on the list and 'ave been for years. I'm a regular. You can ask anyone. No one said nothing to me about a letter and I'm not writing no letter, so—'

He shook his head. '*You* don't have to write it,' he said. 'I'll fill it in for you.'

'You'd better, else it won't get filled in. Letter indeed! Bloody sauce! If they think we've got time to go filling in letters they've got another think coming!'

He had taken a folder from the satchel over his shoulder and from this he drew a slip of paper. Mrs Batty settled herself on a chair on the other side of the table and folded her arms impassively as he took out a stubby pencil and licked it.

'Now,' he began, 'I will take all your particulars and give you a letter. When the hops are ready you'll be sent a card giving the date they want you to arrive and—'

'I know the date,' she interrupted. 'I always go down on the last Saturday of August. Always the last Saturday.'

'Ah, but they're not always ready, are they?' he said triumphantly. 'They weren't ready last year. Apparently you

were all down there four days too early with nothing to do but
make pests of yourselves. These letters are—'

'Who said we was too early? Who said we was pests?'

'Colonel Lawrence said it. Now this card will tell you the
correct day to go down, the correct time of the train, the
correct station – everything. See?' He held it out for her
inspection but, a poor reader, she regarded it dubiously.

'We've never had to have no letter or card before,' she said.
'And I don't reckon to need one now. Bloomin' fuss and
palaver. Am I supposed to sign it or something?'

'No, no. I do that.'

He spoke wearily. He was finding the same objections at
every house and in a way he sympathised. They were mostly
experienced pickers who were set in their ways. Carefully he
explained the new system: the picker's name would go on the
list, be given a number and guaranteed a bin to pick into when
they reached the hop garden. The same number would apply
to all who picked into the same bin – friends, relatives and
children. They would remain in London until they received
the card telling them how and when to travel; the letter must be
produced on arrival at the farm.

Mrs Batty resented the innovations on principle, as she
instinctively resented all changes. She considered life difficult
enough without complicating it further, but she had to admit
to herself that there was some sense in the new arrangements
and it would be pleasant to have the travel organised by
someone else – *if* it could be done properly. Her own
experience of life suggested that if she wanted a job done
properly she must do it herself. However, she was prepared to
give the new method a fair trial and listened attentively, giving
an occasional nod of her huge head so that her chins wobbled.
Finally Harry Samm put a tick against her name on his
list.

'There's your number on my list,' he said. 'One-three-three
– and there's the same number on this letter. Don't lose it. We'll
send the card when the hops are ready and you all come down
then and not before. Understood? Now, how many of you this
year? Will one bin do you?'

She nodded. 'We're seven this year,' she said, 'because next door are coming. That's her and the three kids, me, my old man and my sister, Hetty Bluett. Next door, that's Mrs Harris, Bertie, Vinnie and Em. Em's only a tot, so don't count her. Well, write it down, then.'

He wrote. 'And the other kids?' he asked. 'How old are they?'

'Bertie's eleven, the girl's five.'

'Five?'

'She can pick,' said Mrs Batty grimly. 'She'll have to an' all. Father's done a bunk at last, I could see it coming a mile off – they're scratching around for every last penny, God help 'em. Not that he was much good when he *was* around. Spent it as fast as he made it. She's better off without that drunken layabout – worse than mine, he was, and that's saying something. Have you got all those names? Bertie, Vinnie, Mrs Harris – Susan Harris, if you want to be particular. Me, my husband—'

He nodded. 'Yes, yes. I've got you all down. And you'll probably leave London Bridge at two o'clock in the morning—'

'What? Two in the morning?'

'Special train,' he said. 'The Colonel's hoping to book a special train.'

'Oh, is he? What's so special about it? Square wheels or something?'

He shrugged. 'Don't ask me, I'm only the agent,' he said. 'You'll be met as usual.'

She gave a short laugh. 'Met? What, at four o'clock in the morning? Who are you kidding, Mr Samm?'

'Look, don't blame me, lady. If they say you'll be met, you'll be met. I'm not responsible for that side of it. List, letters and cards. That's my job. Now, any more questions?'

'Yes. What's the rate?'

'To be negotiated as usual.' He stood up quickly and began to put away his folder.

'Here, where's my letter?' she demanded.

'Here you are. And like I told you, a card will be sent to you when the hops are ready and you're *not* to come down before.

I'm to impress that on you all. You and the lot next door are all on the one letter. So's that all O.K.?'

'No, it's not O.K. Two o'clock in the perishing morning!'

He shrugged. 'Well, if you don't come, you don't pick and if you don't pick, you get no money. Please yourself. There's plenty willing to take your bin.'

Mrs Batty tightened her lips, biting back an angry retort. Without the month in the hop-gardens they would never survive the winter. Grudgingly she followed him to the door.

'We'll be there,' she said, 'so don't come the Smart Alec with me. But you tell the Colonel from me to get his barn roof mended. Three years now he's promised us and three years he's let us down. It's no joke in weather like today. You ever try sleeping on wet straw? *He* wants to try it! Tell him that from me.'

'Tell him yourself, lady. I want to keep my job. Now, where's George Street from here?'

She followed him to the front door. 'George Street? Oh, that'll be the Walkers and the Smiths. Turn right at the end of the road, then right again.'

'Thanks.'

She watched him hurry away, his collar turned up, his head unprotected against the driving rain.

'Letter, my foot,' she muttered, then catching sight of her husband approaching at an unsteady run, she slammed the door and flew indoors to start preparing the meal.

*

Vinnie watched as the clock was wrapped in a sheet of newspaper and put into the tea-chest. There were no vases to pack, for they had been broken during the fight. In fact it had all happened only a week ago but to Vinnie it seemed for ever – so many hushed remarks, strange false smiles and half-truths. They were moving, she knew that much, but one day it was to go hopping, the next they were going next door to share with Mrs Batty. Vinnie was confused. She had tried to learn something from her mother's expression, but the mouth was set in a hard line and the grey eyes were dark with unexpressed

suffering. Even her voice was different: sometimes sharp with
a hint of bitterness, at other times slower with a resignation
born of despair.

Next to Vinnie, Em began to cry and Vinnie put out a hand
and rocked the crib to soothe her. Her mother looked up.

'Pet her a bit, Vinnie. I can't do with that bawling, it's going
right through my head. Bertie, get the knives and forks and
wrap them all together in the towel. Then empty the dresser
drawers. The stuff can all go in the old shopping basket. All the
bills can go in the fire – I've nothing to pay them with – and
then the saucepans and the kettle . . . I said pet her a bit, Vinnie.
Lift her out. My head's aching fit to burst.'

'Lift her out?' said Vinnie reluctantly.

'Why not? Anything to stop her hollering. I expect she's
hungry. Bertie, finish what you're doing, then go and find the
milkman. Take sixpence. Get a pennorth of skimmed and then
run round to Percy's for some bacon bits.'

'And some cracked eggs?' said Bertie hopefully.

'If you like. It's my last sixpence. When it's gone, it's gone
and we'll starve then and not before.'

'Not with the hopping,' said Bertie, with one of his cheerful
smiles.

'Maybe.'

'And I'll get a job when we come back.'

'When we come back?' she sighed. 'We may not be coming
back. It'll be a bit hot for us here then. I don't know, I just don't
know. I'll see.'

Bertie smiled at Vinnie to dispel any uneasiness inspired by
these cryptic remarks. She had lifted the baby out and now sat
on the floor joggling Em on her knees, reciting "Ride-a-cock-
horse". She seemed absorbed in the baby and Bertie hoped she
had not registered his mother's doleful comments. He glanced
round the half-bare room. The chairs, table and beds had
already gone next door under cover of darkness. Now only the
smaller items remained to be packed, then they too would be
stowed away out of sight in Mrs Batty's cellar. He wished that
he were older than eleven – or at least looked older. He was not
big for his age and he would fool nobody if he applied for a job

pretending to be twelve. For a few moments he allowed himself the luxury of imagining that his father returned, sober and in funds. They would all move into a nicer neighbourhood where they would all wear new shoes and spread butter on their bread.

'Hey, Em!' he called, irritated by the child's persistent wail. 'Give it a rest, can't you?'

'She won't stop,' said Vinnie. 'She doesn't want to go hopping. That's why she's crying.'

Bertie grinned. 'Oh, *Em* doesn't want to go?'

'No, she doesn't.'

Her mother looked up and wiped her face with the back of her hand. 'Well, that makes two of us,' she said. ''Cos I'm damned if I do, but beggars can't be choosers and we're going, like it or not.'

At this Vinnie scowled and stopped joggling Em, who cried louder than ever.

'It's O.K.,' said Bertie. 'I told you, Vinnie, it's like picking flowers, that's all. Picking flowers in a garden. You pick lots and lots of little green flowers and this man pays you. He might give you a penny. You'd like a penny, wouldn't you?' She nodded.

'Well, there you are, then. You'll like it. All out in the fresh air and everything, with lots of other children to play with. It'll be just like a holiday. Cross my heart, Vinnie, and hope to die.'

He finished his share of the packing and stood up, his hand outstretched for the sixpence for the shopping.

Was it really the last one, he wondered, as he set off along the cobbled street swinging the old canvas bag round his head to the hazard of passers-by. If so, it was to be hoped the hopping card would soon come. Mrs Batty was a good friend but she had little enough herself and certainly nothing to spare for unfortunate neighbours. He sighed. Tomorrow was rent day and he tried to imagine how it would be when Charlie, the rent man, found the flat empty, two weeks' rent unpaid and the gas bill due. He would doubtless make enquiries of the other tenants, but they would pretend ignorance. Mrs Batty would hide the Harrises in her cellar until the danger was past and then hopefully from there they would escape into the country.

The milkman was nowhere to be seen, so he bought a tin of milk from Mr Percy. The old man put five cracked eggs into the tin bowl.

'Now hold it steady or you'll lose the lot,' he warned. Bertie nodded and, while the old man gathered up the scraps of bacon from the slicing machine, told him about the hop-picking.

'Hopping, eh? Ah well, no doubt you'll come back a millionaire,' laughed the old man. 'And be too stuck-up to speak to the likes of me. Forget all your old friends then, will you?'

Bertie assured him earnestly that he would never do that.

'A bad business,' went on Mr Percy, 'your old man going off like that. Not that it surprised me. Oh dear me, no! Never did think he was a stayer, that one. I remember when your Ma wed him. I thought then, it won't last. A gambling man don't change his spots, you see. He might want to but he can't. Gets in the blood somehow and can't be got rid of nohow. Pity, though. Your Ma could have made something of Stan Harris if it wasn't for the gambling. And he had a good heart, you know that? You remember that, young Bertie. Your Pa had his faults but he wasn't all bad. No one is, see? So remember him kindly and just don't go following in his tracks. A good man gone to ruin, is Stan Harris. More's the pity.' Sighing deeply, he wrapped the scraps in a twist of newspaper, then looked down at Bertie and ruffled the boy's dark hair. Impulsively he snatched up an end of cheese.

'Here, take that to your Ma with my regards,' he said. 'Nice bit of cheddar, that. Nice and strong. Call it fivepence all told.'

Bertie thanked him and hesitated. Now he had a penny left. Was it worth taking home the penny or should he spend it?

'Have you any stale buns?' he asked.

Mr Percy produced three doughnuts. 'That's all I've got left,' he said. 'You'll have to give your Em a bit of yourn. Now 'op it before I change me mind.'

Bertie thanked him and hurried off, feeling very proud of his purchases. Even Stan Harris could have done no better, he told himself. He would never, he vowed, follow in his father's bad tracks. He felt like a provider and it was a good feeling.

*

It was just after three o'clock the following afternoon when Charlie, the rent man, was spied making his way up the street. Over his shoulders he carried the large leather bag with the brass lock into which he put the various rent monies for safe keeping. He was not a popular man by the very nature of his work. He wore the dark suiting and black bowler hat considered suitable for a man of his profession and was sparing with his words, preferring to conduct his transactions with nods or shakes of the head and an out-thrust hand. It was claimed that he kept his mouth shut because he was ashamed of his tongue, which was black from years of boot-licking. Whatever the reason, he was forced to abandon his reticence when he discovered No. 71 empty. The Harrises, hidden in the cellar below No. 73, heard his usual peremptory three knocks and regarded each other nervously. Mrs Harris put a warning finger to her lips and prayed that the baby would not wake and cry out. A second rapping followed, and Bertie put an arm round Vinnie who sat on top of the tea-chest and peered at him through the gloom. Upstairs Mrs Batty went into action. She went out and down the steps, her large body wobbling on large legs. Her husband used to say it would take a 'helluva'n elephant to push *her* over'. The rent collector turned to her enquiringly.

'You'll get no answer from them,' she told him. 'I reckon they've scarpered. Not a peep out of them all day and no sign of the kiddies.' He tutted and stepped back onto the cobbles so that he could look up at the windows.

'No curtains, see?' said Mrs Batty helpfully. 'Of course, they could 'ave took 'em down to wash but they're not hanging out the back. I had a look special, just to see. My old man reckons he heard a few bumps in the night, but thought nothing of it.'

'The husband,' said Charlie. 'Any idea where he works? Local, is he?'

'*Was* he, you mean. Left last week and not been back since. Poor soul, his wife I mean. Three kids to bring up and a disappearing husband. I thought she'd be the next to go. Give 'em a week or two, I told my old man, until the money runs out. Then they'll be off. And I was right.'

She leaned back against the iron railing beside the steps, folded her arms and smiled triumphantly.

'What about the kids?' he said. 'Where'd they go to school?'

She shrugged. 'Search me. I suppose they must've gone somewhere but she wasn't the chatty type, you see. Never said much and I never asked. Not my business, was it?'

Charlie looked at her, then turned to gaze up at the flat above the Harrises. 'Evans still there, I take it?'

'Oh yes, but gone out an hour since. Probably forgot you was calling. Very odd couple, them Evanses. Bit doolally, if you ask me.'

Charlie went back up the steps and raised the rusty knocker once more. Receiving no answer, he took a small notebook from his jacket pocket and wrote carefully in it with a stub of pencil. Then he returned notebook and pencil to his pocket and came round to No. 73. Without a word he held out his hand and Mrs Batty fished in her apron pocket for the money. She slapped it into his hand and he dropped it into his bag.

'I'd better have a look from the back of the house,' he said. 'I'll come through yours if I may.'

She feigned ignorance of his meaning. 'Come through my place?' she repeated, playing for time.

'Just to have a look at the back yard; they might be hiding out there. You've no objection?'

She shrugged. 'Not if you wipe your boots,' she said. 'I don't want all that road muck walked in over my lino. Wiped it over just an hour ago.'

He wiped his shoes on the threadbare mat and followed her through the living-room and scullery into the small shared yard at the rear of the house. From there he tried the back door of No. 71 and then, shading his eyes, searched the upper windows for signs of life. Finally he looked into the small shed which housed seat and bucket, then shrugged.

'I'll be back,' he said and made his way back through the house.

'Going to report it, are you?' asked Mrs Batty conversationally, but he merely nodded.

She waited until he went up the steps to No. 75, then closed her front door. Down in the cellar the Harrises breathed sighs of relief. They were safe.

'If only that dratted card would come!' said Mrs Batty and as though in answer to her plea, it arrived the very next morning to the accompaniment of loud cheers.

Bertie hugged Vinnie excitedly, swinging her round so that she squealed and her short legs swung out.

'We're off to the country!' he told her and some of his excitement rubbed off on her. Her eyes gleamed and later that night she allowed herself a little smile.

The long promised adventure was about to begin.

CHAPTER TWO

The table was set for tea outside the French windows, above the stone steps leading down to the broad sweep of lawn. A white damask cloth was laid and the white bone china was edged with a narrow gold band. A bowl of late yellow roses formed the centre-piece and the silver cutlery glinted in the afternoon sunlight.

Four women were seated round the table. The hostess was Lady Christina Lawrence, the wife of Colonel Lawrence who owned Foxearth. Her fair hair was coiffed to perfection beneath her hat and her gown of coffee lace was the most fashionable that money could buy. Her beautiful face was unlined and her grey eyes tranquil below gently arching brows. On Christina's left was Agatha Braithwaite, then Esme Hart and on her right was her cousin, Louise Tarlton. A young maid was fussing with the silver tea-pot but Christina dismissed her with a wave of the hand and she gave a slight bob and scuttled away into the house.

'Poor little thing. She's painfully new,' said Christina. 'She is so nervous with guests that I think it is easier to pour the tea myself, otherwise we may well have it poured into our laps!' Her companions laughed easily as Christina began to fill the cups.

'Do please help yourselves. The sandwiches are cucumber or potted beef and there are biscuits and – oh, the fruit cake is missing. That girl is more flustered than I thought.' She seized a small bell and rang it. Almost immediately the maid reappeared and stood breathlessly before them. The four women regarded her humorously.

'There is something missing, Janet,' said Christina. 'You will forget your own head one of these days.'

The maid stared blankly at the table.

'The cake, cuckoo!'

'The cake? Oh, the cake, ma'am. I'm sorry, I must've left it on the trolley. I know I—'

'Well, it's not the end of the world. Just fetch it, please, Janet and next time check your trolley.'

'Yes, ma'am. I'm sorry, ma'am.'

The girl hurried off and Christina shrugged. 'She colours up at the slightest reprimand,' she said. 'I really don't know if she will prove satisfactory. We shall have to wait and see.'

'They're all the same these days,' said Agatha. 'I'm sure I have more problems with the staff than my mother ever did. I don't know why it should be so, but it is. Mmm, this beef is quite delicious, Chrissie.'

'I'm glad you like it. It's one of Cook's specialities. She would think the world had come to an end if no one commented on her potted beef. Ah, the cake! Thank you, Janet – and bring a jug of hot water in ten minutes' time.'

Janet nodded and once more withdrew.

For a moment the women enjoyed their sandwiches and watched Christina's two children playing with their hoops at the far end of the lawn. One was Julian, an attractive boy of nine with his mother's good looks and his father's intelligence. The other was Eva, only seven, the apple of the Colonel's eye. She was dark, like him, with heavy auburn hair and brown eyes.

'And where is Henry?' asked Louise. 'I thought you said he would join us for tea. It is such a long time since we last met, I have almost forgotten what he looks like!'

They all laughed.

'And Esme and I have *never* met him,' said Agatha. 'I wonder if perhaps we have frightened him away from his own tea-table, poor man. I suppose four females can be quite daunting.'

'*Not* to Henry,' said Christina. 'He loves to be surrounded by beauty – he says it makes him feel young again.'

'Oh, Chrissie!' said Esme. 'You make him sound like an old man.' Christina looked at her friend with amusement. 'Esme, Henry was born the same year as our gracious Queen! Oh, don't look so stricken. I had quite forgotten that you didn't know. I'm Henry's second wife; his first wife died in India, soon after they were married.'

'But he's *so* game!' cried Louise, in an attempt to lessen Esme's confusion. 'He looks years younger and he rides and shoots.'

'He is fairly fit,' said Christina. 'His avowed ambition is to outlive Queen Victoria.' She stood up suddenly, making the crockery rattle. 'Children!' she called. 'Don't go so near the lake with those hoops! Do you hear me? Eva! Julian!'

The two children glanced up at their mother and the boy waved an acknowledgement. They retrieved their hoops and made their way back across the lawn to the tea-table.

'Say "Hallo",' Christina prompted them.

'Hullo,' they choroused obediently.

'*We* didn't have fruit cake,' said Eva. 'We only had seed cake and I *hate* seed cake.'

'Children cannot always have what they want,' said Christina. 'Don't stare at the cake, Eva. You cannot will it to leave the plate and jump into your mouth. Ah, here comes your father. Now you two children run along and finish your game and Papa will see you later before you go to bed.'

They ignored her, however, and ran to the Colonel who was approaching from the side of the house. His hair was greying and he had a large moustache. He stooped slightly and leaned on an ivory-topped cane, but his dark eyes glinted humorously. Beside him was a stocky man in his early twenties, not handsome but pleasing in a rough way, with good teeth and curly brown hair.

'Papa, Papa! May we go to the hop-gardens? Just for an hour. Oh, please say yes, Papa. Just once more before the pickers come. Oh, please, Papa!'

Eva clung to her father and he patted her head affectionately.

'I dare say you can,' he began and they clapped their hands with delight. 'But I shall send what's-her-name – Janet – down for you in half an hour and you are to return with her – and none of your tricks. No hiding from her – you are to come straightway when she calls.'

They promised and darted away, leaving the hoops forgotten on the grass. Seeing them, Christina made as though to call the children back but the Colonel shook his head.

'Let them go, Chrissie,' he said. 'I'm glad to be free of their chatter. Ladies, ladies! How good to see you all!' They had risen and Christina began the introductions.

'You know cousin Louise, of course, Henry.'

Henry took her hand. 'Of course, I remember. You worked *so* diligently and for such a good cause.'

'And Esme Hart who is a friend of Louise – and Agatha Braithwaite, Esme's friend.'

'Esme – what a charming name, it has always been one of my favourites. And no-nonsense Agatha – my grandmother's name! Well, I'm knocked all of a heap. Such an array of beauties and all come to pick in our gardens.'

Henry turned to his companion. 'This is Bryce – Tom Bryce, our chief pole-puller. What d'you say, eh Tom lad? Three pretty ladies come to cheer you through the next four weeks, eh?'

They all laughed and Bryce winked. 'I'll be hard put to keep me mind on me work!' he said.

'But you'll try, eh, Tom?' He nodded.

'I call them our charity ladies,' the Colonel went on, taking a cucumber sandwich. 'Have a sandwich, Bryce. They're very good – and so they should be. We grow our own cucumbers. It's the only way to get a decent cucumber. No flavour, you know, some of them.'

Bryce shook his head. 'My mother'll kill me if I don't go home with a big appetite,' he told them. 'I'd best save myself, but thanks for the offer.'

'Just a biscuit then, eh, and not a word to the mater! Our cook makes jolly good biscuits—'

'Henry, dear, please don't embarrass Mr Bryce,' said Christina. 'I don't think he wants to join us. I expect he's got more important things to do.'

The young man smiled at her. 'I have, ma'am, that's so. But I'll see you three ladies in the morning. We start at six o'clock, mind, so don't be late.'

Saying this he smiled broadly as they all feigned horror at the prospect of such an early start.

'*Six?*' cried Agatha. 'Is there such an hour?'

'He's teasing you, my dear,' said the Colonel. 'Tell them the truth, Bryce.'

'Well, then, 'tis eight o'clock first morning picking. That's when the rules are read and bins allotted, tally numbers given—'

Louise smiled at the dismay on her friends' faces. 'Take no notice of him,' she urged. 'He's trying to frighten you. Believe me, there's nothing to it. By the middle of the morning you'll be old hands with half a bin of hops to your credit. Mr Bryce forgets I was here last year.'

Bryce laughed. 'Oh, I remember you,' he said. 'Picked for the Church Mission in Africa. What is it this year?'

'The Decayed Gentlewomen.'

'Oh aye?'

'Don't look like that,' Esme protested earnestly. 'You make mock, but there are many poor souls fallen on hard times who—'

'Did I make mock?' he laughed, appealing to the Colonel. 'I never said a word. Not a single word!'

Esme looked at him with a provocative glint in her eye. 'You said "Oh aye" in a certain way,' she countered. 'It was not what you said but the way you said it!'

The Colonel held up a hand placatingly. 'Bryce, you'd best go home to your mother's cooking, for you'll not beat these young ladies. They've got an answer for everything; a mere man doesn't stand a chance.'

'I'll do that then, sir.' His keen eyes swept briefly over the four women. 'I'll see you three ladies tomorrow at eight o'clock sharp for the reading of the rules.'

'And very boring they are, too,' said Louise.

The Colonel wagged a forefinger at her. 'But it's required, you see, my dear. If it's required that the rules must be read, then poor old Bryce will have to read 'em – what's in these? Chicken?'

'Potted beef, dear, and do sit down, Henry, if you are joining us for tea.'

He sat down obediently and his wife gave Bryce a dismissive smile. 'They'll be there at eight,' she promised him and he took the opportunity to leave.

'Now, let me see,' Christina continued. 'Another cup of tea, Agatha? And you, Esme? Surely that girl should be back with the hot water. Ring the bell, will you, Louise, and do help yourself to more sandwiches or a biscuit. Henry, I thought we'd take a walk after tea, to show them the hop-garden and the oast-house. The gardens are really at their best this one day of the year. Once the pickers arrive it will be such a shambles, the place will be quite unrecognisable.'

The Colonel nodded. 'Chrissie is right, of course. Today is *the* day. Somehow the poor old hops have survived all the hazards – cold winds and rains and the damnable hop fleas, not to mention wireworms and the ruddy hop-fly. Nature red in tooth and claw, eh? Even in a hop-garden. Every living creature seems intent on its destruction. I hope you've brought plenty of gloves; the sulphur dust leaves a certain stickiness. Still, I expect Chrissie has put you wise to that, eh?'

'Don't worry, Henry,' said his wife. 'The girls are well prepared. Is everything ready now for the morning?'

Janet arrived with a fresh jug of hot water and was sent back to the kitchen for more sandwiches. The Colonel expounded on his favourite subject and Esme and Agatha listened with interest while Louise and Christina – to whom it was already very familiar – put their heads together quietly and talked of other matters.

After tea the Colonel retired to smoke a cigar in his study and Christina conducted her three friends on a tour of the gardens. She had not exaggerated when she described the hops as 'at their best'. The rich clusters of green cone-like flowers hung on the bines like grapes on a vine, a veritable forest of lush green vegetation towering up to a height of twelve feet. The hops were grown on Coley's system – a combination of upright and diagonal poles set in rows, so that the natural profusion of the plants was strangely at odds with the geometric patterns thus produced.

'You're looking at a rare sight,' Christina told them, as they stood admiring the scene. 'This is the last year we shall use this method. Poor Tom Bryce is quite distressed. Most of the farms are going over to wire work and Henry is determined to make the switch. He cannot bear to be thought old-fashioned.'

'What difference will it make?' Esme asked, surreptitiously trying to free her skirt from a persistent bramble.

'To the crop – not a lot, I think. To the work involved – quite a difference. Instead of training the plants solely along poles they'll go up the poles and then along overhead wires.' She shrugged. 'We must move with the times, I suppose. It's called progress.'

She led the way past a huge pile of brushwood faggots and pointed to it. 'One day's fuel for the pickers' fires!' she laughed. 'All that will be gone tomorrow night and we shall replace it daily. It's quite a sight when all the fires are going. We can watch it from the window – it's like a huge encampment.'

They paused at a gate and leaned over. A few ragged children ran forward and then stopped shyly, staring at the four women in their pastel dresses and elegant flower-trimmed hats. Christina waved to them and the children withdrew with whispers and giggles.

'Gipsies,' she explained. 'They always arrive a day or two early and settle in. They're good workers, the gipsies, they work whatever the weather and they pick very clean. Henry thinks very highly of them. You can just see their caravans,' she pointed across the field, 'tucked well back under the over-hanging trees.'

'Something smells good, too,' said Agatha and Louise caught Christina's eye and they laughed.

'Probably a poached rabbit!' said Louise, 'or even a chicken strayed too far from the safety of its coop! There was quite a furore last year, I recall, when chickens and ducks were disappearing.'

Christina shrugged. 'Poor Henry had to apologise to the farmer concerned and reimburse him. It really was beyond a joke. But these things are sent to try us – and they do! Here are some of the barns where the pickers will live – the large thatched one and the smaller tiled one behind it – and at the far end of the lane you can see the oast-house. There's smoke rising from it for the first time since September of last year. It's always quite an occasion when they light the fires.'

They stood silent, regarding the peaceful scene: the large barn with its tattered thatch and beyond it the conical tips of the oast-house. Around and beyond them, acre upon acre, they saw rows of tall poles festooned with leafy hops.

Christina reached up and pulled a single cone from the nearest plant. The others watched as she let it rest in her hand, then rolled it between her fingers and finally sniffed it delicately.

'I love the smell,' she said, her voice suddenly soft. Then she let it fall and sighed deeply. 'Well, tonight's the night,' she said. 'At two o'clock tomorrow morning the "Hoppers' Special" will leave London. At four or five they'll all spill out on to Wateringbury Station. The poor station-master will be at his wits' end wondering how to cope and chaos will reign for an hour or so until they all find their waggons. Then they'll descend on us!' She smiled wryly. 'When that happens these gardens will be transformed. It will become another world.'

*

In the early hours of the following morning all was exactly as Christina had predicted. From Lissom Grove, Islington, Lambeth, Battersea, Whitechapel, Stepney and many more the streets were dotted with groups of people making their way, mostly on foot, to the Bricklayers' Arms Goods Station. Some were unemployed, but many were currently in work and taking the month of September as their annual 'holiday'. They came from an assortment of trades – tailors, sweeps, dress-makers, shoemakers, washerwomen, charwomen – all converging slowly but surely upon the appointed station. Determined not to be left behind, hundreds arrived hours too early and the station was already packed to bursting point with people and baggage. Inevitably they overflowed into the street outside, but fortunately there was virtually no other traffic around at such an hour.

The hop-pickers were destined for many different stations along the newly extended railway which ran through the heart of the Kentish Weald. At these points their ways would diverge once again as they were met by various conveyances provided by the farmers, and literally carted away to their respective farms. For four weeks the mass of eager, industrious people would be thinly spread throughout the hop-gardens of Kent. Some in East Kent around Chartham and Canterbury and northwards to Faversham and Sittingbourne. Others further west in Maidstone, Tonbridge, even as far as Bromley and Bexley, which were still rural, and south again to Hawkhurst and Tenterden. At the end of the season the crowds would reconverge and be assimilated once more into the dense population of London's East End.

It was no mean task for the railway staff to hold back the impatient crowds and a sigh of relief went up when at last the train was seen drawing alongside the platform. The fare was just over two shillings, but babes-in-arms and baggage went free. The pickers carried mattresses, blankets, cooking-pots and – the fortunate few – a change of clothing. Sue Harris carried Em under one arm and under the other a blanket. A bag containing knives and forks, four tin plates and four mugs was slung over her shoulder. Bertie struggled with a rolled mattress from inside which Vinnie listened curiously to the muffled sounds of the outside world. The bottom of the rolled mattress was tied tightly with cord so that she could not slip out, but the top was fastened more loosely. She was not the only child who would thus be smuggled aboard the train; toddlers were carried in sacks and even paper parcels. It was a deception born of desperation, since money for train fares was a luxury which many could not afford. Some pickers would walk all the way from London to the remote Kent villages where they would be employed.

Bertie was worried in case Vinnie could not get enough air,

and kept glancing at her. 'Stop looking in at her!' his mother hissed. 'You'll have the guard after us, acting so suspicious. She'll live, don't you worry. You just get her on to the train, for I've no more money for another fare and if she stays here we all stay, unless you fancy a thirty-mile walk!'

The noise was tremendous as lost children screamed for their parents and tired children sobbed dispiritedly. The lively ones, revelling in the excitement, ran to and fro, getting under everybody's feet and were frequently cuffed and kicked. Arguments broke out as the impatient pickers grew in number and those at the back pressed forward, crushing others against the barriers. Occasionally a woman fainted and had to be hoisted above the heads of the crowd in search of air.

The event assumed nightmare proportions for the station officials, who were forced at last to open the barriers and allow the waiting crowd on to the train earlier than intended. The rush for places became a stampede in which Sue Harris was separated from Bertie, who in turn became separated from Mr and Mrs Batty. Somehow he tugged and pulled Vinnie in her mattress aboard the train and then leaned back, exhausted, against the bare wooden walls of the carriage.

'And do they dare to call this a train?' cried a man beside him. 'Why, it's more fit for cattle than decent folks. Look at it! No seats and the windows all boarded up. Disgusting, I call it, to charge two shillings to travel like blooming animals.'

His sentiments were echoed along the length of the train and for fifteen minutes or more the seething unrest made the platform a dangerous place to be for the harassed railway staff. Constables had been called in and three strolled self-consciously alongside the train, their truncheons in evidence.

Bertie peered down into the rolled mattress. 'Vinnie, are you all right in there?'

'I'm hot,' she whispered.

He could just make out her fair hair and poked a finger in through the string to scratch her head reassuringly. 'When the train starts I'll open it up a bit.'

'I want to come out now.'

'Not yet, Vinnie. I'll tell you when.'

'Are we nearly there?'

''Course not. We haven't started yet.'

He leaned back, his arms round the mattress, and an elderly woman next to him grinned toothlessly.

'What you got in there?' she asked.

'My sister, Vinnie.'

She let out a great cackle of laughter. ''Ere, he's got 'is sister rolled up in there. D'you hear that, Maud? His sister. And they never spotted it?' She roared again, finding the ploy hilarious; Bertie's colour deepened as more faces were turned towards him and the laughter grew.

'Poor little mite'll suffocate!'

'Let her out, mate. She won't get no air in there!'

'Not until the train starts,' said Bertie anxiously. His mother had given him strict orders.

'Oh, poor little cocker!'

'What a shame!'

'Poor devil. She'll die as like as not.'

'Open the top, son.'

'Undo the string.'

'But the guard – the ticket man—' began Bertie.

'We'll hide her. Don't you fret, lad. You do as the man says and undo the string else you won't have no little sister. Leastways, only a dead one.'

With a mixture of relief and reluctance, Bertie did as he was told and as the mattress sprang open Vinnie's tousled head appeared. She gasped for breath, her face almost purple and Bertie looked at her in dismay.

'Are you all right, Vinnie?'

Feebly she nodded her head. At that moment a uniformed figure squeezed his way into the carriage. Immediately ranks closed round Bertie and the mattress.

'Right, show your tickets, please. Hold 'em up where I can see them. Thank you . . . Thank you . . . Tickets everyone, please. No one travels without a ticket except babes-in-arms. Your ticket, please, sir.'

It seemed the unfortunate man did not have one. He began to

explain that the ticket office had been closed when he applied but the official remained unimpressed.

'Two shillings and four pence, then, if you please, sir.' It also seemed that the man had no change about him.

'I'm sorry, sir. I'll have to ask you to step down from the train . . .'

Bertie pushed Vinnie back into the dark depths of the mattress as the unfortunate man was hauled protesting from the carriage and the official resumed his search. He came nearer as Bertie struggled to retie the cord and complete Vinnie's concealment.

'What you got in there, son?'

Bertie looked up, blushing furiously. 'Nothing, sir. That is, blankets, sir. A blanket and a couple of saucepans.'

'Let me see. I'm not daft, you know, son. I may look it but I'm not.'

To Bertie's horror the ticket collector leaned forward, his fingers plucking at the hastily tied cord. Presented with his back, one of the other pickers snatched at one of the two buttons in the centre of the man's coat. Feeling the tug as button parted company with cloth, he jerked round accusingly.

'Oh dear!' said a voice. 'His button fell off! What a pity. Such a nice smart uniform!' There were a few sniggers. 'You should get your old woman to use stronger thread, mate.'

The man bent his arm to feel the back of his coat, cursing under his breath, but then turned back to Bertie and the matter of the rolled mattress. He opened his mouth to speak, but before he could do so the matching button was also tugged free and sailed out of the window.

'Oh dear!' cried the thief. 'There goes another one! You're not having much luck today, cocker. All those buttons falling off! Whatever will go next, I wonder?'

Furiously the official turned and began to remonstrate with his tormentors, demanding the return of his buttons. No one knew anything about it; they all regarded him with expressions of wide-eyed innocence.

A voice at the back cried waggishly, 'You want to watch out for your trousers, chum. They could be next to go!'

A great guffaw of laughter finally defeated the discomfited official. Obstreperous passengers he could cope with, but loss of personal dignity was another matter. Uttering futile threats of dire punishments for the offender if he was ever found, he backed out of the carriage as the whistle finally blew. The laughter gave way to cheers as the ramshackle train slowly gathered speed and the comforting rhythm of wheels on track carried the motley assortment of passengers away from the lights of London and out into the darkness of the unfamiliar countryside.

*

It took time for the hoppers to settle down and make themselves comfortable. However, as soon as this was done to their satisfaction they turned their attention to providing some form of amusement with which to while away the following uncomfortable hours. Some were fortunate enough to have met up with friends from previous years and they now proceeded to regale each other with news of the past year's events. Among others, new friendships were struck and confidences exchanged. In fact it was difficult to remain aloof when pressed closely together in the cramped confines of the 'Hoppers' Special'. Isolated sing-songs developed throughout the length of the train and when the current popular songs had all been sung, the Londoners sang their way through the old ones:

When you've been a'hopping, a'hopping down in Kent,
You'll have lots of money and you'll be glad you went.

They sang loudly and with great enthusiasm, improvising from time to time to include the names and habits of many of the local people who had shared their hop-picking the year before. This caused great outbursts of hilarity and whatever else they did for the first hour, nobody slept.

Vinnie loved every moment of the journey. She revelled in the friendly atmosphere, knowing that Bertie would look after her whatever might befall them before the night was through. Outside the train was the new mysterious world of which she was only a little afraid. The new day would reveal everything, but for the moment she was content to share the feeling of comradeship and unity with her fellow travellers. From time to time Bertie gave her a hug and squeezed her hand in the darkness and she thought she had never been so happy or felt so safe.

Mrs Batty had packed a loaf of bread and a chunk of cheese to sustain them all but the Battys were in another part of the train. Vinnie and Bertie, like most of the passengers, had nothing to eat but were too excited to be aware of hunger. Vinnie was going to a beautiful garden to pick green flowers – Bertie had promised and Bertie did not lie to her. She closed her eyes. Soon she knew they would reach Wateringbury Station. Even the name had a magic sound and she murmured it to herself over and over again. Wateringbury Station meant the end of the old life and the beginning of the new. As the journey went on the pickers became less rowdy. The singing faltered until most of it died away altogether. In the far corner an old man snored and a baby cried fitfully until the movement of the carriage rocked it to sleep again. Vinnie drifted into a half-sleep . . . Wateringbury Station . . . Wateringbury Station . . .

There were several false alarms when the train stopped to put down pickers at other stations along the route, but at last they drew to a halt alongside the platform and heard the long-awaited name called by the porter: 'Wateringbury Station. All those for Manor Farm, Foxearth, Bridge Farm, Upper Hall. Make haste now, ladies and gentlemen, your transport is ready and waiting. All out for Wateringbury. Wateringbury Station – come along there, please.'

Once more Vinnie scrambled back into her mattress and the string was tied securely round the top. Willing hands helped lift her down to the platform and then Bertie was tugging her along towards the exit. He kept his eye open for any sign of his mother or the Battys but there was no one familiar among the crowd. The station-master had sadly under-estimated the number of hoppers arriving at the station and for a few moments all was pandemonium. Families searched for each other and pieces of baggage which had been lost in the mêlée were restored to their rightful owners. Only one porter had remained on duty to help collect the tickets and it was soon obvious that he would not be very successful. Pushing and elbowing their way along the platform, the hop-pickers' one aim was to find their waggon and be hastened through the dark countryside to their beds. Tickets were of little importance and they grew angry and impatient when required to find and surrender them.

However, the crowd on the platform finally thinned out and the retreating train disappeared, whistling eerily in the distance. Now the confusion moved into the station yard, where waggons and carts waited to collect the pickers. Here Bertie and Vinnie (freed once more) were reunited with Sue and Em and joined by the Battys. All the waggoners were shouting the names of their respective farms so that the pickers could identify them. The only lights came from a few hurricane lamps hastily strung from wires between two poles and these cast an unhealthy pallor over the sea of faces. At last the Harrises and the Battys were safely installed on an empty hay-cart and more and more pickers were being hoisted up to join them. An upturned basket on the ground by the rear of the waggon served as a step and stout ladies were pushed and heaved onto the hay-covered floor by the burly driver who was eager to deposit his charges and get off home for what was left of his night's sleep.

All the luggage went into another cart drawn by two horses. Altogether there were four carts goings to Foxearth, for the total pickers engaged numbered nearly a hundred. The cold air had roused the sleepy ones and everyone felt the damp September air keenly as they were drawn along under the overhanging trees towards the farm. Vinnie sat squeezed between Mrs Batty and her mother; her eyes were wide open and she missed nothing of the moonlit ride. Thirty-five minutes later they turned off the road and then pulled up outside a large shed where Tom Bryce waited for them. The pickers knew him of old and realised he was not to be trifled with. He carried a storm lantern and his manner was brisk as he addressed them.

'Right, I want you all down, gathered round me and quiet.

The sooner you hear what I have to say, the sooner you get to bed. It will be seven o'clock all too soon, so let's get you moving in an orderly way.' Obediently the pickers scrambled down again and gathered round him in the half-light. He told them where the other two barns were and then read out a list of names telling them to which barn they had been assigned. Inside the hut, he told them, they would find a space allotted to each family. There were to be no arguments tonight, any queries would be dealt with the following day. Those pickers who had left bedding the previous year would find it waiting for them. No fires must be lit until the following evening, but hot cocoa would be served to everybody within the next quarter of an hour and they should all have their mugs ready. He then wished them 'Good night', but he did not leave the scene. Experience had taught him that it was never wise to do that until the last family was bedded down for the night.

'Come on, you lot,' Mrs Batty urged them. 'Follow me, we're in the big barn.'

They followed her into a large barn with a lofty, raftered roof. Inside, a thick layer of clean hay covered the floor. The large area had been sub-divided by means of thatched hurdles and names on scraps of paper identified each space. Several oil-lamps hung from the overhead beams and by their light Mrs Batty found the area reserved for them. They had no furniture, not even a shelf on the wall; nothing but a few nails on which to hang their clothes.

'Best not to bother undressing,' Mrs Batty told them. 'Just roll out your mattress, cover yourselves with your blankets and get your heads down. If they look lively with that cocoa we'll all get a hot drink, but I shan't be awake long, I can tell you. There's work to be done tomorrow and we'll have to be up at seven o'clock. So make yourselves comfortable. You'll pick up all the little wrinkles tomorrow, you'll see. We'll have it snug and cosy by the end of the week and it'll be just like home.'

The Harrises took her advice. Shyly Vinnie stared round as her mother and Bertie unrolled the mattress and began to spread the blankets. The hurdles were only a few feet high and she could see a man in the next space pulling off his shirt. Everyone could see everyone else; she did not relish the idea of taking all her clothes off in front of strangers and was suddenly aware of the tattered nightdress she would put on. She felt a pang of disappointment, although she had never quite known what to expect. 'The privy?' she whispered to Bertie. 'Where's the privy?'

Mrs Batty, hearing her, laughed kindly. 'There's no luxuries like privies here, love,' she told her. 'Come on, Auntie Batty'll show you.'

She led Vinnie outside to a hedge behind the barn where several other people were making use of the scanty shelter provided by tall weeds and overgrown grasses. As they walked back into the barn Vinnie tugged at Mrs Batty's skirt.

'Was that the garden?' she asked.

'No, love, that's just an old bit of hedge. You'll see the gardens tomorrow. Lovely, they are.'

Reassured, Vinnie was soon snuggled under the blanket between her mother and Em. The Battys' mattress and theirs took up most of the space allotted to the two families. Vinnie stared up into the darkness where the lamps cast long shadows across the roof, but before she could decide whether or not she approved of her new home the cocoa arrived and they sat up again. It came in two large pails carried by a middle-aged woman they had not seen before.

'That's Tom's mother,' Mrs Batty told them. 'She's not a bad sort.' The mugs were dipped into the steaming sweet cocoa and one by one their stomachs were warmed and their minds comforted. 'Goodnights' were murmured all around them and the lights were finally extinguished.

'Good night Vinnie,' said Bertie in the darkness.

''Night Bertie,' she answered and within minutes was fast asleep.

CHAPTER THREE

The early morning mist lay heavy over the water and rose up the steep slopes of the river valley on either side. It was thin and wispy, moving gently in the slight breeze that would soon dispel it completely, exposing the rows of hops to the bright sunshine that already warmed the topmost rows which flanked the roads. These ran parallel to the railway, which in turn ran parallel to the river in the valley bottom. Along the former a goods train clanked its way into Wateringbury Station in a hiss of steam and shudder of brakes.

Clothing the valley, the hop-gardens themselves were bordered with trees – ash, heavy, with clusters of golden keys; a few chestnuts bristling with spiky green fruits; and here and there an elderberry, its slender branches heavy with dark purple berries. In the shadow of the trees a woody plant thrust tiny creamy white flowers into the sunlit air and last year's dead wood lay rotting beneath them like a felled forest in miniature. Brambles jostled for space, dotted with plenty of small red berries and just a few that were ripe and black.

Within this perimeter a broad track ran around the garden. Where the ground dipped the dry earth was embedded with small rocks and broken bricks, to give purchase to the wheels of the carts in wet weather. The mist clung damply to the bines, glistening on the fine short hairs which covered leaves and stem alike, so that both were rough to the touch. The bines clung to the tall poles as they had been trained to do, but here and there a long tendril hung freely, to catch at the hair and face of the unwary, or looped back on itself like a decorative garland. The alleys between the rows were already well trodden but a patchy carpet of thin green moss had somehow survived.

Later in the day the green rows would cast a welcome shade but now they stood silent and cold, while cascades of hops, like dainty green fir-cones, waited for the impatient fingers of the pickers to pluck them from their stems.

It was nearly half-past eight before the weary hop-pickers were finally assembled at the top end of the hop-garden where Tom Bryce waited to address them and make a formal beginning to the work about to commence. After awakening to bird-song and other rural sounds normally alien to them, the pickers had splashed cold water from the nearby stream over their faces and made a hasty breakfast of whatever remained of the food they had brought with them. Some had eaten and drunk nothing. Some had slept badly and were still only half-awake. A very few were still asleep; they would be roused in time by one of the children, sent by Tom Bryce, and would receive one of his cold looks and a sharp rebuke that would ensure it did not happen again. Colonel Lawrence's chief pole-puller had no time for malingerers and they knew that any picker whose work failed to satisfy him would not be on next year's list. There were always plenty of people waiting to replace them. Even now would-be pickers were arriving daily, having tramped all the way from London, only to be turned away at each farm where the quota was already filled. Eventually they might be lucky enough to find a farm where illness or accident left a shortage of pickers. If not, they would be forced to turn back and make their way home, begging or stealing money and food along the way and proving a very real problem to the authorities. Those fortunate enough to be in work knew all this and the majority appreciated their comparative good fortune and behaved accordingly.

'Right, now can you all hear me?' Bryce began from the vantage point of the upturned crate on which he stood. He surveyed the crowd before him: in front, the children – some local, some strangers to him; behind them were the pale-faced Londoners, mainly women of all ages with here and there a husband or father in tow. Most of the women wore hats to shade them from the sun, which even at that early hour promised to be hot later, and their arms were protected by long thick 'mittens'. The latter were made from the legs of old black stockings cut and stitched to shape and would protect their arms from the inevitable scratches. Coarse aprons covered their skirts. To the left a small group stood slightly apart and Tom Bryce recognised them by their defeated expressions. These were the inmates of the workhouses drawn from the surrounding area. Most of the money they earned would be taken to relieve their burden on the rates and even the youngest children were expected to work hard. If they were lucky they would be allowed to keep threepence each at the end of the month. The gipsies were easily recognised by their squat figures and brown weather-beaten faces. The young women were darkly attractive and colourfully dressed; many had babies slung across their backs or tucked into the shawls which crossed their chests and tied behind. The older women, shapeless and taciturn, watched the pole-puller from behind the wisps of smoke rising from the clay pipes clenched firmly between their teeth. They were good pickers, experienced and quick, who were not distracted by adverse weather or the rapidly changing moods of the rest of the hoppers.

Lastly, right at the back, Bryce recognised the local pickers and the three ladies he had met the previous day. Eyes fixed on him with respectful attention, their faces glowed under their fashionable hats and voluminous starched white aprons covered their pastel gowns. He smiled inwardly at their earnestness – their picking would be far slower than any of the others and they would retire frequently to the big house for periods of rest and refreshment. Whatever they earned would no doubt be doubled or trebled by well-intentioned husbands or friends and the 'decayed gentlefolk' would be eternally in their debt.

Tom Bryce raised his voice:

'If you can't hear me, put up your right hand.'

A few hands were lifted and the usual roar of laughter followed his one and only joke. Tom did not aim to be popular – he left that to Adam Forrest, his right-hand man whose natural good humour and ready wit made him a favourite with the pickers. Adam would jolly them along and would frequently dispel tensions or heal any rifts which threatened to disrupt the work.

'Right then, it's now getting on for nine and that's not good enough,' he began. 'So you all had a rough night – I'll grant you that. Mine wasn't that brilliant, but I was here at six and I've already pulled a pole for each bin so you can all make a start when I give you the off. So tomorrow I want you at work before the dew's off the hops. D'you follow? Right. Adam's got your bin numbers and he'll be along to read them out to you when I'm through. As usual, it's four bins to a set and there'll be no changing places once you've started. For the benefit of newcomers, your fingers'll soon blacken but it's not the plague; it's the sulphur we dust the bines with. Don't worry about it, it'll wash off or you can scrub the worst off with a handful of hop leaves.'

He paused and the crowd moved and shuffled impatiently. Now that they *were* ready to start they begrudged the money he was costing them.

'The tally will be fixed at a later date but won't drop below twopence a bushel. Tally man is Jim Everett.'

Here a cheer went up. Jim Everett was well over seventy and had been tally-man at Foxearth for at least thirty of those years. Every year they feared that the winter would see him off, for he was a small frail-looking man. However, he had been spared for another season and the hoppers were glad. Hopping would not be the same without him.

'Right then, now for the Rules.' A loud groan greeted this, but he ignored it and began to gabble at great speed so that to a newcomer it was largely unintelligible. 'You will be in the hop-garden at the appointed time and no one will leave the gardens during working hours without consent . . . all loose hops will be picked up from the ground . . . hops shall be picked free of leaves and branches. For every breach of regulations one bush of hops to be forfeit . . . The signal to start and finish shall be a gong and no hops to be picked during dinner time . . . No lucifer matches . . . No pickers allowed in adjoining orchards. Anyone found stealing fruit or otherwise to be prosecuted . . . Camp fires out by ten o'clock . . . No fighting. No liquor. No immoral language. D'you follow?'

Heads were nodded, then Adam Forrest appeared as if by magic and read out the names of pickers assigned to each bin. Finally Tom called, 'All to work' and within minutes the eager crowd had dispersed and the still, green rows came suddenly alive with movement, colour and sound.

*

Agatha regarded her dirty white gloves with distaste and Louise laughed at the expression on her face.

'I warned you,' she said. 'Hopping is not exactly a dainty occupation.'

'But will it wash out?' cried Agatha. 'I know he said it will come off bare hands but he didn't speak of gloves.'

'That's because no one else wears them.'

They had been picking for nearly an hour and a half, at their private bin. This was a large canvas container set on a rough wooden frame which projected upwards at each end to support the long hop pole which, covered in dense hops, had been laid across its length. The hop bine had twined itself round the wooden pole in a mass of leaves and flowers and these latter were picked off and dropped into the bin below. Only a thin layer covered the bottom as Esme stood up and stretched her arms.

'I'm cramped already!' she protested, laughing ruefully. 'However will we survive the day?'

'You will,' said Louise. 'It's in a good cause, remember.' There were other pickers in sight, but none near enough to overhear their desultory conversation and the three women felt delightfully secluded in their shady retreat. Christina had made a brief visit to see that they were happy and comfortably settled at their self-appointed task and then, satisfied, had left them to their own devices. While they picked, they whiled away the time in an exchange of confidences.

Esme glanced into the depths of the bin. 'We haven't picked

many,' she said. 'I wonder if that's a bushel yet. If so, we've earned twopence.'

It was Agatha's turn to laugh. 'Well, that's hardly going to transform someone's drab existence! Let's hope we speed up a little as the day goes on.'

'Oh, we will,' said Louise. 'It always seems painfully slow at the beginning. I was quite ashamed last season when the measurer came round. There were only the two of us – myself and Jessica Scafe. We thought we'd done rather well, but he just burst out laughing. Not unkindly – he just couldn't help it. Poor Jessica blushed scarlet – you know how she does. But by the end of the first week we had improved quite dramatically.'

Esme returned to her stool and began once more to pluck off the hops. She sat to one side with her two friends facing her.

'Do go on, Louise,' she said. 'You were telling us about Rupert.'

'Was I?' Louise pretended to have forgotten. She was engaged to be married and was easily tempted to talk at great length about her future husband.

'Of course you were!' said Agatha. 'You don't have to pretend. We're both positively green with envy and we love to hear about him.'

'What was I saying?'

'That you were trying to persuade his father to let him leave the Army and—'

'Not leave the Army, you goose!' Louise's trilling laugh rang out. 'To transfer to somewhere nearer home. Nearer to me. He's so lonesome without me, poor man.' Her eyes softened. 'His letters are full of how much he misses me. I suppose it's very flattering, really. It's less than thirty miles, yet he refers constantly to the abyss that separates us! The abyss! He's *so* funny. Goodness knows how he would fare if he were posted abroad. I confess I should die if he went so far away. He's rather keen to go to India, but only if I agree to go with him and I don't think I relish *that* notion! No, he doesn't want to leave the Army. All his family have been military men, you see. It's a matter of principle now, almost a question of family honour. His father would never forgive him. No, I said

I wondered if he could leave the Academy – that's the Royal Military Academy at Woolwich – and transfer to somewhere – Maidstone perhaps – and join the West Kents.'

Agatha stopped and straightened her back with a slight grimace. 'But he's a gunner, isn't he? Is it the same thing? I mean, can he still be a gunner if he changes his regiment?'

'I'm not too sure about the details, but I've written to his father. He's a dear old boy who absolutely worships me.' Louise giggled. 'Whenever I see him, he says, "Ah, here's the mother of my future grandchildren!" I've got a photograph of Rupert in my room up at the house. I'll show you if you like.'

Agatha and Esme agreed enthusiastically and she continued, 'He's wearing his uniform, although it was taken last year before he shaved off his sideburns. He's standing on the axle of his field-gun with the other members of the gun crew. I pray nightly they never have to fire it in earnest.' She laughed. 'It's a quite massive affair. The wheel itself is nearly as high as a man! You must all meet him sometime and tell me what you think of him. I must confess I think the uniform becomes him: the pill-box hat and neat little nipped-in tunic. Rupert thought the sideburns made him look older – he's *such* a baby face, poor dear – but I persuaded him to shave them off. Not the moustache, just the—'

She broke off suddenly as Tom Bryce appeared at the end of the row. He reached them and stood watching for a moment until they all became self-conscious under his scrutiny.

'What's the matter, Mr Bryce?' asked Agatha at last. 'Are we not picking to your satisfaction?'

'Or were you eavesdropping?' cried Esme. 'Hoping to overhear some items of juicy tittle-tattle.'

A grin spread across his face. 'Tittle-tattle doesn't interest me, however juicy it is. And no, I cannot fault your picking. I was just enjoying a sight for sore eyes: three pretty women around a hop-bin. I can't think of anything prettier. Are you enjoying yourselves?'

They assured him that they were, but were slightly disconcerted as he continued to gaze at them in turn, making no attempt to disguise his interest. As though sensing their discomfiture at his boldness, he moved forward to glance into the bin.

'Ah, nicely picked,' he said. 'Clean as a whistle. Not a leaf or twig to be seen.'

'Perhaps we shall earn ourselves a medal,' Esme suggested, catching his eye with a challenging glance of her own. 'For the slowest but cleanest picking.'

He met her look with one of equal openness. 'Oh, if there's medals to be won you might well win one,' he said. 'If not picking why, then, for . . .' He shrugged casually, leaving the sentence unfinished.

'For what, Mr Bryce?' persisted Esme.

'For persistence, maybe?' he answered and Louise laughed lightly.

'Point to Mr Bryce!' she exclaimed. 'I think that's love-fifteen.'

'Do you play tennis, Mr Bryce?' asked Agatha, unwilling to be left out of this exchange.

'I'm afraid I don't.'

'Croquet, perhaps?'

'Not croquet either.'

Esme smiled sweetly. 'Don't you play *any* games, Mr Bryce?'

'Oh yes, I do. Yes, I do play games – but not with a racquet or mallet.' There was a moment's silence while each considered where this line of conversation might profitably be directed; it was Esme who ventured.

'And do you enjoy these games you play?' she asked innocently. He gave her a long, amused look but she did not lower her eyes.

'Oh yes,' he said at last. 'I enjoy them and so does my partner – whoever she may be. Well, now,' he smiled round at them, instantly breaking the tension that had developed, 'since you are obviously managing very well on your own I'll take myself off. If I don't keep my eyes peeled there's some I know will be up to all sorts of tricks. I'll be by again later on. Be good, ladies.' With a nonchalant wave of his hand, he moved on. They watched him without speaking until he was a safe

distance away, then all three broke into peals of excited
laughter.

'Be good! Oh, what a *man*!' cried Agatha. 'Isn't he terrible!'

'And you, Esme!' cried Louise. 'I don't know how you
dared provoke him that way. I hardly dared listen. I didn't
know *what* he was going to say next!'

'When he said he played games but not with a mallet – and
what was it he said about his partner? I thought my face must
be *burning*!'

'Mine too!' cried Louise. 'When he said his *partner* enjoyed
the games! Oh, dear! What a cheek!'

'And yet he wasn't offensive,' Agatha said quickly. 'I mean,
he didn't mean us any offence. It was just so impudent.'

'Dreadfully bold – but in a nice way!' Esme agreed, her face
radiant. 'Oh, we shall have to be very careful with that man. I
mean, we've only been here a few hours and already . . .'

As she stopped they all followed her gaze and saw a little girl
standing only yards away, listening intently to all they said.
Three pairs of abashed eyes met her cool ones.

'Run away, child,' said Esme, recovering rapidly.

The child regarded them silently. She wore no shoes and her
too-large dress was threadbare. Black mittens covered her arms
up to the elbows. Her fingers were stained black, her face was
dirty and there were traces of food round her mouth. Her eyes
were half-closed and her small face was screwed up in a frown
of concentration. Her hair, a dull gold, was tied with a limp
ribbon of an indeterminate colour.

'Do you hear me, child? You must go back to your mother,'
Esme repeated.

Agatha shuddered. 'What a pathetic sight,' she said. 'Is she a
gipsy child, do you think?'

Louise shook her head. 'Too pale,' she said. 'A Londoner, I
expect. What's your name, child? Do you hear me? What's
your name?'

'Vinnie.'

'Vinnie?' The girl nodded.

'Well . . . Vinnie. You can't stay here, this is a private bin.
You must do as you are told and go back to your mother.'

'Perhaps she's lost,' Esme suggested. 'Vinnie, do you know where your mother is?'

Vinnie nodded, half-turned and pointed through the rows of hops.

'Then off you go and find her, there's a good girl. She'll be looking for you.'

'She won't,' said Vinnie. In her experience, her mother never looked for her. If Vinnie was absent her mother was thankful, presuming her daughter to be in the next house with Mrs Batty, sitting on the street steps or playing in the narrow cobbled street. She did not expect her to be in any danger and saw no point in going to look for her. If she missed dinner or tea she would just go without, and if she was required for any reason Bertie would be sent to look for her.

They were nonplussed. 'D'you think she overheard what we were saying?' said Agatha.

Esme shrugged. 'It hardly matters, since we weren't saying anything incriminating,' she said. 'And I doubt if she understood. Vinnie, you're to go away. Wait a moment – see here? A whole penny! It's for you – if you go back to your mother and don't come bothering us again. We are very busy, you see, and you're interrupting us.'

She held out the coin and Vinnie's eyes widened. She ran forward, and her small hand flashed up as she snatched the penny from Esme's gloved fingers. Then she turned and began to run haphazardly along the row, darting between the poles, the wonderful penny clutched tightly in her hand.

'Well, really!' protested Agatha with a sigh of ill-disguised relief. 'A whole penny! I think she would have left us for a farthing!'

'Never mind,' said Esme, 'it was a penny well spent. Now, what were we saying . . .'

Vinnie ran until she reached the other end of the row. Looking cautiously around she saw no one and, believing herself unobserved, slowly opened her fingers to reveal the penny. It was hers, hers alone. A whole penny – just to go away. It was all too easy. Was it a trick, perhaps? She thought not but gave the question a moment's careful thought. No, it was no trick. No one had run after her, they had let her go. She was free and the penny was hers. It was a great responsibility. She must find Bertie and show it to him; he would know what should be done with it. She turned slowly, wondering which direction to take. All around the hops towered up, like giant beanstalks in the fairy tale Bertie had told her. Which way led to Bertie, she wondered? She was lost and knew it but so far felt no alarm. It had been a very strange day and this latest turn of events did not frighten her. Bertie was somewhere among the greeny poles, still plucking the green flowers from the rough bines. Vinnie's mind savoured the unfamiliar words – bine, hopper, tally-man.

A sudden slight noise caught her attention and she whirled round defensively. What she saw quite took her breath away, for two beautiful creatures stood watching her curiously. One was a boy in a sailor suit – she recognised the cut of the collar. The other was a girl dressed all in yellow. After her initial reaction, Vinnie thought of her penny and hastily clasped her two hands behind her back. Wild horses would not drag the coin from her.

'I'm Julian Lawrence,' the boy announced. 'I'm nine. This is my sister, Eva Lawrence, who is only seven. Who are you?'

His tone was not unfriendly, Vinnie decided. He did not sound as though he would send her away or steal her penny. She took a deep breath. 'I'm Lavinia Harris, and my brother is Bertram Harris and my sister is Emmeline Harris and . . .'

To her dismay the children exchanged an amused look and the girl put up a hand to smother a giggle.

'We don't want to know your entire family!' said the boy. 'How old are you?'

'Five, but Bertie is—'

'Oh, it's Bertie now.'

This time they both laughed, but Vinnie bore them no ill-will. It seemed reasonable that such superior people should mock her and enough that they were not sending her away. Remembering the penny, she wondered whether she should impress them with it or let it remain a secret. For the moment she chose the latter.

'So they call your brother Bertie. And what do they call you?'

'Vinnie.'

'Come here, Vinnie. Come a little nearer.'

Obediently she did so and the boy leaned forward slightly and sniffed.

'You smell, Vinnie,' he said and his sister nodded.

'I do not,' Vinnie protested.

'I say you do. She does, doesn't she, Eva?'

'Yes, she does,' said Eva.

'You should wash more often,' said the boy. 'Your face is dirty. Let me see your hands.'

Vinnie hesitated, then held out the left hand with empty palm upwards.

'Horribly dirty,' said the boy. 'Now the other one.'

The coin changed hands behind Vinnie's back and she held the right hand out for inspection.

'See that, Eva?' he asked.

Eva nodded solemnly. 'Horribly dirty,' she echoed.

'You see?' said the boy. 'I was right, wasn't I? You are very dirty and you smell.'

Vinnie was puzzled as to how she should react. She was always dirty but Bertie had never told her that she smelled. Her instinct had been to deny it, but the idea really did not trouble her unduly. Finally she gave a little shrug. Eva had also lost interest in Vinnie's appearance.

'We've been into Maidstone,' she said. 'We went on a shopping trip with Mama. Tomorrow we shall go to church and Papa will fall asleep and snore.'

'Hush, Eva!'

'Well, he will Julian. You *know* he will.'

'It's not a thing you tell,' he insisted.

Eva looked discomfited and Vinnie's generous heart went out to her. 'I won't tell anyone,' she offered. 'I've got a penny, a whole penny. A lady give it me to go away, so I did. I'm going to show Bertie. A whole penny – look!'

Julian and Eva looked at it as it lay in her sticky hand.

'Haven't you ever had a penny before?' they chorused.

Vinnie shook her head.

'Well, you'll be able to spend it later on,' said Julian. 'Old Jessop, the lolly man, comes round the gardens in the afternoon. He sells lollipops and fudge and toffee apples.'

Before Vinnie had fully digested this information she became aware suddenly of a movement among the hops some way behind the other two children. Then there was another movement further over and she saw two boys, a little taller than Julian, with the dark hair and swarthy faces that betrayed their gipsy blood. One of them leaned out from behind a hop-pole and, catching Vinnie's eye, put a finger to his lips. She was surprised and puzzled by their sudden appearance and had not the slightest inkling of their intentions.

Eva was saying something about 'Old Jessop' when suddenly one of the two young gipsies let out a terrifying war whoop and they rushed out from their hiding places, making straight for the defenceless Lawrences. Even before Julian and Eva could turn round, they were seized from behind and handfuls of hops were thrust down their backs. Eva fell backwards, squealing with fright, but somehow Julian managed to regain his balance. Vinnie watched with stunned horror as the fight developed with arms and legs flailing in all directions. Then with a triumphant roar the gipsies wrestled Julian to the ground and the realisation dawned on her that the two beautiful creatures who had deigned to speak to her – the boy and girl who had told her about the lolly man – were being brought low by these two rough louts. A fierce sense of loyalty drove her suddenly forward into the mêlée and, hardly aware what she was doing, she hurled herself at one of the gipsies and began to tear at his hair.

'Let go of him, you useless sod!' she screamed, unconsciously echoing her mother. 'Let him go, I tell you! You idle, no-good, I hate you! Let him go, I say, or I'll tell Bertie. I will! I'll tell him about . . . ah!'

His elbow had jabbed her painfully in the chest and she gasped for breath, releasing his hair for a second. He took the opportunity to push her away and she stumbled backwards into the long grass, striking her head a glancing blow against one of the hop-poles. Her pain increasing her rage, she got up and threw herself upon the second boy who was holding Eva face downward, sitting astride her as a handful of grass followed the hops down the back of her beautiful yellow dress.

'Leave her alone!' screamed Vinnie. 'I'll kill you, if you don't get off her. You're a stinking bully—'

Memories of her mother's outbursts returned to Vinnie with great clarity and lent an edge to her vocabulary. As her small fists rained blows onto the boy's head her language grew worse. Julian came to help her and finally the boy was forced to roll away from the sobbing Eva and turn to face his two assailants.

'You stupid little cow!' he shouted at Vinnie as the flat of his hand met the side of her face and knocked her to the ground. One such blow would have been enough for most five-year-olds, but Vinnie's anger had given her unexpected reserves of stamina. She staggered to her feet again and flew at her attacker, screaming a mixture of abuse and shouting for Bertie to come to their aid.

Julian was dishevelled and flushed with rage and his sailor collar hung lopsidedly, torn in the fray. He put out a foot and tripped his own adversary, then fell headlong under a blow from the other boy. The battle was ended by the appearance at the far end of the garden of an enormous gipsy woman who bellowed two names. Instantly the two boys struggled to their feet, abandoned their victims and ran off towards their mother, who gave them each a hefty wallop round the head and frog-marched them away. She took no interest in Vinnie and the Lawrences, who were now left to sort themselves out as best they could.

Eva still lay face downward in the grass sobbing bitterly, and Vinnie watched as Julian persuaded her to sit up. He took out a clean white handkerchief and wiped her tear-stained face, murmuring soothingly. Vinnie felt a great rush of envy towards Eva. *She* had a brother to make her world right again, but Bertie had failed to appear; Vinnie's champion had deserted her when he was most needed and she felt desolate. Gingerly she began to examine herself for bruises or broken bones but there seemed to be no serious damage. Julian had pulled Eva to her feet and now began to brush down the crumpled dress and rub at the grass stains. When at last her tears subsided sufficiently he turned to Vinnie.

'Are you hurt at all?'

She shook her head.

'You were jolly brave,' he said, 'to try and help us. We both thank you, don't we, Eva?'

Self-consciously he fingered his spoiled collar and Eva gulped, recovering from her fright. There was an awkward pause while the three children regarded each other. The scrimmage had left the Lawrences looking less god-like and Vinnie was dimly aware that they were impressed by her behaviour.

'I shall tell Papa,' cried Eva, 'and he will have those boys whipped. They've put horrible grass and leaves down my back. Ugh!' She wriggled, trying to encourage the offending greenery to fall out, but her bodice was tight-fitting and nothing happened.

'I'll do it for you,' said her brother.

When it was done they all looked at each other again. 'You don't really smell, Vinnie,' said Julian, shamefaced. 'It was just a joke.'

Vinnie could only nod, feeling the moment was too important for mere words. Then, in a flash, her composure was shattered once more and she gave a great wail of anguish.

'My penny! My penny! Oh, it's gone. It's lost!'

Her grief was unassuageable, the tears flowed so fast that while her fingers searched among the grass her eyes saw nothing but pink shapes against a green blur. A terrible sadness welled up inside her, black and all-enveloping. Her recent bravery and the Lawrences' good opinion of her counted for nothing compared with this loss. Julian and Eva helped her, but their combined efforts proved unsuccessful. Julian was first to admit defeat, for he was bruised and shocked from his recent scuffle. The hop leaves were still down his back, irritating his skin, but he would neither humiliate himself by asking either of the girls to remove them nor perform the ridiculous contortions necessary to do it for himself. The young Julian Lawrence took himself very seriously and his dignity was an important part of his self-image. He would not willingly make himself look foolish, even in front of a woebegone hopper's child.

He decided they must return to the house and Vinnie should go with them.

'We will ask Mama to give you another penny,' he told her and without waiting for her answer, he took Eva's hand in his and turned in the direction of the house. After a moment's hesitation Vinnie trailed after them.

Christina Lawrence was in the morning-room writing a letter when the three children appeared. When at last she raised her head her calm expression changed rapidly.

'Julian! Eva! Whatever has happened to you? And who on earth is this child, Julian?'

Briefly Julian told her what had happened. Vinnie meanwhile enjoyed the discreet splendour of the room in which she found herself. The walls were a pale olive green and matching curtains of velvet brocade framed the windows. Tables and chairs gleamed with polish and a thick carpet of intricate design, full of deep reds and blues, covered most of the floor. Huge pictures hung on the walls in ornate gold frames and a small dog slept on a stool under one of the tables. The high ceiling, paler than the walls, was also decorated.

Christina herself was simply dressed in gold-brown taffeta, with lace at the wrists and throat; her fair hair was drawn smoothly back from her forehead and fastened in a chignon at the nape of her neck. Her grey eyes regarded Vinnie as she was pushed forward by Julian.

'So you are Vinnie, is that right?'

A quick nervous nod.

'Vinnie Harris?'

Another nod. Vinnie was dumbstruck by her surroundings and the speed with which things were happening.

'My son tells me you went to his and Eva's aid when they were . . . set upon. Is that true, Vinnie?'

Vinnie nodded, but Julian hissed, 'Say, "Yes, ma'am"!'

'Yes, ma'am,' said Vinnie.

'That was well done. I'm sure the boys meant no real harm –
just boyish high spirits – but nevertheless you acted cour-
ageously. You have my thanks, Vinnie.'

She smiled down at the small face upturned to hers. There
was a strange intensity about the eyes, she thought, for one so
young.

'Since you have lost the penny which someone gave to you,
you shall have another.' She crossed the room, her dress
rustling delightfully as she moved, and opened a small box
which stood on a bureau at the far side.

'One penny!' she said, coming back with the coin glinting
between her fingers. 'And newly minted by the look of it. A
shiny new penny for the one you lost and see' – she held up
another in her other hand – 'a second penny to compensate you
for your bruises. What do you say to that, Vinnie?'

Vinnie did not know what 'compensate' meant. Was the
second penny hers, also? Julian hissed, 'Say, "Thank you,
ma'am".'

'Thank you, ma'am.'

'Good girl! Now Janet shall take you back to the hop-
garden and return you to your mother.' She tugged briskly at a
bell-rope on the wall nearby. 'Julian and Eva, come with me.
We must change your clothes. You look as though you've
both been pulled backwards through a hedge! I don't want
your father to see you in such a state.'

Julian and Eva both muttered 'Goodbye', and allowed
themselves to be whisked away. While Vinnie waited, she
heard their footsteps cross the paved hall and ascend the wide
oak staircase which she had seen as they came into the house.

Janet hurried in, glad of the chance to escape from her duties
for even a short while. She held out her hand for Vinnie's but
seeing how dirty it was, changed her mind.

'Come on then, whatever your name is,' she said. 'Got lost,
did you? I'm not surprised. Like a jungle it is, down in those
gardens. Been helping your ma, have you, to pick the hops?
Well, you are a big girl. D'you like picking? I expect it's fun.
And all that fresh air after smoky old London.' She glanced
back at Vinnie, who trotted at her heels. 'Been crying, have

you? Oh dear. I suppose you got scared when you was lost. Still, no more tears, eh? You'll soon be back with your mother. What's your name again? Harris?'

When they reached the field Janet began to shout for Mrs Harris, and Vinnie very quickly found herself reunited with her mother, Em and the Battys. Bertie, it seemed, had gone in search of her. Once the maid had left Mrs Harris began to grumble at Vinnie for wandering away and causing so much fuss. Her daughter, tired by the events of the past hour, paid little attention, but when at last the tirade petered out she said, 'I want a bit of soap.'

Her mother and Mr and Mrs Batty stared at her in disbelief. '*Soap?*'

'To wash meself.'

'Well, I haven't got no soap, so you'll have to wait,' said her mother.

Mrs Batty shook her head in amazement. 'What's got into *her*?' she asked. 'Soap, indeed! Mind you, she does look in a bit of a state, Sue. What you been up to, Vinnie, eh?'

Vinnie shrugged, 'I want some soap,' she repeated.

Suddenly Mr Batty intervened on her behalf. 'She can borrow a bit of our soap if she's so set on it,' he said. 'Send her down to the stream. It'll keep her out of mischief. Ah, here comes Bertie. Bertie, get your Vinnie our bit of soap – it's in the tin mug on a hook back at the barn; she won't be able to reach it by herself. She could do with a spruce-up, poor little cocker, she's not bad-looking under all that dirt.'

Sue looked up sharply. 'But she can wash herself, Bertie. I want you here picking, you've wasted enough time chasing after her. You're here to make a bit of money, remember, not chase Vinnie round the hop-poles. Get her the soap, then come back here pronto.'

So Vinnie and Bertie slipped away and she told him what had happened, showed him the two pennies and gave him one. They would be in clover, he told her, grinning, when the lollipop man arrived. When they reached the stream she gave the money into his care for safe keeping and then watched him run off.

It was a narrow shallow stream and several gipsy children too young to pick were playing in it under the watchful eye of a wizened old woman. She was too infirm to pick hops but her fingers were not idle; a pile of pegs lay on the grass beside her and she cut and shaped a short length of willow with deft, practised movements.

Vinnie stepped into the water, which was ankle-deep and deliciously cool to her bare feet. Bending forward, she held her skirt up with one hand and rubbed with the tiny sliver of soap at the part of her legs which showed above the water. Then, transferring the soap to the hand holding her dress, splashed water up over her legs and was pleased to see a few bubbles appear. Next, she peeled off the black mittens and threw them back onto the bank before washing her arms; the transformation was really quite satisfying. It was not easy, she decided, but the results were well worth the effort. Her face came last, with a good deal of spluttering and a certain amount of discomfort when the soap hurt her eyes, but eventually content with her appearance she climbed out of the water onto the grass. The warmth of the sun soon dried her arms and it was with some reluctance that she pulled on the ugly black mittens again. The gipsy woman who had watched the performance with interest called to her.

'I reckon you made a good job of that.'

Vinnie smiled shyly. One way and another, it was proving to be a quite exceptional day.

*

The village store in Teesbury sold almost everything. If an item was not in stock Mr Tupp, the proprietor, would send away for it. The small ragstone building stood conveniently to one side of the village green and in fine weather the little shop-front was normally half-hidden by a selection of larger goods – buckets, baskets, cheap fire-irons and the like – which were hung around it. Inside, the sizeable shop would usually be overflowing with bundles of boots, garden tools, stacks of tinned food and piles of doormats. Straw hats and jointed wooden dolls shared the two counters with huge cheeses and

Mr Tupp's black cat. Watering-cans hung on the walls and
flower-pots of varying sizes crowded in where they could.

Today, however, everything was very different. All the
merchandise had been driven back *behind* the counters and a
newly erected wire-mesh partition rose from counter to
ceiling, with only a small gap in the middle through which
goods could be passed and money exchanged. Not even a
flower-pot remained free. Even Mr Tupp looked different;
gone was his sleepy expression and mild good humour. He
now paced nervously up and down the empty half of his shop,
his expression agitated as he referred constantly to the large
half-hunter watch kept in the pocket of his waistcoat. He was a
small, balding man with tiny plump hands which frequently
flew upwards to adjust the ends of his waxed moustache. His
pale eyes were short-sighted, but he would only wear his
spectacles in the privacy of the family quarters and had
consequently developed a habit of leaning forward so that he
could more easily recognise his customers.

'Will!' called his wife. 'Do stop that pacing and come in back
and have a cup of tea. They won't be here yet awhile. They'll
scarcely have pulled the last bine.'

The suggestion irritated him. He knew his wife was right,
but he also knew he could not enjoy a cup of tea because he
could not relax. Instead, he opened the street door and stepped
outside, to the accompaniment of loud jangling from the bell.
A pony and cart was approaching and he knew it was the
bloater man.

'Robbie!' he called.

'Will!'

'How goes it?'

'Fair. And you?'

'Middling.'

'Ah.'

This was the usual extent of the Saturday afternoon's
pleasantries but today was different because the hoppers were
down.

Robbie, slim and neat, jumped down and walked round to
the back of the cart where he began to arrange trays of kippers

and bloaters, tweaking the parsley into place with an air of great concentration. When the display met with his approval he stepped back and glanced expectantly at Will Tupp for his opinion.

'Pretty,' said Will. 'Very pretty.' He fiddled with his moustache and looked across to the far side of the village green.

'You all set up?' asked Robbie.

By way of answer Will waved a hand towards the door of the shop and stood guard over the fish while his friend took a quick look inside, bellowing with laughter at what he saw.

'Looks secure,' he said. 'Keep out an army of ruddy dervishes, that would! I reckon that's secure right enough.'

''Course, next weekend'll be the one,' said Will.

'It will that.'

'Visitors.'

'Visitors,' agreed Robbie.

'Fine old carry-on at the station last night, by all accounts.'

'Oh?'

'You haven't heard, then?'

'No.'

'Oh, a fine how-d'you-do. One lot of pickers weren't collected. No waggon. Not a word.'

'Never!'

'It's true. Hoppers nearly wrecked the station, so I hear. Turned real nasty. Well, you would, wouldn't you, that time of night and no sign of your bed. Station-master was at his wits' end, they say, and him with a dicky heart, poor old lad. Frightened the life out of him, apparently.'

'No!'

'What they didn't do! Door handle tore right off! Windows broke. The whole shooting match!'

'Go on!'

'I tell you it was pretty rough.'

'Who was it, then, didn't collect?'

'Humphreys Farm. His waggoner didn't wake up, so he said.'

'Drunk, most likely.'

'They reckon so.' Will looked at his watch again, put it to his ear and nodded. 'Not long now,' he said. 'They'll come charging across that green like I don't know what.'

Robbie gave a bit of a wink, his head on one side. 'Good money, though Will. Got to make it where we can.'

'Oh, good money all right. *If* they don't pinch too much, thieving rascals!'

Robbie laughed. 'You're well tucked away behind that wire,' he said. 'They'd be hard put to pinch anything off you this year.'

Will shook his head. 'I think that every year,' he said, 'but they always find a way. Marvellous, it is. Ah – I hear something.'

Both men stared across the triangular green. Two boys raced into sight, shouting excitedly as they headed for the shop and the bloater man.

'See you,' said Will hastily as he hurried inside the shop and installed himself behind his defences.

Robbie, defenceless and vulnerable, braced himself beside his cart and waited for the first of the many.

*

By eight o'clock that night dozens of fires were blazing cheerfully as the faggots of brushwood crackled and spat and the orange flames leaped upwards towards the darkening sky. The smell of bloaters, kippers and even bacon drifted on the breeze as the simple items of food bought from Will Tupp's store and Robbie's cart were converted into nourishing and filling meals by the hungry hoppers. The day's work in the sunshine had given them all hearty appetites and huge suppers were expected. Mrs Batty cut thick slices of bread from the loaf while Bertie kept an eye on the billy-can which hung over the fire; it contained roughly-cut potatoes, parsnips and onions and the contents of two tins of bully beef.

'Learnt it from the gipsies a few years back,' Mrs Batty told Sue. 'You won't find them making do with a bit of smoked fish, not on the first night. Oh no, not them. They like to put a proper meal in their bellies.'

'I thought gipsies ate hedgehogs,' said Bertie, lifting the lid to savour once more the appetising smell coming from the dinner.

'So they do, if there's nothing else. They'll eat most things, gipsies will. *And* make it tasty, too.'

'Hedgehogs?' Sue wrinkled her nose at the thought. 'All those prickles! How can they?'

'Wrap 'em in mud and bake 'em. Pull off the baked mud and off come the prickles.'

'Well, they're cheap enough, I suppose. Bertie, stop taking that lid off, will you? You're letting all the heat out. How d'you expect it to cook with you leering in at it every five minutes?'

Vinnie said, 'Ugh!'

'What's up with you?' her mother asked.

'Hedgehogs!'

'How d'you know it's "Ugh"?' asked Mr Batty. 'I bet you've never even seen a hedgehog. Have you seen one, eh?'

Vinnie did not bother to answer. She was trying to imagine Julian and Eva eating hedgehogs baked in mud and it seemed very unlikely that they would.

Mrs Batty smiled. 'Well, if you was a gipsy you'd like it,' she told her. 'You'd get used to it, you see.'

Vinnie nodded. She was finding it difficult to keep her eyes open and hoped the stew would not be too long. If she allowed herself to fall asleep she would miss it. She sighed deeply with a feeling of utter contentment. Bertie had not lied to her – he had promised a garden and it was all around her. She had picked little green flowers as he had promised she would. It was not all quite how she had imagined it, but Vinnie loved it. The day had seemed to last interminably and when she tried to recall Mrs Batty's kitchen in London the picture that she finally raised was hazy. London had already slipped away and hopping was her new existence. Her eyes closed as she remembered Eva lying face down in the grass, sobbing; the pennies; Julian's torn collar and the feel of the moving stream over her feet . . .

'Give her a prod, Bertie, there's a dear,' said Mrs Batty.

'She'll fall asleep else and we'll never wake her up. Goes out like a light, that one.'

'Vinnie! Don't go to sleep. Vinnie! It's nearly ready.'

She blinked up into the familiar face and smiled tiredly.

'The stew is nearly done,' Bertie told her. 'Full of good things. Another ten minutes, that's all. Vinnie, don't go to sleep!'

Mr Batty reached out for her. 'Give her here, Bertie. Poor little mite's had a long day. Come over to Uncle Batty, love, and I'll tell you a story to keep you awake. How's that, eh?'

He took her unprotesting form onto his lap. 'Right, a story about . . .' He waited.

'A princess,' said Vinnie.

'A princess. This princess met a dragon and he was a bad dragon . . .'

Darkness was falling quickly and everywhere flames gleamed on the faces of the people gathered round each fire. There was the friendly clatter of knife and spoon as the only meal of the day was consumed with gusto. Vinnie heard snatches of song, bursts of laughter and the drone of cheerful voices. A few hopeful dogs ran among them and were occasionally rewarded with a few scraps, but this was rare for the pickers were hungry and food was too precious to waste. Further over beyond the gate the gipsy fires glowed and their horses neighed restlessly, a pleasant sound in the September darkness. At the top of the hill lights gleamed in the windows of the big house as the family assembled in the long dining-room.

'Any problems? Everyone happy?'

It was Tom Bryce making his last round of the day. There were a few minor queries, mostly about the accommodation; he dealt with them efficiently and then passed on.

The few local pickers had gone home long since and would very soon be stumbling wearily up their respective stairs to bed. Tom Bryce wanted them back at Foxearth before the dew was off the hops and that meant a very early start, especially for those who lived several miles from the gardens.

'There you are, Vinnie love. Tuck into that and then Bertie

shall pop you into bed.' Mrs Batty handed her a tin bowl and a spoon. 'It's hot, so bunch your skirt up round it. That's the way. And eat every bit, mind.'

Vinnie needed no coaxing. By the light of the fire she dipped her spoon into the steaming mass of vegetables and meat and blew on each succulent piece before sliding it into her mouth. She had never felt so happy in her life before. She just managed to lift the bowl and suck down the last drops of gravy before it fell from her fingers – then sleep claimed her and she toppled slowly sideways into her dreams.

CHAPTER FOUR

At Foxearth the kitchen was a hive of activity. The evening meal would be served to the family at seven o'clock and it was now nearly ten minutes to the hour. The main meal of the day was never a hurried affair but this week, with three visitors staying and sometimes extra dinner guests as well, it had tended to last longer than usual. This did not please the kitchen staff who could not clear the table until the diners had moved into the other room, by which time most of the evening was gone. The precious interval that remained before they made their way to bed was thus curtailed and their only chance for relaxation lost.

The kitchen was a large room. There was a long squat table in the middle, with forms on either side and a chair with arms at one end for Mrs Tallant, the housekeeper. Mrs Tallant was a small woman with unlimited energy and she demanded the maximum effort from all her staff. She always wore black and this, combined with her quick nervous movements, gave her the appearance of a small bird and had earned her the nickname of 'Birdie'. However, since no one ever dared to use this in her hearing, she remained quite oblivious of the fact. If she had a temper, she kept it well hidden; one look from her fierce beady eyes was usually enough to quell any insubordination. Now she stood at one end of the kitchen and surveyed the scene before her like a general watching final preparations for a battle.

Edie, the scullery maid, was straining the vegetables into the big deep sink. Cook was putting the finishing touches to a large succulent ham, pressing cloves into its shiny crust and carefully removing any dark specks which might mar its otherwise perfect appearance. Janet, at the far end of the table, was giving the silver cutlery a final polish with a soft cloth. The room was very hot and Mrs Tallant put up a hand to tuck back a stray wisp of hair which clung damply to her forehead. The bread oven was not required, but the two Dutch ovens were in use and there was also a huge open fire in front of which two large legs of pork sizzled on a spit being turned by young Harry, the stable lad. His long day's work was nearly done. 'Young Harry' did not live in at Foxearth because his family lived less than half a mile away. He came in daily to work but the nightly evening meal in the Foxearth kitchen formed an important part of his wages. Since the kitchen staff did not eat their meal until the family had finished theirs, he was always late going home but the dark homeward walk did not bother him. Tonight his stomach rumbled, for he had not eaten since noon and was very hungry. The smell of the spitted pork made him hungrier.

Above Harry, ranged along the inglenook, were hams and sides of bacon and still more of these hung from the kitchen ceiling. The floor was laid with large flagstones which had to be washed daily with a stiff broom – this job was Edie's, but she was a dull girl and a slow worker and if it grew too late Mrs Tallant would bribe young Harry with a handful of currants to do the job quickly. When that happened he would stuff the currants into his pocket to eat on the way home – he hoped tonight would be such an occasion. Four bins stood at one end of the room containing lentils, oats, beans and flour and on one of these a large ginger tom-cat sat surveying the scene through sleepy yellow eyes.

Mrs Tallant glanced up at the large clock and tutted irritably. 'You have no time now, Janet, to fiddle with that cutlery. I have told you before that the silver should be polished well in advance of the meal. I shall *not* tell you again. Take it in at once and set the table; the mistress will be down before long to inspect the room.'

Nodding guiltily, Janet put down the cloth and returned the cutlery to its portable drawer before hurrying away with it to the dining-room. She was thankful to escape into the cool passages, for her black uniform dress had a high austere collar and was the less comfortable of her two uniforms. By day she wore a flowered cotton dress underneath a voluminous apron, but for serving at table in the evening she wore a smaller apron over a black dress and with it a white lace-edged cap. In the dining-room the long table covered with a white cloth glittered with silver and glass and only the cutlery was missing. Yellow candles stood at intervals along the length of the table and there were small silver dishes full of flowers. Three glasses stood at each place and a white damask table-napkin was folded round a newly baked roll. There was a name card for each setting. The walls were a warm gold and the long curtains were of dark green velvet; the same material up-holstered the dining-chairs. As a token to the cooler evenings a small fire burned in the grate, but the large west-facing room caught the last of the day's sunshine and was never really cold in September. There were several large pictures on the walls and four mirrors created an atmosphere of great spacious-ness.

Janet cursed under her breath, for she had forgotten the matches and the candles must be lit. She went quickly from place to place, setting the knives, forks and spoons in their respective positions. This was a task she enjoyed, one of the few jobs at which she rarely made a mistake. The side table appeared to her inexperienced eye to be ready, set as it was with dishes and plates, jugs of water, bottles of wine and a pile of cloths to deal with any spills. Later, as she finished lighting the candles, the Colonel came into the room leaning heavily on his stick.

'Ah, it's Janet,' he said, 'and what are you up to?'

'Nothing, sir – at least, I mean, setting the table, sir. The knives and forks, sir.'

'The knives and forks, eh?'

He looked at the table carefully and Janet crossed her fingers behind her back.

'Setting the table, are you?' he said again and moved slowly along, pausing to adjust a glass or move a spoon until everything was to his satisfaction.

'Did you do all this, then, eh?' he asked, waving his hand towards the table.

'Yes, sir.'

'Good girl, Janet, good girl.' He regarded her quizzically. 'At least, I expect you are a good girl. Are you a good girl, Janet?' He put a slight emphasis on the word 'good'.

'Yes, sir.'

'Hmm. How long have you been with us, Janet?'

'Nearly a month, sir.'

'And you think you are going to be happy here?'

'Oh yes, sir, I am. Ever so happy, sir.'

'Hmm.'

There was the sound of laughter and voices at the top of the stairs, then footsteps descending.

'I'll get back to the kitchen, then,' she said.

'Get back to your work, eh, Janet?'

'Yes, sir.'

She hurried out of the room. As she passed the bottom of the stairs, she saw the three visitors coming down and gave them a quick bob.

'Good evening, Janet,' said Esme pointedly.

Janet coloured slightly, turned back and gave a deeper bob.

'Good evening, ma'am,' she said.

'We all have names, Janet,' said Esme with an amused laugh.

'I am sorry, ma'am. Good evening, Miss Braithwaite; good evening, Miss Tarlton; good evening, Miss Hart.'

Esme laughed again by way of answer and the three women crossed the hall and went into the drawing-room. Janet poked out her tongue at their retreating backs and then made her way to the kitchen.

'Is everything ready?' Mrs Tallant asked her. Janet nodded. 'Then I shall go and have a look.'

The housekeeper left the kitchen and everyone relaxed slightly.

'Silly bitch!' said Janet.

'Who?' said young Harry. 'Birdie?'

'No, that Esme Hart. "We all have names you know",' she mimicked, 'and then laughing at me in that stuck-up voice.'

Young Harry grinned. 'You don't want to worry about her,' he said. 'All those high-falutin' ways of hers, but she's no better than she should be.'

They all turned to stare at him, astonished. 'No better than she should be?' echoed Janet. 'Whatever do you mean?'

He tapped the side of his nose meaningfully.

'Oh, I hear things,' he said airily.

'What sort of things?'

'Just things,' he said.

Cook snorted. 'He hasn't heard nothing,' she said, 'or else he'd tell us.'

'Go on, young Harry,' pleaded Janet. 'Tell us what you heard.'

He considered thoughtfully for a moment. 'And you all swear not to tell?' he asked. They all nodded earnestly.

'Well, then, Tim reckons she's making up to Tom Bryce.'

Janet's mouth fell open with delighted shock. 'Esme Hart and Tom Bryce?' she repeated. 'I don't believe it, young Harry.'

He shrugged. 'I'm only telling you what I heard. You asked me and I've told you.'

'*Well!*' said Janet and glanced at Cook to see if she believed this piece of news.

'Could be,' said Cook. 'On the other hand, could be a load of old codswallop.'

Janet looked at Harry to see how he had taken this remark, but he merely shrugged again. 'You don't have to believe me – I'm only telling you what I've been told.'

Edie spoke up at last. 'How do you mean "making up"?'

'You know,' said Janet. 'Making eyes at him. Setting her cap at him if you like. Giving him the old "come hither".'

She demonstrated this, putting her left hand on her hip and throwing a provocative glance in young Harry's direction. He burst out laughing. 'If she looks how you look,' he said, 'I reckon Tom Bryce would laugh himself silly.'

Cook reached for the domed meat-cover and placed it over the ham. 'I'll have that pork now, young Harry,' she said, 'and if you have nothing else to do for the next half an hour you can bring in some wood for the morning. Birdie won't want you hanging round the kitchen while we're dishing up.'

Reluctantly, he took himself off to the shed and when Mrs Tallant returned the staff were all dutifully employed about their rightful business.

'Well done, Janet,' she said briskly. 'The table looks very nice. Now go and strike the gong. They drift into that dining-room as though they've got all the time in the world, with not a thought as to how we're keeping the food hot. It won't hurt to get them down a little early for once.'

*

The two children had eaten earlier, so eight people sat down to dinner – the Colonel and Christina, their three house guests and three gentlemen invited to even the numbers: the vicar of the Parish Church and his two sons. The Reverend Parsloe was a widower and lived at the large rectory nearby with his two sons Nathan and Joshua. They were invited every year during the first week of the hopping season, because the spiritual welfare of the pickers was of great concern to the elderly vicar who tried valiantly to see them as more sinned against than sinning. Christina had warned her three friends well in advance that the conversation would almost certainly centre round the Londoners and so they were not disappointed. Even as the gravy-boat circulated, Mr Parsloe, to the embarrassment of his sons, was already launched into his favourite topic.

'My task at this time is quite clear to me,' he was saying. 'I have a duty to my parishioners and another to our visitors from London. My job is to convince the former that there is no real malice in the latter.'

'Bit difficult, eh?' said the Colonel. 'I mean to say, there *is* malice in the beggars.'

'Not malice, Colonel,' said the vicar. 'A misguided wanton-ness, shall we say?'

'*You* can say what you like,' said the Colonel. 'I shall say malice. They've no respect for people or property. They steal, they fight, they blaspheme. They are evil, Mr Parsloe. A necessary evil, perhaps, but evil nonetheless. I thank the Lord that we only need them for one month in the year.'

'But they know no better,' protested the vicar. 'They are like wayward children, the products of the London slums. They are hopelessly ignorant.'

'They are degenerate,' said the Colonel. 'Absolutely degenerate, the whole lot of them.'

'That is because they know no better. We should pity them.'

'The vicar is right, Henry,' said Christina. 'They are a product of their environment and they are not all bad.'

'I say they are,' said the Colonel. 'Show me one that isn't. Show me one that won't pinch the apples off my trees as soon as my back is turned.'

'But that is exactly my point,' said Mr Parsloe. 'Their lives are such that stealing is necessary to them – necessary to their continued existence. They often have no work, yet they still have mouths to fill.'

Christina smiled across at him. 'Take no notice of Henry,' she said soothingly. 'My husband enjoys a good argument and he has been looking forward to your visit all week.'

'Of course I have,' the Colonel agreed with a smile. 'Dash it, I can't argue with you in church and I sleep through most of your sermons—'

'Henry!'

'You know I do, dear, and so does Parsloe. I snore, I confess it, and so everybody knows I sleep through the sermons. That is what sermons are for, isn't it? But if a man can't have an argument at his own table—'

'Really, Henry!' Christina protested. 'Take no notice of him, Mr Parsloe. Sometimes I think he is more wilful than the children. Oh yes, dear, you know you are.'

During this exchange Nathan and Joshua had concerned themselves with the eating of their dinners. Nathan was nearly thirty, Joshua three years younger. Neither was married; this was not because they were unattractive, although in fact they were plain. It was a result of their reluctance to take positive action, a trait which they had inherited from their mother.

They were too lazy to wed and unused to female company. The previous year they had met Louise, but Agatha and Esme were strangers to them and they felt slightly ill at ease. Now, however, Nathan plucked up his courage and spoke for the first time, addressing his remarks to Esme who sat opposite him.

'Do you watch cricket at all?' he said.

'I must confess I don't,' said Esme.

'Nor me,' said Agatha.

'Oh, you should,' said Louise. 'It's a splendid game when it's played well. While I was here last year I watched the village team and thoroughly enjoyed it.'

She looked up at Nathan. 'You played the team from Farleigh, I remember.'

He smiled, delighted that she remembered, and with the smile some of the plainness vanished.

'We did, that's right. How terribly clever of you.'

'I remember it very well. I was most impressed by the standard of play. Perhaps we could all attend a match before we return to London.'

Christina seized on the new topic of conversation gratefully. 'What a splendid idea,' she said. 'Are you playing during September?'

'We are indeed.'

'Then we might come and watch you.'

'Will you come with us, Henry?' Christina asked.

'Where, dear?'

'To watch the cricket. Nathan and Joshua will be playing cricket some time soon. I thought we might go along and watch.'

'I'm not a cricketing man, actually, but I'll see. Horses are more in my line. Have some more meat, vicar, you don't eat enough to keep a flea alive. Janet, give Mr Parsloe some more pork.'

But the Reverend Parsloe shook his head, placing a hand protectively over his plate.

'No, no, thank you, Colonel,' he said. 'Everything in moderation. Even your excellent pork.'

He was annoyed with his son for diverting the conversation and now struggled to bring it back to the welfare of the hoppers.

'There are moves afoot, you know,' he said firmly, 'to improve the accommodation of our visitors. Some of the provision made for them – not yours, of course, Colonel – but some of it, is woefully inadequate—'

'And always will be,' said the Colonel cheerfully. 'It simply is not practicable to spend a lot of money on buildings which will only be used for one month out of twelve. I know, because I've tried it. Christina nagged me several years ago to try to improve the accommodation. That old barn really is almost beyond repair and the roof leaks, but the bank manager just laughed at me. Laughed, Parsloe, at the very idea! They would lend me money for a cowshed or a cottage to house one of my men, but when I suggested building a decent shed for the hoppers to live in during September they cried me down and the answer was "No".'

Christina nodded several times while he was speaking. 'It was very disappointing,' she said. 'Of course we do concern ourselves with their welfare. They may only work for us for four weeks of the year, but during that time they are our responsibility and we would like to see them better housed. But,' she shrugged, 'as my husband says, we can get no financial help and to accommodate nearly one hundred people is a large undertaking. We do what we can.'

The women nodded their understanding, for she was genuinely concerned by outside criticism and spoke defensively.

'Our local ladies,' she went on, 'are already collecting cast-off clothes to be distributed among the hoppers before they return to London, and yesterday morning I was in Maidstone at the chemist's arranging for a large quantity of anti-cholera mixture. We shall have it by Monday, and they will all be given a spoonful. We don't want a repetition of the Farleigh tragedy.'

'Perhaps Esme and Agatha don't know of it,' said the Colonel and the two women shook their heads.

'It was before I was born,' said Christina. 'Back in the forties, but Henry was a little boy then.'

He nodded. 'I remember my parents' shocked faces and the special funeral service. Nearly fifty people died in the outbreak and only a few miles from Foxearth. It was a terrible time. A very terrible time indeed. Thank God nothing like it has happened since, nor ever will again, I hope.'

'Amen to that,' said the vicar, and Nathan and Joshua closed their eyes briefly in support. For a moment nobody spoke, then Louise said briskly, 'That Harris child is a funny little thing. Vinnie Harris. An odd little soul.'

'Odd?' said Nathan. 'In what way?'

'She almost seems to have adopted us,' said Agatha. 'She appears each day and stands staring at us, watching us as we work. She says very little. One or two words perhaps.'

'She has a ferocious scowl,' laughed Louise, demonstrating it, 'and she fixes us with those intense eyes of hers. It really is, as Agatha says, rather odd. When we give her a penny she goes away. Takes it without a "thank you" and then disappears again.'

The Colonel laughed. 'She's not odd at all, she's canny. I told you, they are all the same. When you give her a penny, she goes away. What an easy way to earn a penny a day.'

The three women looked at each other. 'I did wonder—' said Esme and then everyone laughed.

'Her hair fascinates me,' said Louise. 'I think if it were washed it would be a quite beautiful colour. I can only describe it as dirty gold.'

Christina replied, 'Oh, there are many among them who would be quite beautiful in more fortunate circumstances, but their dreary clothes and general air of dirt and neglect render them all equally unsavoury.'

'The gipsy girls are a handsome lot,' said Joshua. The wine was loosening his tongue and his father gave him a sharp glance which he did not see. He went on, 'Of course, they are not very tall and they bear their children so young. The women are quite spoiled by the time they are twenty but at fifteen or thereabouts . . .'

'Damn good workers, too,' said the Colonel. 'Any more pork for anyone – or ham? If not, Janet can clear the main course.'

There were general murmurs to the effect that everyone had had sufficient and Janet was summoned to take away the plates.

Nathan looked enquiringly at the three women. 'And how much longer are you picking?' he asked.

Louise answered him. 'I shall be here for another two weeks,' she said. 'Esme will stay down for one week, poor Agatha is going home on Sunday.'

'What a pity,' said Joshua. 'I was going to suggest a picnic by the river one day next week.'

'Oh, don't speak of it!' cried Agatha. 'I shall be *so* envious.'

'Unless we make it Saturday – then you *could* come.'

'A picnic! Oh, that would be absolutely splendid,' said Esme.

Mr Parsloe coughed discreetly and murmured to his nearest son that *he* would not be able to attend: picnics were for the young, he said. Nathan tried to look sorry. The Colonel agreed with the vicar.

'Damned uncomfortable things, at our age,' he said. 'Perched on a wobbly chair in the middle of a field – not to mention the wasps – persistent little beggars, they are. No, picnics are for the young and foolish. You go and enjoy yourselves. Christina will probably join you, won't you, dear?'

'Perhaps, Henry. The children would adore it, of course.'

'Then that's settled,' said Nathan eagerly. 'We'll arrange it all. Leave it to us. One shouldn't make too many preparations. A picnic should be spontaneous, I think.'

'I do so agree with you,' said Esme, smiling at him warmly, and he began to enjoy the evening.

Janet came in with the dessert – a large mulberry tart, an apple charlotte and a selection of cheeses. Inevitably the conversation returned once more to the hop-gardens and Carrie was mentioned.

'You haven't heard of Carrie?' said Christina. 'Oh, but surely *you* have, Louise. The gipsy woman who tells fortunes.

She comes every year, uninvited, tells a few fortunes, relieves the gullible of their silver coins and moves on to the next hop-garden.'

'Carrie? Is that her name?' said Louise. 'I do recall a gipsy telling fortunes last year. In fact, she told mine. A very tall elderly woman with dark plaits wound round her head?'

'That's Carrie! She is tall for a gipsy, and quite striking to look at.'

'She told me I'd marry a professional man—'

'That's true!' said Agatha. 'Rupert is a professional soldier.'

'And that I would bear eleven healthy sons!'

There was a ripple of laughter. 'Don't tell Rupert that until the ring is on your finger!' laughed Esme. 'It might frighten him away! Mmm . . . Christina, your cook is a positive jewel. This apple charlotte is quite perfect, you may tell her so from me.'

'If you tell her yourself you may wheedle the recipe out of her.'

'Rupert adores apple charlotte,' said Louise. 'If you get the recipe, Esme, do pass it on to me. Then my beloved will be forever in your debt!'

With a great deal more light-hearted chatter the meal drew to a close and it was time for the ladies to retire to the drawing-room and leave the men to their cigars.

Outside night was falling and Christina, looking out of the French windows, saw the mist settling over the lower slopes of the hop-garden.

'I do hope the fine weather holds,' she said. 'That old barn is no better than a sieve in rainy weather and if the pickers get damp and cold their mood changes. There's nothing worse than trying to deal with sullen pickers. They can be most unpleasant, really quite troublesome, when they are roused.'

Louise crossed the room to stand beside her. 'But on Saturday all their weekend visitors will arrive. That will cheer them up, that and the pay-out.'

Christina sighed. 'That's another bone of contention,' she said. 'Henry never allows them to draw more than half their money – unless they are going back to London early for some reason. If they are staying the whole season, then he keeps back half of what is due to them until the final pay-out. Unless he does so, many of the men will drink it all away in the "Horse and Cart" and at the end of the month their families will go home with nothing to show for their month's labour. He does it for their own good, of course, but they don't see it that way. The women appreciate it but the men are sometimes very resentful.'

'Don't worry,' said Louise. 'We'll pray for fair weather when we go to bed tonight and all will be well. You'll see.'

'I do hope so,' said Christina as she turned away from the window.

CHAPTER FIVE

Tom Bryce patted his stomach, turned his chair towards the welcoming glow of the range and stretched out his legs with a sigh of deep contentment.

'You enjoy that, did you Tom?'

'Yes, Mother. I always enjoy your mutton pies, you know that. I always eat too much. It's a wonder I'm not fat as a pig, the amount of food you give me.'

His widowed mother looked at him fondly as her fingers moved along the row and the knitting fidgeted in her lap.

'You'll never be fat, Tom, you work too hard for that. And you take after your father – thin as a board, he was. Never put on an ounce of extra fat, he didn't.'

He grinned at her. 'If you go on feeding me, I'll never leave home, you know. Never find meself a wife and you'll never have no grandchildren. You know that, I suppose?'

'You'll wed, Tom, and the sooner the better. There's that poor little Rose from behind the smithy, eating her heart out for you. She's a nice little thing and you could do a lot worse for yourself. I won't be around forever, you know, to cook and mend for you. If you don't watch it, some other young man'll snap her up and you'll lose her.'

'Plenty more fish in the sea, Mother.'

'But you're not getting any younger, Tom.'

He threw back his head and laughed boisterously. 'You've been telling me that since I was seventeen, Mother! But I can still turn their heads, even though I say it meself. The old charm hasn't deserted me yet, nor won't for a few years yet. If a man can scrump an apple when he wants one, why should he own the tree?'

'Tom! That's not decent, to talk that way. Here, hold your

arm out, let's measure this sleeve. I've taken it back once and I don't aim to do it again. It's got to be right, this time.'

Obligingly he held out his right arm and watched her measure the dark blue sleeve. She never knitted anything but dark blue – a good serviceable colour, she called it. His father's pullovers had been blue and Tom's would be also. He was resigned to it. He thought suddenly of Esme Hart and his eyes narrowed slightly. A nice body, that one, he mused. He liked them well-covered. Nothing worse than a bony woman. Like lying with bent tram-rails!

'What're you grinning at, Tom? No, come on, out with it. I know that look. I ought to, for I saw it often enough on your father's face. And a right devil he was for the women. Like father, like son, they say, and it's true enough. You're up to something, Tom.'

'Don't you trust me, then?' he teased.

'Not farther than I can throw you!' she said. 'Who is it, Tom? Do I know her?'

'No, you don't.'

Esme Hart, he reflected. Esme – a nice name. And she fancied him, he could tell that much. The slightly breathless voice, the shy glances. If only he could get her away from the others. She would never commit herself in front of witnesses. But on her own maybe . . .

'Tom! What's she like, I say?'

'Very pretty, Mother, and plump as a little partridge.'

'And . . . ?'

'And willing. And rich!'

'Rich?' He saw the alarm in her eyes.

'Don't fret,' he told her. 'It's nothing I can't handle.'

'Oh, Tom, do be careful.'

'I will, you can depend on it.'

'It's not one of the Colonel's young ladies, is it, Tom? Oh, it is! Don't deny it, I can see it written all over your face, plain as a pikestaff. You just be careful, Tom. I know the likes of them, they'll amuse themselves with you and then—'

'What, cast me off like an old boot? Where's the harm in that? I don't want to marry the girl, do I?'

She shook her head, worried. 'Mind what I say, Tom. I don't want to see you hurt, nor I don't want no trouble with the Colonel. He won't take kindly to his top man playing fast and loose with his young ladies. If you go breaking her heart . . .'

'She might break mine, Mother.'

'Oh Tom, Tom! You're your father's son and no mistake. Just go careful, son, that's all I ask. You must go your own way, I know that. You're a grown man and don't need me to run your life. But these fancy ladies aren't as soft as you might think and she'll maybe have a trick or two up her sleeve. You take my advice, Tom Bryce, and you go careful.'

*

Next day found Carrie striding along beside the road that led from Farleigh to Teesbury. If she could reach the gardens by mid-afternoon she would have the best part of three hours. Her dark eyes glittered greedily as she anticipated her earnings. She carried a pack on her back containing a selection of pins, needles, thread, ribbons and laces. There were also a few tortoise-shell combs – they were selling a treat – and one or two tiny hand mirrors set in carved wooden frames. A bit pricey for most, but there were always one or two charity ladies there who could sometimes be persuaded to part with their silver. And today was pay-out day; the pickers knew they had money coming to them. Oh yes, she'd take credit, Carrie would. She'd come back this way later in the month. *And* she'd remember everything owed her. No one cheated Carrie – they feared the gipsy curse too much for that. Not even a Londoner would try to make a fool of her.

Carrie smiled grimly as she thought of her reputation and how it had started when a London woman had owed her twopence for a few yards of lace and a paper of pins. She had promised payment when her husband came down at the weekend, but he'd come and gone again and there was no money for Carrie. Denied the debt point-blank, she had, and Carrie cursed her – not loud nor long but with that look in her eye. She'd laughed, the London woman, and spat. Aye, spat at

Carrie and 'all her tribe'. Carrie had moved on, but the next
morning the woman woke with pains in her chest. So bad she
couldn't move her arms. Couldn't pick. The next day she was
worse. And the next the farmer lost patience with her and sent
her away. On the way back to London she collapsed and died.
Nothing to do with Carrie, but no one would believe it. They
thought she'd put the evil eye on the poor woman. No smoke
without fire, they said. Still, no one cheated her after that.
Mind, there were ructions. Fights. The gipsies were feared and
hated for all that season and the next. But it blew over and was
forgotten. All except for Carrie – they remembered Carrie and
nobody cheated her again.

The sun was still shining when she reached the gate and
began to stride through the rows of hops, where the sunshine
dappled the pickers with a greeny light. The word spread at
once.

'Carrie's here!'

She smiled to herself as she made her way along the lower
hedge, keeping a wary eye open for Tom Bryce. It was his job
to keep such as her away because she distracted the pickers
from their work, but she'd give him a few yards of ribbon for
his mother and then he'd turn a blind eye to her activities and
swear he didn't know she was in the garden.

'Carrie! Here, love! Over here!'

A group of pickers waited eagerly, casting anxious glances
in all directions in case they were seen.

'Tell us me fortune, Carrie. Tell me a penn'orth, that's all
I've got.'

'Tell mine next, will you, Carrie?'

'Then mine. I could do with some good luck, I tell you
straight.'

Unsmiling, she told them what they wanted to hear,
promising them good health, better luck, a pleasant surprise or
a legacy. She left them discussing their glittering futures and
moved on to the next group. A long life, a new love, a bonny
baby. Occasionally she included a disappointment or a change
of direction.

'What are you doing here, Carrie?' Suddenly Tom Bryce

blocked her way, feet apart, hands on hips. His words were challenging but his tone was friendly.

She smiled at him. Carrie liked handsome men. She was too old to enjoy their bodies but she still had eyes and could be moved by a bold eye or a brawny arm sprinkled generously with dark hairs. Tom Bryce had all these attributes and more. She admired his youth, for her own was fled and with it her good looks. Once she had been handsome – tall and graceful, strong and desirable. Her fierce dark eyes and tumbling black hair had inflamed more men than she cared to remember. Now her face was gaunt and the tanned skin stretched over the large cheekbones. Her hair was greying and her teeth discoloured and broken.

'Doing?' she repeated. 'Why, selling a few ribbons. Trying to earn a crust like the rest of you. It's a hard world.'

'Telling fortunes, more likely.'

'What if I am? They ask for it. I don't give 'em much. A minute, two at the most. It makes them happy. Shall I tell yours?'

For a second or two he hesitated, then shook his head. 'I've no wish to know what's round the corner,' he told her. 'You just keep out of the Colonel's way if he should take it into his head to look us over. And like you say, make it slippy. We've a good crop this year and it'll take all of a month to see it in.'

She nodded. 'Good luck to you then, Tom Bryce.'

'Thanks, Carrie . . . Wait! I've got an idea. There is something you can do for me.'

'How much?'

'I'll keep my trap shut that you're in the garden.'

'You was doing that any road!'

He grinned at her. 'You strike a hard bargain. Right, here you are. Sixpence.' Her eyes gleamed as she took the coin, bit it and slipped it into her pocket.

'Now here's what you do . . .' As he whispered, a broad grin spread over her face and then she let out a loud raucous laugh.

'You cunning old fox!' she cried. 'That's a dirty trick to pull, Tom Bryce.'

'But you'll do it?'

'I'll do it,' she said. 'Thousands wouldn't, but I'll do it.'

She made her way up between the hops to the top of the field where Esme, Agatha and Louise were working. Agatha fought shy of having the future revealed to her but Louise was promised a large family, a long life and a son who would one day hold a position of great importance in the land. Having discovered their names earlier, Carrie now turned her attention to Esme. She looked into the palm of her right hand and opened her eyes wide.

'What is it?' Esme cried. 'Why do you look that way? Is it good or bad?'

Carrie glanced at the other two women and then whispered to Esme who turned excitedly to her two friends. 'She says that what she must tell me is a secret. Please excuse us,' and she followed the old gipsy into the shadow of the nearby hedge. There Carrie took her hand again and turned it this way and that. 'You have a lover?' she asked.

'Why, no,' gasped Esme.

'An admirer, then?'

'An admirer? No, no – at least I think not.'

'I think you do,' said Carrie. 'I see him clearly. A tall man and strong, with a great admiration for you. You don't know this man?'

'Indeed not.'

Carrie felt the slim hand tremble in her own rough one and kept her face straight with an effort. She traced the young woman's lifeline with her finger. 'I see a long life ahead of you,' she said, 'and great happiness. You are blessed with good health?'

Esme nodded.

'I see a long, fruitful life ahead of you and unexpected wealth.'

'Wealth?' echoed Esme.

'I see more wealth than you dream of,' said the gipsy, 'and you will use it wisely.'

Esme nodded. 'Yes, yes,' she said. 'But this man you spoke of, what else can you tell me? I don't think I know him.'

Carrie ignored her questions and went on, 'I see a tall

woman in your life, a dark-haired woman. Don't trust her.'

Esme looked startled. 'A woman?' she repeated. 'Do you mean a member of my family? A relation of mine?'

Carrie shook her head. 'She is a stranger to you but she speaks falsely. Don't trust her. Be on your guard.'

'I will.'

'Trust your innermost feelings.'

'I will – but the man . . .'

Carrie clasped a hand firmly between her own and closed her eyes as though in concentration. 'He is very near,' she said, 'this man. His admiration grows daily and with it his desire.'

Esme gave a little gasp and Carrie continued, 'He has not yet spoken to you, but he will. Soon, very soon, he will speak to you. He will please you.'

'Please me?' said Esme, glancing round nervously. 'In what way?'

The gipsy shrugged. 'His feelings are very strong towards you. That's all I can say.' She opened her eyes and stared again at the palm in front of her. 'I see a journey,' she said. 'You will go on a journey to another country. A journey before the year is out.'

Esme paid her words scant attention. 'Can you describe this man?' she whispered.

Carrie narrowed her eyes and stared into the hand. Then she put her own hand up to her head. 'Curls,' she said. 'I see curls.' She shrugged. 'Nothing more, that's all. I see nothing more.'

Esme stared at her own hand and then at the gipsy. She fumbled in her purse and paid generously for what she had heard.

'Thank you,' she whispered.

'You understand?'

'I think so. I think so. Thank you.'

With a strange smile Carrie turned away and Esme watched the tall figure stride through the green arches of the hops until she reached the end of the row, turned right and was lost to view. Esme's two friends were waiting for her and she eagerly recounted all that Carrie had told her.

'Curly hair?' cried Agatha. 'Why, that could be Tom Bryce!'

'Tom Bryce?' Esme pretended the idea had never occurred to her. 'Good gracious, I suppose it could.'

'And he desires you! Will *please* you!'

'So she said – and he will speak to me about it.'

'Esme!' said Louise. 'I beg you to be careful. Such a man as Tom Bryce—'

'I know,' said Esme. 'But if it *is* him, what shall I do?'

'Nothing, I hope!' said Louise primly. 'I beg you not to do anything rash – a man like that can mean nothing to you.'

'Of course not,' Esme said hurriedly. 'I know that, but what shall I say if he speaks to me of his feelings?'

Her two friends looked at each other. 'Pretend you are betrothed,' said Louise. 'Tell him that you are in love with someone else.'

'Run away,' said Agatha.

'Run away?'

'I mean, if he tries to – that is, if he makes any advances. Unpleasant advances.'

Esme swallowed. 'He would not dare,' she said.

'Of course not,' said Louise. 'It's more than his job's worth. Take no notice of Agatha, she's trying to frighten you.'

'Indeed I am not. I just thought that perhaps he might – well, try to kiss her or something.'

Esme drew herself up to her full height. 'I trust he will do nothing of the kind,' she said. 'I shall soon put him in his place if he dares to try such a thing. Declaring his admiration is one matter. Trying to kiss me is another. I shall be very polite and very firm and say that his advances are not at all welcome but that I appreciate the sincerity of his feelings for me.'

'Oh, that is nice!' said Agatha. 'But who is this woman with dark hair that you must not trust?'

They discussed the question at great length without reaching any conclusion and Carrie's little joke went un-detected.

*

Adam Forrest, the bin man, was also the measurer and it was his job to measure out the hops with his bushel basket. Jim Everett, the tally-man, accompanied him as he went from bin to bin and kept account of the amount picked by each group. The two of them arrived at Esme, Agatha and Louise's bin at a quarter to six that same Friday. Seeing the men approaching, the three woman had hastily 'hovered' up the hops – plunging their arms into the mass of green flowers and shaking them up so that they did not lie too densely in the bottom of the bin. This meant it would take fewer hops to fill the basket and their final tally would be higher. Adam Forrest peered in at the results of their day's labour.

'You young ladies have done well today,' he said. 'Speeding up, aren't you?'

They nodded, pleased at his praise. Jim Everett opened a hop poke – a large green mesh sack which would hold ten bushels – and Adam Forrest began to scoop the hops into it, counting the basketfuls as he did so. When he reached ten he stopped. 'And there's still a few handfuls left in the bottom there,' he said, 'but not enough to make up another bushel. Best day so far, isn't it?'

'Yes,' said Agatha. 'I think we're getting the knack now.'

'It *is* a knack,' said Adam. 'But you've done very well.'

He turned to the tally-man. 'Right, ten bushels for them.'

Louise produced their tally stick and handed it to him. Round his neck on a leather thong he carried a numbered tally for each bin. Glancing at Louise's stick, he found the tally that matched it, then placed the two sticks together and made a corresponding notch in both to record the ten bushels they had just picked. Then he returned her part of the tally.

'You'll have a nice few pounds for your charity,' said Adam.

'I hope so,' said Louise. 'We have all worked very hard.' Esme nodded and then, glancing past the two men, she caught sight of Tom Bryce. Acting on impulse, she put a hand to her head and swayed slightly.

'You all right, ma'am,' Jim asked her.

'I don't know,' said Esme. 'I felt suddenly dizzy.'

'Most likely the sun,' he said. 'It's been very warm today.

The September sun can be most deceptive although you are wearing a shady hat. You should be all right.'

'You look rather pale,' said Agatha. 'Do you want to sit down?'

'No, no,' said Esme. 'I think I will go back to the house for a glass of cold water and sit a while in the drawing-room.'

'I will come with you,' said Agatha but Esme shook her head emphatically. 'No, please, you go on picking, there's so little time left,' she said. 'I will walk slowly. Perhaps Mr Everett is right and the sun has proved too much for me.'

Fearing that someone would insist on accompanying her, she hurried away in the direction taken by Tom. When she was sure she could no longer be seen by the others, she quickened her steps until she caught up with him. Hearing the rustle of her skirts, he turned and smiled at her.

'Mr Bryce,' she said breathlessly, 'I may not be able to pick tomorrow morning. I feel rather unwell and I am going in to rest.'

'I'm sorry to hear that,' he said. 'What seems to be the matter?'

'It's nothing – at least, a slight dizziness, that's all, but Mr Everett thinks it may be sunstroke and has told me to go in and rest.'

'That's favourite,' said Tom, his brown eyes regarding her keenly. 'You don't want to risk your health, you not being country-bred and used to the sun.'

'You don't think me foolish, then?' she said, smiling bravely up at him.

'Foolish? Of course not. You take care of yourself.'

'You are very kind, Mr Bryce. I am angry with myself for being so frail. I fear I shall miss tomorrow's picnic as well.'

'Going on a picnic, are you?'

'Down to the river with the Reverend Parsloe's two sons, but I think tomorrow they may have to go without me. I will not dare sit out in the sun all afternoon.'

Tom Bryce understood her perfectly.

'Then perhaps we will be honoured with your presence in the garden.'

'To pick hops, you mean?'

'No, just to brighten my day.'

She lowered her eyes hastily. 'Will my presence brighten your day then?'

'It certainly will.'

Her heart began to beat uncomfortably fast. 'Then I shall come and see you,' she said.

She saw the faint flicker of a smile on his face. 'I'll look forward to that.'

'Will you?' Her voice was almost a whisper. Suddenly he put a finger beneath her chin and tilted her face, holding it in that position until she raised her eyes to meet his.

'I'll look forward to that very much, Miss Esme.'

The touch of his fingers against her skin thrilled her. 'You're sure you won't change your mind,' he said, 'and go on the picnic?'

Somehow she managed to speak. 'I won't change my mind.' He nodded slowly, and again the smile touched his lips. 'Until tomorrow, then,' he said.

Esme could only nod and then he was gone, shouldering his way between the green hop-poles while Esme's pretended dizziness threatened to become reality. She put a hand to her chest and took deep breaths in an effort to steady her fluttering heart. Then for a moment she was gripped by an unreasoning panic – whatever had she done? How could she behave so foolishly? To arrange a meeting with this man – her friend's employee! She must be out of her mind, she told herself, yet if the gipsy had foretold it then it was fate. She took comfort in that thought. Fate – it was inevitable. Whatever happened was meant to happen. She clung to that thought as she made her way slowly back to the house.

CHAPTER SIX

That night dozens of visitors arrived from London on the late train. The already overcrowded accommodation in the barns was stretched further to the discomfort of all concerned, but there were no complaints for the weekend provided a welcome break from the week's routine. On Saturday and Sunday, visiting fathers and brothers would all join in the picking and on Saturday afternoon they would finish early and retire to the 'Horse and Cart'. There they would consume large quantities of the rough local cider as well as beer, and the children would drink their way through gallons of freshly made lemonade.

The weather remained fine, the day passed pleasantly enough and the long-awaited evening's enjoyment was finally underway. The 'Horse and Cart' was a very small inn which for eleven months of the year rarely held more than a dozen customers at one time. With all the good will in the world it would not be possible to accommodate all the hoppers, so the proprietor set up trestle tables in the courtyard on which he placed barrels and glasses. The latter he hired out at sixpence a glass, thus ensuring their eventual safe return.

Those pickers fortunate enough to have a change of clothing changed; those less fortunate combed their hair and washed hands and faces in preparation for the evening's entertainment. One by one the groups made their way off the farm and along the lane to the 'Horse and Cart'. They sat where they could, for no chairs were provided; the earliest arrivals enjoyed the luxury of the grassy banks and hedges and a few more sat along the fence and on the gates leading into the adjoining fields. The rest sat and sprawled in the road, making it impossible for pedestrians or traffic of any kind to pass through. The local

policeman was there and another stood by to be called in if the
need arose, but for the time being the mood of the hoppers was
cheerful. Being reunited with their loved ones, they were
content to rest from their week's labours and enjoy a drink and
a song. Within an hour of the last hops being picked that
afternoon, almost all the pickers were to be found in and
around the yard of the 'Horse and Cart'. Vinnie was there with
Bertie, Em and their mother. The Battys were there too and
Hetty Bluett. The children had a mug of lemonade each, the
women were drinking beer and the men – more daring – were
sampling the cider. Vinnie, however, was feeling particularly
resentful.

'Why can't *we* go on a picnic?' she grumbled. 'Eva and Julian
are going on a picnic. I want to. Why can't we, Ma?'

Receiving no answer, she tugged at her mother's skirt. 'Ma,
why can't *we* go on a picnic to the river? I want to, Ma. Ma,
what is a picnic?'

Irritably, her mother slapped her hand away and Vinnie
wailed automatically although the slap was only a small one – a
token of her mother's displeasure.

'Don't cry, Vinnie,' said Bertie. 'We'll go on a picnic one
day, I promise you, but not tomorrow.'

'Why not?'

'We just can't, that's all.'

'But *why* can't we?'

Sue Harris was very tired and her own mood was not a
happy one. Surrounded by so many affectionate couples, she
felt the loss of her erring husband. Mrs Batty had Mr Batty, for
what he was worth, she thought sourly. Even Hetty had found
herself a boy-friend – one Sam Piggott. He was no great
shakes, but he was a partner and that was something Sue Harris
lacked. She drained the last of her beer and sent Bertie off to
refill the glass. Then there was another tug at her skirt.

'Why *can't* we go on a picnic like Eva and Julian? Why *can't*
we go to the river?'

'Because I say so,' her mother snapped suddenly, 'and you
can give over talking about your precious Julian and Eva. I'm
sick to death of hearing about them! Don't get any fancy ideas,

Vinnie Harris. They get to go on picnics because they live in a big house with lots of servants and lots of money – you don't and that's why you don't get to go on picnics. Now, give over before I land you one!'

Vinnie immediately set up a loud wail and tears burst from her eyes. Her mother's hand descended on her bare arm and the resounding slap left red finger-marks on her skin. Mrs Batty looked up from her conversation.

'What d'you do that for?' she demanded. 'Why d'you wallop her like that, poor little cocker! She was only asking.'

'She wasn't only asking,' retorted Sue, 'she was moaning and kicking up hell's delight. That's what she was doing. Nag, nag, nag about the bleeding picnic.'

'Well, she's only a little 'un. There's no cause to wallop her like that.'

Sue's misery turned to anger. 'I'll thank you to mind your own damn business,' she cried. 'She's my kid and if I want to wallop her I will!'

A few heads turned their way curiously and Mrs Batty felt it necessary to have the last word.

'There's no need to take it out on the kid. You've got a nasty temper, you have, Sue Harris.'

'Oh, I have, have I? Got a nasty temper, have I?'

'Yes, you have.'

'Well, you're not so bloody perfect yourself. Put a few pints in you and you're laying about you in all directions.'

'What's that supposed to mean?' snapped Mrs Batty. 'I can't take a few drinks – is that what you're saying?'

'If the cap fits . . .'

'Well, that's rich, that is.' Mrs Batty appealed to the growing audience. 'The times I've carried *her* home,' she began. 'Me and Mr Batty here.'

'Carried me home? You never have, you fat lying bitch.'

Mrs Batty glanced at her husband. 'D'you hear that? Do you hear what she called me? Lying bitch, she called me. You going to let her get away with that?'

Mr Batty leaned forward and wagged a reproving finger at Sue. 'Just watch it,' he said, 'that's all. Watch it.' He seemed none too pleased at the way things were developing. He did not feel up to an argument, and already his stomach was churning uneasily after two pints of the strong rough cider.

'Don't you wag your finger at me, Sid Batty,' cried Sue, "cos you're not so hot when you've had a few. The things your old woman's called you on a Friday night. Oh yes, I've heard her.'

Now it was Mr Batty's turn to glare at his wife.

'Oh, don't deny it,' Sue went on, seeing Mrs Batty open her mouth in protest. 'You know it's true. You know the times of a Saturday morning how you've cursed and swore, washing his stinking clothes.'

Mr Batty roared, 'Stinking clothes?' Someone in the crowd shouted, 'You tell him, love. You sort him out,' and roared with laughter.

Vinnie listened anxiously, wishing Bertie would come back.

'Stinking clothes,' repeated Sue. 'Sick all down his jacket and pee in his trousers. Don't deny it, it's written all over your stupid face.'

The raised voices woke Em, who was sleeping in her mother's lap, but she now raised her small fists in the air and began to cry. 'Oh Christ!' cried Sue, 'don't *you* start your racket!'

'What you going to do, then?' Mrs Batty taunted. 'Going to wallop *her*, are you? Poor little sod's only a year old. Going to hit her like you done the other one? Fine mother you've turned out to be.'

By way of answer, Sue's hand flashed out and caught Mrs Batty a stinging blow across the side of her face. Taken by surprise, she jerked sideways and knocked the best half of Mr Batty's third pint of cider over the man next to him, who in turn let out a roar of protest.

'Look what you're bloody doing!' cried Mr Batty.

But already his wife was retaliating by seizing a handful of Sue's hair and jerking her head forward. Hetty Bluett hastily snatched Em from Sue's lap and the crowd edged back a little from the two combatants. If there was one thing they enjoyed more than a sing-song it was a fight, and they watched avidly as it developed. The two women, both slightly the worse for drink, screeched abuse at each other. As they struggled together some in the crowd jeered, others shouted encouragement. Mrs Batty, the heavier of the two, landed the most punishing blows but they did not always find their mark. Sue Harris's fist did less damage when it did strike home, but she was more agile and managed to avoid most of the blows intended for her. Soon they rolled together on the ground, kicking and screaming. Mr Batty made a few ineffectual attempts to separate them, but received a cut lip for his trouble and retired, cursing them both soundly.

'Let them bloody get on with it,' he muttered thickly and was patted on the back for his efforts.

Apart from the dust, neither of the women was marked until Sue's finger-nail caught Mrs Batty's cheekbone and a thin dark line appeared. Mrs Batty put a hand up to her cheek; seeing the slight smears of blood, she let out a fierce scream of rage and hurled herself upon Sue once more.

'I'll murder the bitch!' she shouted.

At that moment there was a disturbance in the crowd. 'Look out, here comes the copper!' someone shouted and people melted apart as the blue-uniformed figure strode towards the two women.

At once Mr Batty ran forward to help him separate them and after a brief but fierce scuffle, the two women were parted. Seeing the policeman, the crowd murmured disapproval at such unseemly behaviour and Hetty Bluett found herself apologising for her friends' rowdy conduct. By the time Bertie returned, the fight was over and the policeman was cautioning the two offenders, threatening to take action against them if the scene was repeated.

There was no sign of Vinnie. She had slipped away through the crowd and now ran as fast as her legs would carry her back towards the comparative safety of the hop-field. Having received the initial slap, she felt somehow to blame for the whole shameful incident. She ran blindly, terrified, not seeing where she was going, and as she made her way through the gap in the hedge she was brought suddenly to a halt. Astonishment drove out all other emotions, for in front of her she saw one of the ladies from the big house and standing beside her, his arm around her waist, was Tom Bryce.

The two adults stared at her in dismay and Tom withdrew his arm suddenly, glancing at the woman beside him. She turned to Vinnie, saying, 'What do you want? What are you doing here?'

Vinnie said nothing, but instinctively took a step backwards. She didn't recognise the expressions on their faces but knew she was not welcome.

'Hop it!' said Tom Bryce. 'Go on, you've no business here. Hop it, I say.'

Vinnie turned and ran – past the barn, through the gate and into the field where the gipsy caravans were parked. These were deserted, for all the gipsies were down at the 'Horse and Cart' with their fellow pickers. A little more slowly, the child made her way past the caravans, the dying embers of a fire and a dog that barked furiously and strained at its chain. She passed three or four horses tethered to a post and then more caravans. At the far end was a small cart containing some hay and a pile of sacks. Vinnie hesitated, glancing behind her to see that she was not observed, then climbed into the cart and snuggled down into the hay. She pulled a few sacks over her and, thus hidden, fell asleep almost immediately.

Several hours later, Vinnie's disappearance began to be taken seriously. The local policeman was informed and the idea of a search party was mooted. The village sergeant made his way to the cottage where Tom Bryce lived with his mother. She opened the door and at once took fright. 'What is it? What's happened?' she cried.

'Nothing to fret about, Mrs Bryce,' said the sergeant. 'I just want a word with your Tom. We've a bit of a problem up at Foxearth. One of the little ones is missing and I've a mind to organise a search party. I could do with his help.'

His words did nothing to reassure Mrs Bryce, who knew her son did not want to be found. 'I don't know where he is,' she said guiltily. 'He's out, you see. Out for the evening. I don't know where and that's a fact.'

'Out, is he?' said the sergeant. 'Have you any idea when he'll be back?'

'No, I haven't. Lateish, I reckon.'

'But you don't know where he's gone?'

'Well, that's to say I don't know *exactly* where he's gone. He's out with a friend, you see.'

'What friend would that be, Mrs Bryce? If you could tell us, we might be able to find him.'

'I can't tell you,' she said quickly. 'He didn't say – just that he was going out to meet a friend.'

'I see.' It was obvious he didn't believe her and she felt her cheeks burning with embarrassment.

'I'll tell him you're looking for him,' she said. 'When he gets back, I'll tell him.'

'That might be too late, Mrs Bryce. We have a child missing, you see.'

'A child?'

'That's right, Mrs Bryce. So, if you could remember where he is or who he's with, it would be very helpful.'

After a long, painful pause she said, 'He has gone out with a lady friend.'

'Ah, I see, and her name?'

'I don't know her name.' That at least was true. She knew it was one of the three guests from the big house but Tom had not given her a name.

'And you've no idea where we could find your son with this young lady?'

'No, sergeant.'

That, too, was true. She could hazard a guess but she had no real knowledge.

The policeman sighed. 'Thank you, Mrs Bryce,' he said. 'If your son returns, perhaps you'd tell him to contact us. He may be in time to help. I shall make the "Horse and Cart" the centre of operations.'

Mrs Bryce nodded and watched the sergeant walk back along the path between the clumps of marigolds of which she was so proud. 'I'll tell him,' she called out and he gave a brief wave of his hand.

Mrs Bryce closed the door and leaned against it. 'Oh, Tom,' she whispered, 'I told you no good would come of this, but you wouldn't listen. You never do.'

Without Tom Bryce's knowledge of the area, the search that followed was a haphazard affair. Some areas were searched more than once, others missed altogether. Time passed and there was no sign of the missing child. Many of the pickers, willing though they might be, were unable to help in the search because they were too drunk to understand what was expected of them and their vision was too blurred to see anything clearly. Bertie searched frantically, calling Vinnie's name again and again. Sue Harris was beside herself with remorse and fear and although advised by the sergeant to wait at the 'Horse and Cart' for news, she refused to do so and stumbled away alone to search for her lost child. Vaguely she remembered that Vinnie's last words were concerned with the river; convinced that she would find her there, she made her way through the dusk towards the bridge.

The picnickers, repacking the hamper, saw her pass, weaving her way erratically across the grass, calling and sobbing, a pathetic figure. They watched her go, astonished.

'What was she saying?' asked Louise. 'It sounded like "Vinnie".'

'I thought so, too,' said Agatha. 'Perhaps she's Vinnie's mother.'

'Wretched woman!' said Christina. 'She's drunk.' She was holding the tablecloth as she spoke and then handed it to Nathan who replaced it in the large wicker basket. Joshua shook the dregs from the wine glasses and packed them too, while Agatha threw the remains of the uneaten sandwiches into the river for the ducks.

'Those potted shrimps were awfully good,' said Nathan, 'but I'm afraid I ate too many.' He patted his stomach and they all laughed.

'I think I drank too much,' said Joshua and he hiccuped loudly.

'What will your father say?' said Agatha. 'He will say we have led you astray.'

'Lucky old Joshua,' said Nathan. 'I wish somebody would lead me astray.'

Louise was watching the dwindling figure of Sue Harris. 'Whatever is she up to?' she asked curiously. 'She looks so wild.'

'She does rather,' Christina agreed. 'Perhaps Vinnie is lost or has run off to hide somewhere. They're a wild lot. No doubt we shall hear what has happened when we get back. Now, have we packed everything?'

Nathan checked the contents of the wicker basket: 'Knives, forks, spoons, plates, glasses, napkins, napkin rings. We certainly did not leave much.'

'Did we leave *anything*?' laughed Louise.

'Actually, no,' said Nathan, 'apart from a few sandwiches. It was a jolly good picnic and I shall tell the housekeeper so when I return.'

By now Sue Harris had disappeared from sight and Louise turned back to her friends. 'Henry should have come with us,' she said. 'I'm sure he would have enjoyed it, he just pretends not to. You should have persuaded him, Chrissie.'

Christina laughed. 'Nothing would induce Henry to go on a picnic,' she said. 'As he says, picnics are for the young.'

'But he is not all that old.'

'He *thinks* like an old man,' said Christina, her mouth tightening. 'I don't think Henry was *ever* young.'

Agatha glanced at her curiously but said nothing. There was a hint of bitterness in Christina's voice which discouraged any further conversation on the subject of her absent husband. Louise had asked her recently whether or not they intended to have any more children. The Colonel had pretended not to hear the question and Christina had said that she thought it most unlikely.

'Are we all set, then?' Joshua asked.

Having made a final search amongst the grass to ensure they had not overlooked anything, they began to walk slowly back towards the bridge. As they climbed back on to the road and turned in the direction of Foxearth, Sue Harris was already forgotten.

*

The light was fading rapidly as Sue stumbled along the edge of the river bank. From time to time she called Vinnie's name but received no answer. Her mind was confused, her steps unsteady. She slipped suddenly and fell, sprawled across the edge of the bank with one arm in the water. With a scream of fright, she struggled into a sitting position; now her feet dangled and her toes were in the water.

'Vinnie,' she called. 'Vinnie, where are you?'

There was a plop and a splash in the middle of the river and she started violently. 'Vinnie!' she cried urgently, imagining that her child had made the sound. Without another thought, she allowed herself to slide down into the water which pulled seductively at her skirt.

'You come out of there, Vinnie!' she cried.

Now the water was up to her knees; then past her knees, cold and dark. As the current drew her further forwards, her feet slipped on the smooth pebbles of the river bed and now and then slimy weed brushed against her legs, making her shudder.

'Vinnie, d'you hear me?' she called again and then stopped to listen. All around her the wind rustled the leaves of the trees and the water gurgled over the stones and lapped against the river bank.

She was surprised to find herself up to her thighs in the river now and suddenly realised she had made a mistake: her child was not here. Half-turning, she began to retrace her steps but trod on a sharp stone and gave a cry of pain. Lifting her foot sharply, she lost her balance and threw out her arms with a shriek of panic. Then she fell and went under, the cold water shocking her into sudden awareness of her danger: as she surfaced she screamed, but there was no one near enough to hear. She was almost in the middle of the river where the current ran faster and the long strands of weed twined themselves round her legs, hindering her movements. Terror gripped her, paralysing her, and she tried to scream again but could make no sound. Her wet skirt hampered her and the weeds clung more closely. Underfoot, a layer of mud covered the bottom so that she could not find a secure foothold. With a strangled cry, she sank beneath the water again, down into the dark depths where the long weeds tangled round her arms and made her prisoner. She threw up her head in a last desperate attempt to reach air, twisting and turning in the cold water, but the more she struggled the faster the weeds held her. Then her lungs filled with water and she did not breathe again.

Much later when it was discovered that she, too, was missing, the search was renewed and went on until dark.

Vinnie awoke several hours later and cried for her mother. A kindly gipsy returned her to the hoppers' barn, where Mrs Batty comforted her with the promise that her mother would surely be back by morning. When the search was resumed at daybreak, they found Sue Harris's body. It had finally freed itself from the clinging weeds and had washed up in the shallow water which lapped against the stonework of the bridge.

CHAPTER SEVEN

The Colonel's study had been furnished to his own taste and did not reflect the elegance of the rest of the house. It was what he called 'a man's room'. The woodwork was dark brown and heavy lace curtains hid the view across the grounds – a view which the Colonel found distracting when he was dealing with matters of business. His large mahogany desk stood just in front of the window where it received whatever light filtered through the lace. The walls were covered with book-shelves and the books themselves were mostly of a fine quality, covered in leather with gilt lettering on the spines. The small fireplace was rarely used, but the usual fire-irons and a filled brass coal-scuttle were placed in front of it. Several large well-stuffed armchairs stood around and there was a small table in the middle of the room on which fresh flowers were regularly placed. To the left side of the fireplace was a folding screen; when this was opened up and placed behind the Colonel's chair, it indicated that he was not to be disturbed as he was probably fast asleep. Now it remained folded and the Colonel was very much awake, striding up and down the worn carpet which had once covered the floor of his father's study and *his* father before him. Christina stood with her back to the window, watching him, waiting for the tirade to come to an end. The Colonel was very angry and when he was angry he usually raised his voice, but not on this occasion. Today was different. He struggled to keep his voice down in case curious servants should overhear the conversation.

'There is no excuse for it!' he stormed. 'It's quite monstrous. Monstrous! Bryce will have to go. I won't hear a word said on his behalf. There is absolutely no excuse for his behaviour. If the man had been where he should have been, this might never have happened. Don't argue with me, Christina, for you know I speak the truth. Now the damned press will be hounding us – what are we to tell them? That when we needed him, my right-hand man was not to be found? God damn it, Christina, a missing child is bad enough but a drowned mother is a damned catastrophe and you know it. What a Sunday! There is no work being done, you realise that I suppose? They are not picking. Well, if they don't pick, I don't pay them. There are hops to be picked and I brought them down here to pick them. One drunken picker drowns herself and now see what a mess we are in! Don't stand there staring at me, Christina. Say something, for God's sake! Do I have to take this whole business on my own shoulders?'

Christina's look was hostile. 'I am allowed an opinion then, Henry?' she said.

'I have just asked for it, haven't I?'

'Very well, Henry, if you ask my opinion I will give it to you but you may not like it.'

'That will be for me to worry about.'

She took a deep breath. 'I think it will look very bad if you blame this whole disaster on to Tom Bryce,' she said. 'His day's work was done. He was entitled to spend the rest of his time how and with whom he chose. You cannot blame him for that, Henry.'

'I do blame him, damn it! I tell you, his work was *not* over. The pickers might have finished but his responsibility does not end there. I do not pay him to go wenching. When I need him, I expect him to be there. I needed him last night to organise the search party and he was not to be found. How can you say the blame does not rest on his shoulders?'

'You asked for my opinion and I gave it to you. You don't necessarily have to agree.'

'We have to agree on what to tell the press!' cried the Colonel. 'If we don't get the story right, then we are really in trouble and I shall never be able to hold up my head again. Even that parsimonious old Parsloe was murmuring about "a farmer's responsibility to his workers". Confounded impudence! What does he know about a farmer's responsibility? All he has to do to earn *his* money is to stand up in church and preach at the rest of us.'

'I am sure he did not mean it as a reproach, Henry. More of a hint, perhaps.'

'A hint? A hint of what?'

'A hint of how we should approach the problem with the press. I think we should accept responsibility and tell them how we intend to make reparation.'

'*Reparation?*' he roared. 'Reparation to whom? To a damned Londoner who chooses to lose me a day's work?'

His wife turned away from him. 'Oh, that will sound very well in the papers, Henry,' she said sarcastically. 'Yes, that will make very good reading. A damned Londoner has chosen to drown herself and has lost Colonel Lawrence of Foxearth a day's picking. Really, Henry, sometimes you are quite intolerable. A boy and two girls have lost their mother today, their father has already left them. What are we going to do about them, Henry? That is the point of this conversation.'

'She was drunk,' he said stubbornly. 'You know it, I know it, everyone knows it.'

'They were *all* drunk. Are you going to say that, too, Henry?'

'Of course I'm not.'

'Then what are you going to say? All these recriminations are getting us nowhere.'

She took a deep breath and turned to face him once more, then moved round the desk and half sat on it, looking at him.

'I have given the matter some thought,' she said. 'I have a suggestion to make and if you are calm enough, Henry, I will make it, but I don't want to be shouted at.'

He glared at her but said nothing, then flung himself into an armchair, thrust out his legs and waited to hear what she had to say.

'Firstly, I think we must agree to see the press,' she began. 'There is no point in waiting. If we object to answering their questions it will look as though we have something to hide – something we are ashamed of – and that is not the case. I think we should tell them there has been a tragedy, that three young children are orphaned, that they have our deepest sympathy and we are concerned for their welfare. I think we should go as far as to say we will make some provision for them.'

'Make provision for them?' he shouted and made as though to get to his feet, but Christina rose and held up a warning hand and he sank back into his chair.

'I think we must ask Mrs Batty to care for them and offer financial assistance. It will show good faith on our part. Your friends will be impressed with your charity, Henry, and the rest of the pickers will be reassured.'

'And if she says no?'

'I don't think she will, Henry. She is no doubt as greedy as the next woman and if *she* is not greedy, then no doubt her husband is. The money will be a great temptation for him. As for Tom Bryce, I think we must absolve him from any blame. We must say that at the end of a hard week's work he was entitled to spend his leisure time as he chose.'

'But damn it, Christina, I won't let the fellow go scot-free and you know why.'

'Do I?'

'You know you do.'

'Be careful what you say, Henry.'

'Careful be damned! I will say what I like in my own home. Tom Bryce was with one of my guests! I would like to horsewhip the fellow.'

'We don't know that for certain. They deny it, and we shall never know what happened.'

'*I* know,' he said, facing her angrily across the few yards that separated them. 'I know that he was not there when I needed him because he had a damn fool assignation with Esme Hart. How is that going to look if the press get hold of it? I shall be a laughing-stock, Christina. That woman is never to set foot in this house again. Do you hear me? Never!'

'I hear you, Henry, but I ask you not to raise your voice unless you want the servants to hear also.'

'To hell with the servants!' he said, but nevertheless lowered his voice a little. 'There is nothing that goes on in this house that the servants don't already know. They have ears and eyes everywhere, make no mistake about that.'

Christina shook her head wearily. 'I still can't believe it,' she said. 'Esme and Bryce. It does not seem possible. Whatever could she be thinking of – and to deceive us in that way, pretending to be sick. But we must pretend to believe her, Henry. We must accept her version of what occurred. If she says she felt recovered and went for a long walk *alone*, we must accept that; if Bryce says he was with Rose whatever-her-name-is, we must accept that too.'

'I'd like to thrash the pair of them,' he growled. 'That would give me great pleasure.'

She smiled faintly. 'I could almost enjoy it myself,' she said.

For a moment neither of them spoke, then Christina straightened her shoulders. 'But the children,' she said. 'We must let it be known that we intend to provide for them in some way. We must make some form of compensation to them for the loss of their mother.'

'Compensation? Was it our fault she drank herself into a stupor and fell into the river?'

'Henry, please be reasonable. You employ them and you must be seen to take some responsibility for their welfare. I wonder if the Battys *would* care for the children if you made them an allowance weekly for their food.'

'Well, you can stop wondering, Christina, because I shall not agree to it. I absolutely refuse to give the Battys a penny. God knows how they would spend it! Drink it all away on a Friday evening, most likely. No, Christina, that is not a good idea at all.'

She shrugged hopelessly. 'Then do you have a better plan?' she asked. 'We must have some idea what we are going to say when the man from the *Kentish Gazette* arrives. The children have lost their mother and their father has already left them. They will end up in the workhouse, Henry, if we don't do something. Perhaps we could find somewhere round here for the older one – put the boy to work on one of the farms. I don't know . . .'

The Colonel glanced at the large carriage clock which stood

in the centre of the mantelpiece above the fireplace. 'We are going to be late for church,' he said.

'We need not go,' said Christina. 'I have sent Louise and Agatha in the carriage to Tunbridge Wells, recommending the Church of King Charles the Martyr. I thought it would get them out of our way while we were discussing the matter.'

He nodded. 'And sly Miss Esme took herself off home,' he said. 'That confirms her guilt in my eyes.'

'She said the drowning had upset her and she could not face working any longer among the pickers.'

'And you believed her?'

'No, Henry. I tried to, but I did not believe her.'

'She should find herself a husband – a suitable husband – if she needs a man that badly.'

'Henry, please! I wish you would not speak in that way.'

'Well, it's true. A woman of her breeding with a man like that – it's disgusting! She need not show her face here again!'

Christina was silent. After her initial anger had cooled, she had felt only curiosity. How could a man like Tom Bryce appeal to a woman like Esme, she wondered. He was not unattractive – a rough diamond, perhaps, but surely his wooing would be rough also. Briefly, she considered the idea and was surprised to find it not altogether unpleasing. With an effort, she dismissed the thought from her mind and said, 'I think it would be better if *I* spoke to the press, Henry. You are likely to lose your temper and say something you may regret. I could tell them you are unwell, that the tragedy has been a terrible shock and you have been forced to rest. I think I could be more diplomatic, Henry. I am not as angry as you are – distressed and hurt, perhaps, but not quite so angry. We must make up our minds quickly what is to be said and done; they will be here soon. What *are* we going to do about the children?'

'Well, the boy's old enough to work. Bryce shall find him employment on one of the farms in the area.'

'And the girl, Vinnie?'

'I don't know, dammit!'

Christina had a flash of inspiration. 'I wonder if Mrs Bryce would take her. She's a nice woman and she said once she has always wanted a daughter. Tom is her only child. If we gave her something for Vinnie's keep . . .'

The Colonel nodded irritably. 'Well, that will do, that will do. Tell the press what you like. Just give them a damned story and get rid of them. I shall ride into Maidstone and see what arrangements I can make for the funeral. It can be very simple, there's no point in throwing money away.'

Christina sighed wearily. 'What a terrible way to die.'

'Tell me a good way to die,' said her husband.

'But to drown – ugh!' She shuddered at the prospect.

There was a knock on the door and Janet came in, her face flushed with excitement. 'Oh, sir,' she said, 'it's the gentleman from the *Kentish Gazette*, a Mr Sanderson. He's got a photographer with him, to take photographs, sir. Shall I show them in?'

'Not just yet, Janet,' said Christina. 'Ask them if they will be kind enough to wait in the drawing-room for five minutes. Then I will see them.'

'Damned news-hound!' said the Colonel. 'I suppose I'll have to see him but he'll get short shrift from me, I can assure you.'

'Henry! I thought we had agreed *I* should talk to him.'

'Well, you thought wrong, then. It wouldn't look right, Christina.'

'Then we must see him together, Henry. I do not want you to—' She broke off. 'What's the matter?'

The Colonel had risen to his feet but now stood awkwardly clutching the arm of the chair. He put one hand to his head and a soft moan escaped his lips.

'Henry? Oh my God!'

Too late Christina darted forward as her husband crumpled to the floor, unconscious. She knelt beside him and put out a hand to touch him, then drew back in sudden revulsion from the sprawled arms and legs. Realising that he still breathed, she stood up, her own breathing rapid with shock. With trembling fingers she smoothed her dress, not taking her eyes from the forlorn figure huddled on the carpet.

'He's had a stroke,' she whispered and still watching him, she reached out for the bell-rope to summon help.

*

Several days later Christina sat by her husband's bed, reading aloud to him an article in the *Kentish Gazette* entitled RIVERSIDE TRAGEDY.

The article occupied a large area of the front page and included two photographs – one of Vinnie and Bertie standing in the hop-garden, another a view of the bridge where the body was discovered. It was disclosed that Colonel Lawrence was taking responsibility for the dead woman's children. The boy would be found employment, the girl placed in the care of Mrs Agnes Bryce, mother of the Colonel's chief pole-puller. Baby Emmeline would be brought up by Mr and Mrs Batty, close friends of the dead woman, helped financially by a sum of money given by Colonel Lawrence. The pickers would take a morning off for the funeral, which would be held in Teesbury Church on the 11th September, all expenses to be borne by the Lawrence family. The Colonel and his wife received high praise for their handling of the affair and for their generosity and public spirit. It was to be hoped, the article concluded, that in similar circumstances other farmers would be inspired by their example.

Christina, having finished reading, folded the paper and put it on the bedside table. 'So that's that,' she said. 'I must confess I am very pleased the way everything has turned out.'

The Colonel moved his head slightly in agreement. The stroke which he had suffered had left him with some loss of movement in his right arm and leg and a certain impairment of vision. The doctor had prescribed complete rest for at least three weeks.

Julian and Eva stood by the foot of their father's bed. They, too, had attended the funeral of Sue Harris.

'Is Vinnie staying with Mrs Bryce for ever?' Eva asked.

Her mother smiled. 'Hardly for ever, Eva. But if she behaves herself and causes no trouble, she will stay for many years. Mrs Bryce is quite taken with her.'

'But where has Bertie gone?'

'To Merryon Farm, the other side of Wateringbury, where

he is to help with the oxen. They are very fortunate children.'

Eva looked up at her mother innocently. 'Would *we* be fortunate if *you* died in the river?'

'Don't be foolish, Eva. I didn't mean fortunate in that respect.'

'Can Vinnie come to play with us?'

'Certainly not. She is not a suitable playmate for you, you know that quite well.'

'But can we visit her?' asked Julian.

'No, there is no need. We have made provision for the children and there's an end to it. Now, if either of you have work to finish you had best do it now. Your tutor will be here in less than half an hour. Say goodbye to your father.'

'Goodbye, father.'

'Goodbye, Papa.'

'Now off you go.'

They disappeared obediently. For a moment Christina looked at her husband as he lay helpless in the large four-poster bed. 'If you are quite comfortable, Henry, I shall leave you now. Janet will come at regular intervals to see if you need anything and you have a bell beside you.'

He gave a slight nod of his head.

'You need not keep nodding, Henry,' she said sharply. 'There's nothing the matter with your voice.'

By way of an answer he closed his eyes and she turned away with a tightening of the lips. At the door she paused, turned and said less sharply, 'There's nothing you want then, Henry?'

He did not reply and she went out of the room. She was a beautiful woman with a beautiful home and two attractive children: many would consider her very fortunate, but she was a passionate woman beneath the cold exterior and the thought of her husband's useless body filled her with revulsion. She went downstairs with an overwhelming feeling of self-pity.

*

Vinnie did not recognise Tom Bryce in his Sunday best. When he emerged from the bedroom, she stared at him open-mouthed while his mother made approving noises. He wore a dark suit with a waistcoat across which a watch-chain glittered, and beneath this a white shirt with a high collar. The top button of his jacket was fastened and a clean white handkerchief protruded from the breast pocket.

'Oh Tom,' cried Mrs Bryce, 'you do look a treat, although I say it myself. You're my son but you do look a treat, doesn't he, Vinnie? That Rose is a lucky girl. But aren't you going to wear your hat? And what about the gloves? You've got a pair of gloves somewhere, Tom, I know you have. You had them for your father's funeral, remember? And what about taking your father's cane? I do think a cane improves a man's outfit.'

Tom stood in the middle of the room while she fussed about him, flicking real and imagined specks of dust from the dark cloth of his suit. His good-looking face wore a resigned expression as he caught Vinnie's eye and smiled. 'What do you think then, Vinnie?' She smiled shyly.

'Tell him he looks a treat, Vinnie, because he does!'

'You look a treat, Mr Bryce.'

'Thank you, Vinnie.'

'And just wait till Rose sees you,' said Mrs Bryce. 'She'll be knocked all of a heap, I know she will. She's such a nice girl. I am so glad it has all turned out this way, Tom. It really is for the best, you know, you had to settle down sometime.'

Six weeks had passed since the death of Vinnie's mother and those six weeks had seen a great change in Tom Bryce's life. He was now engaged to Rose Tully and today they would all be at the church to hear the first banns being called. Rose was not a hard-hearted girl and she had loved Tom for as long as she could remember. After Sue Harris' death Mrs Bryce had approached her, explaining Tom's predicament, and had asked her to swear that Tom had been with her that evening and not with Esme Hart. The knowledge that he *had* been with Esme distressed Rose immeasurably but she agreed to do as Mrs Bryce requested. She spent an unpleasant twenty minutes talking to the village sergeant, lying to save Tom from whatever trouble might threaten him. Tom was grateful, naturally, and agreed to take her to Margate for the day by

way of a 'thank you'. They strolled on the beach and listened
to the band and then walked hand in hand along the pier. Much
to his surprise, Tom enjoyed her sunny company more than he
expected, and tentatively arranged another meeting. One thing
led to another, until one evening Rose's father discovered them
in the hay together and suggested that he make an honest
woman of her. Tom was reluctant at first, but his mother
added her entreaties to Rose's tears and eventually he gave in.
Christina, on her husband's behalf, gave the union their
blessing and wrote immediately to Esme casually mentioning
the engagement and adding, rather unkindly, that everyone
considered the two of them well-suited.

'I must say you do look a treat, Tom,' his mother repeated.
She seized a duster and polished his already highly polished
boots. 'Vinnie, look in the cupboard and see if you can find the
cane with the carved top. Tom, you fetch your hat and the
gloves. If you are going to dress up you might as well do it
properly, and hurry! She'll be here in a moment.'

Vinnie opened the door of the cupboard and peered
carefully around. She, too, was wearing her Sunday best
bought for her by the Lawrences: a pair of boots with buttons
up the side, a coat edged with fur and a matching bonnet. She
found the cane, which looked like a small version of a walking-
stick, and hurried back with it.

Mrs Bryce nodded. 'That's it, Vinnie. You'll see. When
Tom holds that he'll look like a real gentleman.'

As she spoke, a large artificial flower on her hat bobbed
about and Vinnie waited for it to fall off but was disappointed.
Tom came downstairs again wearing his hat and took the cane
and gloves in his hand. He struck a pose, his weight on one leg,
the cane held across his shoulder.

'Would you take me for a gentleman, then?' he asked and
Vinnie and his mother assured him that they would.

At that moment there was a knock on the door and Vinnie
was sent to open it. Rose Tully was a cheerful girl, with dark
hair and grey eyes. Perhaps her eyes were set rather too wide
apart and her mouth was over-generous, but when she smiled
her face lit up and today she smiled radiantly. Today the banns

would be called and in four weeks' time the man she desired would become her husband. Fate had played very nicely into her hands and she gave thanks nightly in her prayers.

'Why, Tom!' she cried. 'What a dandy you look! A real city gent, don't you think so, Ma?' she appealed to Mrs Bryce, who nodded. 'Don't you think so, Vinnie? And *you* two look a real picture!' she said. 'How about me? Do I look a picture?' She spun around and Mrs Bryce thought she could hardly have chosen a nicer daughter-in-law. Rose wore a warm coral coat with a small stand-up collar and large sleeves which tapered in to her wrists. On her head she had a boater trimmed with ribbons and flowers. Her dark hair was swept back into a bun at the nape of the neck and her face gleamed from the application of soap and water.

'You look lovely, dear. A real treat,' said Mrs Bryce.

Rose grinned cheerfully around. 'We *all* look bonny,' she cried. 'I can't wait to get to the church and have everyone admire us. Look at Vinnie there, a real little princess. It is Vinnie, isn't it?' She peered into Vinnie's face, pretending not to recognise her and the child nodded delightedly.

'Come along, then,' said Rose eagerly. 'If we start straightaway and take our time we can walk to the village as slow as we like – give them all a chance to see us,' and she slipped her arm through Tom's. 'Do we make a handsome couple?' she asked.

'You do, indeed you do,' said Mrs Bryce.

She took Vinnie's hand and the four of them went outside and down the steps. Mrs Bryce locked the door behind them and slipped the key underneath the mat.

As they walked through the village under the admiring glances of all who saw them, Rose's heart was full of joy. She thought fleetingly of Esme Hart and her heart momentarily contracted, but the pang of jealousy was soon forgotten. Generously, she pitied the grand London lady, for she had lost and little Rose Tully had won.

*

The gardens ran with water, lashed by the heavy November rains which turned the earth into mud and drove against the hop-poles from the west, darkening the wood on one side only. The last of the autumn leaves from ash and chestnut were brought down to mingle with their sodden fellows on the rain-soaked ground. An old dog fox sloped across the top of the garden with head well down and brush just clear of the mud, its manner disconsolate. Above, a squirrel peered down and chattered a desultory warning, smugly aware that its position half-way up the trunk of a poplar rendered it safe from harm.

The rain slid down the poles to the waterlogged earth below and ran into rivulets, which in turn made their way down the sloping ground to the hedge at the bottom where they swelled the water already brimming in the ditch. Beneath the ground the water drained downward into the river so that it flowed, brown and deep, to the very tips of the rushes, causing the moorhens to squawk in alarm as the current seized them and threatened to carry them downstream.

Tom Bryce trudged through the mud, his head down, making his way to the barn which two months earlier had echoed to the voices of the Londoners but now stood empty, creaking with the weight of the rain in the thatch. As he entered, he was surprised to see Christina Lawrence who turned at the sound of his footsteps.

'Ah, there you are,' she said. 'I thought I might find you here. I wanted to be sure we had enough suitable dry wood for the bonfire – the day after tomorrow.' He did not answer and she continued, 'It will be the fifth. The children have made a guy.'

He nodded, regarding her humorously. 'You've forgiven me, seemingly,' he said.

'Forgiven you?'

'Well, you're speaking to me, first time since the drowning.'

Christina flushed slightly. 'I only spoke as my husband would have done, had he been able.'

Tom nodded again. 'You did very well,' he assured her, his tone slightly mocking. 'You set me back by the ears, I can tell you. A right rollicking, I told my mother.'

His manner was relaxed and Christina found herself ill at ease, disconcerted by his frank scrutiny.

'You deserved it,' she said.

'So you say.'

'About the wood—' said Christina, hoping to return to a less controversial subject.

'So you've forgiven me?' he insisted, smiling now.

She made a gesture of impatience. 'I suppose so,' she admitted. 'Is it so important to you, to establish the fact?'

'Oh yes, very important. You're the gaffer now, you're the boss. It's important to be forgiven. Got to keep on the right side of the boss.'

He touched his forehead with a gesture of exaggerated humility and Christina laughed in spite of herself.

'Enough said, Tom,' she assured him. 'You *are* forgiven. Can we change the subject?'

'The firewood, ma'am, will be available whenever you want it. Over there.' He pointed to a pile of wood in the corner behind her. 'And I'll be on hand as usual to see they don't burn the place down. Weather permitting, that is. If it goes on like this, you'll no doubt put it off until the following weekend?'

'Yes, I will. Thank you.'

'It was Carrie's doing in a way, you know,' he said provocatively.

'Carrie's doing? What was Carrie's doing?'

He told her about the fortune-telling and she laughed aloud in genuine amusement.

'You're a wicked man, Tom,' she said. 'Poor Esme!' Her expression changed slightly. 'But no doubt she—' She stopped, confused.

'No doubt she enjoyed herself?' Tom suggested. He shook his head. 'Not really. Just a kiss or two. That's all, I swear it.'

'Is that all?' She tried to mock him but her voice betrayed her. 'Poor Esme.' There was a long pause and then she said, 'I almost pity her.'

Her voice was very low but Tom heard the words. 'Maybe *you* would not have escaped so lightly,' he said.

Christina caught her breath, never taking her eyes from his face.

'But now,' she said, 'you are a married man.'

'And you a married lady.'

She nodded and swallowed. 'And Carrie is no longer with us,' she said.

'Perhaps I should send for her?'

'I should not be fooled so easily.'

Tom Bryce grinned, amused by her uncertain manner; by the knowledge that his bold talk disturbed her.

'Perhaps we do not need Carrie?' he suggested and saw the colour rush into Christina's face.

'Don't!' she begged, suddenly vulnerable, her defences down.

'Perhaps,' he went on, 'I only need to reach out and take what I want.'

Her eyes implored him silently and he knew it was now or never. Very slowly he moved closer and let his hands rest on her shoulders. Christina seemed to hold her breath as he leaned forward and she made no resistance as he lowered his head towards her. As he kissed her, she trembled and then her arms moved slowly to encircle his neck, her slim fingers exploring his hair and sliding through the thick brown curls. Her long fair lashes lay fringed against her cheeks. Suddenly she drew back and looked at him searchingly as though she had never seen him properly before.

'Oh, Tom!' she whispered and then began to return his kisses with an abandonment which astonished him.

*

During the following year Vinnie saw her brother from time to time when he drove over with manure for the hops in a cart pulled by two oxen. Always she was awestruck by their large eyes and wide horns. Foxearth used only horses.

'They won't hurt you,' Bertie had assured her. 'They're good old beasts.'

'They're cows,' said Vinnie. 'I know.'

'They're not cows,' Bertie slapped one of them affectionately. 'This is an ox, silly. This is Tugger and that one's Titch. Welsh Runts they are, if you must know.'

Vinnie had looked at him admiringly, impressed by his knowledge and increased stature.

One day when he arrived, however, he drew her to one side and sat beside her on the grass.

'I've something to tell you,' he said to her. 'A secret and you mustn't mind. I have come to say goodbye, Vinnie.'

'Goodbye?' She stared at him.

'Yes. I can't stick it there any longer. I'm going to run away.' She tried to grasp what he was telling her and when she understood the familiar scowl settled over her face.

He grinned. 'You haven't changed much, Vinnie – a bit cleaner, that's all. When are you going to start growing?'

'I don't know. Why are you going away, Bertie?'

'I told you, I can't stick it there. It's the farmer's wife, she's got it in for me. I don't know what I ever done to her but she's got her knife into me proper. Always cursing me and name-calling and half-starving me.'

This last Vinnie could understand. 'Are you hungry, Bertie?' she asked.

'I'm always hungry.'

Tugger tossed his head in an effort to drive away the flies that buzzed around the dung-cart and settled over his face. Both animals were panting and their tongues hung out.

'They're tired,' he said, 'they had a hard day yesterday. We was ploughing and the ground was heavy. Lay down in the end, they did, sulking.'

Vinnie laughed.

'It's true,' he said. 'And they wouldn't get up. Pulling at them, I was. I thought they'd never get to their feet again. I had to call Ted. He soon fixed 'em. Know what he did?'

She shook her head.

'Dropped a bit of water in their ears. You should've seen 'em jump.'

Vinnie laughed, then she became serious again. 'Don't go away, Bertie. I won't know where you are. I won't see you.'

He shrugged. 'You don't see me much now, Vinnie. I'll

write to you if you like and send you a postcard with my name on it and my address; then you *will* know where I am.'

'But where will you be, Bertie? London?'

He shook his head. 'I'm going to Margate,' he said. 'I reckon I'll find work there. I'm tall for my age, see? I'll say I'm fourteen or fifteen. I'll get a job, easy.'

It was all too much for Vinnie. 'But why don't you like it at the farm?'

'I've told you, it's *her*. She hates me. Seems she had a boy of her own and he died. He would have been the same age as me, but he got killed, see. She never talks about him. I think she hates me because I'm alive and he's dead. Leastways, that's what Ted reckons. She's never going to take to me, that's what he says, and I reckon he's right. But what about you, Vinnie, what do you do? Are you all right here? They kind to you, are they?'

She nodded. 'I scrub the table,' she said 'and feed the chickens and scare the birds with a rattle. Sometimes I go in the hop-garden with Tom and I go to school.'

'Do you, now. School, eh?'

'I go to school and the teacher said I am a fast learner and I'm learning to read. She says I've got a good head on my shoulders – I heard her tell Mrs Bryce.'

'Well, that's fine, Vinnie, that's just fine.' He looked round. 'Where's Tom Bryce?'

'Up at the top.' She waved her hand towards the higher slopes of the hop-garden.

'I've got to dump this load and then go back for another. Do you want to ride with me?'

Vinnie's eyes glowed and she nodded.

'Come on, then, we'll ask him.'

The manure was ideal as a mulch for the hops and Foxearth bought as much as possible from Merryon. It was richer than horse manure and because Merryon Farm kept eight oxen in all, there was never a shortage.

Tom and Bertie between them emptied the cart of its load and Tom gave Vinnie permission to ride with her brother on the return trip. For Vinnie it was a great excitement to be perched up on the cart beside her beloved Bertie, looking down on the broad red backs of Tugger and Titch as they moved steadily forward with a rolling gait, happier now that the cart was empty. At Merryon Farm Bertie made a detour so that they would not meet the farmer's wife. While he reloaded the cart Vinnie remained on her perch, watching nervously for any sign of Bertie's enemy. Luck was with them, however, and with a jubilant grin, he finally rejoined her and took the reins into his hands.

'Off we go again,' he said. 'Come on, young Vinnie, you can help me drive them,' and he laid part of the reins across her lap and laughed at her momentary panic. Vinnie wanted the journey to go on for ever, but although she was only six she knew already that joys do not last. When the moment came for Bertie to return to Merryon without her she was resigned to it.

'And I *will* write to you, Vinnie,' he said, hugging her. 'I swear it on my honour. Cut my throat and hope to die!'

'Don't!' she begged in alarm.

He grinned and gave her a little shake. 'You be a good girl, Vinnie, and one of these days I'll turn up to see you and I'll bring you a present. How's that?'

'A present, Bertie, for me?'

'Yes, I promise it.'

'Thank you, Bertie.'

'And if you get unhappy, Vinnie, you let me know. Do you hear me? You just let me know.'

She nodded.

'If anyone hurts you, Vinnie, they'll have me to reckon with. Don't you forget it. Ma's gone and Pa's gone but you've still got me.'

She nodded again and he hugged her once more, so hard that it hurt. Then he climbed back on to the cart, touching the oxen delicately with the tip of his whip, and they were rumbling away along the lane. He waved to her until he was out of sight.

Vinnie wondered what to do. She knew that running away was a bad thing and a secret not to be told. She wondered what

Margate would be like and she thought of the present he would give her when he came back. If running away meant presents, it could hardly be all bad and perhaps in Margate Bertie would not be hungry any more. She certainly hoped it would be that way.

CHAPTER EIGHT

In 1893 the best school in the immediate area was undoubtedly Teesbury and it was this school that Vinnie attended. An ugly grey stone building, it stood under a slate roof and boasted a small playground which served also as a drill area when the weather permitted. In one of the classrooms Miss Maude Babbit sat on the high stool behind her desk and listened to the chanting which came from the room next door:

My help cometh from the Lord,
which made heaven and earth.
He will not suffer thy foot to be moved: He that keepeth
Thee will not slumber.
Behold, He that keepeth Israel shall neither slumber nor
sleep.

There were only two classes in Teesbury School – the infants and the juniors. Maude Babbit taught the infants and Miss Gibbs the juniors, but at the moment the children were separated into boys and girls: the girls learned needlework with Miss Babbit while the boys chanted Psalm 121.

Miss Babbit's gaze travelled over the bent heads in front of her and any girl glancing up from her work met the stony stare for which the teacher was famous. It was a stare well remembered by all the pupils long after they had left school. Her trained ear caught a slight whisper from the back of the room and she reacted automatically.

'Joan Dolling, stop talking at once and get on with your work.'

'Yes, Miss Babbit.'

'And I hope that your hands are cleaner than they were last week.'

'They are, Miss Babbit.'

'Are they? Then perhaps you would be good enough to come out and show them to me.'

All eyes followed Joan Dolling as she put down the apron on which she was working and walked to the front of the class. She held up her hands, palms forward for the teacher's inspection, then turned them round. Maude Babbit was a fair woman.

'Good, you may sit down again.'

As she sat down Joan flashed a look of triumph at the girl next to her. Lavinia Harris, now nearly twelve, was her closest friend and as Joan was thirteen they were the oldest girls in the school and as different as chalk from cheese. Joan was a harum-scarum child, Lavinia was more serious. Too serious perhaps, thought Maude Babbit, but with her background it was hardly surprising. A runaway father, a drowned mother and her brother too had run away. But at least she had a comfortable home with Mrs Bryce and the old woman was fond of the girl. Her gaze moved on. Sally Yates, ten years old, slightly deaf in her left ear; poor Ann Bishop, amiable but dull-witted; Sheila Stevens, nearly nine, lethargic and unimaginative; her younger sister, Harriet, bright as a button.

Next door they had started the psalm again.

– I will lift up mine eyes unto the hills, from whence cometh my help –

Maude Babbit sighed. Thirty-two years old and a spinster, she had taught at the school for the past eleven years. Before that she had been a pupil teacher and as a child had attended the same school. She had never known any other life but now, suddenly and unexpectedly, Joshua Parsloe had proposed to her and was impatiently awaiting her answer. It was this problem that absorbed her thoughts and made concentration difficult. She had never expected to be anything other than a school-teacher, but she was still young. Nevertheless, did she want to give up her work and marry Joshua Parsloe? She was not in love with him and did not pretend to be, but he was a decent man by all accounts and lived comfortably on a small private income. She was young enough to bear children, but whenever she tried to imagine the preliminaries that would result in a child she hastily put the idea from her. The marriage bed did not appeal to her, but no doubt it would be a necessary part of the bargain if she said, 'Yes'.

A scraping of chairs in the next room told her that the boys' study period had ended and they were now on their way outside to drill in the open air. She did not envy Miss Gibbs, for the July sun was very hot and there was no shade at this time of the day. One or two heads turned as the lesson outside began:

'Up, down, forward and back. Up, down, forward and back.'

She smiled to herself, resisting the temptation to cross the room and look out of the window. Miss Gibbs, the head-mistress, was sixty years old and shaped like the proverbial dumpling, but she was full of energy and was no doubt performing the exercises with the boys. Some of the girls saw that Maude Babbit smiled and allowed themselves a snigger of amusement at the headmistress's expense.

'Get on with your work, girls. Vinnie Harris, bring your work out to me.'

Vinnie carried her almost completed petticoat to the teacher. Already she moved with a natural grace and she was growing taller. Her hair, now regularly washed, gleamed like gold as it passed through the slanting sun which came in at the window.

'Don't look so worried, I'm not going to bite you.'

Vinnie smiled shyly and handed the petticoat to the teacher who inspected it with a pleased expression.

'Good girl, you have done very well. You may now choose the lace.'

Vinnie crossed to the cupboard and drew out a big cardboard box containing a variety of trimmings and braids and from these, after much consideration, she selected a piece of heavy cream lace.

'Take note, girls,' said Miss Babbit, 'that the lace on the bottom of a petticoat must measure one and a half times the length round the bottom of the garment, which will allow sufficient for gathers. Lavinia will gather it up on a single thread and pin it into place before tacking it.'

As Vinnie went back to her seat, Maude Babbit eyed her speculatively. Had the child heard anything, she wondered? Did she know of the rumours that abounded in Teesbury – the rumours that concerned Christina Lawrence and Tom Bryce? If so, she showed great discretion for a child of her age. She was in and out of Rose's tiny cottage and took a great delight in the three children. If Vinnie knew anything, it seemed she said nothing to Rose who appeared blissfully ignorant of her husband's infidelity.

'Ten minutes more, girls. Finish off the thread you are using, but don't start another length. Sarah, did I see your lips move? I do hope not. Please save your comments for the playground. If it is worth saying, you will remember it.' The familiar words sounded suddenly trite.

Mrs Joshua Parsloe, she thought, wife and mother. Somehow the words lacked conviction and the whole idea seemed impossible.

'Ann Bishop, open the window, please, it is very stuffy in here.' A few moments later the bell rang and she watched the class troop silently out into the sunshine. She gazed round the empty classroom which was her second home. Was this what she wanted for the rest of her life, or was it Joshua Parsloe? Aloud she whispered, 'I don't know: I just don't know.' It was a cry from the heart.

*

Jarvis Tupp watched the two girls walk across the playground towards him, as he waited beside the old tree-trunk which was reserved by common consent for the oldest girls in the school. It was dry as a bone and completely free of bark and the surface was shiny with use. Jarvis, nearly fifteen, was the son of Will Tupp who kept the store in the village. He was an awkward, clumsy child and his father did not look forward to the day when he would join him in the shop, so had left him at school longer than most of the village boys.

Joan and Vinnie pretended not to notice him until they had almost reached the tree-trunk. They walked slowly, almost languidly, their arms draped round each other's waists, their heads close together. Jarvis considered them much too young for him, but there was no one else since Emily Drew had left to become a lady's maid. Emily, at fourteen, had been very mature for her age and had taught Jarvis Tupp a great deal in the area of his education not dealt with by the village school. Eager and willing to put this knowledge to further use, he had turned his attention to Joan and Vinnie, but so far with disappointing results. Now Vinnie looked up and gave a gasp of pretended annoyance.

'Oh, not again!' she said. 'It's Jarvis Tupp.'

'Oh no!' said Joan.

Jarvis smiled. 'Good morning, ladies,' he said. 'You are both looking charming.'

'You said that this morning,' said Vinnie scathingly. 'Can't you think of anything else to say?'

The two girls regarded him pointedly.

'*If* you will excuse us,' said Vinnie, 'we have things to say that we don't want people to listen to.'

They seated themselves on the tree-trunk with a great flurry of skirts and petticoats.

'Go ahead,' said Jarvis. 'Talk away. You won't disturb me.'

'But you are disturbing *us*,' said Vinnie. 'Look, just go away and leave us alone.'

He thrust his hands into his pockets in a way which he hoped was nonchalant and regarded them loftily. Then he said, 'There's no law against me standing here while you are sitting there.'

Vinnie groaned and Joan rolled her eyes. 'Well you don't have to stare at us, do you?' said Joan. 'There are plenty of other things to look at.' She waved her hand airily. 'Trees, sky, the school.'

'I'd rather look at you,' said Jarvis, 'and while I am looking, I think things.' He accompanied these last words with a meaningful leer.

'What do you mean "think things"?' asked Vinnie, knowing very well what he meant.

'Oh, just things,' he said. 'Don't you want to know what things?'

'No, we don't,' said Joan. 'Knowing you, Jarvis Tupp, it's bound to be something unpleasant.'

However, he continued to look at them, his weaselly face screwed up into what he fondly imagined was a sardonic grin. The two girls whispered together.

'I'm thinking about your legs,' he said at last.

The two girls squealed and clung together. 'I shall tell Miss Gibbs,' cried Joan, 'and she'll cane you.'

'She won't, because you won't tell her.'

He knew this to be true. If they did tell her, then these wickedly sinful exchanges would cease and none of them wanted that to happen.

'I'm thinking,' he went on, 'about being in bed with you both.' There was a pause while all three of them considered such a situation.

'How d'you mean, with both of us?' said Vinnie. 'Take it in turns?'

'Something like that,' he said.

The girls both shrieked again. 'You've got a nerve,' said Vinnie. 'You ought to be ashamed of yourself.'

'Well, I'm not,' he said. 'The trouble with you two is you're too young. Emily understood. She had a nice body, too.'

'You don't mean—' gasped Vinnie. 'You didn't see Emily Drew without her . . .' She could not finish the sentence.

He laughed shortly. 'Would I tell you if I had?' he countered, and Vinnie's eyes narrowed.

'Emily Drew would not let you do anything like that,' she said. Since Emily had left the village, there was no way of proving whether what he said was true or not. The girls knew it and so did he.

'If she did,' said Vinnie, 'then she's no better than she ought to be.'

'She enjoyed it,' said Jarvis, 'and so did I and so would you.'

'Jarvis Tupp!' cried Joan. 'You have the cheek of the devil. Don't you dare say things like that! We would not enjoy it, would we, Vinnie?'

'Certainly not,' said Vinnie, 'so stop that sort of talk, Jarvis Tupp, or else go away.'

'You're scared,' he said. 'You're scared to admit that you might enjoy it – that you might learn something.'

'Learn something?' echoed Vinnie. 'From Jarvis Tupp? I don't think so. Not much chance of that.'

'There's nothing you could teach us, Jarvis Tupp,' said Joan. 'Nothing that we would want to learn, anyway.'

He grinned and looked at Vinnie. 'I reckon your legs would be a bonny sight,' he said. At this Vinnie leapt off the tree-trunk but he was too fast and dodged the wild blow.

'Help me, Joan!' cried Vinnie as Jarvis continued to dodge about. Joan slid from the tree-trunk, but at that moment the bell rang and Miss Babbit appeared in the playground with the large brass hand-bell. There was no talking allowed after the first bell had rung, and no movement, so they all froze until it rang again and then hurried into their separate lines. Vinnie was flushed and furious; Jarvis grinned triumphantly, while Joan hid her disappointment that *she* had not been the one finally provoked to action.

'Eyes front!' said Miss Babbit. 'Arms still, feet still. Straighten up, boys. David Warren, did I see your lips move? I hope not. Where is Ann Bishop?'

The girls giggled and Ann Bishop appeared sheepishly from the girls' toilet and joined the end of the line.

'I see nothing at all funny. Lead in, boys.'

Risking a reprimand, Jarvis Tupp threw a final glance in Vinnie's direction and then disappeared through the doorway.

'Girls, lead in,' said Miss Babbit and the girls followed. What is it, Vinnie wondered, that Jarvis Tupp could tell her? And what was it that he and Emily Drew enjoyed so much – if he was to be believed? It must be more than a kiss, probably much more. She wrote her name at the top of the spelling paper and sighed. Presumably one day she would find out for herself. In the meantime she applied herself conscientiously to the work in hand. It was important to Vinnie Harris to get ten out of ten every time.

*

At the end of the afternoon when the bell rang, Miss Babbit asked Vinnie to stay behind. Vinnie's heart sank and she watched reluctantly as Joan left her to her fate with a cheery wave of her hand. Miss Babbit sat on her high stool and leaned forward with her arms resting on the desk, her fingers neatly entwined. Vinnie stood before the desk and looked up at the teacher with a sullen look replacing her usually pleasant expression. Miss Babbit appeared not to notice.

'I hear that Miss Gibbs has spoken to you, Vinnie,' she began. Vinnie nodded.

'Yes, Miss Babbit,' prompted the teacher.

'Yes, Miss Babbit.'

'She tells me you did not seem very taken with the idea. That surprised me, Vinnie. You are a clever girl and the position would suit you. Most girls would be flattered and delighted at the prospect.'

She waited, while Vinnie fidgeted from one foot to the other.

'I don't want to be a school-mistress,' she said at last.

'Why not, Vinnie?'

Vinnie shrugged without answering and the teacher counted to ten. 'Why don't you, Vinnie?' she persisted. 'It would give you financial security and you would be well respected.'

Vinnie sighed deeply at this and Miss Babbit felt her patience slipping away.

'Don't you want security and respect?' she asked. 'You really do not seem to understand exactly what we are offering, Vinnie. You would stay on here and assist me for a year or two – maybe less – and you would eventually replace me.' She wondered whether to tell Vinnie of her possible betrothal and decided to do so. 'In fact, it may be sooner than you imagine, Vinnie. I may be marrying shortly and then, if I should—'

'You're to be wed?' Vinnie was surprised into speech. A

broad smile lit up her face and the sullen expression vanished. 'Oh, Miss Babbit! Who are you going to marry?'

The teacher smiled faintly and made a nervous gesture with her hands. 'I only said "might",' she insisted. 'I haven't yet made up my mind. But you can see, can't you, that if I *do* and if I should – well, if God sees fit to grant us a child – you would be an invaluable replacement. You know the ways of the school and are familiar with the—'

'It's Mr Parsloe!' cried Vinnie. The slight blush on Maude Babbit's cheeks gave her away and she nodded confirmation.

'But it is a secret between us,' she warned. 'As I've told you, I am still undecided, but if I should leave the school, for whatever reason, you would take my place and when you have completed your training—'

'I don't *want* to be a school-mistress,' interrupted Vinnie, the excitement fading once more from her eyes.

'Then what *do* you want to be?' cried Miss Babbit. 'You surely do not mean to spend your life among the hop-poles? Is that all you want from life? With your brains, Vinnie, you are worth more than that. Work on the land is for those less well endowed with intellect.'

'I don't want to work in the hop-gardens. I want to go to London.'

To Vinnie it seemed that her words hung in the air.

'To London?'

'Back home with Emm and the Battys. Mrs Batty said I might lodge with them for a bit until I find work. I'm going to talk to them when they come down in September.'

'Vinnie! Have you taken leave of your senses? Go to London? Leave Mrs Bryce?'

Vinnie looked away. 'I've got my own family,' she muttered.

'Well!' For a moment Miss Babbit was lost for words, but Vinnie looked at her defiantly.

'I could work in an office,' she said. 'I could learn to use a typewriter, lots of girls do. I could learn – you said I have a good brain.'

Miss Babbit's mouth closed in a thin disapproving line.

'That will do, I think, thank you. We will talk about it some other time when you have returned to your senses. No! I said that will do. Save your arguments. I am tired and I have no time for such nonsense. Go home, Vinnie Harris, and think carefully about what I have said.'

Vinnie opened her mouth to protest, changed her mind and closed it again.

'Goodnight, Vinnie.'

'Goodnight, Miss Babbit.'

On the way home Vinnie considered the prospect of stepping into Maude Babbit's shoes. She thought about the teacher, seeing again the thin face with its brown eyes and small, prim mouth and the plain clothes she wore, even to church on Sundays. Would she, Vinnie Harris, be forced into the same mould if she allowed herself to be persuaded? Miss Babbit was plain and still a spinster. If she wed Joshua Parsloe, she would relinquish her accustomed role and play, instead, the dutiful wife. Vinnie shuddered at the thought of life as Mrs Joshua Parsloe. If *only* they would let her go to London, she thought. London was different. In London life would be exciting and she would meet wonderful people who would appreciate her. She would *be* somebody. Quite how it would all come about Vinnie did not know, but she was quite certain that it would. As she neared home she squared her shoulders with sudden resolution. She would pray hard; she would explain her dilemma and then she would leave the problem in God's hands for he was better able to deal with such matters. Vinnie pushed open the gate with a heart grown suddenly lighter and as she made her way round to the back door, she was humming cheerfully.

*

Later that same evening Mrs Bryce and Vinnie sat in the small kitchen, the former darning a pair of Tom's socks, the latter struggling with a list of dates which must be memorised by the following morning.

'I don't know what Tom does to his socks,' grumbled Mrs Bryce, peering shortsightedly at a blue sock which was stretched over a wooden mushroom, 'but he has always been the same even as a lad. You would think he had no boots, the way he went through his socks. Pair after pair and he's no better now.'

Vinnie nodded without answering.

'Just look at that!' Mrs Bryce held out the sock with its offending hole for Vinnie's inspection. 'I told him,' she went on, '"Rose has got her hands full without all your socks to darn." Poor Rose, all those children to care for and another one on the way. I told him, "You're not a rabbit, Tom", but he just laughed. He takes no notice of me, but then he never did.'

Vinnie tried to concentrate on the list in front of her. Tom was virtually his mother's sole topic of conversation and with an effort Vinnie could let her words flow in one ear and out of the other.

'Henry the First, 1100–1135, Stephen, 1135–1154, Henry the Second, 1154–1189, Richard the First, 1189—' There was a sudden tap at the window and Vinnie cursed silently.

'Well, I never!' said Mrs Bryce. 'There's that tapping again. Every night at the same time. Are you sure you don't know who it is, Vinnie?'

She looked at Vinnie curiously, but the girl had turned her face away to hide her guilty expression – she guessed rather than knew that it was Jarvis Tupp.

'How would I know?' she said.

'Well, dear, no one is going to come tapping for me at my age. I reckon you've got an admirer.'

'I have *not*,' said Vinnie.

'Well, how can you say that, dear, if you don't even look outside. It might be Prince Charming on a white horse come a-wooing!' She laughed at the flight of fantasy but Vinnie was not amused. The tapping was repeated a little louder.

'Just pop your head out of the door and say "Hullo".'

'I don't want to.'

'Well, you know how persistent he is, dear. He will just go on tapping if you don't. Shall *I* have a look outside?'

'No! I'll go.' Reluctantly, she put down her notebook and opened the back door, making as much noise as possible, thus giving whoever it was time to hide. She glanced outside, then hastily withdrew her head.

'I can't see anyone,' she said. 'Whoever it is must have gone.'

'You didn't have much of a look, dear.'

'I haven't got time to waste,' said Vinnie. 'I'm trying to do some work and anyway I don't care who it is.'

Mrs Bryce smiled gently. 'Well, you're a growing girl, Vinnie, and you're bound to have admirers. You'll have to get used to the idea. You really are getting quite bonny with that lovely hair of yours. You'll be wanting a young man before long and Jarvis Tupp is not a bad lad.'

'Jarvis Tupp! Who said it was Jarvis Tupp?' Vinnie felt herself blushing.

'Well, whoever it is, dear, you could do a lot worse. His father's got that nice little shop and when he's dressed up in his Sunday best—'

'I don't like Jarvis Tupp,' protested Vinnie, 'he's horrible.'

'Do you think so?' Mrs Bryce was genuinely surprised. 'He looks quite nice in that blue suit of his. I've seen him in church once or twice and thought what a nice-looking lad. He could grow up very handsome.'

'I don't care if he never grows up,' muttered Vinnie.

'Vinnie, that's not a nice thing to say. The lad's done you no harm. Just comes knocking at the window hoping you will go out and say a few kind words to him.'

'Well, I won't.'

Mrs Bryce shrugged. 'Well, that's up to you, dear. I don't suppose you could do any better. He really isn't a bad lad.'

'You wouldn't think so,' said Vinnie, 'if you knew how he talked at school – if you knew the things he said and what he thinks.'

'Really, dear? What sort of things?' She stopped darning.

'Nothing,' said Vinnie. 'I don't want to talk about it.'

Mrs Bryce bit off the wool and surveyed the darn with satisfaction. 'Well, when you've finished that homework,' she said, 'you can give me a hand with these socks. There're two more pairs here and I shall be all night at it.'

There was another tap at the window and Vinnie threw down her book in exasperation.

'Now don't take on, dear, just pop your head out of the door and say a few friendly words. Tell him you've work to do and you're going to give me a hand with the darning. Then there's an end of it.'

But Vinnie refused to go out again and to her great relief, the tapping eventually ceased. When she was sure she had memorised her dates, she put away her books, dutifully took up one of Tom Bryce's socks, threaded a needle and began to darn.

'Have they said any more to you about being a teacher?' Mrs Bryce asked her.

She nodded. 'They keep on about it,' she said.

'Well, I don't know what to say. I think you'd best go up and have a talk with the Colonel's wife. It's really up to them to decide whether you should stay on or not. I'll speak to Tom about it and ask him to put in a word for you, to see when it's convenient for you to go and talk to them.'

Vinnie nodded again.

'You don't look very pleased, Vinnie. Most girls would jump at the chance.'

Vinnie took a deep breath. 'I want to be a typewriter lady,' she said.

'A what?'

'A stenographer, then. I want to learn to type, so I can work in an office in London.'

Mrs Bryce was dumbfounded. 'Work in an office?' she said. 'Vinnie Harris, the very idea! You'll do no such thing. Lord knows what would happen to you in an office. Don't you let the Colonel hear you talking like that, he won't be at all pleased. Oh, it's no good looking at me like that. Head in the clouds, that's your trouble. You think yourself lucky if you get the chance to do school-teaching. The Lawrences have been very good to you all these years and you can't expect them to support you forever – and get on with that sock, unless darning's beneath you!'

'I hate darning. It's boring.'

'Maybe so, but you've got to learn all these things. You'll have a husband of your own one day.'

'I don't want a husband,' said Vinnie, scowling. 'If I can't work in an office, then can I be a lady doctor?'

Mrs Bryce threw down her darning. 'I'm tired of hearing what you want and what you don't want. Lady doctor? Whatever next? You'll have a husband like the rest of us, like it or lump it. And since you can't talk sense, I'll thank you not to talk at all. Typewriter, indeed!' She snorted her disapproval. 'You're a girl from the London slums, Vinnie Harris, and don't you forget it.'

CHAPTER NINE

Three days later, wearing her best blue cotton gown and a straw hat, Vinnie made her way towards Foxearth. She kept to the road although there was a shorter way through the hop gardens. This was a formal visit and she had been told to go about it in the proper manner – she must approach the front door and give her name to the maid, as the Colonel's wife would be expecting her. As she went along she rehearsed a highly rebellious speech in which she announced her intention to return to London and become a lady 'typewriter'. Or maybe a telephonist. Anything other than the job she was meant to plead for. She did not want to be a school-teacher, nor did she want to remain in Teesbury for the rest of her life. London was full of adventure and Vinnie wanted a share of it. If they would not allow her to go to London, then perhaps they would agree to Margate. Bertie was in Margate, so it obviously had a lot to offer in the way of excitement.

She turned in at the broad driveway, her footsteps crunching on the newly raked gravel. Pausing, she examined her almost-new boots, fearful that the sharp edges of the gravel would spoil the leather, but was reassured and went on. Suddenly she heard laughter and the sound of wheels, followed by the ringing of a bell. Her view of the curving drive was restricted by large rhododendron brushes, but when she had gone another fifty yards or so she came in sight of the house and saw the reason for the merriment. Eva was riding a tricycle! Julian was nearby, his hands on his hips, a smile on his face as he watched her efforts to turn the machine in a tight circle. The gravel was well churned up and there were even tracks across the lawn.

Julian caught sight of Vinnie and beckoned her forward.

'Vinnie, what d'you think of it? My lovely new toy!' He grinned. 'It was delivered yesterday. Eva, get off and let me show Vinnie how well it goes.'

'I'll show her,' said Eva, weaving an erratic course towards the lawn.

'You can't. You don't ride it as well as I do. Oh, Eva, *do* get off – and say "Hullo" to Vinnie.'

'Hullo to Vinnie. Let *me* show her. Oh, Julian, you pig!' He had seized one of the large rear wheels and held it grimly so that it would not turn.

'Hullo,' said Vinnie.

She saw Eva from time to time because she was educated at home, but Julian had been sent away to Rugby and only came home for the holidays. She looked at him carefully while his attention was focused on his young sister. His hair was so fair it was almost white and he wore it in the fashionable short cut. He was tall for his sixteen years and very slender with narrow shoulders. Vinnie wondered if his pale complexion was due to poor health or if that was his natural colour. She felt a sudden longing to 'fatten him up', as Mrs Bryce would say, and was worried that perhaps the school did not provide nourishing food. Mrs Bryce's words came back to her – 'a husband of your own to care for'.

'Eva, *do* get down. It's *my* machine and *I'll* show it to Vinnie.' Eva was finally persuaded to dismount and the three of them stood round the tricycle admiringly.

'There, Vinnie, what do you think of it, eh?'

She noted that he had picked up his father's habit of adding 'eh' to many of his sentences and wondered briefly if Bertie had grown more like *their* father.

'It's a Royal Salvo,' Julian told her. 'Isn't she a beauty? Made by Stanleys. You can't get a finer machine, I swear it. And such a joy to ride – I'll show you.'

'I wanted him to have a penny-farthing,' said Eva, 'but he wouldn't. The Salvo's too easy.'

'Too easy! Then why did you end up riding all over the lawn, you cuckoo? There's quite an art to it, Vinnie. Watch, then you shall have a go.'

'Oh no!' she protested.

'Oh yes, you must! It's a real thrill, Vinnie. See, you take the hand-grips – so – and put your feet on the pedals. That's how you steer it – by the small front wheel. The penny-farthings are very unstable. A friend of mine had one and he came a nasty cropper. Broke his elbow, poor fellow.'

'His elbow? How awful.'

'Yes. Fell off, straight on to his elbow. Now, run along beside me, Vinnie, and watch me. Round we go, not too sharply. Eva finds turning rather tricky—'

'I don't at all, Julian! It simply doesn't steer very well.'

He ignored her and continued to issue instructions to Vinnie, who ran alongside, nodding her understanding of the mechanics of the Royal Salvo.

'Why is it called "Royal"?' she asked. 'Does the Queen ride one?'

'I doubt it. Not at *her* age. But maybe she approved the design. I'm thinking of joining a cycling club, that would be great fun.'

Satisfied that he had taught her all she needed to know, he jumped down and Vinnie took his place.

'Tuck your skirt up,' cried Eva, 'otherwise it might tangle in the struts.'

'They're spokes, not struts,' Julian corrected her. 'But Eva's right. Forget modesty, Vinnie, and tuck up your gown. We don't want you to have a fall.'

Slowly, her heart beating wildly, Vinnie set off with Julian and Eva one on either side of her. They both shouted encouragement and advice but she was not able to listen to them. It required all her concentration to co-ordinate the movements of her arms and legs, but she began to master it at last.

'Now try to turn,' Julian told her. 'Steer with your feet. That's the way. It's really too big for you, of course, but at least you can get the feel of it.'

Vinnie gasped with excitement as she manoeuvred the machine in a wide curve and found herself facing back the way she had come.

'I did it!' she cried.

Eva was clapping her hands and Julian laughed delightedly at the expression on her face.

'You're a natural!' he said. 'A natural cyclist. That's a splendid effort.'

A quarter of an hour later Vinnie remembered the purpose of her visit. 'I'd best go on up to the house,' she told them, 'but thank you, Julian, for the ride. I have to see your mother and father about my schooling.'

'Father will be resting at this time,' said Julian, 'but Mother is somewhere around. Ask Janet.'

At the front door Vinnie paused to tuck up a few stray strands of hair and smooth her gown. Her buttoned boots were dusty and she rubbed at them with the hem of her petticoat. One day she would own a tricycle, she decided, and she would cycle into Maidstone. The idea appealed to her and she was smiling when the maid opened the door. Mrs Bryce had told her exactly what to say.

'I'm Lavinia Harris,' said Vinnie, 'and I'm come to speak with the Colonel or his wife.'

Janet looked at her, seeming undecided how to answer, and Vinnie waited. She had expected to be invited to wait in the drawing-room – Mrs Bryce had assured her that this was the correct procedure. There she was to sit with her feet together and her back straight until the Colonel or his wife came into the room. Then she was to stand up.

'The Colonel's sleeping,' said Janet.

'Oh.'

'And the mistress—'

Vinnie waited, puzzled. 'Could I see the Colonel's wife?' she asked.

'You could but—'

There was a strange expression on the maid's face. Vinnie thought it amusement and put up a hand to check that her hat was set straight on her head. It seemed to be all right.

'But what?' Vinnie prompted.

'But she sometimes goes to see the horses on a Friday – when the groom's away.'

'Oh, I see.' In fact Vinnie did not see. Nor could she understand Janet's apparent reluctance to give her the information she needed.

'She'll be in the stables,' said the maid.

'Shall you tell her I'm here, then?'

'No, I think not.'

'What then?'

The girl shrugged. 'I don't know.'

'Shall I go to the stables and find her?'

'If you want to, I suppose you can.'

'Or should I come in and wait in the drawing-room?'

'You'll have a long wait.' For some reason she giggled.

'Oh, then I'd best go to the stables.'

There was no answer. For a moment the two girls looked at each other, then slowly the door closed and Vinnie heard the sound of muffled giggles. It was all very confusing.

As she made her way to the back of the house she was wondering if perhaps she could be a maid intead of working at a typewriter. The stable yard was cobbled and she stepped carefully. There was no sign of the Colonel's wife or anyone else. Six of the stalls were in use and the horses watched her with interest over the half-doors. She patted each velvety nose and murmured lovingly to each one. At the end of the yard she turned and walked back. The door was open at one of the empty stalls and she glanced inside. Narrow wooden steps led up to a loft and Vinnie's curiosity overcame her. She would have a quick look in the loft, there was no one to see her.

Quietly she began to ascend the steps when her ears caught a sound from somewhere above. She frowned, then smiled. Maybe she had found the Colonel's wife. When her head was level with the trap-door she suddenly heard a voice that was unmistakably male. Janet was obviously mistaken: the groom *was* here. Another step and she could see right into the hay-loft. And what she saw astonished her: a pair of corduroy breeches lay in a crumpled heap not a yard away, and beyond that in the hay a man lay on top of a woman. The man was bare except for a shirt and his buttocks rose and fell. Most of the woman was hidden from Vinnie's gaze by the hay, but her arms were clasped round the man above her and Vinnie saw a long grey sleeve of fine silk and a slim white hand which glittered with rings. She remained staring at the sight before her, as though turned to stone. The man was supporting his weight on his arms so that he was looking into the woman's face; Vinnie recognised Tom Bryce's curly hair, but the sounds he made were unfamiliar. Then she heard the woman begin to moan, whether in agony or a kind of ecstasy, Vinnie could not tell.

'Oh Tom! Tom! I want it, Tom!'

Tom's body moved faster.

Suddenly the ladder creaked, but only Vinnie heard it. Slowly, hardly daring to breathe, she began to descend the steps, half-paralysed with shock and terrified that she would be discovered.

'Tom! Oh my God! My love!'

The voice was that of Christina Lawrence and she was in the hay with Rose's husband who had taken off his trousers to lie above her!

Vinnie left the stable yard and went back towards the house. What was she to do now? It seemed likely that the Colonel's wife had forgotten her visit. It seemed unlikely, moreover, that even if she remembered it she would want to leave the hay-loft and talk to Vinnie about her possible future as a school-teacher. Christina Lawrence and Tom Bryce were enjoying what they were doing, thought Vinnie dazedly. The woman's sounds were *not* agony. She had called Tom, 'My love' and she had sounded happy. So Jarvis Tupp and Emily Drew – he *had* told them the truth! Emily and Jarvis *had* enjoyed it. Some of the tightness went out of Vinnie's face and her expression softened into one of relief. She was comforted to know that whatever it was *exactly* she would find it pleasurable.

Once, a long time ago, she had heard those same sounds from her own mother and father. Vinnie was beginning to understand a lot of things.

As she walked past the front door and down the driveway she saw that Eva was once more perched high on the tricycle and Julian was sprawled on the grass watching her.

Seeing Vinnie, he called, 'Did you find her?'

Vinnie hesitated. She thought, that was your mother, Julian, in the hay with Tom Bryce, and hoped he would never know.

'No, she must have forgotten I was coming,' she improvised. 'It doesn't matter. I'll come back another day.'

'D'you want another ride before you go?'

'No, thank you.' Vinnie wanted time to think over what she had seen.

'Come up again some time,' said Julian.

'Yes, do,' called Eva. 'Watch me, Vinnie. I'm getting very good at it. Even Julian says so.'

Vinnie nodded, smiling, and kept on walking. She felt suddenly much older and wiser – she felt that, after today, her life would never be quite the same again.

*

Christina groaned. 'Move over, Tom. I've told you before – you're no light weight.'

He kissed her and rolled over to lie beside her. 'I thought you liked it,' he teased. 'You give a good imitation of a woman enjoying herself.'

'Like it? Good gracious, no! What gave you that idea?' She slid her hand up under his shirt and ran her fingers over the hairy chest, seeking out the familiar curves and hollows of his body.

'What makes me think you like it? Let me see – perhaps it's the way you keep asking for more!'

She laughed softly. 'You always seem willing to give it!'

'I try to satisfy your demands, ma'am.'

'Tom!'

'It's true, I do. I'm not saying I don't enjoy it.'

'I'm pleased about that.'

'You're pleased about all of it!'

Christina turned on to her side and he took her into his arms. For a while they were silent, drowsy, sated. She gave herself up to the luxury of her thoughts, reliving the ecstasy which had just ended. Tom's thoughts veered away from their passion towards the more mundane aspects of his life. In another month the hopping season would be upon them once more and there was a great deal still to be done before the Londoners arrived.

'We haven't ordered the brushwood,' he told her.

'Tom Bryce!' she protested, her languor vanishing at his words. 'What a time to tell me. Have you no delicacy?'

'I leave such luxuries to you. You're the grand lady, I'm just an oaf. Remember?'

The jibe was justified, she knew, for they had quarrelled once and she had called him just that. But his timing was unforgivable. She tensed slightly in his arms.

'Don't, Tom,' she said. 'You promised to forget that, but you keep reproaching me with it. You know it hurts me, you do it deliberately.'

'I'm sorry.' He did not sound it and she struggled to remain untouched by the careless tone of his voice. She loved him and she needed his body. She also knew him very well and admitted to herself that his personality was not wholly endearing. He could be indifferent, callous even. It was his way of 'evening the score'. Aware of the vast difference in their life-styles, she tried to sympathise and make allowances. He was an arrogant man and her social superiority was not something he could accept easily. His spiteful remarks were somehow intended to redress the balance. Now she made an effort not to be distracted by the problem of the hoppers' firewood.

'It was very good,' she said softly.

'What was?'

Oh, dearest God, don't let us quarrel, she pleaded silently. Recently his moods had become more changeable, his manner less predictable.

'Tom, please . . . You used to say you loved me. Always, afterwards, you used to say—'

'You know I love you. What was all that about if it wasn't love?'

'That was lust, Tom. There's a difference.'

'Oh, is there, ma'am? Forgive me. I didn't know.'

'Tom! Why can't you say it, to please me? I say I love *you*.'

'God! You women are all the same – you sound like Rose talking.'

'Don't, Tom! Please don't talk about Rose. You know I can't bear it.'

'You talk about "poor Henry".'

'I'm sorry. But Henry is helpless, he's no competition. Rose is – well, Rose is . . .' She could not put it into words.

'Rose is fruity again? She *is* my wife.'

'I know. I know. Please let's not talk about it, Tom.'

'She's not getting anything you're not.'

'Tom! You can be so crude. You do it to offend me, I know you do.' She withdrew her arm and lay on her back, staring wretchedly up into the rafters.

'You ladies are so easily offended.'

'Stop it!'

She rolled over, facing away from him, pulling her skirts down over her legs and fumbling with the row of tiny buttons that fastened her bodice.

'D'you want a child, is that it?'

'No!'

Her denial deceived neither of them. Christina longed to bear his child but knew it was impossible. There was no way she could pretend it was her husband's baby – he would never again father a child.

'You might fall for one.'

'I mustn't.'

'Accidents do happen.'

'No. It's out of the question.'

In her mind's eye she saw Tom with Rose, but immediately tried to push the image from her. She sat up abruptly, her fingers busy with the last few buttons at her neck.

'This wretched loft!' She sighed deeply. 'When we have so many bedrooms, it's quite preposterous.'

'Ask me up to the house then.'

He grinned up at her and her ill-humour vanished. Tom Bryce commanded her emotions even though she would not admit it. She felt the familiar lurch as her inside contracted with a rush of love for him, and smiled back at him as he propped himself up on one elbow.

'I dare you to!'

'No, I daren't.'

'Why not? Who's to know?'

'The servants.'

He shrugged. 'That won't worry me.'

'They're not *your* servants. How would I keep their respect if they caught us together?'

'They know already.'

Her smile faded. 'They know?'

'I reckon so, don't you?'

'No. At least, I hope most sincerely that they do *not* know. Tom, are you teasing me?'

He shrugged again. 'They'd have to be blind and daft if they don't put two and two together and make four.'

Christina bit her lip, vexed and disturbed at the prospect.

'Don't let it worry you,' he said. 'They'll not tell.'

'But . . . I'd rather they didn't know.'

'Then maybe I'm wrong. What's the matter – are you ashamed of me?'

'Of course not. But if they know, then it won't be long before Rose hears about it.'

'She probably knows already.'

'Oh no! Dear God, I hope not. Has she said anything?'

'Not a word. She's got her pride, same as you.'

'Damn!'

'Tut, tut! Not a very ladylike expression.'

'That's enough, Tom. Don't try to provoke me.'

'No, ma'am. I won't, ma'am.'

Grinning, he pulled her into his arms and rolled her over in the hay. At once her blood raced and her spirits soared. All the time he wanted her she knew she could keep him. She struggled ineffectually beneath him, pretending dismay.

'Not again, Tom! *Tom*! Dear God, you're a greedy devil, Tom Bryce. You're never satisfied.'

'Not true. I get satisfied, but I don't stay satisfied. Why did

you do up all these damned buttons? I want to get to those rosy
nipples—' He was pulling clumsily at her bodice.

'Stop, Tom! You'll tear it. Let me undo them.'

'You've plenty more gowns. There!' With a fierce tug he
ripped it open, ignoring her half-hearted protests. Tom Bryce
knew his lady. He knew that his roughness stirred her body
and quickened her desire. Christina Lawrence knew real
passion; his poor little Rose no longer thrilled to his touch, but
merely suffered his advances, too tired and harassed to enjoy
their lovemaking. And she was big with child and the sight of
her clumsy body did not inspire him. Some men found pregnant
women desirable – he did not.

'And up with those petticoats!'

She struggled, wriggling helplessly as he reached and
snatched up a handful of grey silk, pulling it up around her
waist. He knew she wore no underclothing when they
met.

'Oh, Tom! My very dear Tom—'

'Tell me you love it!' She shook her head.

'Say it!'

'No!'

'You'll be sorry!'

'I won't – say – it – Oh!'

'Tell me you love it!'

'You're hurting me – Tom! Oh, my dearest Tom, I love
you! I love it! It's true. I've said it. I do! I do! Oh Tom—' As
Tom Bryce went into her he grinned. The Colonel's wife was
happy again.

*

June came and by the twenty-first day of the month a morose
Tom Bryce had found too many hop bines 'up top' of their
poles. A heavy rainfall in May had encouraged the plants so
that they made too much growth, covering the poles with a
profusion of thick stems and an over-abundance of leaves
which would sap the strength of the bine. Later the hops
would be undersized and the crop small. It was disappointing,
but hops were unpredictable. If conditions were right, a

bumper crop would make a fortune for its owner; if conditions were contrary, the results could bring ruin. To guard against such disasters the growers diversified, putting a few acres under fruit or barley, and most of them kept a few pigs and chickens as well as a cow.

By July, the bines were well advanced but the first week of the month brought another familiar problem. The blight known as downy mildew appeared, colouring the underside of some of the leaves with its dark spores. Vinnie and Joan were employed after school to pick off the affected leaves and earned themselves a few shillings. It had seemed a localised attack, but by late August their efforts had proved insufficient to arrest the spread of the disease and Adam Forrest was sent through the gardens with a sulphuring machine. This consisted of a large drum on wheels containing sulphur powder, from which extended a long hose. Every few yards he would stop and pump the powder through the hose and up into the hops.

Adam, usually cheerful, shook his head as he worked. It was not going to be a good crop, he forecast gloomily, and that meant fewer pickers would be employed. Those that *were* employed could consider themselves among the fortunate few. Mrs Lawrence, knowing this, would be able to offer a lower price per bushel and the Londoners would feel resentful. He emptied the drum and returned home as the first few drops of rain began to fall. Too late, he thought despondently. First it had rained too early and now it was too late. The hops had formed and were already ripening – it was sunshine they needed now, not more rain. He pushed the machine out of the gate on to the lane and found Vinnie hurrying to meet him.

'Mr Forrest!'

'Aye, Vinnie.'

She fell in alongside, one hand held over her hair to protect it from the rain.

'Don't tell me, Vinnie,' he teased. 'You've a favour to ask me.'

'I have, yes!' she laughed.

'The answer's "No",' he told her, 'as it always is. You come bothering me every year and the answer's always the same.'

'But just this once!' she cried. 'I would so love to see their faces—'

''Twill be dark, Vinnie. Two in the morning, it's black as the grave and they'll be tired and wanting their beds.'

'But Mr Forrest, they'd be so surprised to see me waiting there. I'd be no trouble to you, you know I wouldn't, and I could help with the luggage. Oh, just this once, Mr Forrest! Take me to the station. *Please!*'

He shook his head stubbornly. 'You know it ain't allowed,' he told her. 'I've asked other years and 'tis always the same. You'll see them the next morning. What difference does a few hours make?'

'They're my *folks*,' said Vinnie desperately.

'There's only Em as is folks,' he reminded her. 'The others is just neighbours.'

'I'll give you two shillings,' offered Vinnie.

He came to an abrupt stop and stared at her. 'Two shillings? Where d'you get two shillings?'

'The downy mildew,' said Vinnie. 'I saved it specially.'

She saw that he wavered. 'Three shillings,' she said, 'and that's all I've got. Just take me this once and I'll never ask you again, I promise I won't.'

'But Mrs Bryce'll have my guts for garters!' he protested.

'She won't know. I'll get out of the window and down the pear tree. Then you will?'

He sighed noisily and scratched the back of his neck. 'If it means that much to you—' he said, 'but I won't take your money. You keep it, Vinnie. And only this once, mind. If the mistress finds out, I'll be catching an earful, good and proper, and I'll never hear the—'

The rest of this homily was lost as Vinnie, overjoyed, flung her arms around his neck and kissed him.

*

To Vinnie it seemed that they sat and shivered in the dark for ever, waiting for the train. Her mood alternated between joy at the forthcoming reunion and black despair at the thought that maybe there had been a derailment and they would never arrive. In front of them, barely discernible in the feeble light from the hurricane lamps, the horses tossed their heads and scraped their hooves impatiently.

'They don't reckon much to the dark,' said Adam.

'No more do I,' Vinnie told him. 'It's lonesome and I keep hearing things in the air. It's not bats, is it, Mr Forrest?'

'Maybe.'

'Ugh!' She shuddered and then presently said, 'You don't think there's been an accident, do you?'

'I don't – and that's the fourth time of asking! Pipe down, Vinnie, there's a good girl. Train'll come in its own good time and you pestering won't make it come any sooner.'

She relapsed into silence, somehow comforted by his manner. If he sensed disaster he'd be less sharp-tempered. Around them in the darkness, other horses shuffled and other drivers coughed and mumbled, weary but resigned. At last they heard the clang of the signal and the distant whistle followed by the chatter of wheels on track. Vinnie was down from her perch in a flash and running towards the narrow gateway through which the hundreds of passengers would all have to pass. She climbed onto the wooden fence and peered into the blackness. The platform was better lit than the forecourt and she saw the station-master consulting a large watch.

'Dead on time,' he remarked loudly.

'It never is!' cried Vinnie. 'It's late. It must be!'

'Dead on time,' he repeated. 'Give or take a minute.'

'Ah!'

Satisfied, she turned back to stare along the track as the train approached. She could feel the vibration. In her imagination she heard their exclamations of surprise; she was hugging her sister and Mrs Batty was remarking on how tall Vinnie had grown in the past year.

'They're here!' she whispered. 'They're here!'

The train juddered to a halt in an eruption of steam and the carriage doors flew open. Within seconds the tiny platform was crammed with people and luggage and the noise was incredible.

'Em!' shouted Vinnie. 'Em! It's me, Vinnie! I'm over here!' She stood up, balancing precariously on the fence, wildly waving her arms to attract attention to her whereabouts. Above the commotion, the station-master was bellowing instructions to anyone who would listen, but he was mostly ignored. The one thought in everyone's mind was to reach the waggons and be on their way to bed. They pushed, screamed, laughed and swore, elbowing each other in their haste. Vinnie searched frantically for a familiar face – Mrs Batty in the old straw hat which she tied on her head with a blue scarf; or Em, with her long pigtails. Or maybe she'd look different this year – maybe she'd wear her hair tied back or even cut short. Vinnie hoped she would look the same as last year, her eyes huge in the pale, angular face. Em took after her father.

In the dim light of the overhead lamps, eyes showed whitely in grey faces above the shapeless, shadowy forms which, crowded painfully together, pressed relentlessly along the platform towards the exit. Once outside in the courtyard the mass broke up into smaller groups which criss-crossed the area, blindly following the cry of their particular waggoner: 'Merryon'. 'Foxearth'. 'Upper Hall'. 'Manor Farm'. They were weary and excited but at every cart reunions were taking place as people who had missed each other on the train finally met up with cries of delight. Vinnie abandoned her position on the fence and made her way to the exit where the crowd was thinning a little.

'Tickets, please. Now come along there. You've all got tickets, I hope, so let's be having them!'

Behind her the noise and confusion grew as children and the elderly were hoisted on to the carts and waggons, along with some of the luggage.

'They must be here,' whispered Vinnie, but she was growing anxious and a cold dread nudged at her uncomfortably. 'They must be here, or they'd have said. They'd have sent word, I know they would.'

Suddenly the station platform was empty once more and the station-master was preparing to put out the lamps. With a creak of wheels the first cart rolled away into the night with cheers from its occupants and a lot of good-natured banter.

'Vinnie!'

It was Adam Forrest, calling to her to join him.

'They *must* be here,' she repeated, but the station-master was bidding her 'Good night' and she heard the key turn in the lock as he padlocked the gate behind the last picker.

'Vinnie! You're keeping everyone waiting.'

She wanted to call, 'I'm coming', but the words stuck in her throat.

'*Vinnie!*'

Other voices joined his. 'Come on girl! For Pete's sake, let's get moving! We don't want to be here all night.'

Vinnie moved back to the fence and, stepping up, took a last look at the deserted platform. The train had long since gone on its way towards Beltring, the next stopping place along the line. Dazed with shock, her face crumpled in despair as huge desolate sobs forced their way from the depths of her being, obliterating everything else from her mind. She no longer heard the voices which urged her to hurry; she was unaware of the darkness which surrounded her and the fluttering shapes that swooped overhead.

'Vinnie!'

She did not hear him. All she heard was the terrible clamour of her thoughts and all she felt was an overwhelming misery. Slowly she bent her head, as though weighed down by the volume of her tears, and abandoned herself to her sobbing. She made no demur when Adam Forrest arrived to put an arm round her shoulders and lead her gently back to the cart. The pickers, most of whom knew her from previous years, murmured their sympathies and regrets as she was helped up on to the seat beside the driver. Vinnie sat with bowed head as they rattled through the quiet lanes and gradually her grief lessened, giving way to a sense of deep loss. As they pulled into the gateway at Foxearth, she turned to Adam Forrest and put all her agony into three words.

'They didn't come,' she said, and then cried anew all the way home.

CHAPTER TEN

April of 1897 was mild, but Vinnie shivered on her way home for she had come out without a shawl. Around her as she went through the hop-gardens the wind rustled the poplars, but she scarcely registered the familiar sound. Vinnie knew the hop-garden in all its moods, for she spent most weekends and many evenings working there. She was familiar too with all aspects of the work and there was little that she could not turn her hand to if required. She helped with the planting out of the young plants or 'hills' and watched them mature from year to year, reappearing each spring from beneath the frozen ground to climb and twist round the upright poles and wires which formed part of the new system. Each winter she dug round the plants with the three-pronged 'spud' and later spread the manure which came over from Merryon. She knew how to cut away the spare shoots so that only the leader remained, and joined in the hop-tying by which means the young plants were discouraged from growing haphazardly. She had spent many hours hoeing between the rows and more than once had gone home with bleeding knees after an evening spent kneeling on the hard earth, planting small pieces of turnip with which to lure click-beetles away from the tender young hop plants.

As she crossed from one row to the next, she saw Tom Bryce and he called to her. 'Evening, Vinnie.'

'Hullo, Mr Bryce.' Vinnie was fifteen now and it was four years since she had seen him in the hay-loft.

'Where are you off to?' he asked. 'Going home?'

She shook her head. 'Mr Parsloe has asked me to look in on his wife. She's feeling poorly.'

'What's Parsloe doing up at the house?' Tom asked.

'They're all playing croquet.'

'All?'

'Louise arrived this morning and is staying for a few days.'

'Ah yes, I'd forgotten. So it's croquet, is it? In April?' He snorted. 'Nice to have nothing better to do.'

'I suppose so.'

'And Mrs Parsloe's sick, you say? That poor woman!' he said. 'She deserved better.'

Vinnie did not answer, although she knew what he meant.

'Been reading to the Colonel?' he asked.

'Yes.'

'Poor old devil,' he said, but Vinnie did not meet his eyes. She liked the frail old man and reading to him in the elegant sunny bedroom was pleasant enough. He could still only talk with difficulty, but the doctor believed he would improve with time. The Colonel smiled a lot and his eyes were kind. Unconsciously she resented Christina and Tom for cheating him, but no word of what she had seen had ever passed her lips.

'Heard from that brother of yours?' he asked.

Vinnie's face clouded over. It was over a year since the last postcard had reached her and she fretted in case some harm had befallen him.

'I reckon he'll be married by now,' said Tom. 'How old is he?'

'Twenty-one,' said Vinnie proudly.

'How long since you've seen him?'

'Three years, four months,' said Vinnie.

'He'll turn up,' said Tom, seeing her downcast expression. 'Turn up with a wife and a baby and then there'll be some celebrating.'

At this prospect, a smile lit up Vinnie's face and Tom looked at her curiously. 'And how old are you?' he asked. 'You're shooting up faster than a hop plant. Fourteen, is it?'

'Fifteen.'

'Fifteen!' He whistled by way of exclamation. 'Fifteen, are you? Almost a young woman, then.'

Vinnie shrugged, but he was suddenly seeing her as though for the first time. Her heavy golden hair was drawn back into a long plait fastened top and bottom with ribbon. Her face was a delicate oval and her eyes were clear and calm. She no longer scowled as she had when a child and the set of her head upon the slim neck was almost proud.

'Got a young man, have you?' he asked.

'Maybe,' said Vinnie, reluctant to admit that she had not.

'And who's the lucky man? Do I know him?'

'I only said maybe,' said Vinnie. 'You may ask away but I shan't tell you.'

He grinned. 'Lucky lad,' he said.

Vinnie realised suddenly that he was trying to flirt with her in a mild way and she eyed him speculatively. Over the last two or three years he had put on weight. The handsome face had lost its firm lines and too much ale had thickened his waistline. Vinnie wondered why the Colonel's wife found him attractive. She shivered again.

'I must go,' she said.

He opened his arms wide. 'I'll cuddle you warm,' he said.

'You'd crush my ribs,' Vinnie retorted. 'Rose says you have a hug like a bear.'

He laughed, pleased at the compliment. 'Oh, you two talk about me, do you?'

'Sometimes.'

'All good, I hope,' he said.

'Some of it good,' said Vinnie.

He had dropped his arms to his sides again.

'Tell your young man,' he said, 'that if I did not have my arms full with Rose, I'd be after you myself.'

'I'll tell him.' She eyed him warily and when he made a sudden lunge in her direction she was ready and side-stepped neatly. He heard her laughing as she ran away, weaving in and out between the poles.

'You tell him,' he shouted after her.

Her voice floated back. 'I will,' and she laughed again.

*

The small fire in the bedroom, neatly laid, had not been lit. On the bed Mrs Joshua Parsloe shivered. Her eyes were closed and she was fully dressed. She did not care that she was cold, in fact she welcomed the discomfort; she was so abject that comfort of any kind would have seemed an intrusion on her wretchedness and it was for this reason that she had not lit the fire. She sprawled across the bed, her face ashen, her jaw tightly clenched against the pain that racked her. She no longer glanced down at the bed with its spreading red stain; she had lost a lot of blood and hoped to lose much more. Not only did she mean to lose Joshua's child, she also wanted to lose her own life.

The last two years since Maude had married had been the most unhappy of her whole life – so unhappy, in fact, that her desperation had given way to a determination to end her existence. She hoped she would bleed to death, that it would be all over before anyone found her. The thought of her child did not prick at her conscience. She hated to think that she carried Joshua's baby within her and she did not want to bear him a son. Their union had proved disastrous. Not only did his shapeless body revolt her – with time she might have overcome that – but Joshua Parsloe had a very vivid imagination and the normal delights of the marriage bed were not enough for him. During his bachelor days he had created a variety of sexual fantasies which he now expected to play out with his wife's co-operation. At first she had agreed, albeit reluctantly. Later, as the fantasies grew more obscene, she had protested passionately but Joshua was not one to give up his pleasures easily and many times he had beaten her into submission, taking an extra pleasure from the violence. Humiliated and afraid, Maude told no one of the degradation she endured nightly, but she could not always conceal the bruises and before the first year was out the village was full of rumour and speculation. Joshua's sexual appetite was insatiable and Maude lived a perpetual nightmare – each day filled with dreadful anticipation of the approaching night. Under the strain, her health began to give way and in moments of deep despair she feared for her sanity. Miss Gibbs' concern for her grew as the weeks passed but try as she would, the headmistress could not persuade her erstwhile colleague to confide in her and no one was fully aware of the depths of Maude's despair.

The final horror had come when she discovered she was pregnant. She was sick with loathing, but ironically the first three months passed with no ill-effects and no one guessed her secret. Maude had prayed for help and now it seemed that her prayers had been answered. God had seen fit to terminate her pregnancy and on bended knees that morning she had thanked him for it. She felt that the blood that flowed from her would clean her spirit as well as her womb. Suddenly the thought had struck her that the bleeding might not stop and she had welcomed that too as a merciful way to end her misery. If God saw fit to take her life, she would accept without protest. She would not fight against her fate, she was in His hands.

Hours passed and she grew weaker, making no effort to eat or drink but merely waiting hopefully for death. She did not allow her thoughts to dwell on the absent Joshua, nor on the period since her marriage. She recalled instead her happy childhood and the pleasant years she had spent as Miss Babbit and thought, too, of the children who had passed through her care; she knew that the last two years could not take away the achievements of her life prior to her wedding. It occurred to her that she should pray again, so she put her hands together and tried to concentrate on her thoughts. If her last hour was upon her she should spend it wisely and prepare herself for heaven:

'Dear Father, look down and pity me. You find me in a sorry state and yet I know you understand and still love me. I thank you for all the happy years you gave me . . . If the last two were sent to try me, I'm sorry I have not been able to rise above them and for that I ask your pardon. I hope you will be merciful. I thank you for my dear parents and my friends and all who have brought joy into my life. I did not mean to end it, but you have shown me the way and so I hope you will not punish me for what I am doing. The world is hateful to me and I long for death and whatever is to come after death. I should ask, I know, that you forgive Joshua for all he has done to me and yet I cannot find it in my heart to do so. This is a sin and I will surely answer for it . . . I pray you that when I am dead my friends remember me kindly . . .'

It was at that moment that Vinnie knocked on the door and, receiving no answer, went round to the back of the house and let herself in at the kitchen door. She called out, 'Mrs Parsloe! It's Vinnie, Vinnie Harris. Your husband said I was to call.'

Maude closed her eyes, willing her to go away.

'Are you upstairs, Mrs Parsloe?'

Receiving no answer, Vinnie was puzzled. She went to the bottom of the stairs and called again.

'Mrs Parsloe, may I come up? Your husband sent me,' she repeated. Someone was obviously in the house, for the back door was not locked. She began to go upstairs and Maude, hearing her footsteps, groaned. Surely this girl, for whom she had done so much, was not to be the instrument of her undoing? There was a tap on the bedroom door. Maude did not answer but it opened and she knew Vinnie stood there. Maude's head was turned away from the door and now she did not move, not even to look at the girl.

Vinnie whispered, 'Mrs Parsloe? Are you asleep?'

Thinking this to be the case, she took a few steps closer to reassure herself that all was well. Instead she saw the huge dark stain and let out a scream of horror. Assuming that Maude Parsloe was already dead, she stepped back but at that moment Maude turned towards her.

'Oh, Miss Babbit, I thought – I thought you were – oh, what has happened to you, Miss Babbit, I mean Mrs Parsloe?'

The pallor of Maude Parsloe's face did nothing to reassure Vinnie and as she stared into the dark, haunted eyes, speech failed her. As the woman on the bed moved, the sickly sweet smell of blood reached Vinnie and instinctively she put up a hand to cover her mouth and nose.

'The doctor, Mrs Parsloe,' she stammered. 'I'll go for the doctor.'

'No, child, wait.' Maude held out a hand beseechingly. 'Don't leave me, Vinnie, I beg you.'

'But all this—' Vinnie could not bring herself to say the word, but indicated the red stain. 'I *must* go for the doctor.'

'No, Vinnie. I forbid it.'

Vinnie's expression changed to one of panic.

'Wait, Vinnie. Come here, dear. Come closer. Don't be afraid.'

Very reluctantly, Vinnie moved forward, fixing her eyes determinedly on the haggard face and when she was near enough Maude Parsloe seized her wrist so hard that it hurt. Vinnie tried to withdrew but the grip was tightened.

'Please, Miss Babbit, let me go. Let me go for the doctor.'

'No, Vinnie, it's too late and I don't want the doctor.'

'But—'

'I tell you, Vinnie, it's too late. There's nothing he can do for me now and if you leave me I shall die alone.'

Vinnie's eyes widened with horror as she tried once more to pull her wrist free of the vice-like grip that held her. 'Don't talk of dying, Mrs Parsloe, I beg you. I'm sure it isn't too late.' To her dismay the other woman's eyes filled with tears which began to trickle slowly down the pale cheeks. 'Oh, don't cry. Please don't cry.'

Awkwardly, she sat on the edge of the bed, compassion overcoming her fears, as Maude Parsloe began to sob helplessly. 'Please understand, Vinnie,' she gasped. 'I want to die. You must let me die. My life isn't worth living. I've told no one but now you at least must understand. Listen, Vinnie. You mustn't wed. It's – it's not what you expect, Vinnie. Do you hear me? Do you understand?'

A fresh storm of tears racked her. Wildly Vinnie looked around the room, unable to bear the sight of her one-time school-teacher brought to such a hideous state.

'Please say you understand. I don't want the doctor. I want to slip away quietly. Try to understand. Have pity on me, Vinnie, and do as I ask.'

'But if I don't go for help you'll die,' Vinnie protested, 'and it will be my fault.' Feebly, Maude Parsloe shook her head and Vinnie fancied that the grip on her wrist grew weaker. Seeing that she frightened Vinnie with her tears, Maude made a desperate effort to control them. 'Just sit with me, Vinnie. Don't leave me to die alone. Do this one thing for me, I beg you.'

'Oh, Miss Babbit, I shouldn't stay. You shouldn't ask me. I don't know what to do.'

'Stay with me, child.' She gave a sudden gasp as a fierce pain seized her and she screwed up her eyes and face in an effort not to scream. The constraining hand fell from Vinnie's wrist as Mrs Parsloe was brought suddenly very near to death. If Vinnie ran for the doctor, the woman would die alone. Perhaps there *was* nothing the doctor could do. Vinnie hesitated.

'Vinnie—' the voice was very weak. 'Read to me, Vinnie, from the bible.'

Vinnie looked round and saw an old leather-bound bible on the bedside table. She picked it up and sat down again on the edge of the bed.

'What shall I read?' she asked.

For a moment there was no answer, then Maude Parsloe gathered her remaining strength and whispered, 'The psalm, Vinnie. Psalm one hundred and twenty one.' With an effort Maude kept her eyes open, fixed on Vinnie's face. 'Read, Vinnie,' she whispered. 'Read to me, quickly, child.'

It seemed to Vinnie that she would never find the right page but at last the bible lay open in her lap and she began to read:

'I will lift up mine eyes unto the hills, from whence cometh my help. My help cometh from the Lord, which made heaven and earth . . .' Maude's hand reached across the coverlet and plucked feebly at Vinnie's skirt. Her right hand lay palm upwards and gently Vinnie took the hand in her own and felt the fingers close against hers in a gesture of thanks. She read on, making a conscious effort with the beautiful words. Once she had read the lesson in church and Miss Babbit had congratulated her; now she wanted her to enjoy every word.

'The Lord shall preserve thy going out and thy coming in from this time forth, and even forever more.'

As she came to the end of it, she looked at the woman on the bed and saw that Maude's lips curved in the ghost of a smile. Then the fingers relaxed their hold on her wrist. Mrs Parsloe's eyes were already closed and Vinnie regarded her fearfully. Was she still breathing? Vinnie leaned nearer, looking and listening for signs that she was, but there was no movement.

'Miss Babbit,' Vinnie whispered. 'Please—' She swallowed hard. A small hand mirror lay on the dressing-table and Vinnie recognised it as part of the set that the school had given her as a wedding gift. In a second or two she held it in her hand.

'Oh, poor Miss Babbit,' she whispered. Hastily she returned to the bed and held the glass to Maude's open mouth. There was no misting of the glass. Vinnie returned the mirror to the dressing-table and then stood at the bottom of the bed. The bloodstain unnerved her and she lifted the lower corners of the bedspread and arranged it over Maude Parsloe's legs. Miss Babbit was dead, she knew it as surely as if the doctor had told her. Someone, she felt, should bid her farewell. Vinnie picked up one of the limp hands and put it to her lips. 'Goodbye, Miss Babbit,' she whispered and added, 'God be with you.' With a last look at the still form on the bed, she tiptoed out of the room, closed the door behind her and then went downstairs and out into the sunshine. There she took a deep breath and then began to run for help.

*

Over the next two days the mild weather gave way to a cold east wind, but this did not prevent most of the village from attending Maude Parsloe's funeral. Many people were in tears, Mrs Bryce among them, but Vinnie remained dry-eyed throughout the simple service. She had cried all her tears on that terrible day. She sat at the back with Mrs Bryce, Tom, Rose and the children and was embarrassed to find herself the object of many interested stares. She desperately hoped that no one would ask her further questions about Maude Parsloe's death, for she had already given an account to the Colonel's wife, to the doctor and to the police sergeant, as well as the members of her immediate circle. She had also suffered severe doubts as to the wisdom of her behaviour on that fateful afternoon and asked herself over and over again if she might have saved the school-teacher if she had gone for help sooner. The doctor's insistence that nothing could have been done at that late stage went some way to reassure her on this point, but she still felt keenly that other people less well-informed than the doctor might consider her irresponsible.

The school-children sang two hymns, the vicar gave a moving oration and Miss Gibbs read the 121st psalm in a voice choked with emotion. Vinnie had been asked to do the reading, but her natural reticence had prevailed against the vicar's persuasion. The coffin, covered with flowers, stood on two trestles at the front of the church and in the front row Joshua Parsloe sat with his head bent avoiding all eyes. His father was conducting the funeral service and he, too, felt the awkwardness of the situation, for since Maude Parsloe's death many people in the village had shunned Joshua as a mark of their disapproval of his behaviour towards his unfortunate wife. When the children stood up to sing, the congregation were moved to see their mourning tokens – black hair-ribbons for the girls and black armbands for the boys. Outside, as though in protest at her death, the heavens opened and the rain, slanted by the east wind, spattered against the church window, making the sad occasion even more dismal. At last they all stood up and watched the coffin as it was carried past them on the shoulders of the bearers. In ones and twos, many weeping openly, they moved out of the pews and followed the bier out of the church porch and into the driving rain. Many went home then, for only family and close friends had been invited to the graveside to watch Maude Parsloe's coffin lowered into its final resting place.

'Ashes to ashes, dust to dust . . .'

The familiar words imprinted themselves on Vinnie's brain with an awful finality. One day that would be her fate. One day she would be surrendered to the darkness, removed for ever from the sight of those she loved and who loved her. She sighed heavily and wished for tears to relieve her pent-up grief and fear, but none came. She glanced up and saw the Colonel's wife, beautiful in black: beside her stood Julian, with one hand holding a black umbrella over her head and with the other holding Eva close to him. Next to Eva stood Joshua Parsloe. His hands still covered his face and his shoulders shook. Vinnie

felt sure that his grief was feigned but was immediately
ashamed of the uncharitable thought. To one side, in the
shelter of a tree, the gravedigger waited to complete his sombre
task when the last of the mourners had left the graveside.
Finally it was time to go. They had paid their last respects and
there was nothing anyone could do for the frail corpse. The
downpour increased and hurriedly the mourners dispersed and
made their separate ways to the vicarage where the funeral
feast awaited.

Vinnie was one of the last to leave the graveside. She felt
strangely drawn to the woman abandoned there – it was as
though she herself was Maude Parsloe's replacement. She
would become the next school-teacher at the village school and
her life would be a continuation of Maude's own. She
whispered a last appeal to the departed spirit, 'Don't let me die
that way. Please don't.'

A heavy hand on her shoulder made her jump and she turned
to see Joshua Parsloe. There was no one else within earshot,
she noticed, and her heart sank as she saw that the expression
on his face was not a friendly one.

'What did she say to you?' he hissed fiercely. 'Did she say
anything before she died – about me? I insist that you tell me.'
Vinnie shook her head but that did not satisfy him.

'Tell me, I say,' he demanded. 'You were there. She must
have told you something. Did she speak . . .' he hesitated,
'about our life together?'

Again Vinnie said, 'No', but he shook her roughly. 'Don't
try to deceive me, child,' he said, 'I'm not a fool. She must have
said something, I'm certain of it.'

'She said nothing,' said Vinnie. 'Only what I told the doctor
and the police sergeant. Only what I have already told – that
she knew she was going to die and that she wanted me to stay
with her so she would not die alone.'

'But *is* that all?' he insisted. 'Think. If you are hiding
something—'

'Indeed I'm not,' cried Vinnie, her indignation overcoming
her nervousness. 'She said nothing. Nothing at all – nothing
that I have not told. She did not speak of you at all.'

His eyes narrowed. 'If you're lying to me, Vinnie Harris—'

'I'm not lying, sir,' she protested. 'She did *not* mention your name once, I will swear it on the bible if you will let me do so. She did not speak of you, I tell you. Not one word. She said only—'

'Only what?'

'Only told me that I shouldn't wed,' said Vinnie reluctantly. 'She told me I should stay a maid.'

Her earnestness seemed finally to convince him and he released the pressure on her shoulder. Fumbling in his pocket he drew out a coin which he pressed into her hand. 'I want you to forget that last remark, do you understand me, Vinnie? Forget it, forget that Maude ever spoke to you that way of marriage.'

Vinnie stared at him without answering and he closed her fingers around the coin. 'You understand, Vinnie, this is a sovereign – a golden sovereign. It is for your silence. You are not to repeat a word of this remark concerning marriage or the marriage bed – nor any other remarks you may remember at some later date. Do you hear me, Vinnie Harris? Do you understand me?'

'Yes, I do,' said Vinnie, hating the nearness of his face and the frightened look in his pale eyes. She felt a great loathing for the man and her pity for Maude increased tenfold. She knew suddenly why the woman had longed for death – it was her only escape from this horrible man.

But Joshua Parsloe was already striding away towards the carriage which would take him back to the vicarage. Slowly Vinnie opened her fingers and looked at the coin that he had given her. It gleamed dully in her palm and she thought of Judas Iscariot and his bag of silver. Impulsively she flung it from her and watched it sail through the air and fall into the long grass. She drew a great shuddering breath of relief. The others were calling her to hurry and she realised suddenly that she was soaked through and chilled by the heavy rain. Gathering up her sodden skirt, she hurried out on to the street and climbed up into the waiting carriage where Mrs Bryce had kept a place for her.

*

In the large parlour of the vicarage the mourners stood about dispiritedly in their damp clothes while the housekeeper served wine and a selection of sandwiches and biscuits. The conversation was stilted and the strained atmosphere did not relax. As soon as was decently possible, most people made their excuses and left. Vinnie and the Bryce family were among the first to depart. As Vinnie followed them down the steps, she felt a touch on her arm and turning, saw Julian Lawrence smiling at her.

'Don't look so sad, Vinnie,' he said kindly. 'You did all you could for her, all that she asked. You have nothing to reproach yourself for. Please believe me.'

'I hope not,' said Vinnie. 'I do hope not.'

'She is at peace,' he said. 'We should be thankful for her. Look at it that way, Vinnie, and you need not feel so sad. You have had a wretched time these last few days. A bad shock. We think – at least—' he corrected himself, 'Eva and I think, you should have a holiday and mother has agreed that we may take you to Margate for the day when we go next week – as our guest, of course. Will you come with us, Vinnie?'

Vinnie was amazed at the change in her fortunes and her depression lifted immediately at the prospect of such a glittering event.

'Margate?' she echoed. 'Oh, Julian!'

Eva, seeing that her brother spoke with Vinnie and guessing the reason, now joined them. 'Do say you'll come,' she said. 'It's such fun at Margate. We love it there, don't we, Julian?'

Julian nodded.

'Have you ever been to the seaside?' Eva asked Vinnie and the latter shook her head. 'You mean you've never seen the sea?'

'Never.'

'Then you're in for a great experience, isn't she, Julian? It's such a glorious sight and of all the resorts Margate is our favourite. We have been to Dover and Ramsgate and last year we went down to Folkestone. That was when those two ships were driven on to the beach by the storm: the *Agder* and the *Baron Holburg*. Oh, you must remember, Vinnie.' But Vinnie shook her head.

'That terrible gale last September,' Eva continued. 'We went down on the train to see them. We were too late to see the rescue operation of course but the beach was still crowded with people. The press photographers were there . . .'

'It was exciting,' Julian confessed, 'and Folkestone is very pleasant but we do much prefer Margate, and you will enjoy it too, Vinnie. We need not talk about it now, but some time during the next few days we will call in at the cottage and make plans.'

'We will go to Palm Bay,' cried Eva, 'and if Mama is not coming with us, we could go to Newgate Gap,' she said. 'Do you fancy a donkey ride, Vinnie?'

Vinnie nodded. She fancied everything. Margate sounded like another world to her and her eyes began to gleam with excitement.

'And we can listen to the band,' said Julian. 'Above Fort Steps. The poor old bandstand may not be there much longer, for they are talking of building a winter garden and if they do they will cut into the cliffs below and the bandstand will have to go.'

At that moment the Colonel's wife called to Julian from the other end of the hallway.

'We will see you another day and talk about it again,' Julian promised, and brother and sister went back into the house leaving Vinnie in a whirl of excitement. The nightmare of the last few days began to fade and in its place came a delightful expectancy. Vinnie Harris was going to Margate! She could hardly believe it. Not only that, but she was going in the company of Eva and Julian and her joy was complete.

The next morning Vinnie went back to the churchyard and stood beside Maude Parsloe's grave. The gravedigger had done a hurried job, shovelling in the wet earth as fast as he could and now, unlevelled, it had a careless look about it as though the person buried below was no longer of any significance.

'I'm going to look for my money,' Vinnie whispered. 'I hope you don't mind, Miss Babbit. It's for Margate, you see.'

She felt sure that Miss Babbit's ghost would understand this cryptic message and she set about the task of reclaiming her sovereign untroubled by conscience. She had very little money of her own and did not want to feel like a charity child when the day of the great expedition arrived. For nearly an hour she searched amongst the wet grass, but her patience was finally rewarded and she pocketed the coin thankfully and went home.

CHAPTER ELEVEN

The following day Julian stopped by at the cottage for a couple of minutes to leave various brochures for Vinnie to look at and that evening when her school work was finished, she settled down to enjoy them.

'Listen to this,' she cried, reading aloud from one of them. '"The Clifton Bath supplies warmed baths from one shilling each and ozone baths from three shillings".'

'Ozone!' said Mrs Bryce. 'What's ozone?'

Vinnie shrugged. 'Some sort of bath,' she said helpfully. '". . . softened water specially for drinking, fourpence for two gallons". That's very reasonable.'

Mrs Bryce hid a smile. 'Oh, very reasonable,' she agreed. 'It all sounds very nice. I suppose you'll go looking for that brother of yours while you're there?'

'I'd dearly like to,' said Vinnie, 'but I don't know if there'll be time. Eva and Julian have such plans and there's so much to do, but if there *is* time – I would so like to see Bertie again. Tom said he's most likely married by now with a baby.'

'Well, let's hope not,' said Mrs Bryce. 'He's a bit young for that and if he's a sensible head on his shoulders, he'll stay single a bit longer. So don't you fret on that score, Vinnie, but I dare say you would like to see him again as much as he would like to see you.'

Vinnie sighed and turned her attention to the railway guide.

'If ever I'm rich,' she said, 'I shall visit all the seaside places – Folkestone, Ramsgate, Margate, Dover. I'll see them all.'

'That will be nice, dear.'

'If we went to Folkestone,' said Vinnie, 'we could go on a ship to Boulogne.'

'Boulogne?' said Mrs Bryce, startled. 'Isn't that foreign?'
'It's France.'

'Ah, I thought so. I shouldn't go to France, dear. Anything could happen to you in a foreign country, and they say the food isn't at all like ours.'

'I don't care,' said Vinnie. 'I'd try it anyway.'

'You don't speak French, dear.'

'I could learn.'

'Shall you want to take some lunch?' asked Mrs Bryce, but Vinnie shook her head.

'No, Julian is going to buy our lunch at a hotel. We are going to eat our lunch in a real restaurant.'

'My! Well, I hope he's paying for it.'

'He is. They are paying for *everything* but I am taking the sovereign just—' She broke off. She had not intended to mention the money, for she had told no one about it. Mrs Bryce, however, had noticed her slip.

'Sovereign?' she asked. 'What sovereign? What have you been up to, Vinnie Harris?'

'Nothing, I haven't been up to anything. It was given to me by Joshua Parsloe, if you must know.'

'I certainly must,' said Mrs Bryce. 'And what's *that* dreadful man giving you money for, I'd like to know?'

Reluctantly, Vinnie explained what had happened, crossing her fingers behind her back that Mrs Bryce would not make her return the money.

'I wonder how many more sovereigns he's handed out,' said Mrs Bryce. 'I wouldn't be in his shoes for all the tea in China. He might be able to buy folks' silence but he will never buy off his own conscience. Don't you fret about the money, Vinnie. I am sure Mrs Parsloe would have wanted you to spend it and enjoy yourself. Very fond of you, she was, and she would like to think you were having a good time at Margate with your friends.'

'I shall bring you back a souvenir,' Vinnie began, then looked up suddenly. 'If folks from London go to Margate, why then Em could be there as well. Then there would be me, Bertie and Em all together again.'

It was still a source of deep grief to Vinnie that the previous year the Battys and Emmeline had not arrived for the hop-picking and no one knew what had become of them. The Walkers had known only that they had moved, but no one seemed to know where. Vinnie sighed and Mrs Bryce smiled at her.

'Now don't you go setting your hopes too high, Vinnie,' she warned. 'Or else you'll be disappointed. Never mind Bertie and never mind Em. You just tell yourself that two very nice friends are taking you to Margate for the day and that ought to be enough for any girl. Now drink up your tea and off to bed with you or you'll never get up in the morning.'

*

That same evening in a small hall in Whitechapel, a handsome young man was holding forth with passion on a subject very dear to his heart. His name was Roland Fry and he was just twenty-two years old. He stood behind a lectern and addressed a group of between twenty and thirty people who filled the front three rows. On the lectern was a sheaf of papers and a pile of magazines, one of which he now picked up and waved at his listeners.

'And there's more,' he told them. 'Listen to this extract from the Salvation Army magazine, *The Deliverer*.' He glanced at the cover.

'True, this was five years ago, but I am told on the very best authority that these conditions still prevail.' He cleared his voice with a little cough and began to read:

'"Where the hoppers' huts *are* rain-proof and draught-proof the space is frequently so limited that men, women and children are much more often herded together than accommodated. Much evil comes of it – drinking is freely indulged; foul language abounds; quarrelling rages; in the spoiling of tempers consequent upon great inconvenience and overcrowding, the children suffer, often painfully."' He lowered his voice suddenly. '"Indecent habits are common and open and many a hitherto pure girl goes back to the city contaminated, to drift ultimately to the streets".'

There was a murmur from his audience and a few whispered comments as he laid down *The Deliverer* and picked up a newspaper.

'And this,' he cried, 'from no less a journal than *The Times*: "Meanwhile, the whole rural population in the hop cultivating district of Kent is demoralised, not only in the matter of drink".' He turned the page. 'And here's a letter from an anxious correspondent. I quote ". . . the society is fatally promiscuous. Mothers come back drunkards or immoral; daughters even at fourteen or fifteen years of age, are debauched and ready for the streets and little children glib-tongued in obscenity and blasphemy."'

He ran a finger round the inside of his collar and his blue eyes shone with fervour as he gazed as his audience.

'Now, I don't pretend that nothing is being done for these unfortunate people. We know, indeed, that something is being attempted. Parliament has passed many acts on their behalf and the Society for the Employment and Improved Lodgings of Hop Pickers has done a great deal to help them. Of course the owners of the hop-gardens are aware of the problems and many more God-fearing people are anxious to do what they can. But *I* maintain that there is always room for more. We are only a few people, but with determination and perseverance and with our trust in God, I suggest that we can go among these people and better their lives.'

There was a murmur of approval at these words and he leaned forward, resting his arms on the lectern. 'I believe,' he told them earnestly, 'that if at the end of the month after all our endeavours, we can say we have saved *one* girl from a life of immorality, then it has been a month well spent.'

A young woman began to clap and he smiled warmly in her direction.

'We are the fortunates of this world,' he told them. 'We have shoes and we have comfortable homes; we have enough to eat and we have interesting work to fill our lives; we also have friends with whom to share our leisure. These people who need our help have none of these things.'

An elderly gentleman in the second row put up a hand and

Roland nodded to him encouragingly. He stood up slowly.

'I don't for a moment doubt,' he said, 'that these people need our help, but I do wonder if it is necessary to help them down in Kent. As you say, they are local people. Surely if we are to make special efforts on their behalf, we can do it much more easily while they are at home?'

There were a few murmurs as he sat down and immediately the young woman who had clapped earlier raised her hand. Receiving a smile from Roland, she stood up; she was unused to speaking in public and a faint blush tinged her smooth cheeks.

'I don't agree at all,' she said. 'The point surely is this. Many of these people don't go to church. So how do we make contact? If we want to reach them we must be prepared to go in search of them. We *ought* to go into their homes, but are not always welcome. Down in the hop-gardens, however, they are all gathered together almost literally under one roof. We can reach them so much more easily there. Possibly away from their own environment they may even be more receptive to what we have to offer. I have never actually been to a hop-garden but I have heard what Mr Fry has told us and I would like to say right away that I am willing to go down if I am needed and will do all I can to help them.'

As she sat down, Roland gave her a dazzling smile of approval, then took a pencil from his pocket with a flourish. 'May I have the young lady's name?' he said. 'For she is our first volunteer. Please let us show our approval of her generous offer.'

The short burst of applause which followed deepened the colour in her face. She rose once more to her feet: 'My name is Mary Bellweather,' she said. Roland wrote it down. When he had returned the pencil to his pocket, he continued, 'Now I don't want to waste any more time. It's getting late and the caretaker will soon be waiting to lock up and go home. I have explained the conditions in the hop-gardens, I have explained the way in which other groups are helping and I have told you what I would like to do for these people. What I suggest is that we take a vote on whether or not we can contribute our share, small though it may be. If we decide in favour, then we can consider the details of what we can do and how best we can achieve it.'

'I will second that proposal.' It was Mary Bellweather.

'Then can we have a show of hands,' said Roland. 'All those in favour of action?'

The decision was unanimous. 'That is absolutely splendid,' said Roland. 'I can't tell you how encouraged I am by your warm response. Has anyone any ideas they would now like to put forward? I certainly don't want to remain in the limelight. I have said quite enough, probably more than I needed to, but you must forgive me. This cause is very dear to me. I now throw the meeting open to discussion. In fact, I will come down off this high horse,' – he indicated the dais on which he stood with a light laugh – 'and join you in the body of the hall.'

He came down the steps, found an empty seat and the others shuffled their chairs around to form a rough circle. Immediately the elderly man began to speak: 'Surely the most obvious thing to offer them is a church service,' he said. 'An open-air service when the weather permits and when it's inclement perhaps we can beg a temporary shelter or if necessary huddle under a tree.'

'Splendid idea!' said Roland. 'Of course, taking the word of God among them must be our prime concern. At this stage, I think perhaps somebody might act as secretary and take these suggestions down in note form. I wonder if Miss Bellweather would be kind enough?'

She nodded and Roland produced a notebook which he handed to her. She flipped it open and began to write:

'Point one,' she said briskly. 'Offer church service.'

'What about advice?' asked another woman. 'Perhaps we could go among them while they work, asking if they have problems and offering to help wherever we can?'

Miss Bellweather scribbled again. The elderly man said, 'What about clothing? From what we've heard, some of them have no shoes. Perhaps we could collect old clothes and take them down and distribute them to the needy.'

'It's the drunkenness which appals me,' said another man.

'Supposing we offer them some other form of drink – something much cheaper. Even if the men insist on their beer, perhaps we could wean some of the women away from their stout.'

'Orange juice and lemonade for the children—'

'A tea-urn perhaps.'

'Milk from one of the nearby farms—'

Roland held up a hand. 'Now here we must add another point – that if we are to provide these things, then we need capital and shall have to find a way of raising money.'

A young woman with bright auburn hair spoke next: 'I am not sure I understand how this is going to be organised. I can see that all these possibilities have great merit, but are you proposing to travel down in the train each day or are we going to have to live with them?'

There were hasty murmurs of, 'I hope not!' and, 'Surely that won't be necessary.'

'Another good point,' said Roland. 'I think we must go down there, but certainly not live among them – that would be intolerable and we could not expect anyone to do it. No, I think we must arrange accommodation in farm-houses where possible or in the local inns.'

'One of us could go down in advance,' suggested Miss Bellweather, 'and arrange accommodation for the rest.'

'But for how long?' cried another. 'Would we all be required to put in a whole month's work?'

'That is another point we must consider,' said Roland. 'Many of us will not be able to spare a whole month, so we must draw up a roster. We certainly don't want to have everybody down there during the first two weeks of the period and nobody there for the last two.'

'It's going to involve us in an awful lot of work,' commented the auburn-haired woman. 'I propose therefore that those of us with the most time carry the heaviest burden. Having no family, I am free to offer my services wherever they are needed and would be perfectly willing to spend two weeks in Kent.'

Miss Bellweather smiled at her. 'And what is your name, please?'

'Emily Gerrard.'

A dark-haired woman who had not spoken previously now stood up. She told them her name was Sylvia Grant and that she was training to be a nurse. She was willing, she said, to spend part of her annual holiday among the hoppers if her nursing training could be of any value. As the meeting continued, it soon became obvious that among the number of people present there was a great variety of talent which could be utilised. Ideas came thick and fast and the growing enthusiasm proved very infectious. Before the meeting ended they had drawn up a rough plan of action and had a list of names. Several suggestions had been made regarding ways in which they could raise money, and it was agreed that they would meet again at the same time the following week.

'We all know the problems,' said Roland, 'and we all know what we hope to achieve. Perhaps we can give the matter serious thought during the coming week.'

He then declared the meeting closed.

The chairs were returned to their proper places and people drifted away in ones and twos. Mary Bellweather took a long time collecting together her gloves and bag, so that she and Roland Fry were the last to leave.

'I think you live in my direction,' he said to her. 'Perhaps I can escort you to your door?'

She accepted eagerly. He did not know that for the past six months -- since moving into the area – she had greatly admired him and had hoped to find a way to get to know him. As he locked the door of the church hall behind them, he was quite oblivious of her excitement and his thoughts revolved entirely around the newly formed mission.

*

The tea-table with its white damask cloth and silver cutlery was set in the shade of the large chestnut tree so that the cream and butter would not be affected by the warm sunshine. Eva took a third scone and spread it liberally with jam and cream. Then she took a large bite which left her with traces of cream on her upper lip and these she wiped away with a white napkin.

Her mother drew her eyebrows together in a slight frown of disapproval.

'You eat too fast, Eva,' she told her. 'I have been telling you that ever since you were a child. It simply is not an acceptable way to eat your food in company.'

'But I'm not in company.'

'Well, you are certainly not eating alone.'

'But it's only you and Julian. Julian doesn't mind, do you?'

'Of course I do,' he said. 'The sight of you wolfing your food quite turns my stomach. How you will ever find a husband I can't imagine.'

She groaned at the familiar topic and he laughed. 'We do have to find you a husband,' he mocked.

'I find nothing amusing about that,' said Christina. 'We do most certainly have to find her a husband.'

'I might elope,' said Eva with a wink at her brother. She put the rest of the scone into her mouth and reached for a fourth.

'Eva, please!' said Christina. 'Surely three is sufficient? Unless you want to ruin your figure.'

'I don't care a fig for my figure,' said Eva. 'Oh, that's rather nice – a *fig* for my *fig*ure.'

Her mother's exasperation increased. 'It is not a joking matter, Eva, you really *must* curb your appetite. I hope you will not eat too heartily on Sunday when the Marlowes are here. Andrew Marlowe is a most eligible young man, but he will hardly be attracted to you if you gobble your food.'

'I don't want to find a husband just yet,' said Eva. 'Surely one more year can make very little difference. One year at a school in Paris—'

'No, Eva. We have talked about it and I have made my decision. The answer is "No".'

'Julian, that is your fifth scone!' cried Eva indignantly. 'Why isn't Julian being scolded?'

'Julian is a man,' said Christina, 'and men have larger appetites than we do. Really, Eva, sometimes you are very childish for a young woman of seventeen. Do try to behave a little more decorously. Too much cream will spoil your complexion.'

Just then she caught sight of Vinnie, who came down the front step and turned to walk down the drive. She gave a slight wave of her hand and Julian and Eva turned their heads. 'Can Vinnie join us?' asked Eva. 'I'm sure she would enjoy cream and jam scones.'

'I think not,' said Christina. 'You make too much of the girl. These people are all the same. If you give them too much encouragement they take advantage.'

'Not Vinnie,' said Julian. 'She is too proud for that.'

'Proud?'

'Julian's right,' said Eva. 'She has a sort of dignity. Do let her join us.'

'Eva, I said no. Let that be the end of it, please, and after this trip to Margate I hope you will leave the girl alone.'

Eva and Julian exchanged a look which Christina chose to ignore. Julian excused himself from the table before Christina could protest and ran after Vinnie's retreating figure. He caught up with her and as they spoke their obvious animation increased Christina's displeasure. For a moment the idea crossed her mind that his interest in the girl might be more than platonic, but she dismissed this as ridiculous.

'I am going to take a spare set of bathing clothes for her,' said Eva as they watched Julian walk back across the grass towards them. He sat down cheerfully, but made no reference to his brief conversation with Vinnie.

'I have just told Mama that I am taking a spare set of clothes so that we can all go bathing tomorrow.'

Julian nodded absent-mindedly. 'I would like to use the telephone once more, Mother,' he said. It had recently been installed but, still an innovation, was not freely used. 'I am trying to trace that brother of hers, but having no success so far. It would be wonderful to bring them together again after all these years.'

'But you have made about five calls already,' protested his mother. 'The telephone isn't a toy, Julian, it is a costly piece of equipment . . .'

'I am not using it as a toy, Mother, I am trying to trace Bertie Harris and that involves getting in touch with the various hotels in Margate. I wrote to most of them, but by the time they replied there simply was no time to write to any more. The telephone is the obvious answer.'

Christina sighed. 'Well, I shall be glad when tomorrow is over and there's an end to all this nonsense. Please don't arrange any more jaunts with the child.'

She picked up the fly-swatter as a solitary wasp began to hover over the jam pot, saying, 'Wretched things, I can't abide them.' She swatted it neatly and it fell into the grass where Julian stepped on it. 'Team-work,' he said with a smile, and the vexing subject of Vinnie was allowed to drop.

From the opposite side of the lawn Tom Bryce now appeared, making his way towards them. With a polite nod to Eva and Julian he addressed himself to Christina, explaining his concern for the state of the crops which were suffering from lack of rain. Almost too readily she excused herself from the tea-table and offered to accompany him back to the hop-garden. Eva and Julian watched them go without speaking.

'I don't believe him,' Eva murmured when they were safely out of earshot. 'I don't believe there's anything wrong with the crop.'

She could not bring herself to put her thoughts into words on the subject of Christina and Tom Bryce. Neither of them had ever referred to their mother's relationship with the Colonel's top employee and now Julian avoided her eye.

'There has been very little rain,' he said. 'It might well become a problem – the hop is a delicate plant.'

'So is Mama.' Immediately she regretted her words and Julian knew that she did. 'I feel for Papa,' she said. 'Oh, damn!'

Confused, she covered her face with her hands, her elbows resting on the white cloth. After a moment Julian said quietly, 'I don't think we should judge them, it is an unhappy situation.'

For a moment she removed her hands from her face. 'Unhappy – for Tom Bryce? I don't like the man.'

Julian shrugged. 'We all depend on him a great deal,' he said. 'We need his expertise. Mother could not manage the hop-garden without him.'

Eva picked up the silver napkin ring and began to roll it round her fingers. 'He is a married man,' she said stubbornly. 'He has a wife of his own. Poor Rose – I think he's a swine.'

There was another silence and then Eva said, 'Bryce has a wife, mother has a husband, but poor Papa—'

'Exactly. Father is a helpless, bedridden, old man.'

'It's not his fault.'

'No one is to blame,' said Julian, 'but he can give mother no companionship. What sort of life is that for her?'

'Must you always take her side?'

'Need we take sides at all?' he asked. 'I don't think we should judge her, Eva. We can't really understand all her problems. I think we must be tolerant.'

'I can't be tolerant, I hate him,' she protested stubbornly. 'I can't bear to think of it.'

'Then don't. Let her be, Eva. We must all live our own lives as best we can. She is past forty and the best years of her life are over. We must all find our happiness where we may.'

'How very Christian of you!' Her tone was mocking and she would not look at him, concerning herself with the napkin ring.

'Christian? I don't know. I merely try not to condemn too readily.'

Eva's eyes flashed. 'Have you never heard of the ten commandments?' she said. 'Thou shalt not commit . . .'

'That's enough, Eva.' He stood up abruptly. 'If we say any more we shall quarrel and tomorrow will be spoiled. Tomorrow is Vinnie's day. I shall go and make that last telephone call. Are you coming or will you stay here?'

'I'm coming.' She got up reluctantly. 'I'm sorry, Julian. I didn't mean us to quarrel.'

'Let's not talk about it,' he said. 'If you are good I shall let you make the connection but then I shall speak to the hotel.'

He glanced back at the table and saw that another wasp was showing interest in the food. 'You had better ring for Janet to clear,' he said and, striding on towards the house, he left his sister to ring the small bell which brought Janet scurrying out into the garden with a large tray.

*

The railway deposited them on Margate station in the middle of the morning, where a stiff breeze made it necessary for the two girls to hold on to their hats. They left the station and, dodging the traffic, made their way to Palm Bay where the cliff gave a little protection from the breeze. The tide was out, leaving a large expanse of yellow sand, and the greeny blue sea and pale sky brought a gasp of admiration from Vinnie which made her two companions smile.

'It's so beautiful!' said Vinnie. 'So huge and wide and bright.'

She stood stock-still, taking in every detail of the scene before her so that later she could describe it to Mrs Bryce.

Elderly ladies, their bonnets tied securely under their chins, sat beneath parasols admiring the sea view. Others, less able, were pushed and jolted across the sand in Bath chairs by hired servants. Further out on the firmer sand, a game of cricket was in progress and further still children and adults alike paddled in the sea, skirts and trousers tucked up out of reach of the waves. A photographer had persuaded a family to pose for him and they stood smiling self-consciously into the lens while he busied himself under the black cloth. Old men tried to read their newspapers, clutching them firmly against the breeze which threatened to tear the pages from their hands. One had already escaped its owner and the separate sheets fluttered along the sand. A donkey was led past with two children perched precariously upon his back, while an anxious mother ran alongside urging them to 'Keep a good hold'.

While Julian, Eva and Vinnie were making their way slowly across the beach, he took the opportunity to tell Vinnie of his lack of success the previous day. He had telephoned all the hotels in Margate, he told her, planning to find Bertie and bring the two of them together. However, the very last hotel had disappointing news – Bertie, it seemed, had become very friendly with one Adam Turner who also worked there. When the latter decided to become a trooper in the Army, Bertie had been persuaded to join him and the two of them had left several months earlier. All that the hotel knew was that they were on their way to Woolwich, where they hoped to become troopers in the Royal Artillery.

'I hope you are not too disappointed, Vinnie,' he said. 'I am telling you now because I feared that if I did not speak of it you might go on hoping for the rest of the day – hoping to meet up with Bertie.'

'I would have done,' said Vinnie. 'I did very much want to see him, but you did all you could and I am very grateful.'

'Don't let it spoil the day,' Eva urged. 'I'm sure you will see him again soon. At least now we know where he has gone. Julian could make further enquiries for you.'

Julian nodded. 'Of course I will,' he said. 'I will do anything I can to help.'

'Julian will find him for you, I am sure of it,' cried Eva, 'so don't be gloomy, Vinnie. We have so many marvellous things to do today and so much to show you. We are determined that you will see everything,' she went on, 'in case you never come again. Have you seen enough of Palm Bay? If so we can go on to the bandstand and listen to the music. What do you say, Julian? Then we could take an early lunch and go to Newgate Bay.'

This was agreed and they made their way to the green above Fort Steps where a band played military music under the ornate canopy of the bandstand. They settled themselves in deck-chairs and Vinnie, looking around her, was thrilled to think she was in the company of so many fashionable people, all of whom seemed to accept her as one of themselves – at least no one stared at her or pointed an accusing finger. For a 'child of the London slums' Vinnie felt extraordinarily comfortable among so many of her social superiors and this fact gave her great and unexpected satisfaction.

When they had heard enough music, it was decided that they would patronise the restaurant in George Sanger's Grand Hall. This was aptly named because the restaurant formed only a small part of the large establishment. Also on the site was a zoo, an Italian garden, a ballroom, concert hall and a roller-skating rink.

It was the first time that Vinnie had ever eaten in a restaurant and at first she spoke in hushed whispers as though she were in church; Eva soon laughed her out of her nervousness and the meal proceeded gaily. To celebrate the occasion, Julian ordered a bottle of white wine and Vinnie's excitement was doubled by its heady sparkle. After coffee, Julian persuaded them to their feet once more, assuring them that the walk to Newgate Gap would shake down their meal.

'Then,' he told them cheerfully, 'we shall be ready for our dip.' Vinnie walked along between them in a haze of contentment which was not dispelled even when they discovered that all the bathing machines were already hired out and that none would be available until much later in the afternoon.

'At least there are donkeys for hire,' cried Eva and they joined the short queue. Newgate Gap, as its name implied, was cut through the steep chalk cliff which led down to the sea. It was spanned at the seaward end by a decorative bridge and there were steps at one side leading up to the cliff-top. A dozen or more donkeys waited patiently along one side of the gap, tended by an old man and three younger men, all of whom shouted repeatedly to attract customers for their rides. The rides themselves extended to the edge of the sea and back, a fairly short distance, so the queue dwindled rapidly and Vinnie soon found herself sitting side-saddle on a dark brown donkey who carried his ears well back. The leather saddle had been polished by much use and Vinnie felt very insecure as she clung for support to the front of the saddle while the man tugged at the reins and urged the donkey to 'Come on up'.

Eva's donkey was a pale, creamy colour and Julian's almost black with a white blaze on its forehead. They set off one behind the other, rolling uncomfortably as the donkeys' hooves slithered on the stony surface of the road which was in fact little more than a broad track.

'I'm going to fall off!' cried Vinnie. 'I know I am. I'm going to fall.'

Eva turned back, laughing. 'No, you won't,' she said. 'It feels as though you will, but you won't.'

The man leading Vinnie's donkey stopped to speak to a friend and she waited anxiously, watching Julian and Eva disappearing towards the far end of the gap. The two men, exchanging a muttered joke, seemed to have forgotten her existence.

'Do you mind?' she began. 'My friends are well ahead.'

The man glanced at her briefly, said, 'Right you are, miss,' and continued his whispered conversation.

'Please!' said Vinnie desperately, for by now Eva and Julian were almost indistinguishable from the rest of the crowd below the bridge. By the time the man condescended to continue the ride, Vinnie saw that the others were on their way back.

'What happened to you?' shouted Eva. 'We thought we had lost you.'

'I thought you had,' cried Vinnie but Julian grinned at her as they passed. Glancing back, she saw them dismount at the end of their ride while she was being carried down the road in splendid isolation.

It was while they were turning below the bridge that the donkey took fright. Rather recklessly, a boy was trying to climb the sloping cliff-side and half-way up he dislodged a large number of stones which came rattling down on to the road. One of the stones bounced up and struck Vinnie's donkey in the neck and the frightened animal squealed in pain and plunged forward. The reins slipped from the man's hand and as the animal galloped on Vinnie found herself alone, clinging on desperately. Hearing her screams, people scattered out of the way as the runaway donkey raced back towards its fellows. Twice Vinnie almost fell off but somehow she managed to stay on. She felt herself slip on the saddle* and gritted her teeth, expecting at any moment to be flung on to the hard stony surface of the road. She closed her eyes fearfully, then opened them as she felt the animal abruptly slowing down and saw Julian standing before them, his arms outstretched. The donkey braced itself and then turned suddenly sideways to elude the outstretched hand which sought for the dangling rein. Vinnie slipped but Julian was there to catch her and for a moment they clung together. Shaken and trembling, she fought back the tears of fright that now threatened to spill over and shame her.

'My poor little Vinnie,' Julian murmured, holding her very close and patting her shoulder comfortingly. 'You're safe now. Quite safe.'

Vinnie, with her head on his shoulder and his arms closed tightly round her, wanted the moment to last forever. She felt safe, loved and cared for: Julian Lawrence was holding her in his arms and seemed unwilling to release her. Then she heard Eva's voice beside them and reluctantly raised her head.

'Oh, say you aren't hurt, Vinnie!' she cried.

'No, Eva, I'm not hurt.'

Julian took a small step back so that the distance between them was increased and immediately Vinnie yearned for the nearness of his body and the warmth of his embrace. She looked up at him and knew intuitively that he also regretted the brevity of their closeness.

'You have had a bad fright,' he said, his eyes on hers, 'but luckily you weren't harmed.'

'Thanks to you,' she said, steadying her voice with an effort. He shrugged lightly. 'I think the wretched animal would have stopped anyway,' he said.

'What happened along the road there?' cried Eva. 'We suddenly saw you charging towards us.'

Vinnie explained the cause of the incident. 'But I'm not at all hurt,' she ended and wanted to add that even if she had been it would have been well worth it for those few moments in Julian's arms.

She quickly recovered from her fright and the rest of the day passed pleasantly. First they returned to Sanger's Grand Hall and went round the zoo; then they found a small tea-shop where they ordered cream buns and a pot of tea for three. By the time the train was due to take them home Vinnie was delightfully weary. The two girls sat opposite each other by the windows and Julian sat down next to Vinnie. For a second or two Vinnie saw the surprise in Eva's eyes but knew that the surprise in her own must be even greater.

Exaggerating the extent of her weariness, she let her eyes close from time to time and leaned towards Julian as though unaware that she did so. Daringly she let her hand fall between them under the cover of her skirt while fixing her eyes on the view from the window. She willed him to take her hand or at least to touch it but was forced to wait in an agony of frustration for most of the journey. Julian continued to talk cheerfully and Vinnie forced herself to answer. Not until they were almost home was her prayer answered when, as the train gave an unexpected lurch, Julian let his own hand slide from his knee and suddenly she felt the pressure of his fingers on her own. Then their hands were clasped and remained so for the final ten minutes of the journey.

For Vinnie it was a time of wild ecstasy. But for Julian? She could not tell, for outwardly he remained quite composed. Perhaps, thought Vinnie, she too appeared composed – perhaps only she was aware of the wild fluttering of her heart. Surreptitiously, she glanced across at Eva who seemed unaware of the tension and chattered away quite normally. How would Eva look, Vinnie wondered, if *she* had been swept by such new and wonderful emotions?

At the station Julian alighted first and helped both girls down from the carriage. His eyes met Vinnie's briefly and a secret spark leapt between them. Tim Bilton was in the station yard to meet them with the pony and trap. This time Julian sat next to his sister and Vinnie sat alone but when they reached the cottage and it was time for her to alight, he called out to Tim, 'I'll see Vinnie down,' and was out of the trap before the groom could protest. His arms reached up for her and his hands went round her waist. As he swung her to the ground, Vinnie was aware that Eva watched them curiously and she hastily lowered her eyes.

'Thank you for a very nice day,' she said. 'It's been so wonderful.' As she said this she raised her head and met Julian's gaze so that he knew to what it was she referred.

'We enjoyed your company,' he said with a faint smile and then he had climbed back into the trap and they were bowling away. Vinnie stood in the road long after they were out of sight, watching the dust settle; she closed her eyes, wondering once more at the touch of his fingers, and sighed deeply. For a moment she let her imagination take over and visualised further meetings and closer intimacies and then, with another sigh, she put such notions aside and – remembering the ornate plate which she had bought for Mrs Bryce – hurried up the path, eager to give it to her.

CHAPTER TWELVE

One day in August Vinnie made her way down to the village
store and, finding it unattended, rapped sharply on the counter
with her knuckles. When nothing happened she called, 'Mr
Tupp – shop!' but it was his son who finally appeared. Jarvis
was eighteen now and a little taller than his father. He was
trying to grow a moustache without much success and still had
a full head of hair, but apart from these differences, Vinnie
thought he was going to grow up very much like his father.

'I've brought the order down from the big house,' Vinnie
told him, holding out a list which was carefully written in Mrs
Tallant's neat hand.

Jarvis took it and laid it on the counter. 'Not my
department,' he told her triumphantly. 'I'm "mobile", you
see.'

After several uncomfortable years of sharing the shop with
his son, Will Tupp had stumbled upon the ideal solution. He
bought a second-hand carrier's cart and a horse to pull it and
sent his son out daily to tour the outlying areas with a selection
of food and household items from the shop. This had the
twofold effect of increasing his sales while removing Jarvis
from his presence and the arrangement suited father and son
very well.

'I've painted up the cart. I expect you noticed.'

'Yes, I did,' said Vinnie, who had not in fact noticed it. 'It
looks very smart.'

'I don't do things by halves,' said Jarvis.

'I'm sure you don't.'

There was still no sign of Will Tupp and Vinnie was
anxious to get home. Edie normally brought down the order,

but she was in bed with a fever and since Vinnie had been reading to the Colonel, Christina had asked her to do it. Vinnie had agreed reluctantly, for she was embarrassed by Jarvis's recent advances.

'Will your father be long?' she asked.

'He's out in the back,' said Jarvis. He gazed at her with his pale eyes. 'You going to the hopping supper?' he asked.

Vinnie hesitated. She didn't wish to lie but felt immediately that he hoped to invite her.

'I may do,' she said. 'Bit too early to say really. We haven't started hopping yet.'

'I just wondered.'

'Ask me again later on,' she said, reluctant to hurt his feelings.

'I might – I might not. I might have asked somebody else by then.'

Vinnie hoped very much that he would have done so too, but she smiled without answering.

'How's things up at the big house, then?' he asked. 'Young folk still away, are they?'

Vinnie nodded. Eva and Julian were still in Wiltshire, where they had been staying with friends for the past five weeks. After their excursion to Margate she had only seen them once before they left for their holiday. She had prayed they would come back in time for the hopping, but there was still no mention of their return and she was too proud to ask anyone.

'Nice little business I'm working up with the cart,' said Jarvis. 'Quite profitable. I think Pa's quite surprised. Mind you, nothing comes easy and I work hard at it. Only common sense, isn't it? I mean, one day it will all be mine. Mobile *and* shop.' Vinnie nodded cautiously.

'Quite a prosperous little business, all in all,' he continued. 'You could say I was nicely set up for the rest of my life. All I need now is a wife.' He gave her a meaning look and Vinnie's heart sank.

'Trouble is finding someone I fancy,' he went on. 'Can you think of anybody who would make me a good wife?'

'I thought you fancied Emily Drew,' said Vinnie a trifle

tartly. 'You were always telling us how well the two of you got on together.' She put a slight emphasis on the words 'got on' and Jarvis, taking her meaning, laughed.

'Oh, we did. We did,' he said. 'But Emily Drew is engaged to another, as you well know. More fool Emily Drew.'

'She's probably very happy,' said Vinnie, but he shook his head as though he knew better.

'What about Sheila Stevens?' said Vinnie. 'If you wait a few years she'll be old enough to wed.'

'I don't choose to wait a few years,' said Jarvis. 'So that just leaves you and Joan Dolling.'

'And she's moved away,' said Vinnie. 'Anyway, she's never done you no harm, so why should she have to marry you?'

He grinned. 'Oh, you don't want me to wed Joan Dolling,' he said. 'Perhaps you would rather I chose you.'

'Perhaps I wouldn't,' said Vinnie. 'Perhaps I'd rather marry a gorilla or a three-legged dwarf! Your father is a long time out in the back. I think I'll just leave this order with you.'

'I shouldn't, because I shall be leaving in a moment and shan't be here to give it to him. I'm off round Teston and Farleigh today. Care to come with me for the ride?'

'No, thank you. I've something better to do.'

'Such as?'

'I've a letter to write.' Vinnie had meant to keep her letter secret but the desire to speak of it was too much for her. She had bribed Janet to find the address of the house in Wiltshire where Julian was staying and she meant to send him a letter asking him when he would be coming home. If he cared for *her* at all, she reasoned, this would tell him that she cared also for *him* and might hasten his return. Jarvis Tupp's eyes narrowed thoughtfully.

'A letter? Who are you writing letters to?'

'That's none of your business, Jarvis Tupp, but perhaps I've got an admirer.'

Jarvis's mouth fell open at the very idea. He was well aware that none of the young men in the village were courting her and it had never occurred to him that there might be a rival for his attentions elsewhere. Before he had time to recover from the shock, the door opened and a stranger came into the shop. Vinnie turned and they both regarded the newcomer with unabashed curiosity. He was a tall, slim young man with dark hair and deep blue eyes and he carried a bulging suitcase. He seemed quite unperturbed by their scrutiny, but looked weary, his face beaded with perspiration.

'I wonder if either of you good people could help me,' he said. 'My name is Fry, Roland Fry, and I'm rather at a loss for somewhere to stay. The thing is, I wrote to book myself a room at the "Horse and Cart", but somehow the letter never reached them, or so they say, and the room's not ready. They weren't expecting me at all. I've walked all the way from Wateringbury with my suitcase, but I simply can't carry it another yard.'

As though to prove the truth of this last statement he set it down, took out a handkerchief and mopped his face.

'You visiting then?' asked Jarvis. 'Friends, like?'

The young man smiled. 'Not exactly,' he said, 'although I suppose one could look at it in that light. I am a member of the Brothers in Jesus and I have come down to find accommodation for the other three members of my party who will be arriving at the end of the week.'

'To do what exactly?' asked Jarvis.

Roland Fry's expression changed from weariness to earnestness. 'To bring help and relief, both physical and spiritual, to the London hoppers,' he told them. 'There are many unfortunates among them in need of help and guidance. But we believe we are all brothers – all neighbours. I and my three companions will go among them giving help and advice wherever we can. Oh, I know what you'll say. You'll tell me there's a criminal element among them who don't deserve help but will merely take advantage of our generosity. But how can you separate the sheep from the goats? I believe—'

Fortunately this little homily was interrupted by the belated appearance of Will Tupp and once more Roland explained his predicament. Will scratched his head.

'Room to let?' he repeated. 'I don't know of anyone with rooms to let. Leastways, only the "Horse and Cart" and they've just got the one room and you say that's not ready. I don't think I can help you there.'

'You should have brought a tent,' said Jarvis, but the young man did not find that suggestion very amusing.

Vinnie was thinking rapidly. 'If it's just a bed,' she said, 'and a bite to eat, I may be able to help you. Mrs Bryce might take you in.'

He turned to her eagerly. 'Mrs Bryce, you say? I'd be so grateful. If I could just stay somewhere and settle myself in . . . I'm terribly late already.'

'Late?'

'For my appointment with Colonel Lawrence, the owner of the hop-gardens. He is expecting me for dinner at seven o'clock to discuss the various problems which occur most frequently among the hoppers. I would like time to change my clothes and freshen myself a little before I go up there.'

'I'm going that way,' said Jarvis. 'I could drop you both off at the cottage.'

Vinnie hesitated, having refused several similar offers over the last three months, but Roland Fry had no such reservations. 'I should be most awfully grateful if you could,' he said and so she agreed. After she had explained several items in the Lawrences' order to Will Tupp, they went outside.

'Just finished repainting it,' Jarvis told the newcomer, waving a hand towards the cart.

Vinnie looked at it properly for the first time and was forced to admit that Jarvis had indeed made a good job of it. Both horse and cart did him credit. The horse, a piebald, looked clean and sleek from regular grooming and the harness was well polished. The horse turned its head to look at them curiously, jingling its harness as it did so. The cart, supported by two bright yellow wheels, was dark brown with yellow and white lettering: J. TUPP : PROVISIONS FRESH DAILY. A curved canvas top gave it the appearance of an early pioneer waggon.

'*When* I persuade my father to install a telephone, I shall add a telephone number,' Jarvis told them.

Roland Fry and Vinnie made admiring noises and when

Jarvis felt they had been sufficiently appreciative, he allowed them to climb up on to the narrow seat in front of his cart. He left the two of them together for a moment while he darted back into the shop for a word with his father. Roland looked properly at Vinnie for the first time and liked what he saw.

'It's most awfully lucky for me, meeting you like this,' he told her. 'I don't know what I would have done—'

'Don't thank me just yet,' said Vinnie. 'Mrs Bryce may not be willing.' She thought it unlikely though, for Mrs Bryce would be very glad of the extra money.

'Is Mrs Bryce your landlady?'

Vinnie was about to explain the situation when Jarvis returned. He climbed nimbly up into the seat beside her and shouted to the horse. She found herself wedged between the two men. On her right, Jarvis leaned against her and, as they went along, managed from time to time to let his left arm rest on her thigh. With every small jolt of the cart he contrived to lean closer and in order to avoid him, Vinnie was forced to lean the other way, much to the ill-concealed delight of the man on her left. Both men found the nearness of her body very exciting, but while Roland talked earnestly of other matters in a determined effort to distract his thoughts, Jarvis allowed his to wander along forbidden paths, and by the time they reached the end of their short journey he was aroused to a state of pleasurable discomfort. Both men jumped down simultaneously and held up their hands to assist Vinnie, who laughed suddenly, looking from one to the other. To Jarvis's dismay, she chose the other man, and Roland soon had his hands round the neat waist and was helping Vinnie to the ground. As his arms encircled her, she steadied herself with her hands on his shoulders and although she could not bring herself to meet his eyes, she felt the tension in his body. Hastily she ran indoors to announce the arrival of the newcomer, but soon came out again, followed by Mrs Bryce herself who assured Roland that she would be pleased to offer him a bed for a few nights if he was willing to 'take us as you find us'. It was quickly agreed that he would stay and that Mrs Bryce would provide all his meals at a reasonable price.

'It will be like old times,' she told him, 'to have a young man about the place. Come along in and bring that case of yours.' And she bustled back into the house to make him a pot of tea.

Roland turned to Jarvis. 'I would like to get a message to the Lawrences,' he said. 'I wonder if you would drive up there for me and tell them I shall be delayed. I would of course pay you for your trouble.'

'I'm not going that way,' said Jarvis sourly. He saw Roland Fry as an interloper who had made advances to his woman. 'I've no time to run errands.'

'I'll go,' said Vinnie, 'I don't mind walking back,' and she pretended not to see Jarvis's scowl deepen. Without another word, he climbed back on to the seat of his cart and whipped up his horse, jerking the reins so violently that the startled animal set off at a great pace with the cart swaying wildly from side to side.

Ten minutes later, with a hastily scribbled note from Roland in her hand, Vinnie was on her way back along the road towards Foxearth when she heard the rattle of an approaching cart behind her and turning, was surprised to see that it was Jarvis overtaking her. He pulled up alongside with a flourish.

'Jump up!' he said. 'I'll take you up there.'

Surprised by his apparent change of heart, Vinnie hesitated. It did seem churlish to refuse in the circumstances, so she nodded her thanks and once more climbed up on to the seat beside him, although this time she was able to keep her distance. For a while they rode in silence, then without any warning he turned the horse sharply so that they jolted off the road along a track that was only just wide enough for a single cart.

'What are you up to, Jarvis Tupp?' said Vinnie. 'Where are we going?'

'Don't panic. I'm taking a short cut. I want to show you something.'

The track was badly rutted and the cart shuddered and shook. There was a sudden crash from inside, but Jarvis paid it no heed.

'You broke something!' cried Vinnie. 'You're going too

fast. Slow down or you'll have a wheel off the cart! Are you mad, Jarvis Tupp? Slow down, I tell you. You've no right to take me down here. This doesn't lead to Foxearth, it doesn't go anywhere near there.'

He glanced at her, adopting an air of exaggerated surprise. 'Doesn't it?'

'You know it doesn't!'

'Oh, dearie, dearie me!' he mocked.

The track became narrower and the hedges on either side scraped along the sides of the newly-painted cart. Vinnie clung to the edge of the seat as the jolting increased.

'You're going to ruin all that new paintwork,' she told him, 'and serve you right if you won't slow down!' Jarvis's mood was worsening. He had quite forgotten the unsuitability of the track for horse and cart, but there was no way he could go now except onward and this he did with a very ill will. Somehow he managed to blame Vinnie for whatever was broken inside the cart and for the scratches he would find on his newly completed handiwork. It was Vinnie's fault – it must be, for it was she who had inflamed him.

'When we do stop I'll show you something you won't forget in a hurry,' he muttered. 'There'll be no airs and graces then.'

Vinnie was frightened now. Had it been possible, she would have thrown herself from the cart, but the overgrown hedges allowed no escape and she cursed her own stupidity at not guessing the reason for Jarvis's 'change of heart'. Angry with herself and full of apprehension, she relapsed into silence and the two of them continued grimly side by side until at last the lane opened out into a clearing in the middle of a hazel coppice. It was a small area of moss-covered ground and the crushed appearance of the plant life revealed it as a popular spot for lovers. As soon as the cart stopped, Vinnie scrambled down and began to run back the way they had come, but Jarvis was faster and he caught her arm in a painful grip.

'Stuck-up little cow!' he said. 'Planning to be a virgin for ever, were you?'

Frantically, she struggled to free herself from his grip but he managed to catch hold of her other hand and dragged her back towards the clearing.

'If you lay a finger on me, Jarvis Tupp—' she began.

'I'll lay more than a finger on you,' he said thickly. 'After I've done, you'll be *begging* me to marry you. There'll be none of your high and mighty talk then. Oh, struggle and kick me as much as you like, it will make no difference. You're damn well going to get what you've been asking for, Vinnie Harris, and you're going to get it from me. Feel that!'

He forced her hand down his body and laughed at the shock in her eyes. 'I'm going to give *that* to you, Vinnie Harris, and you're going to love it.'

'No!' she cried. 'I won't and you're not! You are not going to lay a finger on me.'

She twisted her arms but his grip did not relax for an instant and the pain in her wrists brought tears to her eyes. When she tried to kick him he retaliated swiftly and this time her tears did flow as the toe of his boot cut into her shin. She suddenly wanted to vomit from fear and pain but fought back the sense of nausea. She must not give way to her fears, that much she knew; if she were to outwit him she must keep her nerve. Suddenly he threw her backwards and she fell heavily to the ground. Before she could struggle up again he had snatched off his jacket and tossed it behind him on to a fallen log. She tried to stand up, but he caught her by the shoulders and flung her down again, his hands going down to the buttons of his breeches.

'You *won't!*' screamed Vinnie.

She managed to roll away from him, searching desperately for a piece of wood or a stone with which to defend herself. There was nothing on the ground, so she snatched at a low branch but the wood was green and pliable and would not break. The effort had wasted precious seconds, for Jarvis's crumpled breeches lay on the ground and suddenly he had her by the hair. She clung to the branch, but he pulled her away from it and slowly forced her head down.

'Look at it, then!' But she shook her head and closed her eyes.

'Don't let it be like this,' she prayed silently. 'Not the first time . . . not Jarvis Tupp.'

If Julian were here, instead of Jarvis, she would surrender willingly because he would be gentle and loving. Jarvis was neither – he was a greedy, insensitive animal. His body was hateful, she told herself, and she would die rather than look at it. Suddenly his right hand dealt her a painful blow across the side of her head while his left, holding her hair, jerked her off her feet and she found herself sprawling on her back on the moss, her petticoats and skirts momentarily protecting her as he straddled her body. He leaned forward, pinning her arms to the ground and leering into her face.

'You've got a shock coming, Vinnie Harris,' he gloated. 'Christ! You've got a shock coming. You can wriggle and scream and curse as much as you like, but you won't leave this clearing until I've had what I want. We can do it nice and friendly or we can do it this way. Maybe this way's more fun. Please yourself, it's all the same to me but get one thing into that head of yours. Your virgin days are well and truly over.'

He laughed at the fear in her eyes and his laughter distorted his face, making him ugly.

'I'll scream,' she began. 'Someone will hear me.'

'Scream away.'

She was silent, knowing her words were a bluff. Wherever they were – and she was not quite certain – they were certainly not near a habitation of any kind. She might 'scream away', as he put it, but it would be to no avail. She had best conserve her energy; no one was coming to her rescue. If she was to be saved, she must save herself. She renewed her efforts and, freeing one arm, begun to punch his neck and chest.

'I can't feel a thing,' he assured her but she saw that he lied and knew that at least some of the blows had hurt. Then she was helpless again, once more pinned to the ground under his weight. Suddenly, however, she realised that the horse and cart had moved and were now facing the other way. If only she could get to the cart and climb up she could drive herself back to the road, leaving Jarvis to follow on foot. A mere nine or ten yards separated her from the cart, yet it seemed unlikely she could ever reach it. She had never driven a horse and the prospect daunted her but it was certainly the lesser of the two evils and she was prepared to try anything.

'Get off me, Jarvis Tupp,' she said through gritted teeth. 'I swear if you take me I'll kill you for it.'

This threat seemed to delight him. 'I like a bit of spirit,' he told her. He was wondering how he could open her dress, for if he freed her hand she would be able to defend herself. Shifting his weight sideways, he held both wrists back above her head with one large hand and with the other began to unbutton her bodice.

'Don't you dare!' she screamed. 'Take your hands off me! You let me be or I swear I'll make you sorry.'

'You'll be a lot sorrier!'

'Your father will have something to say to you!'

Jarvis grinned. 'Oh yes, he will indeed. He'll say "marry the damn girl" and that's how it'll end, Vinnie Harris. You might as well give in now as later. You'll be Mrs Jarvis Tupp before the year's out and be thankful for it too.'

With a sudden supreme effort, Vinnie jerked him off balance so that he rolled to one side and for a moment they wrestled together, kicking and cursing, until he was once more master of the situation. This time she found herself on her knees with both arms bent up behind her, his prisoner once more.

'I could tie you up if I'd a mind to,' he told her, his breathing fast and furious. 'Do you hear me? If you try that again, I'll tear a strip off your skirt and tie you to a tree and then we'll see how you fight back. How would you like that, eh?'

The more Jarvis thought about it, the more he liked the idea. He pulled her to her feet and glanced around in search of a suitable tree. Vinnie's panic deepened as she saw the resolve in his eyes and she made another frantic effort to escape, but with his free hand he tore open the front of her bodice and then pulled it down over her shoulders so that it pinned her arms by her side. Then he put his arms round her and drew her closer. Some of the anger had left him, to be replaced by desire, and he leaned forward and kissed her throat.

'Don't fight me, Vinnie,' he whispered. 'Please don't fight

me. I don't want to hurt you, but I won't take no for an answer.
I'll make you a good husband, I swear it. Don't make me hurt
you.'

'I'll never marry you, Jarvis Tupp, whatever you do to
me.'

'If I get you with child—'

'Don't!' she shouted.

Horrified by his words, she pictured again the bedroom
where Maude Babbit had died so tragically. She saw herself
lying there in a pool of blood and cried out again, 'I *won't*
marry you! I won't marry anyone!' and began to struggle once
more.

'By Christ, you *are* a stubborn bitch!' he raged, and this time
it was his fist that struck her. As she reeled back she tripped and
fell with Jarvis on top of her. There was a rending sound as he
tore at the waist of her dress and then to her shame he had
pulled it off completely and she finally wore only her petticoat.
Frightened and furious, Vinnie burst into tears, but just then
there was a sound from behind them and for a moment Jarvis's
attention was distracted as he glanced back. The horse was
beginning to move away, the cart lurched and there was
another crash from within as something else was dislodged.

To Vinnie it seemed her one and only chance: she pushed
him with all her remaining strength and he fell back, striking
his head on a fallen tree-trunk with a cry of pain. She picked
herself up, snatched up her dress and ran towards the cart,
forcing herself between its side and the prickly hedge which
scraped at her bare arms and shoulders. Somehow – she was
never sure how – she climbed up on to the seat, snatched up the
reins and jerked them, shouting, 'Get along, get along!' as
Jarvis had done earlier. To her relief, the horse responded
without hesitation and gradually horse and cart gathered
speed. Suddenly there was a pounding – Jarvis was behind
them, beating an enraged tattoo on the back of the cart. Surely,
she thought, he would not follow them far, for he too was only
half-dressed. For a moment she wanted to laugh at the vision
thus conjured up – she was almost hysterical, but at least she
was free. He was shouting now, cursing her, but she could tell

as his voice receded that he had been unable to keep up and she muttered a prayer of thanks.

Soon they would be back on the road and she must decide what to do. She was not in a fit state to deliver Roland Fry's message, nor could she go home in her present distressed state for Mrs Bryce would almost certainly insist on knowing exactly what had happened and for the moment Vinnie felt unable to speak of it. Then she thought of Rose: she was not too far away. To reach their tiny cottage she could go through the woods on the other side of the road and no one else need see her. Rose would understand, Rose would help mend her gown and then she could continue to the Lawrences.

Vinnie congratulated herself on this solution to her problem. She dared not glance behind her but guessed that Jarvis must have gone back for his coat and breeches. This would delay him, but not for long. Somehow they reached the road again and, turning on to it, narrowly missed a pony and trap approaching from the opposite direction. The other horse, startled by their sudden appearance, reared wildly and Vinnie caught a glimpse of the trap's two occupants as they stared at her, but then they had gone and other more pressing problems remained. She reined the horse to a standstill and climbed down shakily. There was no one else in sight now and she knew that several minutes must elapse before Jarvis reappeared. She would go to Rose for help. Hitching the reins over a low tree-branch, she abandoned horse and cart and, still carrying her gown, ran across the road and into the shelter of the woods on the other side.

The emotional shock of her experience had left her shaken and tearful, but her anger had given way to a feeling with which she was unfamiliar. Briefly, she thought it might be disappointment but that was impossible. 'Frustrated old spinster'. Who had said that and why did the phrase present itself to her now? Was she frustrated? Was it frustration she felt so fiercely? Vinnie did not know, she only knew that a strange restlessness had taken hold of her and that her body ached. As she stumbled on through the woods, making her way between the trees, every footstep was an effort and her heart thumped painfully. A stitch in her side made her gasp. In her mind's eye she saw herself once more sprawled on her back with Jarvis pinning her down. She paused for a moment, leaning against one of the trees to regain her breath. Julian would have treated her kindly, would have spoken softly and lovingly. She would write to him, she thought disjointedly, but would say nothing of what had happened.

To her dismay the cottage, when she reached it, appeared to be empty. There were no children playing in the garden and the front door was closed. She peered in at the window and, seeing no one, made her way wearily round to the back door which to her surprise stood open. She pushed it wider.

'Rose, it's me, Vinnie.'

There was no answer and after a moment's hesitation, she went inside. The cottage seemed deserted. She went to the bottom of the stairs and called up, 'Rose, are you there, it's Vinnie. I must talk to you.' Perhaps she was sleeping – possibly the children were with their grandmother and Rose had snatched the opportunity for a well-earned rest. Vinnie went up the familiar staircase, pushed open the bedroom door and gasped in dismay. Tom Bryce, sitting up on the bed, was rubbing his eyes sleepily. He was still fully clothed except for his jacket and his shirt was unfastened to the waist so that the dark hairs on his chest were evident. For a moment they stared at each other.

'What the hell—' he began, seeing the state she was in. 'Your lip's bleeding,' he told her, without moving from the bed. 'What's happened?'

For a moment Vinnie could not answer. She leaned against the door beseeching him with her eyes not to pursue his questioning. All she could do was to shake her head while her lips trembled and fresh tears trickled down her cheeks.

'Who was it, Vinnie?'

She shook her head again, then whispered, 'He didn't—'

'But he tried to? Ye Gods, I'll kill him, whoever it is.'

'No,' she whispered, closing her eyes. 'He said—' she began again, then stopped. He had said she had been 'asking for it'. She couldn't tell Tom that. She couldn't tell anyone that, it wasn't true. She sighed heavily. When she opened her eyes she saw that Tom still sat on the bed but now he held out his arms to her. She hesitated, then slowly crossed the tiny bedroom to stand before him. His hands went round her waist and quietly he pulled her down to sit beside him. He put an arm gently round her shoulders and she laid her head against him while he rocked her, murmuring soothingly. Neither spoke. Vinnie closed her eyes and as his caresses continued the unfamiliar ache within her grew until it became a yearning. When he kissed her she made no effort to stop him. She imagined that it was Julian's mouth and then pretended that the whispered endearments were Julian's also. A warning bell rang somewhere in the recesses of her mind, but it was drowned by the clamour of her reeling senses. The voice of her conscience whispered to her urgently, but her body thrilled to the new voluptuousness that threatened to overwhelm her. When at last her body surrendered, it was to Tom Bryce. While Roland Fry's note to the Lawrences fluttered among the branches of the hazel coppice, Vinnie Harris tasted, for the first time, the heady delights of passion.

CHAPTER THIRTEEN

The Colonel lay in the large high bed and stared round the familiar room. The bedstead was highly polished brass and from the small wooden canopy above him heavy velvet drapes reached to the floor. He looked down at the shape of his own body beneath the sheets and felt frail, almost intangible. 'I'm fading away', he thought. 'Soon I shall be gone and perhaps then Christina will come back and sleep in this bed.' She had moved out several years ago, ostensibly to give him more room but he was well aware that was not the true reason. There was only one thing to be done and he had done it. He allowed himself a wry smile of satisfaction. Yes, one day she would find out what he had done about it. He was not a malicious man, or so he believed, but her behaviour towards him had been less than charitable and he could not find it in his heart to forgive her. She had taken a lover and had made little effort to conceal the fact from him, seeming to delight in the small hints she dropped from time to time which hurt him more than he would admit.

He sighed, wishing the bedroom faced the sun, but it was on the cool side of the house and by the middle of the afternoon the sunlight had gone and the mahogany furniture looked dark and sombre. He found it depressing. The floor was of polished wood, with rugs scattered over it, and at the end of the bed was a chaise-longue upholstered in rich brocade and heavily fringed. He could only see the top of it but remembered it well, for he had given it to Christina on their tenth wedding anniversary. 'Oh, Christina, you have not been a good wife. Not a good wife at all.'

There was a mahogany dressing-table against the far wall

with a chair in front of it, but Christina never sat there; it was never used. He was bedridden – a stupid, hateful word but terribly apt. His world had shrunk to this one dark bedroom which various vases of flowers did little to brighten. The clock on the mantelpiece ticked loudly but he no longer looked at it, for his eyesight was blurred. It chimed on the hour and that was enough for him.

He wondered why Vinnie had not come and thought wistfully of the young woman with the golden hair. She was almost beautiful and would become a handsome woman. He liked to watch her as she sat by the window reading to him, and sometimes her words were lost as he fancied himself a young man again – a young man with a maid. It all seemed a long time ago. He thought of his own Eva, vivacious and wilful but with a loving heart. Christina must make sure she married well, she deserved only the best. She and Julian would be home tomorrow and he was looking forward to seeing them both again.

Sometimes he thought he would linger on in this half-life for ever, but at other times he felt keenly that each day might be his last. When he died he wanted those he loved to be near him so that he might take one more look at them before closing his eyes for the last time. Christina had assured him that his children would be home tomorrow. She gave him such information reluctantly, as though she no longer considered him part of the family and entitled to know what was happening. 'You are cold and heartless, Christina. But you misjudge me sadly if you think you can treat me this way.' He tried to remember how it had been between them when they first married. Had she always been so cold? She had no right to be cold, he told himself. He had given her everything, including a fine son and daughter. Poor Julian, he takes life too seriously – not like his father at that age! The Colonel chuckled, but the effort made him cough and it was some moments before he regained his breath.

There was an oval hand mirror on the bedside table but even if his sight had been better, he would not have used it. He did not want to see himself as he now was, a frail old man with wispy white hair and faded brown eyes. He wondered if he should ring for Janet, but decided against the idea. Poor Janet, he thought. She deserved a husband, but it was out of the question: Christina did not like her servants to have followers. He would ring for her later and ask for news of the hop-picking. Janet had a ready ear for gossip and might know what happened to Vinnie . . .

His thoughts rambled slightly as he almost dozed. He had not always been a frail old man. He had once been strong, a military man, a leader of men. It was ironic that he had survived the Crimean War only to succumb to a series of strokes which left him helpless. He had led a full life and a good one. He had fought in the best wars, ridden the best horses, sampled the best women! He had eaten well, drunk the finest wines he could afford and had ruled his own little empire with considerable success. His regrets were few: that Christina had only borne him two children and that he had missed seeing Persimmon win the Derby the previous year. He began to chuckle again but remembering the earlier coughing attack, stopped himself and smiled instead, thinking that now his only ambition was to outlive Queen Victoria with whom he had shared his lifetime. Surely that small pleasure would not be denied him? But the Queen was a very stubborn woman who knew how to take care of herself. She took a holiday each spring in the south of France where the sun shone and the air was bracing. He smiled again and his head lolled to one side on the crisply laundered pillow. His mouth fell open and he was almost asleep when there was a tap on the door and Janet came into the room.

'Are you all right, sir?' she asked.

He opened his eyes and smiled. 'Only just, but stay, stay,' he said as she made to withdraw. 'I want someone to talk to.'

'I have brought your new medicine, sir,' she said cheerfully. 'I've tasted it and it's not at all bad, so don't pull that face.'

'Don't bully me, Janet.'

'As if I would, sir.'

Janet smiled fondly at the old man. With no man of her own she had taken the elderly Colonel to her heart and spent as much time as she dared with him, even taking it upon herself to initiate what she secretly termed 'his treatment' since his last stroke five months earlier. His speech – badly impaired – had gradually improved and although no one else realised it, this was entirely due to Janet's efforts. She had talked to him whenever she was able to slip into the room, and would not take his incoherent mumbles as answers. She nagged him good-naturedly – and sometimes not so good-naturedly – forcing him to make greater efforts to recapture his failing speech. Even when she guessed what he was trying to say to her she would pretend otherwise, urging him to repeat himself more clearly. Slowly but surely the continued practice brought about an improvement which the doctor had commented upon with approval.

Now she poured a spoonful of medicine and slipped it into the old man's mouth, then wiped his lips with the napkin she had brought for the purpose.

'You're a good girl, Janet,' he praised her and she laughed.

'I've no chance to be anything else but good,' she told him.

'If I were ten years younger,' he assured her, '*I* would lead you astray.'

'I don't doubt it,' she laughed. 'I bet you were a real one for the girls when you were a young man.'

She knew how much he enjoyed talking about his youth and often encouraged him to do so. Now she busied herself about the room, rearranging the flowers and tidying the bed, but they both knew she was merely finding reasons to justify an extended visit.

'I've seen those pictures of you as a military man,' she told him. 'Real smart you were, a very fine young gentleman. The Guards, wasn't it?'

'Scots Guards, Janet, that's right, although we were called the Fusiliers then.'

He raised a feeble hand towards a row of photographs above the mantelpiece and Janet moved over to them.

'Ah, here's one of you on horseback, sir.' She peered at the writing, pretending not to have seen it before. 'Inkerman

1854', she read, 'and who is this other gentleman, with the dark beard?'

'That's Captain Duberley,' he told her, holding out his hand for the photograph. 'I always knew I'd come back in one piece, you know, Janet. Always knew I would. Pass me the other one, there's a good girl.'

'Albany Barracks, London,' she read. 'Looks like a parade with all those rows of horses.'

'It is a parade. They called it the Drawing Room Parade.'

'Which one's you, then?'

The bony finger traced its way along the line and finally came to rest.

'Ah, that's you is it, sir? One of these days I'll get meself a magnifying-glass and have a proper look. And these others? They're wearing different uniforms. Is it a band?'

'The Queen's Trumpeters, they are,' he told her. 'See the jockey caps. Very smart, they were.'

'But not as smart as your lot, sir, with those helmets.' For a few moments his eyes gleamed with the pleasure of recollection and then a shadow crossed his face and he handed the photographs back to her.

'They say war's a glorious thing, Janet, and so it can be but there was nothing glorious about the Crimea. Never seen so many dead, so many wounded, so many sick.' He shook his head. 'I saw the bay at Balaclava full of floating arms and legs. Can you imagine that?'

She shuddered, her horror genuine.

'So many amputations, you see. It was incredible. Like a bad dream. Nothing glorious in that sight, Janet.'

'Don't talk about it, sir. Don't even think about it. It was a long time ago.'

'Was it, Janet? Sometimes it seems like yesterday. And Sebastopol. Terrible disaster. I was thirty-six years old.' He sighed heavily. 'Comradeship can be glorious, Janet. So can victory. Even defeat can be glorious. Not like Redan. That was a fiasco – a shameful fiasco – but can you blame the men?'

'I'm sure you all did the best you could, sir. Now, let's not talk about—'

'They wouldn't fight, you see. The men just wouldn't fight. All the stuffing knocked out of them, you know. Nothing glorious about that, is there?'

'No, sir. Now what—'

'But I didn't lose my courage, Janet. I was a good officer. I was lucky, you see, because I had this notion that I'd come through and it kept me in good spirits . . . You're right, it was a long time ago. And look at me now,' he said. 'Only half the man I was.'

'Don't talk so daft, sir,' said Janet. 'You're the same man inside. 'Course you are. Same as you were when you were fifty and thirty-and-ten. You may look a bit different, but you're the same Henry Lawrence inside.'

Hastily she turned away, for these kind words had brought tears to his eyes and she gave him time to brush them away before turning back to the bed.

'Now,' she said cheerfully, 'no more sad talk. Let me tell you all the news.'

He nodded without speaking and pointed to the chair beside the bed. Janet perched herself on it, her back straight, her hands in her lap. The Colonel hated to see anyone slouch.

'Let me see now. Have you heard about Jarvis Tupp? Well, it seems a few days back he went off in his cart with Vinnie Harris and they were on their way up here to bring you a message from that Mr Fry from London. You know – Brothers of Jesus or something like that. The Mr Fry that came to dinner one evening, but maybe you didn't see him? Well, next thing anyone knows is the horse and cart is in the ditch and no sign of Jarvis Tupp or Vinnie Harris neither. Then Jarvis comes wandering home an hour later in a rare old temper.'

'And Vinnie?'

She shrugged. 'Nobody knows and she isn't saying anything.'

'That's very odd.' He frowned.

'Jarvis was supposed to be bringing her up here, but they never arrived.'

'And no one is saying anything?'

'Not a word, sir, from either of them.'

'Hmm. I don't suppose we'll ever know what happened.'

She searched her mind for other tit-bits. 'Oh, the new washing machine's broke down again and Mrs Tallant says what can you expect from such new-fangled nonsense. The handle won't turn the mangle part, it just keeps slipping. Edie got all hot and bothered and had to spread everything outside to dry on the grass. And did you know about the fair, sir?'

'I daresay Christina has told me about it, but tell me again, Janet. I forget these things.'

Without further encouragement, Janet launched herself into an account of the coming attraction. Christina had decided that a fair would be held on the last Sunday of the hopping season. This would involve her in considerable financial outlay but her reasons were not as generous as they appeared. The fact was that the last Sunday, when all the hoppers were paid off for the month, often proved to be very difficult. With their packing done and a longish wait for the train home, the hoppers found themselves with little to do except spend their money and get into mischief. It was a day which the local people dreaded. A fair, Christina reasoned, would provide them with a comparatively harmless form of entertainment and hopefully would reduce the amount of drunkenness. It was only an experiment but if it worked, it could be repeated in future years. If it was not successful, the idea could be abandoned.

'It will be held in the lower meadow,' Janet told him, 'and there'll be a Punch-and-Judy and an organ-grinder and performing dogs and monkeys. The local folks can sell their dahlias and the mistress says we can all have a couple of hours off to go to it. It's going to be quite a do. Pity old Mr Everett will miss it – he loved a good fair.'

The old tally-man had died a few months earlier and no one had yet been chosen to take his place. Vinnie had been persuaded to stand in for him with an account book, but she did not relish the idea and had made up her mind not to be talked into it again.

'I expect you'll be able to hear the music if your window is open,' Janet told him kindly. 'We'll see what the weather's like, sir. If it's a fine day it wouldn't do you any harm.' He nodded absent-mindedly, his thoughts already elsewhere.

'Eva and Julian,' he asked her. 'When are they coming home?'

'Why, tonight, sir. Cook's expecting them off the half-past eight train and young Harry's going down to meet them. If you can stay awake sir—'

The old man smiled. He rarely managed to stay awake after eight o'clock these days and it was a little joke between them.

'I will be awake, Janet.'

'Of course you will, sir. Now I'll have to be going.' She stood up and gave the pillow a final tweak.

'When is Vinnie coming? he asked.

'I don't rightly know, sir.'

'Send word to her, Janet, somehow. It is all very odd and I want to talk to her.'

'I'll try, sir.'

'If you can't go yourself, send young Harry.'

'I'll do that, sir. Now I'd best be off before Birdie – I mean Mrs Tallant – misses me.'

She patted his hand briefly. 'I'll be up again later with your tea. Cook's made you a custard with nutmeg on top the way you like it.'

As she reached the door, he called out, 'No one rode a horse like me. You know that, Janet? No one in the whole damned Regiment.'

'I am sure they didn't, sir,' she said.

*

Roland Fry's mission had got off to an unfortunate start, for when he arrived at the Lawrences on the first evening Vinnie had not delivered his note and Christina, irritated by his late arrival, treated him rather coldly. However, his youthful good looks, profuse apologies and obvious eagerness to please finally won her over. It was agreed that the Brothers in Jesus could erect a small tent at the northern end of the hop-gardens and Christina also offered to accommodate the two young ladies who were to join him shortly. Gareth Brooks, the other male member of the group, would stay at the 'Horse and Cart' alone, since Roland had decided to accept Mrs Bryce's hospitality for the rest of his month's stay. This was partly because it seemed a convenient and homely place, but was also due to Vinnie's presence. In spite of her strange behaviour, he had taken a liking to her and hoped to get to know her better.

Within the next few days the rest of the party arrived and settled in and for two days the four of them made their way individually among the pickers, introducing themselves and generally making themselves agreeable to everyone concerned.

The first actual meeting was arranged for Wednesday at noon when the pickers stopped for a brief lunch break. Roland Fry had a concertina which he only played indifferently, but it was decided that a little music would help the proceedings along. It was therefore the sound of the concertina that drew a small crowd of 20–30 pickers to that first meeting. Roland beamed at each new arrival, and his deep blue eyes added a radiance to his smile which the female pickers found quite irresistible. Many in the crowd were children who stood impassively, staring at the four men and women in their smart clothes and straw boaters. Half a dozen or more of the hoppers had come because rumour had it that tea and buns would be distributed free of charge and their meagre finances extended only to an evening meal. Mary and Lydia smiled nervously at the children, reluctant to meet the eyes of the older members of the crowd. Their solitary forays among the pickers had produced a variety of responses, not all of them polite and they felt very keenly, although none of them spoke of it, that to many of them they were figures of fun. At last, when it seemed obvious that no one else was going to turn up, Roland lowered the concertina and cleared his throat.

'Welcome, one and all!' he cried with rather too much enthusiasm so that his voice took on a high-pitched note and he hastily lowered it before continuing.

'This is a wonderful response,' he said. 'A quite wonderful response to all our hopes. Already we look upon you as our friends and we want you to look upon us as *your* friends.'

He had decided that a simple approach was best and used

words of one syllable as though addressing young children. Gareth Brooks and the two ladies nodded their heads and deepened their smiles. Out of the corner of his eye Roland saw someone lurking at the rear of the crowd, half-hidden by the hops, so he raised his voice a little.

'Come on, don't be shy. We are all friends here.'

Everyone turned to see who he was talking to and he saw to his surprise and pleasure that it was Vinnie Harris. She moved reluctantly forward and stood at the back of the group.

'Ah, Miss Harris,' said Roland heartily, for here at least was a name with which he was familiar. 'I am glad you could join us. I am just telling these good people that we want to be looked upon as friends and helpers.' His eye roved over the crowd.

'Bring us your troubles,' he said, 'and we will give you the benefit of our advice. Bring us your cuts and bruises and this lady' – he indicated Lydia – 'will attend to them. She is training to be a nurse and has given up part of her holiday to come down to Kent and be of service to those who need her. Now let me introduce my colleagues. Mary Bellweather' – she gave a little nod – 'Lydia Grant' – she smiled broadly – 'and Mr Gareth Brooks.' Gareth took off his cap, gave a little bow and replaced it.

Roland's glance returned to Vinnie, who was watching him with a strange expression on her face. A strange, rather withdrawn young woman, he thought, and yet she had seemed so cheerful that first day in Tupp's store. Every time he caught her eye now, she glanced away as though unable to meet his gaze and it disappointed him.

'Here in Kent,' he said, 'at Foxearth, we are all one big happy family working together to bring in God's harvest bountifully given. In a moment we will give thanks for his generosity, but before that I would just like to tell you that we have brought from London a large supply of second-hand clothing which may be of interest to some of you. They are all clean things in good condition and will be given away to those who are in genuine need. We have also several dozen pairs of shoes of varying sizes.'

There was a murmur of interest from the crowd, many of whom were bare-footed. Roland felt a thrill of satisfaction. We are going to reach them, he told himself; our little mission is going to succeed.

'A number of bibles have also been donated –' he went on, but now they regarded him blankly. 'These also will be given away free to those who wish to read the good book for themselves. Above all, we want you to know that there are people in London – and of course locally – who care deeply about your spiritual and physical welfare and who want to help you. We can only do this, however, with your full co-operation. You must tell us your problems and let us help you to deal with them.'

He hesitated, aware that he was repeating himself. The beautiful speech that he had prepared in his head the night before had deserted him under the influence of Vinnie's gaze. He was honest enough to admit this to himself, and almost wished she had stayed away from this meeting on which so much depended, but the Lord had seen fit to send her along and he struggled to come to terms with her disturbing presence.

'We have one thing in common,' he said, 'and that is our birthplace. We are all Londoners. We all come from that large metropolis and we all know how easy it is to feel lost and neglected among the thousands of people that inhabit its many dwellings.'

He liked that line: it had a nice biblical ring to it, he thought, and he continued more hopefully.

'But I don't want to do all the talking,' he said. 'What about you, haven't you anything to say to us, anything to tell us, any questions to ask? Don't be shy, we are here to help you.' A small boy raised a grubby hand and pointed at the nearby fire.

'What's in that kettle?' he asked abruptly.

Roland smiled at him. 'Ah, a good question. That's tea and the box on the small table beside it is full of buns.'

'Can I have one, mister?'

'Of course you can,' said Roland. 'If you—' But his young listener didn't wait for the rest of the sentence. He made a dash for the box containing the buns and was swiftly followed by the rest of the children. Mary Bellweather darted over to intercept them, but already a confusion of hands were opening the lid and reaching inside.

'Not yet!' cried Roland. 'Not yet, children, please come back. I haven't finished what I have to say and we haven't said our prayer.'

His words fell upon stony ground. A woman in the crowd said defensively, 'You told 'em they could have one.'

'I did, indeed I did, but I had not expected—'

'You're a bit long-winded, that's your trouble.'

Roland felt his cheeks burn, then another voice chimed in. 'We 'aven't got all day.'

Gareth leaned across and whispered to him, 'Let's cut out the prayer for today' but Roland refused to abandon their original plan. All the children were now running off among the hop-poles, a bun in each hand, while Mary looked ruefully after them. They had provided two dozen buns and already more than half of these had gone. Some of their listeners would have to be content with a mug of tea, she thought. Oh well, they must learn from their mistakes. Roland raised his voice.

'Let us pray.'

He put his hands together in front of his chest and pretended to close his eyes, though in fact he peered through the slits to watch his audience. An elderly woman put her hands together, but for a moment no one else did. Then the old lady glanced round her and said sharply, 'Well, you heard what he said, let's get it over with or we'll have no time for the perishing tea and buns.' Hastily, palms were joined and eyes were closed. She winked at Roland. 'Well, get on with it, then,' she told him.

'Blessed Father in Heaven,' he began earnestly. 'Look down upon thy servants gathered here and give us Thy blessing. We are all involved in Thy work harvesting the fruits of Thy handiwork. Grant us, I beseech you, good health and peace of mind and let there grow up between us the feeling of brotherly love—'

'Right, that'll do!' said the old woman firmly and she headed towards the small table and plunged her hand into the box of buns. The rest followed as one man. They did not make the orderly queue which Mary Bellweather had expected. Instead they jostled and pushed and snatched and within seconds the box was empty and those who were disappointed were at no pains to hide their dismay. Mary Bellweather poured tea into the assembled mugs and handed them out while Gareth offered round a bowl full of sugar. The old woman, spluttering crumbs, addressed herself to Roland.

'You'll do all right,' she said, 'but we want more buns and less chat. And where are these shoes? I could do with a spare pair.' She raised one foot and Roland saw that she wore a pair of men's boots which gaped at the toes and were without laces.

'I mean,' she went on, 'they'll never let me in to Ascot like this.' There was a hoot of laughter and Roland said, 'Er – tomorrow we shall be in the tent from eight until nine in the morning and we shall be distributing clothing then.'

'I'll be there,' she said, 'and I've a narrow foot, mind!'

'A narrow foot,' said Roland. 'Right.'

'D'you want to write that down? Lizzie Potts – narrow foot, size five.'

'I think I shall remember.'

'A narrow foot and a decent 'eel. I'm no lightweight and I don't fancy tottering about on any of them fancy 'eels.'

'Indeed not,' said Roland heartily. 'A narrow foot with a firm heel. I'm sure we shall find something suitable for you.' She swallowed the last mouthful of her bun and washed her mouth round with tea which she then swallowed.

'Nice drop of tea that,' she said. 'Always tastes better in the open air, tea does. That's one of the things I like best about 'opping, tea in the open air. Well that's it for now then. Quick pee and it's back to work.' She threw the dregs of the tea and the breeze carried them over Roland's trousers and shoes, but he made no comment. Cheerfully she handed him the mug and with a wink disappeared in the direction of the nearest hedge.

Roland wished it was not quite so hot. The so-called 'privy' was beginning to smell abominably and when the wind was in a certain direction it made his delicate stomach heave. Next year, he decided, they must pitch their tent further over. When at last the four of them were alone, they looked at each other and Mary Bellweather laughed.

'Well, it's over,' she said. 'I don't know whether to be pleased or sorry.'

'I'm pleased,' admitted Lydia.

Roland smiled at her gratefully. 'I'm sorry there were not more buns,' he said.

'That old woman!' said Gareth.

'A narrow foot!' mimicked Mary. 'I don't know how you kept your face straight, Roland. We shouldn't laugh, I know, but she was a funny old thing – and those awful children!'

They all laughed and began to relax a little. 'Never mind,' said Gareth, 'we survived, that's the main thing.'

'You mean we have survived so far,' said Roland. 'At eight o'clock tomorrow morning no doubt they will descend on our tent. I shudder to think how we shall sort out all those shoes to everyone's satisfaction.'

Lydia was counting the mugs and groaned. 'Three missing. Those wretches have stolen three mugs.'

Mary, beginning to giggle, covered her face with her hand. 'I'm sorry,' she spluttered. 'I can't help it. It's all so funny.'

'Who was that girl at the back?' asked Gareth. 'The one that came late? She didn't stay, not even to have a mug of tea.'

'Oh, that's Vinnie Harris,' said Roland lightly. 'She is at my lodgings, the one I spoke of whose mother was drowned here. She is a strange girl.'

Mary looked at him sharply but said nothing.

'She could be beautiful when she grows up,' said Lydia. 'That beautiful hair! Is she still at school?'

He nodded. 'She thinks she's going to be a school-teacher, but at present she seems to be a jack-of-all-trades. Sometimes she reads to Colonel Lawrence. At other times during the year she helps with the hops. As you say, she could be beautiful.'

Mary began to pack the mugs back into the cardboard box. 'Well,' she said, 'I shall take these down to the stream and wash them, but we shall need to buy a few more. If they keep disappearing, we shall soon have none left at all.'

Roland suggested they might buy a few from Will Tupp.

Gareth took up the kettle and poured the remaining water over the fire to damp it down. Then Roland folded up the table and looked round for his concertina.

'What's the matter?' Mary asked. 'Don't say they have taken that as well? They have? The devils! Would you believe it? I wonder if there's the slightest hope of getting it back?'

'Probably not,' said Gareth. 'You had best resign yourself to its loss.'

At that very moment the sound of a concertina being played very badly floated towards them across the hop-garden and Roland threw up his hands in a gesture of despair.

'Lord give me patience!' he begged.

'He will,' said Mary and on that note they made their way back to the tent, already making plans for the next day.

*

When the supper had been cleared away and the washing-up done, Vinnie took the boots and shoes into the back garden and sat on a bench in the last of the evening sunshine. The bricks underfoot, which had absorbed the sun's heat all day, now gave it out again and were delightfully warm to her bare feet. Beyond the small bricked area the garden sloped down to a hawthorn hedge at the bottom and the two side hedges were yew. Once they had been neatly clipped, but now they were trimmed whenever Tom had time to spare, which was rarely. The grass had been cut but not raked and the chopped dried grass lay like hay. To the right was a large elderly crab-apple tree on which the small apples already glowed like red decorations on a Christmas tree. The one rose tree, grown tall by neglect, supported three heavy blooms of a deep pink colour. A small hen-coop occupied the far left-hand corner and half a dozen chickens strutted among the grass, ignoring Vinnie, busy with whatever it was they pecked at among the grass. On the clothes-line a sheet and pillowcase flapped whitely next to an apron, three towels and several lace-edged undergarments. A pigeon chuntered sleepily on the roof. In the vegetable patch beetroot sprouted and tomatoes reddened on the plants. There was a cucumber frame with a cracked pane and a riot of marigolds which had seeded themselves and flourished unheeded.

Vinnie surveyed the scene dispassionately for a moment, then applied herself to the task in hand. Beside her were two cloths and a large stone jar containing a mixture of beeswax and mutton fat. She dipped the cloth into the mixture and began to rub it into one of the boots. It was familiar, soothing work and left her attention free for other more pressing matters. She was 'late' and it worried her, for her body was fairly regular in its habits. Vaguely she remembered Rose soon after her wedding being 'late'. Then she had 'missed'. Vinnie remembered the glee with which Rose had told them and Mrs Bryce's excitement.

'Missed what?' Vinnie had asked.

'You know,' Rose had answered and the two women had laughed at her ignorance. Now Vinnie was late. If she also missed, would she have a child? It was a distinct possibility and the fear nagged at her like toothache, giving her no peace. She did not want to think about it. She did not want to think about Tom Bryce and tried hard not to do so, but the memory of that evening was printed indelibly on her mind and she could not ignore it. What had happened could never be denied. She had spoken of the events of that evening to no one, for now Rose's company was denied her and she could no longer seek comfort and reassurance from that quarter. She could not confide in Mrs Bryce, for she was Tom's mother and Vinnie could not imagine how *she* would react if she knew what had happened. The waiting was the worst part. But if Tom had made her with child then everyone would know soon enough, for her body would fill out and whispers would fly around the village like angry bees. It would be obvious then that she had lain with someone and when the truth came out . . . she dared not even consider it. And poor Rose who had pretended for so long to know nothing of her husband's affair with Christina Lawrence . . .

Vinnie rubbed the mixture well in and then took up the other cloth and began to polish the boot. She wondered vaguely if she was damned for ever in the sight of God – she had not previously paid Him much attention, but suddenly it was important for Him to think well of her and not cast her off. She tried to remember what Roland had said at the meeting. Had he said that God forgave sinners? He certainly had not said they would be damned, or she would have remembered it. She was not yet sixteen and did not want a child. Please, Tom, she thought, don't let it be. I know you did not mean it but please don't let it turn into a baby. Tom was already married and there was no question of a union between them, so who would care for her and the child? Sighing deeply, she picked up the other boot of the pair, took up the first cloth again and dipped it into the jar. At that moment a shadow fell across her and she looked up to see Roland Fry beside her. Her heart sank but she smiled briefly.

'May I sit with you?' he asked. 'Mrs Bryce sent me out to keep you company. She's worried about you.'

'Worried?'

She lifted down the pair of newly cleaned boots to make room for him on the bench beside her. He was a good man, she reminded herself, not exactly a vicar but a well-meaning man who spoke of God as though he knew Him intimately. He could have proved a very useful ally, but soon he would be going back to London and she would probably never see him again.

'Worried about me?' she repeated. 'There's nothing wrong with me.'

He smiled gently. 'But Mrs Bryce thinks there is. She says you have grown so quiet suddenly. *Is* there anything wrong, Vinnie?'

'Nothing. Nothing at all.'

He stretched out his legs and leaned back against the wall of the cottage. After a while he said, 'You are making a good job of those boots.'

'I'll do yours if you like.'

'That's awfully kind.' He picked up the jar and sniffed the contents.

'Mutton fat and beeswax,' Vinnie told him. 'Keeps out the rain. Take off your boots and I will do them for you while you wait.'

He hesitated, for there was a small hole in the heel of his left sock. 'Perhaps tomorrow,' he said. 'You've got plenty for today.'

'Please yourself.'

He regretted his answer and sought for another topic. 'I saw you at the meeting,' he said. 'What did you think of it?'

She shrugged. 'You were nervous, I could tell.'

'I was very nervous,' he agreed, 'but you did not stay. We gave everyone a mug of tea and a free bun.'

'I wasn't hungry.'

'But you did listen,' he said, 'and I hope you will act upon it. I hope you *will* bring us your troubles.'

Vinnie looked at him. 'Some troubles can't be mended,' she said.

'Indeed they can, Vinnie. With God's help everything is possible. So you *do* have a problem?'

'I didn't say that,' she corrected hastily. 'I didn't say I had a problem. Yes, that was a nice little meeting,' she went on hurriedly in an effort to distract his attention. 'Next time maybe I will stay for the bun.'

'I hope you will.'

'And . . .' she hesitated. 'And if ever I am in trouble, which I'm not, I'll remember what you said.'

'Vinnie, I would like to ask you something.' She waited for the inevitable question.

'What happened to that note I gave you for the Lawrences, the first day I was here?'

All the colour drained suddenly from her face even though she had half-expected the enquiry. Now that it had come, it was a shock.

'I lost it,' she stammered. 'It blew away as we were going up to the big house. There was no point in going then, without the message.'

'But whyever didn't you tell me?'

'I thought you'd be angry.' She rubbed furiously at one of Mrs Bryce's best boots, avoiding his gaze.

Roland was puzzled by her attitude but remained silent.

Glancing up at last, Vinnie saw the expression in his eyes.

'What are you looking at me like that for?' she demanded.

He shrugged. 'Mr Forrest tells me you are a very good tally-man,' he said. 'Or should I say tally-woman?'

Her face remained frozen into its grim lines. 'I don't know,' she said finally. 'The pickers don't like it. They don't like the account book, they prefer the tally-sticks but I can't use them.'

'They will get used to it.'

Vinnie wondered suddenly if she could take her problem – if it was a problem – to one of the two women who had come with Roland. No, she dared not. They would almost certainly tell Mrs Bryce and Mrs Bryce would tell Christina Lawrence. And *she* would tell Tom! The irony of such a situation did not escape her. Would Tom deny it? Could he? She gave a deep sigh.

Roland longed to put an arm round her slim shoulders. Gently he began, 'Jarvis Tupp seems fond of you. He says—'

She turned on him, her eyes blazing.

'Jarvis Tupp is a liar!' she cried. 'Whatever he told you is a lie. If you trust Jarvis Tupp, then you're a bigger fool than you look.'

Jumping to her feet, she threw down the cloth and the boot and made to run inside, but he put out a hand and caught hers.

'Please, Vinnie,' he said. 'Please sit down. I'm sorry I made you angry. I'm sorry I have upset you. I like and respect you, and all I want to do is help you if you are in any kind of trouble. Sometimes it is easier to confide in a stranger than in someone you know. I didn't mean to distress you. Please forgive me. Do sit down again and get on with your polishing.'

Slowly, Vinnie sat down. She knew his little speech came straight from the heart and she was touched by his concern for her.

'I'm sorry, too,' she said quietly. 'I didn't mean what I said. You don't look like a fool.'

Roland laughed gently. 'I have been called much worse than that,' he said, 'in the last few days. There's nothing mealy-mouthed about London hoppers.' He picked up a boot and a cloth and handed them back to her.

'Suppose you put on the polish and I take it off again,' he

offered, 'and we will say no more on that other matter. But do think over what I have said. I am here if you need me, Vinnie.'

When Mrs Bryce went out ten minutes later, she was surprised to find Vinnie and Roland, deep in animated conversation, working together on the boots and shoes.

*

It seemed to Rose Bryce, toasting bread over the kitchen fire, that she had been married for ever. It was hard for her to remember the time when she had not been surrounded by children of various ages all demanding her attention. Although she loved them all dearly, there were times when she wished herself single again. She inspected the toast, turned it over and pressed it back on the prongs of the fork.

'Nearly done,' she said cheerfully. 'This is for Bertha.'

'See!' said Bertha triumphantly.

Tommy set up a wail. 'Why Bertha? She hasn't finished and I have.'

'That's because you gobble your food,' Rose told him. 'And you can take that look off your face. You've all had one slice and you'll all have a second – *if* you are good.'

'It's not fair!'

''Tis, so,' said Bertha. 'You should chew each mouthful twenty times, like Pa told you, but you never do.'

'Nor do you.'

'I do sometimes.'

'I've never seen you.'

Rose counted to ten, inspected the toast and straightened up. She spread the slice with dripping and handed it to her eldest daughter. Then she put her hand to her back, which ached, and tried to straighten further. She was expecting another child but the idea brought her no pleasure. Surely five was enough for any woman? She took the next slice of bread and returned to the hearth. The youthful bloom in her cheeks had faded and her face looked drawn and white. Her dark hair was almost hidden under a white muslin cap, but she had pinned a small spray of fresh flowers over one ear and knew that she was still an attractive woman.

'I want butter on mine,' said Tommy, and an immediate wail went up from the others.

'You'll get dripping and like it, like the rest of them!' said Rose.

The fender needed a polish, she noticed, so did the kettle. That was a job for Bertha later on. Above the fireplace shirts and petticoats, newly ironed, hung over a string to air. Rose was most particular about airing; she had been brought up that way. A flat-iron stood beside the fireguard and next to that was Tom's clay pipe awaiting his return. He seemed later than usual, but he would come when he was ready. She knew better than to question him when he was late, for his temper grew shorter with each passing year and for nearly a week he had hardly spoken to her. Something bothered him – Rose had an idea that it had to do with Jarvis Tupp, but so far she had not mentioned it to him.

The cottage consisted of a living-room and scullery downstairs and two small bedrooms above. She and Tom slept in one of the rooms with their youngest child in a cot in the corner. The other four children already shared the second bedroom, so where was the next child to go, she wondered. And how many more would there be? Her husband was a lusty man – a little too lusty perhaps, but she would not think about that. From a small wicker cage in the window a bird sang shrilly and a cat was curled up on the small table immediately below. The floor was of red brick and had to be scrubbed daily. The beamed ceiling was grey with the smoke of countless fires. The walls were hung with samplers and on top of the cupboard at the far end was a washing-basket full of clothes which waited for the copper to be lit.

The door opened, Tom came in and the children shouted greetings. He kissed the girls and ruffled the hair of the boys. Rose stood up and he put his arms around her waist and kissed the tip of her nose. To the children he said, 'There was a time when your Ma was so light I could swing her off the ground.'

'Oh Tom!' she protested, laughing easily while the children giggled.

'She's too fat now,' said Tommy.

'You watch your tongue, young-un.'

'Do you want a piece of toast, Tom, before I get your supper?' He shook his head.

'Sorry I'm late, but I stayed to give young Harry a hand. Trying to dig out a wasps' nest, he was, and making a rare mess of it. Wasps everywhere. It's a wonder he wasn't stung.'

He pushed the startled cat off the table and perched himself on the edge, gazing out of the window. His head caught the wicker cage and it swung wildly, making the bird flutter.

'Tom, that poor bird! You do that every time.'

He put up a hand and steadied the cage, shifting his body slightly to be out of its way.

'We burnt it out in the end,' he said. 'Sometimes it's the only way.'

Tommy suddenly excused himself from the table and slid out of the room.

'What's he up to?' Tom asked.

'He's been scrumping,' said Bertha treacherously. 'Pinching apples off the school tree and Miss Gibbs sent a note. She gave him the cane.'

'I'm asking your mother, not you,' said Tom.

'That's about it,' said Rose. 'The note's on the mantelpiece.'

Tom grunted. 'No apples on that tree worth scrumping,' he said. 'Never was.'

Rose was troubled and stared into the fire instead of watching the toast. The children pulled exaggerated faces as the smell of burning reached them and seeing the ruined bread, Rose took it off the fork and threw it into the fire with a gesture of irritation. Tom had kissed her every day for the last six days and now he was apologising for being late – not only apologising but volunteering an explanation. Rose knew her husband well enough to realise that he was troubled by a guilty conscience. For a long time now she had lived with the secret knowledge of his liaison with the Colonel's wife. That was old news, but something else had happened, and whatever it was disturbed him deeply.

As she cut another slice of bread, the disgruntled cat sprang back on to the table and sat beside Tom, purring loudly and blinking its yellow eyes lovingly at him. Out of the corner of her eye, Rose saw him fondle it, the large fingers gentle around its throat and ears. She wondered suddenly about the new young school-teacher who had taken poor Maude Babbit's place until such time as Vinnie was old enough, but she was as skinny as a broom and pasty with it. Some even said she was consumptive-looking. No. She had been seen more than once in the company of George Lennox of Merryon Farm whose wife had been dead two years now. That seemed a likely match. But she was not Tom's type. No, she would not ask, it was not her way. She loved Tom and she loved the brood of children he had given her. She was often tired and sometimes depressed and this was one of those times, but she could live through it. If she knew nothing, then it need not trouble her too much. Whatever other folk might suspect about her husband and Christina Lawrence, they could not possibly know for certain and that was enough for Rose.

'Your mother called by,' she told him cheerfully.

'Oh yes?'

'It seems her gate has fallen off at last. The post is rotten. Says you promised to see to it.'

'I did. I'll pop over there later tonight.'

The toast-making finished, Rose made a fresh pot of tea and sent the children out into the garden so that her husband could have a little peace and quiet.

'Her leg is bothering her again, too,' she said. 'Worried about Vinnie, as well.'

His answer was a long time coming, then he said, 'Worried? What's the matter with Vinnie, then?'

'That's just it, she doesn't know. Says the girl's gone all moody and won't talk to people. Doesn't want to see anyone.'

'She's at a funny age,' he said.

'What's funny about it?' said Rose. 'I wasn't funny at that age. It seems the only person she talks to is that Mr Fry from London. Doesn't want to read to the Colonel any more and when they sent that young Harry down to take her back for a game of croquet, she wouldn't go. Then after young Harry had gone, she burst into tears. Always had a soft spot for that

Julian, so your Ma says, and time after time she's said she
wanted to play croquet. Then when she gets the chance she
turns it down. Quite a little madam at the moment, she
is.'

'Roland Fry isn't the man for Vinnie,' said Tom. 'I know his
sort. All talk and no action, that's Roland Fry.'

'Oh, Tom!' Rose protested. 'That's hardly fair. He's come
all the way from London just to help folk and you say he's all
talk and no action. He may not be very successful, but he *is*
trying.'

'Trying? He's trying my bloody patience, I know that.
Preachings and bun-fights and that awful business with the
clothing.'

Rose giggled suddenly, remembering her husband's description.

'I'm sorry, Tom,' she said. 'I can't help it. I would so love to
have been there. I do love a good laugh.'

'It's a wonder he lived to tell the tale,' said Tom.

The distribution of free shoes and clothing by the four
members of the Brothers in Jesus had proved disastrous. On
arrival at the tent at a quarter to eight, Roland had discovered
to his horror that at least half of the shoes had been stolen
during the night. Most of the hoppers who turned up at the
appointed time were therefore disappointed, which gave rise to
a certain amount of bad feeling and even worse language. To
add insult to injury, Mary Bellweather suddenly realised that
the pickers who protested the loudest about the shortage of
shoes were actually wearing some of those stolen the night
before.

The clothing, which had been locked away more securely in
a large tin trunk, was fought over and all Roland's pleas for 'a
little calm' went unheeded in the scuffle. The Brothers in Jesus
stood by helplessly until the last garment had been seized and
then watched the last picker disappear through the tent-flap
with a feeling of un-Christian thankfulness.

'Roland Fry is a born loser,' said Tom. 'I know his sort.
What's for supper, then, love?'

'I've got you a bit of fish. Robbie had a nice bit of hake and there's a few potatoes left from yesterday. I'll hot them up for you with a bit of parsley sauce.'

Tom stood up, took Miss Gibbs' note from the mantelpiece, read it and replaced it. 'Fry's not the man for Vinnie Harris,' he said again and went in search of his erring son.

*

Vinnie's letter took an hour and a half to write and was the result of much deep thought and agonised soul-searching. She wrote it in her best copperplate on a sheet of notepaper which the Colonel had given her some time earlier.

'Dear Julian, I am sorry I was out when you called—' That was a lie, for she had in fact been hiding upstairs in her room refusing to come downstairs and face him.

'—and also that I cannot accept your kind invitation to go with you to the hopping supper. You will never know just how disappointed I am, but the reason is a private one and although I cannot tell you I hope you will believe me and trust me and – O, please do forgive me.'

Since her intimacy with Tom Bryce she felt quite unable to look at Julian or to let him look at her. It seemed to Vinnie that her shame must show in her eyes and she was terrified he would recognise her guilt. Only Julian, she was sure, could draw a confession from her unwilling lips and therefore she dared not risk a confrontation.

'Something bad happened while you were with Eva in Wiltshire. How I wish you had not gone, but you did and I longed for you to come home and now you have I cannot see you. It is so sad.' She had considered carefully before adding the next paragraph and had finally decided that as this was the only letter she could ever write to him and as they would not meet again, she could be totally honest about her feelings.

'I thought I would never tell you this but now I will. I think I love you. I think it happened the first time I saw you which you will not remember, but I do and you were like a prince to me then and also now and I respect you so much. Mr Fry has also asked me to the hopping supper and I could go because he is nothing to me so it does not matter, but I will not for fear of seeing you. Dear Julian. I am sorry that we must part. You were the best thing in my whole life and I have lost you, but maybe it is God's punishment. He knows best, at least I think so. Goodbye, Julian. Yours truly for ever, Lavinia Harris.'

She read it and re-read it while tears coursed silently down her cheeks. Then she folded the letter, matching the corners precisely and pressing the folded edge with her finger-nail. For a few moments she delayed sealing the envelope, for to Vinnie that meant the end of the relationship. She sat with it in her hands, admiring the smooth feel of the heavy quality paper, and tried to imagine how Julian would react when he read the letter. Surely he would feel *some* regret and maybe he would be a little flattered. Did he have another woman in his life, she wondered? He had never spoken of one, but that might have been in consideration of Vinnie's feelings. There might be a female cousin in Wiltshire – they had stayed there such a long time. The thought was unbearable to her, but she told herself sternly that she should want Julian's happiness if she truly loved him, even if that meant wishing him into the arms of another woman. She, Vinnie, could never be a suitable match for him – or for any other decent man. The thought depressed her utterly, but she knew she must accept it. Julian must marry and she could only pray that his wife would love and honour him and make him as happy as he deserved to be.

Reluctantly she sealed the flap and addressed the envelope, placing the writing to the left-hand-side as Miss Babbit had taught her: 'Julian Lawrence – by hand.' She was proud of that last touch. It had a professional look of which Miss Babbit would surely have approved. Gently she pressed the envelope to her lips with a terrible feeling of finality. She was nearly sixteen, almost a woman, and her life stretched before her, empty and uninviting.

*

Julian read her letter and was completely bewildered. Immured at Foxearth, he had heard no rumours and paid little attention when his father complained that Vinnie no longer came to read to him. He decided not to show the letter to anyone and locked it inside a drawer in the desk in his bedroom. Then he made what he hoped were discreet enquiries about events during the previous month's hopping. Only Edie would admit to knowing anything and she was very vague and hardly to be relied upon.

'It's all gone very peaceful, sir. In the gardens that is. A few fights, so young Harry says, and one of them hoppers' weddings.'

'Hoppers' weddings?'

'You know, sir, where they jump over a hop-pole and bin man says they're wed legal – 'til they go home, that is.'

Julian felt a shiver of apprehension. 'And who was it, that was "wed"?'

'I dunno, sir. A girl and a lad, I suppose.'

'You don't know their names?'

'No, I don't. No one as I've heard of, anyway, but the mistress was that mad! And that nice Mr Fry. All hot and bothered, he was, and said it wasn't right in God's sight.'

'Who's Mr Fry?'

'The parson man – only he isn't a real parson. Lovely blue eyes, he's got, and comes from London. I went to one of his meetings once and he's a lovely talker, sir. Have you heard him talk?'

'Do you mean *Roland* Fry?'

'I dunno, sir. Do I?'

Julian frowned. 'And nothing else has happened?'

She shrugged. 'I dunno, sir, it might have. Jarvis Tupp got into a scrape, but his lips are buttoned. His father threatened to thrash it out of him but he's not big enough. Jarvis just laughed in his face and won't say nothing.'

'What sort of scrape?'

'I dunno, sir, but his cart ended up in a ditch, so they so. Run off without him, the horses did. Leastways I think so.'

Nothing added up, thought Julian wryly. There was only one way to discover the truth and that was to ask Vinnie herself. But would she tell him? Would she ever even talk to him?

He found her in the hop-garden, acting as tally-man to

Adam Forrest and he watched her for a while, unobserved. Another bin man held open the large greeny-yellow hop-poke into which Adam Forrest tipped the hops. Vinnie counted each bushel, her lips moving silently, until the tenth bushel. Then the bin man drew a length of pre-cut cord from his belt and secured the top of the poke which was then dumped beside the bin. Immediately the next poke was shaken open and Adam continued his measuring. The pickers watched him carefully. Each time he filled the basket he wiped his arm across the top to level the hops. If he pressed the hops downward with his arm instead of brushing off the surplus, the pickers would be credited with fewer bushels per bin and would complain bitterly that they were being cheated. Adam Forrest was generally judged to be a fair measurer, but the Londoners considered it foolish to be *too* trusting.

While Julian watched, a second poke was filled and set beside the first and then a third followed. Later the waggon would drive along the alleys between the rows and the driver would load the pokes and take them to the oast-house where the hops would be dried. Vinnie worked carefully, a frown of concentration on her face. When she had made the final entry she added the total and showed the result to the pickers for approval. A nod from the pickers, a brief smile from Vinnie and then bin man, Adam and Vinnie moved on to the next full bin.

'Vinnie!'

She turned and Julian saw the shock in her eyes. 'Oh no!' she whispered.

'I must talk to you, Vinnie,' he whispered. 'Please don't look at me like that.'

'I can't talk,' she stammered. 'I mean, I don't want to. I've nothing to say – I'm working.'

'I shan't take no for an answer. You're not being fair.'

'I've told you everything in the letter—'

'You told me *nothing* in the letter. Vinnie, what are you afraid of? You can talk to *me*, surely.'

She looked at him and her eyes were dark with misery. 'Please, Julian, don't you understand? You're the one person I can't – I'm coming!' Adam Forrest watched them impatiently. 'Oh, I must go, Julian. Do please go away. It will do no good to pester me, for I won't tell you any more. Not just for my sake . . .'

'For whose sake, then?'

'I can't tell you.'

The bin man added his voice to that of the measurer. 'Vinnie! Are you coming? You're holding us all up.'

'Right away! Julian, I *must* go.'

'Then when will you meet me?'

'I can't—'

'As soon as they call last bines?'

'No, I—'

'I'll be around waiting for you to finish.'

'No, Julian.'

'Yes, Vinnie.'

He waited until the end of the day's picking, never letting her out of his sight yet never getting too close. When the last bin had been emptied he waylaid her, ignoring her air of desperation and her entreaties to 'leave me alone'. Little by little he extracted the story from her unwilling lips and eventually he knew everything except Vinnie's final surrender.

'Go on,' he said inexorably as her voice faltered to a stop. 'What did Rose say?'

'She wasn't there.'

'Did Jarvis follow you?' Vinnie shook her head.

'So was that the end of it? Is that what all the fuss is about, Vinnie? He didn't rape you; he molested you, but that wasn't your fault. Why do you blame yourself this way for something that didn't happen? You've nothing to be ashamed of – nothing at all.'

'Oh, but I have!' Suddenly her eyes were blazing and her voice rose. 'You think you're so clever, Julian. You think because you're rich and clever that you understand everything. Well, you don't! Oh, why couldn't you leave me be? I'm tired of your questions!' Her wretchedness gave way to anger and she hated him for the light he cast into the dark corners of her mind. 'You want to know it all, then I'll tell you and *then* you'll go away. Oh yes, you will!' Her lips trembled. 'Someone was there. Tom Bryce was there—'

'But he's a friend—'

'Oh yes, he's a friend. A good friend. A very good friend. He's a sight too friendly and it was my fault just as much as his. *He* took me, you see. He did what Jarvis wanted to do – oh, now it's your turn to suffer! Yes, Julian, Tom Bryce took me, but that's not the worst of it. I let him do it. D'you understand? Do you know *now* why I'm so ashamed?'

Her breath came in painful gasps as she struggled to express the inexpressible. 'I let him do that to me because – well, because right then I *wanted* it to happen. I can't explain it because I don't understand it. It was as though my body took over and told me what to do. My mind said it was wrong, but the rest of me wouldn't listen. At that moment it didn't seem at all terrible.' Her voice faltered. 'It was only afterwards. But no one can blame Tom. He didn't force me; didn't threaten me; didn't hurt me at all. No, not one blow. I've no bruises, nothing. Oh—' She burst into sudden passionate weeping. 'I'm so ashamed. I'm ashamed for Rose, for him and for me but it's too late, you see. I want to undo it, but I can't. What *am* I to do? How can I look at Rose who is my friend? How can I face you or anyone else? I almost wish Jarvis had got his way. At least I'd have hurt no one else and I'd—'

Julian was shaking his head. 'You and Tom Bryce? My God!' The revelation stunned him. He was barely able to grasp what she was saying. He stared into the wild eyes and noted the dishevelled hair and quivering mouth.

'Are you satisfied now?' she demanded bitterly between her sobs. 'Now that you know how low I am, are you pleased you badgered and pestered me? Now you're hurt too. Can you imagine *my* pain? How do you think I feel, Julian Lawrence, telling you this? Cheap and nasty, that's how I feel – and that's what I am. Go back to your big house and your—'

He swallowed hard, trying not to see her with Tom Bryce. 'Stop it, Vinnie! Don't say those things.'

'Why not? It's the truth and that's what you wanted, isn't it? That's why you've made me say what was best left unsaid. I wanted to spare you the truth, but you wouldn't let me. Well, now you know it all. The very worst.'

They stared at each other white-faced and there was a long silence. At last Julian said slowly, 'So what about my invitation?'

She stared at him. 'What invitation?'

'To the hopping supper.'

'Don't ask me, you don't mean it. You're just trying to be kind.'

'Will you, Vinnie?'

'No!'

'Then I shan't go, for I shan't go without you.'

'Take someone else.'

'I want to take you.'

'Julian, please—'

Fresh tears filled her eyes and rolled down her cheeks. She began to rub at them with her hands, regardless of her looks.

'Vinnie Harris, you look horrible,' he said, 'but I still want to take you to the ball.'

She tried to smile. 'You make me sound like Cinderella,' she said shakily. 'Are you going to wave a magic wand and make me—' She intended to say 'beautiful' but instead she said 'clean', and they were both silent again and serious.

'I want to go back and start again,' she said, her voice low. 'If only God would let me have that day again – but I know He can't. I wouldn't do it then. I swear I wouldn't! If only I could undo it—'

'Don't talk about it any more. Come here.'

He held out his arms but she hung back.

'Don't be so kind to me, Julian. I can't bear it. Oh Julian, how do you think of me now? I must know and yet I'm so afraid. You must be shocked and disappointed—'

'Shocked? Yes, I confess I am. Disappointed? Perhaps.' She lowered her eyes hastily, regretting her question, but he went on, 'But most of all – if I'm honest – then I think I'm jealous.'

'You can't mean it!' she gasped.

'I think I would have liked to be the . . . first,' he said. 'Will you come to the supper with me, Lavinia Harris?'

She flung herself into his arms and then cried out as he hugged her too tightly.

'Yes, I will, Julian Lawrence.'

'I think I love you, Vinnie,' he began, but quickly she put a hand over his mouth to silence the words she had once hoped, but now could not bear, to hear.

CHAPTER FOURTEEN

Steven Pitt, at fifty-two years of age, was as skilful as his father had been before him. For one month in the year he spent twenty-four hours a day in the oast-house supervising the drying process of the hops. An error of judgement could ruin the entire crop and he was not a man to take chances. He made up a bed in the alley bodge – a narrow, high sided cart – and slept there whenever he could snatch an hour or two. The room was warmed by the constant temperature of the nearby furnace and he was quickly lulled to sleep by the soporific smell of the drying hops.

As soon as the pokes were delivered to the oast-house, he cared for the hops with a devotion that many a wife envied – his own included. For the rest of the year he did a variety of jobs around the farm, but for the month of September he was king, the highly respected ruler in his little kingdom and he revelled in this situation. No one, not even the Colonel's wife, could gainsay him. There was another bonus too: for four weeks he was free of his wife's nagging tongue! Free of what he called her 'whims'. He could make do with a hasty wash in the morning and could go for days without changing his socks, assuring himself that he was too busy to attend to such unimportant details. He could snatch a bite to eat whenever he fancied and gobble his food if he wished. He could not be expected to chop wood or pump water or milk the goat. For this short time he was released from 'petticoat rule' and he made the most of it.

Now Steven stood in the upstairs room, leaning his elbows on the window and looking out at the scene below where willing hands were preparing the long-awaited hopping supper.

His wife was organising the helpers, who were setting up trestle tables and covering them with white cloths. The courtyard around the oast-house was the favourite place for the hopping supper, but if the weather was bad it was held in one of the barns. His wife, Ellen, was a large woman with a voice to match and even as he watched she was shouting instructions at the top of her voice and waving her arms imperiously. The trestles were being set up on three sides of the square, the fourth being reserved for the fires where already the first sausages and kippers were cooking, scenting the air with their savoury smell and splashing fat on to the coals beneath them. Bread was piled on the table with bowls of home-made pickle. His wife's voice reached him thinly:

'Maisie, where are those potatoes, they will never be done in time? Joan dear, fetch the butter will you, and check up on the forks. They'll be arriving any minute now and we are nowheres ready.'

Her face, he knew, wore the familiar harassed expression but he knew also that she was enjoying every minute of it. As wife of the head drier she, too, had her moment of glory and the hopping supper was the crowning achievement of *her* year.

As though suddenly aware of his scrutiny, she turned and cast a look towards the upper window of the oast-house and he hastily ducked back out of sight. Even now, he thought ruefully, she could well find him a job to do and that was something to be avoided at all costs.

He surveyed the room, which was almost empty because most of the other driers had gone home to rest and clean themselves up in time to accompany their wives to the supper. A few feet in front of him was the hop-press and below it a circular hole cut in the floor. Into this a deep sack called a pocket would be inserted which would project eight feet into the room below. The dried and cooled hops would be shovelled into this, Danny Wootton would turn the handle of the press and a plunger would compact the hops. When the pocket was full, it would be lowered down to the room below to await collection for the final trip to the brewery.

Steven crossed the room to the drying area. This consisted

of a slatted wooden floor covered by a horse-hair blanket loosely woven to allow warm air through from the furnace below. On the blanket the hops were laid to a depth of ten inches, and as they dried the moisture rose into the conical roof and was taken out through the cowl. He nodded to John Burrows, who sat half-dozing against the wall watching the hops.

'Any problems?' he asked.

The man said, 'Nope' without turning his head and Steven turned away. John Burrows' wife had died a few months earlier and he had therefore offered to work on while the others were at the supper. Satisfied, Steven Pitt went downstairs to check on the furnace and add another handful of sulphur to each of the two long-handled pans which rested on the coals. The sulphur fumes would give the hops a nice bright colour. He prowled around checking a pile of hop-pockets and inspecting the various tools. He found a broken hop shovel, its sacking free of the wooden frame and – pleased to have something to do – he settled himself down on a pile of pockets and set about repairing it.

Suddenly Ellen put her head in at the door. 'If you've nothing to do, Steven Pitt,' she said, 'you can give us a hand out here. There's one or two arriving already and still plenty to be done.'

'What do you mean, nothing to do?' He indicated the scuppet. 'What do you think this is?'

'I know well enough what it is,' she said. 'It's a scuppet, but I'd scarcely call that urgent.'

'It may not be urgent to you but it's urgent to me. You get on with your job, love, and leave me be to get on with mine.'

'But surely you could spare ten minutes?' she began.

'Not ten, not five, not one,' he said dogmatically. '*I'm* drying hops, *you're* setting out a party. Now you go and get on with it.'

She gave him a withering glance but his head was already once more bent over his task and she withdrew.

'And good riddance,' he muttered, making a yapping motion with his left hand.

'I heard that,' Ellen said, reappearing round the door. 'Thought I'd gone, didn't you, Steven Pitt? Well, I haven't and I'll thank you to treat me a bit more courteous. If a wife can't ask her husband to give a bit of a hand when she's rushed off her feet—'

'I've told you before, Ellen, if it's too much for you, give it up. There's plenty of younger women willing enough to take over if you're finding it too much at your age.'

'What do you mean at *my* age?'

'What I say, love. If it's too much for you, let someone else take it on.'

This was his trump card and they both knew it. There were plenty of women younger than his wife who would willingly shoulder the burden of organisation.

She snorted. 'And a fine mess they'd make of it!'

'I don't doubt they would,' he said, 'but at least the worry would be off your shoulders and no one could blame you. Might make them appreciate you then.'

'Appreciate me? They appreciate me now, Steven Pitt, so don't you go thinking otherwise. Oh, they appreciate me all right. Nineteen years I've done this supper and nineteen years it's been a success. They appreciate me, don't you worry, because I have got it all at me finger-tips and I know exactly what I'm doing. I could do it single-handed if I had to.'

'You don't need me then, do you?'

She sighed heavily, silently admitting defeat. 'Well,' she said, 'I suppose you'll want a bit to eat later. Two sausages and a couple of taters?'

'That will do me nicely, thanks, love.'

When she had gone he settled himself more comfortably on the pile of pockets and resumed his task. In a few more minutes he would go up once more to check if there were any problems in the drying chamber. He knew there would not be, but it was as well to make sure.

Outside in the courtyard all the helpers gathered together while Ellen Pitt briefed her little army on the final details.

'Now, Maisie, you are going to do the sausages and they are going on in half an hour – right? Sue, check the first batch of potatoes, take them off if they are ready and put the next lot on. They should be done in another quarter of an hour. Let me see, chairs for the Foxearth lot. We had better send someone up for them. Will you see to that, Linda? Thanks, love. Bread's done, butter's done, pickles, cruets? Have we got enough cruets? And mustard? Last year the Colonel's wife was asking for mustard and there was none to be found. Now let me see – the fiddlers should be here in a minute and we have made them a little platform, so that's ready. Meg, perhaps you could make sure they get something to eat? Tell them to go one at a time for food, then there's always music going. We don't want half an hour's silence like we had the year before last. Raffle? That's you, Moyna. You want a tin for the money – oh, you've brought one, good girl! Mrs Lawrence is going to judge the best dancing couple and have we got the rope for the tug-o'-war? Good, for we must make sure they hold it well away from the tables. We nearly had a disaster last year. So, anything else I've forgotten?'

She looked round challengingly. No one could think of anything and few would have dared to mention it if they could. Ellen Pitt had a sharp tongue and was not afraid to use it. She turned slowly, surveying each table in turn, checking finally before dismissing her helpers.

'Cider and ale, cider and ale, cider and ale. All tapped ready, I hope?' There were nods.

'Good, and don't forget after the first rush for food is over, there will be a side of cooked beef coming down later from Foxearth. By that time most of their bellies will be already full and the meat will go round comfortably. Remember the Colonel will be here in his Bath chair, so give him a smile, poor old fella! He does so hate to be left out. Off we go then and the best of luck!'

They echoed her sentiments and then disappeared about their appointed tasks.

An hour later the little courtyard was transformed. It was crowded with hop-pickers all dressed up in whatever finery they had managed to assemble. For some of them this might be merely a clean ribbon or a newly washed shirt, but those who had shoes had given them a rub and those who had none had washed their feet. They crowded on both sides of the trestle tables and around the fire, helping themselves to sausages, bread, chops and the jacket potatoes which were split open and filled with butter. Many sat around the grass edges of the courtyard, some perched in the various waggons, a privileged few had chairs to sit on. There were two fiddlers and one accordionist and they played a succession of lively tunes. Some people sang but no one danced: that would come later. The important business at present was due to show proper respect for the feast provided and this they did. The light had faded, for it was gone eight o'clock, and a variety of lanterns adorned the oast-house wall, casting a flickering light over the proceedings.

The Lawrences sat near to the fire, Christina resplendent in crimson with a small bustle, the Colonel so well wrapped up in blankets that he was scarcely visible. Steven Pitt looked down on them in solitary splendour from his vantage point in the oast-house. Even John Burrows had gone down to mingle with the crowd under strict orders from Steven Pitt to, 'Enjoy yourself lad.' Steven had turned the deep layer of hops. Now one more day, he told himself, then all the excitement would be over for another year, but it had been a good harvest. A good crop.

Almost opposite him across the yard, behind the trestle tables, he picked out the plump figure of his wife but she had sent him some food and then forgotten him – too busy to spare him even a glance. She was in her element and he was pleased for her. He saw Tom and Rose Bryce and Tom Bryce's mother – and there was Eva Lawrence, beautiful in a white gown with flowers in her hair. She would be a beauty like her mother, he thought. The Lawrences were a handsome family. He looked for Julian and was surprised to see him with his arm round Vinnie Harris's waist. That would set a few tongues wagging! At the opposite end of the courtyard were the four Brothers in Jesus. Mr Fry was beside the Bellweather lass and that fellow Brooks with the outlandish name he could never remember, was arm-in-arm with a dainty young woman with blonde hair who had taken Lydia's place when she returned to London. Well-meaning people, he thought, but they were more trouble than they were worth. Such help as they could give was a drop in the ocean and he doubted if it was appreciated. The Londoners were a wild lot and no one would tame them but by golly, they knew how to enjoy themselves!

Will Tupp was there from the store, and old Robbie had turned up even though they had declined to buy his bloaters. But where was Jarvis Tupp? Up to no good, most likely. He was a sly one and not to be trusted if all they said about him was true. Funny business about that cart . . .

There were sounds in the room below and he made a move towards the stairs thinking it was a young couple in search of privacy, but he suddenly recognised Christina Lawrence's voice and hesitated.

'Tom?'

'Christina!'

'Don't you Christina me. What the hell are you playing at?' Steven Pitt froze in horror.

'Playing at?'

'Yes, playing at. Don't act the innocent, you know exactly what I mean. You didn't turn up that Thursday night and you've been avoiding me and I want to know why. I think I'm entitled to an explanation.'

'I've been around.' The tone was evasive.

'You have not been around, Tom, and even if you had been around, it's hardly enough. Do you expect me to come chasing after you? As it is, I have been to your home twice.'

'For God's sake, why?' He sounded agitated.

'Why, Tom? Why? Because I wanted to see you, that's why and each time you were not there – "Gone to see his mother", said dutiful Rose. So why the sudden interest in your mother?'

'I'm not suddenly interested in her.'

'Oh, then perhaps it's Mr Fry who interests you? Hardly your type, I should have thought.'

'Lower your voice, Chrissie.'

'Don't you tell me how to behave! Then if it's not Roland Fry, perhaps it's Vinnie Harris.'

There was a moment's silence. Steven Pitt wondered frantically whether to brave it out and go downstairs pretending he had heard nothing, but felt that it was already too late. His only course was to remain where he was and hope he was not discovered.

'You are being ridiculous.' It was Tom Bryce speaking.

'Then where were you that Thursday? I waited for you until nearly midnight.'

'I'm sorry. I can't remember now what happened. I was obviously delayed.'

'Even I know that. What I want to know is who delayed you.'

'I've told you, I can't remember. Please keep your voice down, else somebody will hear you.'

'So they hear me? Perhaps I don't care! Perhaps I don't care any more. All I want to hear from you is the truth, Tom Bryce, because if I don't then you and I are finished. If you think you can treat me like a toy to pick up and throw away when you are bored, then you are mistaken. Very seriously mistaken. I have given you the last ten years of my life.'

'You gave it willingly enough.' There was the sound of a scuffle. 'Don't you raise your hand to me, you bitch, unless you do want us to be finished.'

'You swine! Let go of my wrist – you're hurting me!'

Steven Pitt could hear the suppressed fury in her voice.

'Then calm down. You're making a fool of yourself.'

'Oh no, Tom, it's you who is making a fool of me, or trying to, but that's something I will never allow. Either you tell me why you stayed away, or you can stay away for ever.'

'Hysterics don't suit you, Christina.'

'Tom! Tell me what I want to know and tell it truthfully or I'll make you suffer.'

'You'd enjoy that.'

'Maybe I would.'

'You really want the truth? You're not going to like it.' There was another long silence and when Tom Bryce spoke again his tone had changed.

'Don't press me, Christina. Let's forget it, let's write it off and carry on as though the last ten days had never been.'

'No, Tom, I can't take that. I can't accept anything but the truth.'

'I wish you would, Christina.'

'So do I, Tom, but I can't. Things have gone too far after all these years.'

'Christina, please.'

'No, Tom, I want the truth. Who were you with that night?'

Another pause.

'That night – nobody,' said Tom, 'but that evening, Vinnie.'

'My God. That little trollop! So it's true.'

'What?'

'That she was seen near your house, half-naked.'

'That's how she came. It was none of my doing, she was running away from Jarvis Tupp.'

'Oh, my God!'

'I was there on my own. Rose had taken the children to her mother's for the afternoon.'

'You and Vinnie Harris! But Tom, she's only a child, barely sixteen. Are you mad, Tom?'

'I think I was that evening. It just happened. It didn't mean anything, nothing. Not to her, or to me. It was one of those things best forgotten.'

'Forgotten? You expect me to forget something like that?'

'No, I don't. That's why I didn't want to tell you. I knew you wouldn't understand.'

'I understand. Vinnie Harris is new territory for you – another conquest. I am no longer enough for you. I understand perfectly.'

'That's not true. You've always been all I wanted.'

'Then how can Vinnie Harris take precedence over me and why didn't you come to me afterwards?'

'Would you have wanted me to?'

There was another silence.

'I was shocked and upset,' said Tom, 'and so was she. It should never have happened, but it did. It should have been forgotten.'

'Until the next one, I suppose. Until your next chance meeting with a young girl who throws herself into your bed and then I'm supposed to forget that one as well, am I?'

'I couldn't face you afterwards, Christina. I wanted time to think and time to sort myself out. I wanted to make sure she was not going to make trouble. She is a decent girl, Christina.'

'Decent? She is a tramp. A sly little tramp – and with a man old enough to be her father. Well, she goes!'

'Christina, please!'

'No, Tom, she goes. If this is the thanks I get for all the time and money I have spent on that wretched little slut, then the quicker she goes the better.'

'You can't mean it, Christina. You can't punish her and not me. Are you going to send me away as well?'

'I'm certainly going to give it a lot of thought.'

'You really are a vindictive cow.'

There was another scuffle and Steven, white-faced, heard Christina cry out in pain.

'Take your hands off me, Tom Bryce and don't ever lay another finger on me. Do you hear? I don't care if I never set eyes on you again. Do you understand that?'

'Chrissie!'

'Don't Chrissie me! And what about your wife? How much does *she* know? How much does she know about Vinnie Harris and how much does she know about us?'

'There's no need to involve Rose.'

'Oh, but I think there is. I think there is every reason to involve her if she can't satisfy her own husband. If he has to search for satisfaction elsewhere, then perhaps she ought to be aware of it.'

'You leave her out of it, do you hear me?' Tom's voice rose angrily.

'My God, Tom Bryce, you have got the cheek of the devil. You think you can insult me this way and still give me orders as to how I should behave? Well, I have news for you, Tom Bryce, you are in for a shock. My God you are!'

'Christina, come back here! . . . Christina . . . Hell and damnation!' There were three thuds as though Tom Bryce struck the door-jamb with his fist. Steven Pitt prayed that he would follow his mistress outside and not take it into his head to come upstairs. His prayers were answered as he heard Tom's steps fade.

After a moment, Steven stretched his cramped legs and moved cautiously to the window. Christina Lawrence was nowhere to be seen. Tom Bryce had rejoined his wife. Slowly he sank to his knees and let out a low whistle of astonishment and relief. Sparks were flying, he thought, and this was only the beginning. However he, Steven Pitt, would keep his mouth tightly shut. He was a peaceable man who valued his job and the cottage that went with it. He sighed heavily and shook his head. Not one word of that overheard conversation would ever pass his lips, he vowed as he turned back to his plate. The potato was barely warm but he held it cupped in his hands and sat for a long time, staring into space. When at last he began to eat the potato it was quite cold.

*

The beef arrived on time and was quickly cut into large succulent slices. Each one was laid on a thick slice of bread, trencher fashion and handed across the table. The reasonably orderly queue stretched right round the courtyard, but the music continued to play and everyone was in high spirits so that for those at the end of the queue the waiting was less irksome; by the time *their* turn arrived, those at the head of the queue would have finished and would envy the last few. Christina had reappeared and was supervising the distribution. Her smile was brittle but this passed unnoticed. Only when Vinnie and Julian drew near did she turn aside, unable to bear the radiant expression on the girl's face.

Vinnie, unaware of Christina's hostility, was blissfully happy with Julian beside her, but still unable to believe her good fortune. The worst had happened – she had told him – and he was still fond of her. It was incredible, yet true. She could tell by the way he looked at her and the pressure of his fingers as he held her arm, and he had said that he loved her. At least, he had said he thought he loved her and that was enough for Vinnie. It did not matter that she was a poor girl from the London slums and he the son of a wealthy man. They were just a boy and girl in love with each other and the evening was theirs alone. The future was another matter, but for Vinnie at this moment it did not exist. She was aware only of the closeness of their two bodies and the beating of her heart. When finally the last of the food had been devoured, the tables were quickly cleared away and the men prepared for the tug-of-war. This took place amidst a mixture of hearty jeers and shrill cries of encouragement. The local team pulled against the hoppers and as usual, the locals won, sprawling into an undignified heap as their opponents were edged over the line and thankfully relinquished the rope. The village constable, invited in the line of duty to preserve the peace, watched warily for any sign that the Londoners were taking their defeat badly – as sometimes happened – but on this occasion his fears were groundless. The beer and cider they had consumed was small in comparison with the amount of food they had eaten and none of them was yet drunk enough to be aggressive. Later, perhaps, although he hoped not.

'Vinnie, you look really beautiful!'

She turned to see Mary Bellweather smiling at her with Roland Fry beside her.

'You do, indeed, Vinnie,' said Roland. 'I quite envy your escort, but I am very glad you changed your mind and decided to come.'

He turned to Julian. 'How did you work the miracle?' he asked. 'She refused *my* invitation.'

The smile went out of Mary Bellweather's eyes although her lips still curved. She had not known that Roland had invited Vinnie first and the news hurt her.

Julian looked at Vinnie and laughed. 'It wasn't easy,' he said. 'Vinnie can be very stubborn when she wishes.'

They all laughed and for a moment Roland's eyes met Vinnie's reproachfully. 'Well, the least you can do is to save me a dance,' he said.

'I'll do that with pleasure,' she told him.

'Not the first dance,' cried Julian, 'for that one is mine. Come on, Vinnie, they have started and we are wasting precious time.'

Already the courtyard was swirling with people attempting to polka. The tune was being played very fast and there was not a great deal of space, but some couples seemed to manage it satisfactorily. Others, less nimble, contrived to bump into as many other couples as they could, so that within minutes the music was almost drowned out by the shrill laughter and good-natured repartee. As soon as Julian and Vinnie started to dance, however, the rest of the pickers dropped back respectfully, for Julian was the first of the Lawrences to take the floor. The hoppers watched the handsome young man and his glowing partner as they circled the floor gracefully. When the music stopped, there was a spontaneous round of applause, as much for their evident happiness as for their dancing. Then the fiddlers struck up again and the courtyard was once more a mass of swirling couples. Roland and Mary danced past and Tom danced with his mother while Rose watched approvingly from the side until one of the farm-hands swept her also into the throng. To Vinnie it was an enchanted evening and one that she wished would last for ever. She could not ever recall such joy. Even the trip to Margate had not held the essential element of requited love. Whatever might happen tomorrow, she thought, she would give herself up to the delights of the evening and her radiant expression and joyful exuberance were generally remarked upon. But she alone failed to see the grim expression on Christina Lawrence's face.

Roland claimed his dance and she thought he held her a little too tightly for a man with another partner, but she smiled and laughed with him and was genuinely unaware of Mary's misery. Then she was back with her beloved and the hours rolled by in a happy confusion. Other couples discreetly slipped away from time to time, to reappear later – dishevelled and bright-eyed – to face the laughing taunts of their friends. The older men drank too much and their wives began to scold. Here and there the inevitable squabbles broke out, but there was no serious trouble and Vinnie and Julian were unaware of it.

Before the Colonel was carried back to the house, he sent word to Vinnie that he had missed her and hoped she would read to him again the following day at the usual time. He added that he was an old man and that old men take rejection most unkindly. Vinnie, receiving this message, ran after him up the hill, kissed his cheek, begged his forgiveness and promised to be there at the appointed time.

When at last the musicians gave up and the party came to an end, Julian insisted on walking Vinnie home. The air had grown chill and now they had stopped dancing they were aware of it. Vinnie shivered and Julian took off his jacket and put it round her shoulders. Then he put an arm round her waist, she rested her head against his shoulder and in this way they walked back along the road to the cottage. On the doorstep they clung together in a long goodnight kiss.

'I love you, Vinnie,' he whispered. 'I don't know how it has happened and I know it should not have, but I want you to know I do love you.'

'In spite of – everything?' she asked again.

'In spite of everything or because of everything. I don't know.'

She stared at him, trying to see the expression in his eyes, but the moon was behind the clouds.

'Shall I see you tomorrow,' she asked, 'when I come to read to your father?'

'Of course. We will talk again then.'

She nodded. 'I'd best go in.' They kissed again, then Vinnie found the key under its mat and he took it from her and opened the door.

'Remember I love you,' he whispered.

'And I love you.'

She closed the door and leaned against it, unable to watch him walk away. With her eyes closed she could imagine that he was beside her still. If she opened them, she would know that he had gone.

'Oh, Julian!' she whispered. 'My very *dearest* Julian.'

She saw him in her mind's eye, slim and fair, and saw the love in the cool grey eyes. Was there anything, she wondered, that she did not love about him? His voice was gentle, almost too soft for a man, but she found that reassuring after the harsh, loud voice of her father which had dominated her early years. His mouth was small and sensitive; his hands moved with a nervous elegance that fascinated her. There was nothing brash or crude in his nature, she was sure, and no unwholesome thoughts disturbed his mind. Julian, in Vinnie's eyes, was a perfect example of chivalrous manhood – a Prince Charming.

'Oh, my beloved boy!' she whispered yearningly. 'I wish I could care for you, always.'

She wanted to protect him from the ugliness of life but that pleasure, she reflected, would fall to another woman's lot. How she would envy the future Mrs Julian Lawrence! She took off her shoes and made her way up the stairs, avoiding the fifth step which creaked. She was a dandelion, she told herself, to Julian's rose and he could never be hers. But for the present – she worshipped him and he had said he loved her. That must suffice. Once in bed, she drifted into sleep on a wave of joyful thoughts. Had she been able to foresee the events of the next morning, she would have felt very differently.

CHAPTER FIFTEEN

Wateringbury Station at half-past-six the following morning was still shrouded in mist from the river which ran parallel to the railway line. The sharp angle of its gable and the tall ornate chimneys were softened and shrouded and the tall rectangular windows reflected nothing, making it look blank and unattractive.

Vinnie sat on one platform and stared across the line. Her eyes, robbed of their lustre, also looked blank and there was nothing attractive about her pale, shocked face. She sat motionless, a small huddled figure wearing a coarse blue gown with a pinafore made of sacking. From the opposite platform the station-master eyed her curiously. She had appeared like a waif out of nowhere, a single ticket to London already clutched in her hand. She had nearly an hour's wait for the train, yet she was not dressed for travelling. He began to whistle cheerfully as he carried the few parcels that would go up to London on the train. Vinnie, unaware of his existence, stared dully into space – her eyes open, her jaw clenched tightly as though to prevent speech. He made his way along the platform, crossed the line and strolled back towards her.

'Going to be nice later,' he told her. 'Proper hopping morning this, even though it's all over bar the shouting.'

Slowly she turned her head and nodded without answering.

'Going home early then, are we?' he persisted. 'You'll be missing the fair. All the fun of the fair this afternoon! Most folks are going back tonight or tomorrow. I didn't expect to see anyone here this morning.'

She looked at him as though she did not understand; as though he were speaking a foreign language.

'Back to smoky old London, is it, then?' he said. 'Back to the big, bad city?' He laughed to show that this was not meant unkindly. 'Another hour, nearly,' he said, 'and then the train will be here. You'll be a bit warmer then. I'd let you into my office only it's against regulations. It's being so near the river – it's always misty here first thing in the morning at this time of the year.'

She nodded, wishing he would go away.

'You all right?' he asked. 'Not sick or anything?'

'No, not sick.'

'Good. Only you look a bit pale, I just wondered.'

'Pale?'

'You know, white. You look a bit white, as though you've seen a ghost.' He laughed again.

'Oh.'

'You'll have the train to yourself, I should reckon.'

She nodded, once more changed her mind and shook her head and then put up a hand and touched her cheek as though to test its paleness. The station-master was coming to the conclusion that she was slow-witted.

'The – train – will – be – along – soon!' he said clearly and distinctly. 'The – train,' he pointed up the track in the direction from which it would come.

'Thank you.'

He smiled. 'Well, have a nice journey.'

'Thank you.'

As he had predicted, the train was almost empty when it finally arrived. She climbed into a third-class carriage and sat down by the window on the Foxearth side so that she could take a last look at the farm as they passed. The station-master passed her window, tapped on it and smiled, then moved on and she heard him exchanging a greeting with the driver. She gazed round the carriage as though she had never been in a train before. The seats were upholstered, the walls wooden and there was a luggage-rack, high up on each wall, made of strong mesh netting. The train on which they travelled to

Margate had been lit by candle-lamps, but this one had electric lighting and a window in the door that could be adjusted with a leather strap.

'"Cord Communication,"' she read in a whisper. '"To call the attention of the Guard and the Driver, passengers must pull down the cord which will be found outside the carriage . . ."' She began to hope there would be an emergency – a train crash, perhaps, in which she would be the sole victim. Or a murderer might get into the carriage with her and do her the favour of ending her life. Accidents happened; murders were less common, but it was just conceivable. Vinnie wanted her life to end as quickly as possible, for there was nothing left in it for her. The shivering in her limbs increased rather than decreased as she sat in the train, but this was from shock rather than cold. Once the train gathered speed, she leaned forward as the familiar countryside slid past her. At last she could pick out Foxearth, the farmhouse and the hoppers' barn, and further along the oast-house. The hop-gardens were almost bare, for this Sunday they were picking the last few rows and she saw only a few figures at work. Rows of grey hop-poles towered above the bare earth which had been trodden hard by the feet of countless pickers. Then she passed the row of poplar trees which acted as a windbreak, and the view of Foxearth was hidden from sight.

She sat dry-eyed and alone in the carriage, stunned by the suddenness of events. Christina had waylaid her on her way up to the hop-garden and one look at her face had told Vinnie that she knew what had happened between herself and Tom Bryce, but she had not been prepared for what followed.

'Don't bother to protest your innocence, for Tom Bryce has told me everything exactly how it happened,' Christina told her. 'He is quite as disgusted by your behaviour as I am and as you should be. No, don't you dare interrupt me, Vinnie Harris! You will listen to what I have to say and then you will get out of my sight for ever. To think how we once admired you and all the time you had the morals of a whore – no, don't interrupt me, for I can scarcely keep my hands to myself as it is and I won't be responsible for my actions.' Her eyes glittered

with hate. 'I'd like to take a whip to you, Vinnie Harris, yes, a
whip! What kind of creature are you? First Jarvis Tupp and
then Tom Bryce. One man should be enough for any woman
and you are nothing but a slip of a girl, not yet sixteen. Oh,
Tom has told me everything, he was quite shocked, in fact. We
have obviously misjudged you. You hoodwinked us all: Mrs
Bryce, poor Miss Babbit, even my own son. But don't worry, I
shall tell Julian the truth as soon as I return to the house and I
know he will be sensible.'

Vinnie opened her mouth to protest, but Christina slapped
her across the face. 'I said don't interrupt me,' she hissed. 'You
will hear what I have to say. I have brought my son and
daughter up to be decent people with an appreciation of right
and wrong and I won't have them contaminated by someone
like you. What you did that night is quite abominable, but
apart from telling Julian for his own good, I shall keep the
sordid details to myself. Unless, that is, you ever set foot in this
village again, in which event I shall tell everyone exactly how
depraved you are. For now I can see you as you really are and I
intend to throw you back where you belong, in the London
gutter. Take this –' she held out her hand '– it's a one-way
ticket to London. From now on you are on your own, Vinnie
Harris, and God help you, though that's more than you
deserve.'

Vinnie positively shrank from the hatred that glowed in
Christina's eyes. She was so horrified by Christina's account
that she could only attempt a few words in her own defence
and those had been swept aside as worthless.

Now, in the train, Vinnie faced up to the full horror of her
situation. She believed that Tom had told Christina a garbled
account of what really happened. It did not for a moment occur
to her that Tom had not betrayed her so cruelly; she accepted
what she was told and was certain that nobody would take her
word against Tom's. There was no way she could clear her
name and she groaned aloud.

And now Christina would also tell Julian the terribly
distorted version of what had happened and Julian would have
to decide which to believe. Surely he would believe Vinnie –

yet Christina was his mother and what reason did he have to doubt her word? Dear God, she thought, don't let him believe all those vile things that she has said of me.

Vaguely her eyes roved the tiny compartment and she read and re-read the cord warning. If only there was an accident – a derailment, perhaps – but no, it would not do, for then she would be forgotten and no one would ever clear her name. She closed her eyes and understood for the first time how easy it had been for Miss Babbit to throw her life away the way she had. Here Vinnie pulled herself up sharply and snapped her eyes open – no, she would not think along those lines, she would not let herself sink that far. Surely nothing would give Christina greater pleasure than to hear of Vinnie's death. Of course, Julian would not believe Tom's version . . . it was quite impossible. He had said he loved her. Surely they trusted each other – and yet the nagging doubt persisted.

For nearly an hour her thoughts revolved around the morning's happenings until suddenly, she realised she had given no thought at all to her future! Whatever would become of her? She had no work, no money, no home. As Christina had told her, she was being thrown back in the gutter, but at least she could sink no lower. She would find a job somehow; she would earn money; she would buy food and shelter. She did not know how any of this would be achieved, but her determination grew with each click of the wheels on the track. Her mother was dead and her father had disappeared, but she would find Bertie and Em and they would be reunited. She would *not* starve, even if she had to beg or steal her food. She had intelligence and somehow she would survive – she would deny Christina the satisfaction of hearing that Vinnie Harris died in squalor . . .

Her thoughts were interrupted when the train door opened and a small plump woman heaved herself up into the carriage. Automatically, Vinnie held out her hand to help her. The woman smiled, then lowered herself on to the seat opposite and bounced up and down.

'Nice bit of springing,' she said. 'Better than some.' She wore a dark woollen dress and a blue wool tartan shawl covered her shoulders. Her bonnet was sewn with a blue ribbon and she carried a hat-box over one arm. She looked around her critically, then leaned forward to examine the woodwork behind Vinnie's head.

'Vandals,' she said, 'heathens. I'd birch them, I would. Damaging other people's property. There's no excuse for it. Look at that! A penknife done that.'

Vinnie turned her head and saw the marks. 'Yes,' she said. 'It looks that way.'

'Caught one at it once, I did,' the woman went on, 'and he had the cheek to go on scraping away, but I gave him short shrift. Boxed him round the ears, I did! Then opened the window and yelled for the guard. That scared him – he climbed out the other side and took to his heels and they couldn't catch him. Maybe it will make him think twice next time.'

'I should think so.' Vinnie forced herself to reply.

The woman settled herself comfortably and set down her hat-box.

'Do you travel by train much?' she asked Vinnie.

'Not much,' Vinnie replied.

'You should, my dear. The best way to travel there is. You can sit nice and quiet in a train. Don't talk to me about the motor car, they're such smelly things. No, this is my favourite way to travel. I've been all over the country. It's a sort of hobby. I've been in a sleeping-car, you know.'

'Have you?'

'They can be quite comfortable, you know, and very private. Top bunk I had, but the lady below kept snoring. There's no cure for that, you know. Snoring. I don't snore, I'm happy to say. But it can be a nuisance.'

'I'm sure it can,' said Vinnie dully.

'I've been on the Midland, you know, and the London and Birmingham. 'Course, I was only twelve then and don't really remember it, so perhaps it doesn't count. I've been on the London and South Western, too. That's a nice railway – very well organised. Polite, they are, and I do like a bit of politeness.

But in all the years I've travelled, I've never seen anyone pull the cord. Not once. Funny, that.'

Vinnie nodded. In one way she resented the woman's intrusion into her private grief, yet she was also glad of the distraction.

'I was on that train in sixty-four – you know, when that Briggs was murdered. Mind you, I was only a babe at the time and I didn't know what was happening. I didn't know he was being murdered, but I *was* on the same train. Got on at St Neots on my way to see my aunt. Makes you think when you've been in a train with a murderer. Going up to London for the day, are you?'

Vinnie hesitated. 'Not exactly,' she said. 'I'm going *back* to London. It's my home.'

'Oh, your home, is it? You don't sound like a Londoner.'

'I've lived in Kent for a long time.'

'Kent, eh? I like Kent. I was nearly in a derailment once, but I missed the train. If I *had* caught it, I'd have been in it! My husband says I'm asking for trouble, travelling around the way I do, but it's a sort of obsession with me so I take the chance. If you want a tip when travelling by train, I will give you one for nothing. Take your own food with you on the day. If I'm going to be on a train for more than a couple of hours, I take a picnic with me: some chicken or a cold chop and maybe a slice of cake. Such a scrimmage on the station buffets and the dining-cars are so expensive, *if* you're lucky to get on a train that's got one. I've tried them all and I've come to the conclusion your own food is the best.'

She patted the hat-box. 'I suppose you thought this was a new hat?'

'I hadn't thought about it,' said Vinnie truthfully.

'Well, it isn't dear, it's my lunch.'

The woman continued her monologue almost without pausing until the train pulled into the London station. Vinnie helped her down on to the platform and watched her waddle away, towards the barrier, then slowly followed her. Her instinct was to turn and climb back into the train, as the small compartment might well be her last shelter for some time.

Instead, she made her way to the end of the platform, handed the ticket to the collector and walked out into the October sunshine.

Where to now, she wondered? She must think calmly and not panic. She had eaten a breakfast of porridge and milk so food was not an immediate problem. Glancing up at the large station clock, she saw that it was only twenty-past ten, so she had ten hours before nightfall. In spite of her determination, panic bells rang, her stomach churned with fear and for a moment her mind went quite blank. Thank goodness she was wearing her shawl, she thought, and wrapped it closer round her shoulders. Well, standing still would do no good, she might as well walk. She would walk for an hour and then take stock of her situation. In that time anything might happen, but she would walk towards Whitechapel for in that area she was most likely to find someone she knew. Mrs Batty, perhaps, or Hetty Bluett, even the Walkers. She stopped a man to ask directions.

'You're a long way from Whitechapel. Keep left, turn at the corner, down to the cross-roads, then ask again.'

Vinnie thanked him and began to walk, keeping her head erect. There was no need for anyone to know of her predicament, she reasoned. No one in London knew her or cared about her. Her shame was of no interest to them. London was a large, impersonal place and if necessary she could lose herself in it. She could even change her identity – this thought intrigued her. She made her way towards Whitechapel, stopping frequently to ask directions, often being misdirected but gradually moving closer to her home ground. Vinnie felt a detached curiosity about Whitechapel, of which she could remember very little. Two young boys, barefoot and ragged, overtook her, one on each side, and ran laughing and shrieking along the pavement. Then they deliberately collided with a barrowful of fruit, dislodging a mound of apples and oranges. In the confusion they seized one of each and made off with them into the crowd, while the owner of the cart shook his fist and screamed abuse after them. Vinnie went to pick up some of the apples and oranges and began to replace them in the barrow. The old man helped her, still muttering furiously, but when the fruit was restored to its former position, he thanked her grudgingly and gave her an apple.

Vinnie found London strangely exhilarating. There was so much to see that for long periods of the time she was able to steer her thoughts away from Foxearth and all that the name stood for. After the comparative peace of the village of Teesbury, London seemed to seethe with life of all kinds. Every street was crammed with vehicles, for the rich rode in their carriages and the middle classes patronised horse-trams. The poor, she noted, still relied mainly on their own two legs, weaving a path in and out of the traffic; others drove their own carts which were pulled by donkeys or broken-down horses. Children skipped and ran, sometimes in the road. To add to the confusion, a few bowled hoops made of iron, while others swung ropes and chanted their skipping songs.

Dogs barked, horses neighed, motor cars honked their horns and at every crowded junction the drivers of millers' drays confronted the drivers of coal carts and exchanged curses, each one insisting that *he* had right of way. In some cases a policeman struggled to untangle the chaos much to the amusement of bystanders. Instinctively, Vinnie kept away from the policemen of whom she was very wary. She could not rid herself of the feeling that she had no right to be there, that she was an intruder in this teeming town. She half-expected that at any moment she would be accosted by one of the uniformed figures and asked to give an account of herself.

By late afternoon she was growing hungry and, stopping to listen to an organ-grinder, almost envied the monkey who was being fed by passers-by. She lingered outside a baker's shop but the sight of the food made her feel hungrier than ever, so she hastily moved on.

'Is this Whitechapel?' she asked repeatedly and at last she was answered in the affirmative. Immediately she felt a great surge of confidence. She had succeeded in her first objective and had done it entirely on her own. She had not been harassed, robbed or run over and that in itself was a matter for congratulation. Not that she had anything worth stealing, she reminded herself with a faint smile.

Soon she had found the road in which they had lived – the road of which Bertie had spoken so fondly – and then she was standing outside No. 71. Without allowing herself time to hesitate, she went up the steps and knocked loudly on the door. It was opened by a tired-looking woman with a young baby in her arms. Vinnie smiled, trying to look calmer than she felt.

'I'm sorry to trouble you,' she began. 'My name is Vinnie Harris and I used to live here and –'

'Well, you don't live here now, love, so do me a favour and don't come pestering.'

'Oh please!' cried Vinnie. 'I don't want to pester you, I just want to ask if you know anyone called Hetty Bluett or Mrs Batty?'

The woman shook her head. 'I don't know 'em,' she said.

'Do you know of anyone who might know them or anyone who might know where they've gone?'

'No, I don't.'

From inside the house there came the sound of children crying and the woman's mouth tightened. 'So, 'op it,' she said, 'and don't bother us with your problems. We've all got plenty of our own.'

She shut the door in Vinnie's face and Vinnie struggled with her disappointment, trying not to let the small setback destroy her new-found feeling of confidence. She would ask around, she told herself, she would go into the next road and ask for the Walkers. They might still be living at their old address, although she could not remember the number of the house and would have to knock on all the doors. She hoped, nervously, that not everyone would treat her enquiries with the same indifference.

Half an hour later she had knocked on every door in the next road. The Walkers, it seemed, had moved away and no one knew where they were. Many of the people were kind, some were helpful, some were openly suspicious but whatever their reaction the answer was the same: no one knew anyone who could or would help. Now Vinnie had no names left. She looked up at the sky which had grown overcast and from which the first drops of rain were beginning to fall. Her confidence evaporated with the darkening sky and she was seized with a fresh wave of panic as she noticed the lamp-lighter making his rounds. Soon the streets would empty and become mysterious places in which all manner of danger might lurk unseen. She was cold, frightened and hungry. The rain fell harder and her spirits fell with it. She pulled the shawl up over her head and held it under her chin, but it was already wet and gave little comfort.

Vinnie wandered aimlessly because now that her search had failed, she had nowhere to go. She moved warily, avoiding a crowd of raucous women who clustered round a standpipe filling jugs and buckets with water. She shunned the men who propped themselves against the damp walls of grimy buildings and who called and whistled to her. Once she fell over a sleeping dog and grazed her knee, but the discomfort was nothing compared with her growing fears. The crossing-sweeper with his broom at the ready, called to her, offering to sweep a clear passage through the horse-dung that littered the street. When she drew closer, however, and he saw that she was not wealthy enough to pay him, he spat and turned away.

At last, the weary girl turned off the main road and made her way along the broad alleys until turning another corner, she discovered a blind alley at the far end of which a group of people were settling themselves for the night. A woman and three children huddled together in one corner. The man in the group wore a battered stove-pipe hat and the collar of his shabby coat was turned up to protect him from the rain. Ranged in front of them was a collection of almost worthless junk – an old saucepan, several stone jars, a set of saucers and a few books with broken spines. The three children eyed her curiously as she approached. Their hair was unkempt, their faces dirty and their clothes in tatters but to Vinnie's surprise, the woman greeted her in a friendly way.

'What's up, ducky? Lost a penny and found a halfpenny, have you?' Vinnie, taken aback, shook her head.

'Lost your way, then?'

'Yes, I have.'

'You don't want to wander round here on your own, ducky,

that's for certain. Unless you want a knife round your throat.'

Vinnie glanced nervously over her shoulder, half-expect-
ing to be set upon at any moment.

'You're scaring the poor kid,' the man protested. 'Take no
notice of her! Where you making for?'

Vinnie hesitated. 'I don't know,' she said. 'I came up to
London to look for friends, but they've moved.'

'Moved, have they?' said the woman. 'Well, it don't surprise
me, not round here. Come and sit down for a bit.' She patted
the pavement beside her and three young pairs of eyes
followed Vinnie as she accepted the invitation and sat down
gingerly beside them on the damp cobbles. The man leaned
forward eagerly.

'Want to buy a saucepan, love, or a bottle or a book, maybe?
I can let you have them cheap.'

'Hark at 'im!' said the woman. 'Let you have it cheap. He's a
fool to himself, practically gives his stuff away. Here, put that
round your shoulders, you look half-frozen.' She tossed
Vinnie a piece of blanket and the girl stammered her thanks.

'I'm sorry,' she said, 'but I've no money. Not a penny.'

'Join the club then, dear, but don't look so worried. We'll get
a free breakfast in the morning – a hunk of bread and a bowl of
soup. Leastways, *they* call it soup. I call it slop but beggars
can't be choosers, love.'

The man protested. 'It's not bad at all. You're a sight too
fussy.'

To Vinnie just then, a slice of bread and a bowl of soup
sounded quite delicious. The man rubbed his hands together
and blew on them.

'Our lad should be back soon, miss,' he said. 'He might have
a bit of something.'

'He might,' said the woman, 'and he might not. That's just
the way it goes.' She glanced up. 'Still, the rain's easing off a
bit. Might be a fine night. What's your name, love?'

Again Vinnie hesitated, fighting the urge to preserve her
true identity, though why she did not know.

'Vinnie,' she said. 'Short for Lavinia.'

'Lavinia, eh? – well, I'm Ada and this is Bert and these three

get called all sorts of things depending on what mood I'm in.'
She chuckled wheezily. 'You'll like our lad, George. Our
eldest, he is. We had another, but he got run down by a tram.
Took his arm off and he bled to death. Our George'll bring us a
bit of something. He's a very good lad. Ah, here come the
girls.'

Two younger women were making their way unsteadily
along the alley towards them and were greeted cheerfully by
Vinnie's new friends. Noisily they settled themselves down in
the opposite corner, obviously the worse for drink.

Ada whispered to Vinnie, 'They make a fair bit at their
game but it all goes on booze. Daft, I call it. Ah, here he comes,
bless 'im!'

'Here comes George!' cried one of the children and Vinnie
saw a tall boy of about her own age, approaching them with a
jaunty swagger. He carried a bundle wrapped in newspaper
under his left arm and when he reached them he swept to
attention and saluted with his right hand.

'Sir George Ponsonby at your service,' he said with an
exaggerated swagger for Vinnie's benefit. 'And what have we
here? A veritable feast, as they say.' He knelt and opened up
the newspaper and there were squeals from the three little girls.

'Oh, George, you have done well,' said his mother and she
jerked her head in Vinnie's direction. 'Can you spare a bit for
her?'

George looked at Vinnie. 'I don't see why not,' he said, 'if
she's not particular.'

'I'm not,' said Vinnie quickly.

'Then pull up a chair, love.'

In spite of herself, Vinnie grinned and moved closer as the
whole family clustered round the contents of the paper. There
was half a loaf of bread, decidedly stale, half-a-dozen overripe
tomatoes and a whole new pie, its crust shiny and golden.

'That's never a meat pie, George?' said his mother.

'It certainly is!'

'Meat? George! Where did you get that? I hope –'

George tapped his nose. 'Ask no questions, fear no lies,' he
said. 'If your conscience pricks, you don't have to eat it.'

His father said, 'Folks like us can't afford a conscience. We don't care how you come by it, lad. That's a fair old pie, that is and you've done us proud.'

George smiled modestly and glanced at Vinnie to see if she was impressed.

'Yes, you have,' she agreed.

Quickly and expertly Ada divided up the food. 'There you are, bit of bread, bit of pie and tomatoes if you want, except Meg here who doesn't like 'em. What a feast! All we want now is the champagne. You've never forgot the champagne, George?'

He snapped his fingers with a look of great dismay. 'I *knew* there was something else,' he said. 'Champagne, of course, it went clean out of my head. Never mind. We'll have champagne tomorrow, eh?'

The children regarded him solemnly and one of them said, 'You always say that but we never do have champagne,' and they all laughed. Then they fell on the food hungrily. The bread was very dry, the tomato bearable but the pie was delicious. While they were eating, Vinnie glanced uncomfortably at the two women in the opposite corner of the alley, but the drink had done its work and they were already asleep, their heads lolling, their mouths open. Silently Vinnie prayed that she would not end her own days that way. But with the food, her courage returned and she pushed such morbid thoughts to the back of her mind. Tonight she would sleep in the alley with these friendly people. Tomorrow was another day. Later she went to sleep feeling strangely hopeful.

CHAPTER SIXTEEN

Mary Bellweather fastened the buttons of her brown jacket and pinned her hat securely to the hair piled on top of her head. She took her fur stole from the hallstand and was fastening it around her neck when her mother came bustling out of the breakfast-room and into the hallway.

'Mary, I do wish you would wear something warmer over your ears. You'll get an ear-ache,' she protested.

'It isn't cold, mother.'

'Not cold? It's nearly November, Mary, how can it not be cold? At least tie a scarf over your hat.'

'I don't need one. It's not far and I shall only be gone for an hour or so.'

Mrs Agnes Bellweather remained unconvinced: 'Well, take a hansom, dear,' she said. 'That way you can avoid the worst of the puddles. There's nothing worse than standing around with wet feet. Or take another pair of shoes to change into,' she said as Mary shook her head.

Her mother sighed. 'Mary, dear, why are you so stubborn?'

'You worry too much, mother. You fuss over me like an old hen.'

'Really, Mary, is that the way to speak to your mother? Your manners these days are quite appalling. Mixing with those terrible people for a whole month has left its mark—'

Mary laughed. 'You know very well father would have approved,' she said. 'And please don't keep referring to them as dreadful people.'

'Then take your umbrella with you, Mary and do be sensible, child.' But with a smile and a wave of her hand, Mary went out, closing the front door behind her.

She was humming cheerfully as she went down the steps and picked her way between the puddles, lifting her skirt as she crossed the road to avoid the worst of the mess. She allowed her thoughts to wander: she had been so happy during her stay in Kent, but only to herself would she confess that her whole happiness had centred on Roland Fry. If that earnest young man had taken it into his head to do good work in the middle of Africa, Mary would have followed him willingly. She still treasured the memory of the hopping supper and the Sunday fair when, free of his responsibilities to what Roland called his flock, they were at liberty to enjoy themselves like any other young couple and Roland had shown her more attention than she had ever dared hope for. Several times while they danced his arm had tightened round her waist and when not dancing they had sampled the delights of the fair hand in hand. He was such a good person, she thought. So earnest and so well-intentioned. The only flaw in her happiness had been Roland's concern for the wretched Harris girl. If she chose to run away, it was her own fault, but Roland saw it differently, of course, and worried on her behalf. Mary had pointed out to him that Vinnie Harris was not one of the London pickers but a local girl and therefore not one of Roland's flock at all. Gareth and Lydia had agreed with her, urging Roland not to let the matter spoil their last day, and finally Roland gave in with a good grace. Now they had been back in London for nearly a month and slowly but surely Mary's relationship with Roland was deepening as she gave thanks daily for the mission work that had finally brought them together.

Breakfast for the needy of Whitechapel was dispensed from a small shed which stood empty for most of the day but was hired by the Brothers in Jesus for two hours each morning for the sum of five shillings. The last tenant had been a rag-and-bone man who kept his cart there, but he was currently serving a sentence for larceny and the owner of the property had sold his cart to compensate for arrears of rent. When Mary arrived, Roland was already there. He looked up and at the sight of her, his handsome face broke into a smile. Mary thought that with his dark hair and deep blue eyes, he was the handsomest man she had ever known, which made *her* the most fortunate girl.

'Am I late?' she asked.

'Not at all. I was very early,' he answered. 'I couldn't sleep, so I thought I might as well come in and sweep the place up a bit. I'm afraid I raised rather a dust. Perhaps it wasn't such a good idea, after all.' He was covering the old trestle table with sheets of yesterday's *Times*. Mary took off her jacket and stole and hung them up behind a screen at the back of the shed.

'It must have rained a great deal in the night,' she said as she slipped her head into the apron and tied the strings behind her waist. 'The road was filthy.'

While he set out the rows of mugs, Mary filled three large kettles, set them on the ramshackle stove and lit the gas. The stove was their latest acquisition, but it was very ancient indeed and Mary eyed it nervously as the jets fluttered unevenly. Roland began to cut slices of bread, but laughingly Mary took the knife from him.

'Let me do that,' she said. 'Cutting bread is not your forte. I will cut, you spread.' She took the beef dripping and handed it to him, he found himself a knife and they were soon at work.

'We make a marvellous team,' he said casually and her heart somersaulted so that she dared not answer in case the tremble of her voice gave her away.

'I telephoned the Lawrences last night,' he went on. 'There's still no sign of Vinnie. Poor Mrs Bryce is quite beside herself. No one knows what's happened or why she went.'

'She'll turn up,' Mary said shortly.

'Do you think so? I do hope you're right. My own theory is that she may have been abducted or have come to some harm. Most people leave a note of some kind when they run away. The rumour is that she set off for the hop-gardens as usual and then took the London train. Apparently she didn't even collect her wages. How is the child going to live? There's a chance she may come right to London.'

Mary kept her eyes on the loaf she was cutting. 'Why London?' she asked.

'Because she was born in London and only raised by Mrs

Bryce. She had a sister apparently brought up by a neighbour, a girl called Emmeline whom Vinnie hasn't seen for ten years. If Vinnie is wandering the streets of London with no money—' he shrugged.

'Well,' said Mary firmly, 'Vinnie Harris isn't our worry. We have enough poor wretches of our own to think about. How is Old Sarah?'

Roland shook his head. 'Not good at all,' he said. 'The doctor says at her age there's no hope at all and it would be a waste of our funds for him to visit her again. Lydia is going to call on her tonight with some fruit, but the poor old girl can scarcely swallow.'

'If she dies it will be a blessed relief,' said Mary. She paused in her cutting and looked up at him. 'Roland, you must learn not to take everything so much to heart. You cannot solve all their problems and death is a problem no one can solve. We do what we can, but our resources are so limited.'

'I know, I know,' he said. 'I get too involved, it's true.' He smiled at her. 'I promise I will try. Ah,' – he glanced towards the door – 'here's our first customer by the look of it.'

An elderly man shouldered open the door and let it bang to behind him. There was a bench along one side of the room and an assortment of chairs. He settled himself on the first chair without speaking, keeping his gaze firmly fixed on his well-patched shoes. Next, a group of youngsters sidled in, eyeing the table hungrily and muttering brief greetings. They did not sit down, preferring to hover near the table. Mary glanced at them sharply. 'I'm watching you,' she said. 'No helping yourselves like you did yesterday. There will be enough for everyone.'

'Can I have two slices, Miss, one for me bruvver?'

'You haven't got a brother,' said Mary, with an amused glance at Roland. She was learning fast.

Two very old ladies then shuffled in, supporting each other and laughing raucously. Mary tried to hide her dislike; between them they had a vast store of crude jokes and obscene stories with which they tried to entertain her, much to her embarrassment. Knowing this, Roland gave them a warning look and waved an admonitory finger at them. This merely sent them into further peals of laughter as they staggered towards the wall and deposited themselves on two chairs next to the old man. The first kettle began to steam and Mary spooned tea into the three large brown tea-pots while Roland added a spoonful of sugar to each mug. More people were now arriving, in various stages of destitution: some bare-footed, some obviously ill, others apparently recovering from the previous night's excesses with the smoke of the tap-room or gin palace still clinging sourly to their clothes. Today, there was a slab of cheese which Roland cut carefully into thirty equal pieces. There were rarely more than thirty people to be fed, but if more turned up, the last to arrive would be unlucky.

'By the way,' he whispered to Mary, 'I've been invited to Foxearth for the bonfire celebrations. They suggested I take a friend. Would you like to come with me?'

Mary's look of delight was answer enough and he went on, 'I did say we might lodge at the "Horse and Cart" but Mrs Lawrence would not hear of it and insisted that we stay with them.'

At last everything was ready and their eager customers lined up to be each given a mug of sweet tea, a slice of bread and dripping and a piece of cheese. For some time the chattering ceased while the food was consumed and Mary and Roland watched them with satisfaction.

'Watching them eat,' Roland whispered, 'gives me more pleasure than eating my own meals. I expect you feel the same way?'

Mary nodded. 'It's a good feeling,' she said, 'to be doing something worthwhile. We are so very fortunate.'

Roland was watching three little girls. 'Look at Ada's three,' he said. 'They are nibbling that cheese like three little mice, trying to make it last. Savouring it, almost.'

Ada herself came forward just then. 'Any spare bread, mister?' she asked. 'We've got this girl, the one I told you about before. Turned up again she has, half-starving. It's not that I begrudge her a bit of my bread, but it's becoming a habit.

I just thought you might spare her a bit. In the family way, if you ask me. She's got that drawn look. A woman can always tell these things.'

Roland looked at her in dismay. 'Expecting a child?' he said. 'And you say she's only a girl?'

The woman shrugged. 'I don't know how old she is, really. She just keeps turning up in our alley.'

Mary and Roland exchanged glances. 'Why won't she come in and get some food for herself?' said Mary.

'Too shy, I suppose, or ashamed. We brought her along the first morning but she took one look at you two and nipped off back along the road. Refused to come in.'

'How very odd,' said Roland.

He looked in the box and produced a single crust. 'This is all that's left, I'm afraid. Your friend is welcome to this, but do try and persuade her to see us. We may be able to help her in some way.'

'Thanks, mister, I'll talk to her. See what I can do.'

She stuffed the crust into the pocket of her coat and waited hopefully to see if a second mug of tea might be forthcoming. Curiously, Mary went to the door of the shed. Half-way along the street a young woman leaned against the wall of one of the warehouses. Her back was towards Mary, but there was something very familiar about her. Mary's heart sank but, ashamed of her reaction, she began to walk slowly along the street. The girl heard her, turned briefly and began to run away in the opposite direction.

'Vinnie!' shouted Mary, although she was still not really sure. She began to run after the girl, but in her heeled shoes she slipped on the cobbles and went sprawling. Roland came to her aid and she was soon back on her feet explaining what had happened. He ran on in the direction the girl had taken, but did not find her and returned bitterly disappointed. Mary met him at the end of the street.

'It may not have been her,' she said. 'I only thought there was a slight resemblance.'

But the woman in the shed reaffirmed the girl's name and Roland's disappointment turned to self-blame.

'I should have guessed,' he said. 'I should have realised. If only I had been in time!'

'No need to take on so,' said Ada. 'I doubt she will go far in her condition and where *can* she go? She's weak as a kitten, but at least she knows where to get a bite to eat. She'll be back, don't you worry.'

'I do hope so,' said Roland but Mary, not wishing to tell a lie, turned hastily away pretending to be needed elsewhere.

*

The Colonel was dozing when Janet went into the room, but he quickly roused himself.

'The paper, Janet, the paper! Why hasn't it been brought up?' Janet fussed over the bedclothes. 'It hasn't come, sir.'

'What do you mean, hasn't come? It always comes.'

'I mean *The Times* hasn't arrived, sir. Birdie thinks – I mean Mrs Tallant thinks – that they've got into a muddle at the store because her *Mail* has been delivered.'

'Dammit, Janet, what the hell is Tupp playing at sending the *Mail* and not *The Times?*'

'Mrs Tallant says you can borrow the *Mail*, sir, if you would like to read it.'

'I would not like to read it, thank you, Janet. No offence to Mrs Tallant, but as far as I'm concerned, there's only one newspaper and it is not the *Daily Mail.*'

'No, sir. I'll tell her, sir.'

With her duster, she wiped the small bedside table, lifting each medicine bottle and replacing it carefully in its appointed place, while the Colonel continued to mutter. Finally, his curiosity triumphed.

'Well, is there any news,' he asked, 'of Salamon Andrée?'

'No, sir, I'm afraid there isn't. It's been a long time now, sir.'

'It has been a damn sight too long. Middle of July they left and where are we now – beginning of October.'

'Yes, sir.'

Salamon Andrée had taken off from Spitzbergen on 11 July with two companions in their balloon 'The Eagle'. They hoped to reach the North Pole, a journey of more than six thousand miles. The expedition had aroused world-wide interest and the Colonel was one of thousands who had followed preparations for the flight with great interest. Now it was Janet's job to search the newspapers daily for items of information about the expedition. So far, there had been only one: a message tied to the leg of a pigeon had been found by the skipper of a sealing ship on 15 July. Since then, there had been no word.

'No news is good news, sir. That's what they say.'

'I'm not so sure,' said the old man. 'I went up in a balloon once, Janet. Wonderful things. Wonderful! So quiet and so still. You don't feel the wind, you see, Janet, because the wind is blowing you along. You travel with it. Can you imagine that?'

'I think I can, sir.'

He sighed. 'Those were good days, Janet. Ballooning was all the rage when I was a young man. If you had enough money you could always get a ride at the Cremorne Gardens or the Crystal Palace, that's where they launched them. They were exciting times.'

'You were very lucky, sir.' Janet had heard all this before and knew which responses were required.

'Hmm.'

He accepted a spoonful of medicine and then said, 'Any more news of the Queen's health?'

'No, sir.'

'Hmm,' he said again. 'She's a tough old lady, I'll grant her that, but I *will* outlast her, Janet.'

'I should hope so, sir.'

'Any news of that Harris child?' He had taken her departure as a personal affront and no longer referred to her as Vinnie.

'We don't know anything for certain, sir. We've heard nothing since that phone call from Mr Fry. The mistress says we will never find her now.'

'Does she, be damned! Well, that's as maybe. And that telephone call last night?'

'That was Master Julian from Cambridge. He was asking if there was any news, but the mistress told him there was none and to stop worrying about her and concentrate on his studies.'

The Colonel sighed deeply. 'She will come to a bad end,' he said, 'and serve her right, the ungrateful madam.'

Janet said nothing. Vinnie's disappearance was a very sore point, but Janet was not entirely sorry that she had gone. Now, without Vinnie's visits, the Colonel depended more and more on Janet and this knowledge gave her great satisfaction. True, she did not read as well as Vinnie but she did her best and her efforts generally met with his approval. Suddenly from outside there came the sound of the lawn-mower and young Harry's voice shouting 'Whoa!' Janet pretended not to notice, but the Colonel's hearing was still very acute.

'What's going on out there?' he demanded. 'Look out and see, Janet. Is that Lancer out there?'

Janet knew very well that it was Lancer, but she crossed to the window and peered out.

'Well,' he demanded, 'what's happening?'

'It's Lancer, sir, pulling the mower.'

The Colonel flew into one of his rages. 'I won't have Lancer used in this way, I've told Christina time and again. That horse has earned his retirement. If I am not to ride him and if Julian's away, then he can graze to his heart's content, for no one else can manage him. I will not have him doing these menial tasks. He is too good an animal to be towing a damned mower. I want to see Christina.'

'She's out, sir. She's gone to Tunbridge Wells.'

'Dammit!'

The maid looked at him in alarm. 'Sir, please don't excite yourself, it won't do you any good. The doctor says you are to stay calm.'

'How in the name of heaven am I to stay calm when my orders are disobeyed and my wishes ignored? Open the window and tell young Harry to take the horse back to the stable at once. What are you staring at, girl, get on with it.'

Reluctantly, she pushed up the window and leaned out, calling several times.

'I'm sorry, sir, he can't hear me, sir, it's the noise of the mower.'

'Confound the mower! I won't have any horse of mine doing such work – and we will have hoof-marks all over the grass. Are they mad?'

'Please, sir, he is wearing leather shoes.'

'Leather shoes? Who's wearing leather shoes?'

'The horse, sir, so he won't do any damage.'

She closed the window and then hesitated. 'What shall I do, sir?'

'I've told you what to do, girl. Get downstairs and tell young Harry what I said.'

She was half-way to the door when he added '– and bring up the *Daily Mail* if you must.'

*

It had taken a long time for Roland Fry's father to agree to the installation of the telephone, but at last it stood on the hall table, a handsome and ornate machine which the housekeeper regarded with deep suspicion. She dutifully dusted it each morning and polished its brass parts, but nothing would induce her to lift the receiver on the rare occasions when it rang. Patiently, Roland tried to explain the way in which it worked, assuring her that in times of emergency she might be required to use it, at which she shook her head emphatically and said, 'Never!' She listened resentfully while he named the earpiece, the mouthpiece and magnetic generator handle, but when at last he had made a connection to Mary Bellweather and invited the housekeeper to say a few words, she shook her head firmly and departed to the kitchen with the self-righteous air of one who has resisted temptation.

It rang one Thursday afternoon just as Roland was on the point of leaving the house and he turned back to answer it.

'Is that Roland Fry?' The voice was familiar, but he could not place it.

'Speaking,' he said.

'This is Julian Lawrence. I'm calling from Cambridge.'

'Mr Lawrence, how nice to hear from you. I do hope nothing is wrong.'

'So do I. May I speak to you frankly?' said Julian.

'By all means. I hope you will.'

'It's Vinnie Harris. I am uneasy in my mind about her. Weeks pass and we are no nearer finding her. I am fearful that when we do catch up with her it will be too late. I feel so very helpless, Mr Fry, all these miles away, and for some reason which I don't pretend to understand, my mother is most unsympathetic and gives me very little information.'

'We *have* very little information, Mr Lawrence,' Roland told him. 'Since our one and only sighting of her, she seems to have disappeared completely and I can only assume that if she is still in London she is using a false name. She is obviously determined not to be discovered. But I do share your concern. I must confess I became very fond of the girl while staying at their home.'

There was a silence as Julian digested this piece of information and after a moment Roland said, 'Are you still there, Mr Lawrence?'

'Yes, of course,' said Julian hastily. 'Please understand that I do appreciate all you are doing and I am sure you are being most conscientious in your search for her, but as you say, if she wishes to disappear, it is going to be very difficult to find her. It is for this reason that I should like to suggest offering a reward for her.'

'A reward?'

'Yes. I don't know how you feel about it, but I am prepared to pay ten pounds for news of her whereabouts.'

'Good gracious!' said Roland. 'That's very generous indeed. A reward of ten pounds for information might be a very promising idea. If someone knows where she is, but is keeping silent, a sum like that will prove a great temptation. I think that is a splendid plan, quite splendid.'

'I am very glad you feel that way and I wonder if I could trespass further on your kindness by sending you the money order to hold personally until required. I have also drafted an advertisement which I can insert in *The Times* personal column, although I doubt it will be read by the right people.'

Roland laughed. 'Very unlikely, I should think, but of course we must try every avenue. I am in a good position here to spread the news of the reward by word of mouth. I am on my way to a meeting now and I will add it to the agenda.'

'I would be tremendously grateful if you could,' said Julian. 'I shan't rest easy until we have found her.'

'None of us will,' said Roland. 'She is such an innocent.'

They spoke a little longer and Julian gave Roland a telephone number by which he could be reached at the University. Roland promised to do everything he could.

*

Roland rapped on the table and declared the meeting open. 'I will call on the new secretary to read the minutes of the last meeting,' he said, whereupon Mary Bellweather rose to her feet and read the account in her clear sweet voice. The minutes having been passed unanimously and signed, it was Roland's turn to stand. He looked round at the Committee, smiling with pleasure. In addition to himself and Mary, the members were Gareth Brooks, Lydia Grant and two middle-aged sisters, Agnes and Mary Harper.

'I would like to start promptly, because there is another unexpected item which I would like to discuss when we have dealt with the rest of the agenda. Mr Brooks, I believe you have something to say to us on the subject of temperance.'

Gareth cleared his throat. 'Ladies and gentlemen, as you know at the last meeting it was suggested that one of us investigate the problem of drunkenness in our own area and I volunteered to do this. I have in fact accumulated a large number of statistics.'

There was a loud groan from Lydia, followed by a ripple of good-humoured laughter.

'None of which I will burden you with,' Gareth continued, 'but I will put my conclusions as briefly as possible. I must confess that I did believe our involvement in this particular problem quite unnecessary, but since my enquiries I am utterly convinced that no matter how many people are already trying to tackle it, there is always room for more help. I firmly believe it is a problem we must come to grips with in whatever way we can. I attended a term in our local police courts and discovered that on every day of the week at least three-quarters or more of the cases would never have arisen had it not been for the demon drink.'

He paused to glance down at his notes and then resumed. 'We all know that wives are beaten by drunken husbands. We all know that people under the influence of drink are at the mercy of pick-pockets and thieves. We all know of men who will rob and steal to obtain money to spend on drink . . .'

Gareth went on to enlarge on his findings and the rest of the Committee listened intently to everything he had to say. When he sat down the subject was discussed and a resolution passed that if sufficient funds could be raised, hot tea or soup would be offered in the evening as well as at breakfast-time at half the price of beer. The hope was that men might thus be persuaded to drink two pints of good hot tea instead of one pint of cold bad ale.

The next item concerned the collection of second-hand garments from some of the wealthier residents in the area. Then there was a discussion of the ways in which they might raise more money for various aspects of their work. When finally all these points had been dealt with to everyone's satisfaction, Roland stood to address the meeting on the subject of Vinnie Harris and a great deal of interest was expressed at Julian's offer of a reward. Only Mary had little to say on the subject, but her apparent indifference went unremarked. It was decided that a large notice would be pinned up in the shed where the breakfast was served and that everybody's attention would be drawn to it.

'If we speak of the reward to every person who comes,' said Agnes, 'and urge them to tell everyone in their circle, the news will spread dramatically. May I suggest, however, that we word the notice carefully? I believe we should say that the reward will only be paid for information which leads to her discovery. Otherwise the first "Smart Alec" who pretends to have seen her will walk away with the ten pounds and once it is no longer available, interest in her whereabouts will fade and genuine information will not be forthcoming.'

There was a murmur of assent and Mary scribbled hurriedly.

Lydia offered to design an eye-catching poster describing the reward and then Mary Harper spoke.

'Do we know if the young man concerned wishes to be named in the poster?' she asked. 'Would it be better to refer to him as an anonymous donor?'

This point was debated at length, until Roland said he would be in contact with Julian again and would then ascertain his wishes in the matter.

'And now, before we go our separate ways,' he went on, 'I have one more sad duty to perform. That is to ask for all your prayers tonight for the bereaved families in Margate. It is now confirmed that nine men died when the lifeboat "Friend to all Nations" capsized. Most of us, if not all, have at some time spent a pleasant day in Margate and having seen it at its sunny best, it is hard to imagine it lashed by a terrible storm. But now the deaths of nine men have been confirmed. The funeral service will be held on Wednesday December the eighth, and if any of you wish to attend, please let me know as my father has a cousin living in the town who will let us have further details. If there are no more questions or comments' – he looked around but no one spoke – 'then I declare this meeting at an end.'

*

Vinnie made her way slowly along the crowded pavements, her eyes blinded by tears. It was a bitterly cold December day, but she was oblivious to her discomfort. She heard neither the clip-clop of hooves, the rattle of cart-wheels nor the impatient shouts of the drivers. She had just come from Harry Samm's home – if such a word could be used to describe the hovel in which he lived with his ailing wife. Yet it was not their degradation which had reduced her to tears. It was the news that her sister Em was dead and had been so for the past three years while Vinnie continued to live in false hopes.

In her search for Em, Vinnie had finally remembered Harry

Samm, the hopper's agent. She had discovered him after days of fruitless searching during which she had eaten virtually nothing and had only water to drink. By the time she arrived on his doorstep she was half-fainting with cold and hunger and only the desire to find her sister gave her strength to remain upright. Harry Samm, unaware of the reward offered for news of her whereabouts, had invited her in reluctantly and told her all he knew.

It seemed that some years earlier the Battys had defaulted on their rent and had been evicted. They had gone to Hetty Bluett, taking Emmeline with them, but Hetty's current 'gentleman friend' objected to their intrusion and at the end of the week, Hetty had regretfully told them to leave. In desperate straits by now, Mr Batty had stolen an umbrella from a passing carriage, intending to pawn it, but the coachman had followed him and handed him over to the police. After his first conviction, he had turned to full-time crime and was now serving a sentence for house-breaking. While he was at Wormwood Scrubs serving his first sentence, his wife had developed bronchitis which worsened until pneumonia set in. She never recovered her health and eventually died. Emmeline had been taken into the workhouse where she had lived for nearly three years before succumbing to an unspecified bowel disorder which might or might not have been dysentery.

Harry Samm went on to tell Vinnie that Hetty Bluett lived only a few streets away from him but that she would receive short shrift there. Hetty, it seemed, had married her gentleman friend and lived to rue the day – he earned little and spent most of it on gambling. Distressed and despairing, Vinnie was on the point of collapse. At Mrs Samm's insistence, they had given her a thick slice of bread and a cup of weak tea, but there the hospitality ended and Vinnie found herself once more in the street alone with her grief. At first she had struggled to keep back her tears but now, careless of curious looks from the passers-by, she gave way to the appalling sense of loss and loneliness which overwhelmed her. Only Bertie remained – if he was still living – and possibly her father. Vinnie did not care if she never saw her father again, because she blamed the family's disintegration on his initial desertion. But Em – poor little Em! What would Bertie say when he knew, she wondered. If only Bertie were alive – but she could not be sure even of that and the thought robbed her of any last shred of comfort.

She stumbled on, a pathetic figure, still wearing the clothes she had worn on the day she left Teesbury, though by now the dress was filthy and torn and the shoes let in the rain which fell steadily on to the dirty buildings and ran down the sooty walls to the street below. Ahead of her, at the corner, a crossing-sweeper darted in and out between the traffic to clear a path for the ladies to step along as they crossed from one side of the road to another.

Vinnie turned right and went down some steps into a narrow lane, then right again and down more steps. She had no idea where she was going and cared even less. After several more turns, she was completely lost and half-way down another flight of steps she sank down weary and defeated. Had she been offered the chance to die at that moment, she would have accepted willingly, for Harry Samm's news had effectively pushed all thoughts of survival to the back of her mind, leaving nothing but a black nightmare of despair.

'Are you all right, my dear?'

Vinnie ignored the voice.

'Are you unwell? Are you in need of help?'

The voice was strangely familiar and wearily Vinnie raised her head to look straight into the startled eyes of Mary Bellweather. The latter recognised her immediately and gave a slight gasp of shocked dismay.

'Vinnie Harris!'

Vinnie's eyes filled with tears which rolled unheeded down her face, mingling with the heavy drops of rain falling from Mary's large black umbrella.

'It's Em,' stammered Vinnie. 'My sister, Emmeline. She's dead! She's been dead three years and I didn't know. Buried somewhere and I don't know where – in a pauper's grave.' The words mingled with sobs. 'Poor Em, she was always so sickly, such a tiny little thing and Bertie used to make her laugh.'

Mary, her thoughts whirling, stammered a condolence but Vinnie seemed not to hear. 'Bertie made us all laugh then, even Ma. I was jealous of Em when she was born. They all made that much fuss of her instead of me and I cried when I saw her in Bertie's arms. Poor Em. I envied her her name, too, I thought Emmeline was so much nicer than Lavinia.' She broke off and put her hands over her face. Mary knew she ought to comfort her, but the words stuck in her throat.

'I wanted them to call me Em,' Vinnie went on, 'but they would not, though when I went to bed that night Bertie told me that Lavinia was the best name he'd ever heard. He said it was a name for fairy-tale princesses and I believed him. But it always hurt when I saw her in Bertie's arms.'

She sighed, and stared up into Mary's face. Mary had taken a step backwards and now regarded the wretched girl at her feet with very mixed feelings. She had found Vinnie Harris, the girl they had all been looking for, but she wished most desperately that she had not done so. Stupidly the phrase ran through her mind – 'he asked her to the hopping supper, before he asked me.' Did Roland prefer Vinnie Harris? In her present state she was most unappealing – dirty, haggard, wet and obviously with child. Whose child? It was anybody's guess. But public opinion had marked down Jarvis Tupp as the father.

Suddenly aware that Vinnie was looking up at her, Mary said, 'I'm sorry about your sister. I'm truly sorry.' She held out her hand to Vinnie and said, 'But do get up, you can't stay there.'

Vinnie ignored the outstretched hand, and stared at her blankly. 'A pauper's grave,' she said. 'Do you know what that means? A few planks nailed together in a hurry. That's what she had. That's what they buried her in: a few bits of wood knocked together in a hurry.'

There was horror in Vinnie's eyes as she stared into Mary Bellweather's face and Mary, normally so good with comfort, struggled for words.

'Well, it's all over now. She is at peace,' she said. 'Her soul is with God. The trappings of a burial don't really matter.'

'They matter to me,' said Vinnie. 'They'll matter to Bertie when he knows. He would not want her buried like that. I know he wouldn't.'

Mary looked around her and searched for some way to escape from the unwelcome encounter. She knew exactly where her duty lay but fought against it. She did not want to take Vinnie to Roland Fry, yet this was obviously the most likely moment at which to persuade her to go, for the shock of her sister's death had obviously driven all other thoughts from her mind. The desire for anonymity had probably gone also.

Vinnie closed her eyes and leaned back against the wall. As the rain increased it trickled down her matted hair and ran down her face into her collar. Water ran down the uneven steps and soaked into her skirt too, but if she was aware of any discomfort she gave no sign. While Mary still hesitated between the two courses of action open to her, a large middle-aged woman who was making her way up the steps paused to glare at Vinnie.

'Drunk at this time of the day,' she said to Mary. 'Disgusting, isn't it? They don't deserve your pity, Miss.'

Mary felt herself flush and muttered a reply, but Vinnie appeared not to have heard the woman's comments.

'Poor Em,' she said again, shaking her head slowly. 'Bertie will be that upset when he knows. I must write him a letter.'

'Do you know where your brother is?' asked Mary.

Vinnie shook her head. 'But I must find him,' she said. 'I must find Bertie.' She tried to struggle to her feet and Mary, suddenly unable to put out a helping hand, watched as she sank back exhausted.

Suddenly Mary had a flash of inspiration. 'You can't stay in London, Vinnie,' she said. 'You must go home. You must go back to Teesbury.' She waited hopefully, but there was no reaction from the girl at her feet.

'Do you hear me, Vinnie? Everyone is very worried about you. Mrs Bryce, the Colonel's wife – everyone. You must go home where you belong – where you are among friends. Then the father of your baby can look after you. He must be made to marry you!'

At last Vinnie raised her head. 'He can't do that,' she said.
'But he must,' Mary insisted. 'He must marry you and care for
you and the child.'

Vinnie shook her head. 'He's already wed,' she said. 'With
babes of his own.'

'Oh.' For a moment she was taken aback. Then she went on.
'Well, he must make provision for you, that's the least he can
do.'

'No,' said Vinnie, 'I don't want him to know. I don't want
him to make provision. I must find Bertie – he will tell me what
to do.'

From overhead there was a crack of thunder. Vinnie ignored
it but Mary, terrified of storms, glanced upwards in agitation.

'There's going to be a storm,' she said. 'I must go home, I
must get along. What will you do, Vinnie? Will you go back to
Teesbury where you belong? Do be a sensible girl and say
yes.'

Vinnie shook her head and covered her face with her hands.
There was a flash of lightning and the thunder rolled
ominously nearer. Mary opened her purse, took out some
money and forced it into Vinnie's right hand. 'There,' she said,
'that's the train fare and a little extra. Go now and get yourself
something to eat, then go to the station. Go back where you
belong, Vinnie. I promise you it will be best. Do you hear me?'

Vinnie made no effort to examine the money she had been
given and seemed not to hear Mary's exhortations. There was
another flash of lightning and thunder reverberated in the
alley. Without a backward glance, Mary picked up her skirts
and ran.

Later that evening, she gave Roland a carefully edited
version of her chance meeting with Vinnie. 'But I couldn't
persuade her to come with me,' she ended. 'She absolutely
refused, so what could I do? I couldn't drag her bodily through
the streets.'

'Of course not.' His disappointment was obvious and Mary
felt a deep pang of remorse.

'I don't blame you at all,' he said. 'I am sure you did your
best.'

'She insists that she will find Bertie and tell him of her sister's death.'

'Poor Vinnie,' said Roland. 'If only I had been there. The two of us could have persuaded her, I am sure of it. Oh, Mary, if only you knew what this means to me. Do you remember at that first meeting you attended, I said that if all our efforts resulted in saving just one girl from ruin, then we could count ourselves well satisfied?'

Mary nodded.

'Well, don't you see, Vinnie Harris is that girl? The one girl. Over these last weeks she has become the symbol of everything we have struggled for. At least to me. Oh, I know we give breakfast to the hungry and we do all we can for the unfortunate wretches around us, but we are not really involved. With Vinnie, it's quite different. We know her, her background, her hopes and fears. She's more deserving of our time than any of the others. Can you understand that, Mary?'

'I accept that is how you feel about her,' Mary said cautiously, 'but surely Vinnie is a sinner whether we know her well or not. Surely, no single unfortunate should take up more of our time than another. That means we are judging them, doesn't it?' she went on. 'We are deciding which of them deserves our attention. I don't think we should allow personal feelings to interfere with our work.'

Roland was clearly surprised by her stand and for a moment he made no answer. Then he said, 'But Vinnie is a respectable girl who has fallen upon hard times. If we save her, we can restore her to a state of respectability again. Most of the people with whom we work will never achieve that state. This is no fault of theirs, but the fact remains that they will always need our charity and compassion. Vinnie will not. Are you advocating that we shrug our shoulders and let her remain at the bottom of the heap? You can't mean that, Mary, surely?'

Mary's heart sank and she regretted entering into such an argument, but it was too late to withdraw.

'At least Vinnie chose to be where she is now,' she said with a hint of bitterness. 'She ran away from good and loving friends. Most of the people with whom we deal have been the victims of cruel circumstances, illness and unemployment, or family problems. Vinnie Harris had a life that these people would have envied and she chose to throw it all away. We don't know why, but she did.'

Roland was looking at her strangely and a cold fear touched Mary's heart.

'We don't know that,' he said quietly. 'We don't know that she chose to throw it away. In fact, I think it most unlikely. I think something happened that made her run away.'

'We all know what that was,' cried Mary. 'She is with child, by all accounts. Oh, Roland, don't look at me that way! I know you don't want to believe it but it must be so and she must have done that of her own free will.'

Roland turned his face away. 'You surprise me, Mary,' he said. 'I thought you more charitable. You judge the girl most harshly and seem determined to think the worst of her. The child – if she is with child – may be the result of physical assault. You seem unwilling to give her the benefit of the doubt.'

As they walked on a painful silence developed between them. They had spent the evening at Lydia's home sorting some second-hand clothes which they had collected. Now Roland was walking Mary home before returning to his own.

Mary's heart beat faster and her thoughts were agonised. Surely now Roland would guess that the feeling which overpowered her was one of jealousy. Would he recognise the fear she felt that the difference of opinion over Vinnie Harris could spoil the deepening relationship between them? Mary genuinely believed herself a more suitable partner for Roland and her feelings for him had developed rapidly from affection and respect to deep love. She was in love with Roland and although she knew that his feelings did not match hers in intensity, they enjoyed each other's company and she nursed a hope that one day he would return her love in full. Now, suddenly, it seemed Vinnie Harris' ghost stood between them and in a flash of bitterness Mary wished that she had walked right past the forlorn figure on the steps. She could have pretended not to see her, but her conscience would have troubled her. Roland was striding along and Mary found herself almost running to keep up with him. He stopped abruptly and turned to her.

'In spite of your apparent disapproval,' he said, 'I shall go on looking for Vinnie. I shan't give up until I find her, which with God's help I will do.'

CHAPTER SEVENTEEN

Christina was reading a letter when Eva entered the breakfast room. She was seated at the long table with her back to the window; the bright sunlight silhouetted her well-groomed head and slim neck and the indirect lighting softened her face, making it still beautiful.

'A letter from Agatha,' she told her daughter. 'She has arrived in India and seems to be enjoying herself.' She turned her attention from the letter to butter a triangle of toast and spread marmalade on it, unaware of her daughter's tense manner. Eva sat down opposite her and picked up the silver tea-pot.

'Pour me a second cup, will you, dear?'

Eva obeyed and then filled her own cup, spilling some of the tea into the saucer as her hand trembled.

'Agatha says Louise is determined to find her a husband and has arranged a great many dinner parties and visits,' Christina told her. She turned the pages, searching for the relevant paragraph.

'Ah, here it is. "Louise is a model of domesticity and motherhood and is determined to bring about the same transformation in me." If Agatha cannot find a husband in India, she will never find one.' She read on. '"The bungalow is very charming and the garden as English as they can make it. Servants are everywhere, one to cut the grass, one to feed the dogs, one to stand guard at the door. I think I shall never become used to so many pairs of eyes watching my every movement, but Louise says it is inevitable. She and Rupert seem very attached to one another and the children, all five of them, are well behaved although we see them only rarely as they are in the charge of an ayah, that is, a nurse. Yesterday we went riding – on camels!"' Christina smiled. 'Can you imagine Agatha riding on a camel?'

'No, Mama.'

'Somewhere else she speaks of an uprising . . .' She skimmed the pages impatiently, 'Ah, yes. "During the journey out there was much talk of the Orakzai tribesmen who massacred twenty-one men defending a fort. I was very alarmed and feared I had chosen a bad time to visit India, but Rupert assured me it was an isolated incident and nothing of the kind will ever happen here, for which I was immensely thankful."'

Christina laughed again. 'What women will do to find a husband! Still, already it seems she is being wooed by both a young subaltern and a middle-aged planter. English women are definitely at a premium and the man who cannot snare one is forced to take an Indian mistress. I think it unlikely we shall ever see Agatha again.'

She glanced at her daughter to see her reaction to this last remark and noticed for the first time the girl's uneasiness.

'Have you heard a word I said, Eva?'

Slowly, Eva raised her eyes and met those of her mother.

'Mama, I have something to ask you,' she said nervously.

'And that is?' Christina's tone was not encouraging.

'I would like to invite a friend to visit me,' said Eva. 'At least, he is already on his way.'

She saw her mother's eyes narrow. 'Already on his way? You mean a gentleman friend of yours is about to visit us uninvited?'

'Yes. That is, not exactly. The fact is, *I* invited him.'

'*You* invited him?'

'Well, no. He asked if he might come to Foxearth to speak to father and I said yes.'

Very deliberately Christina laid down the letter, picked up her napkin and dabbed at the corners of her mouth, then laid the napkin down again beside the plate and looked at her daughter with cold eyes.

'And when was all this arranged, may I ask?' she enquired.

'Sunday morning, Mama. He telephoned on Sunday morning while you were at church.'

Christina raised her eyebrows. 'Ah,' she said coldly, 'the headache that kept you at home. He obviously encourages you to be deceitful, this friend of yours. May I ask why he wishes to visit and speak to your father?'

'I am sure you can guess, Mama.'

'Indeed I can't guess, Eva. I am not in the habit of making guesses, as you well know. If a perfect stranger suddenly invites himself to visit us without obtaining our consent, then I cannot imagine what he would want to discuss with your father. But no doubt you will tell us in your own good time.'

'I am trying to tell you now, Mama.'

'You are not being very successful then. Perhaps you had better start at the beginning. Who is this friend, where did you meet him and what are his intentions towards you?'

Unable to bear her mother's cold manner, Eva suddenly pushed back her chair and stood up. She took a deep breath. 'He wants to marry me, Mama. He loves me and I return his feelings. His name is Gerry Cottingham. I have met him several times when I visited Wiltshire. He is Toby's closest friend.' Toby Lawrence was the Colonel's nephew. 'He comes from a very respectable family, Mama, and is a qualified engineer with the railway. His firm thinks very highly of him—'

'Does Toby's father know of this friendship of yours? If so, it's strange that your father was not told.'

'I think he must be aware of it,' said Eva, 'but it hardly matters. What matters is that we love each other and that Gerry is on his way over to ask Papa's permission for us to wed. I am certain you will approve of him, Mama, when you meet him. He is most eligible in every way—'

Christina's expression was grim. 'I wish I could share your enthusiasm, Eva,' she said icily, 'but I can assure you nothing is certain in this world. Least of all, my acceptance of a complete stranger into the family. Surely Mr Cottingham knows this is not the way to conduct a courtship. He has been most secretive, indeed you both have. It is hardly a promising start to negotiations of the kind you are suggesting, and I am quite sure your father would agree with me.'

'But he does know, Mama. I have spoken to him already, before I came down to breakfast, in fact.'

Christina's jaw tightened ominously. 'That was very high-handed of you, Eva. May I ask why you did such a thing?'

Eva stared at her defiantly. 'It's Papa he wishes to speak to,' she said.

'Nevertheless, your father is not fit, as you well know, and I like to think I shield him from most responsibilities. You should have spoken to me and then I would have spoken to your father. I think you knew that very well, Eva, but chose to ignore it for reasons best known to yourself.'

'I think you know the reason why I did it, Mama. I knew you would disapprove and I knew you would try to persuade father not to see him.'

'If I thought it in your own best interests, I certainly would persuade him not to see Mr Cottingham. But perhaps you had better tell me a little more about him. All I know at present is his name and his occupation. I don't want a list of his virtues but I would like to—'

'Mama! He will be here in a moment. There is no time to tell you more. I'm sorry but I had to do it this way. I knew if I asked you in advance you would tell him not to come. I love him and I mean to marry him. Whatever you say of him and whatever you may think of him, to me he is the dearest man in the world.'

'Eva, you are behaving like a child. In fact, you *are* only a child, not yet eighteen and still very immature. This whole matter is most distasteful, but I will agree to see him and if he is to be here to lunch, you had better tell Mrs Tallant.'

'Oh, Mama—'

Christina held up a hand to silence her.

'Save your gratitude, Eva,' she said. 'I am only inviting this young man to lunch out of courtesy, not because I expect to like him. You may rest assured that if I don't consider him suitable, then I shall say so and no entreaties on your part will sway my judgement.'

She stood up, her movements calm and unhurried and quite in contrast to Eva's distracted air. 'I see no reason, Eva, why you should not have told me months ago of your growing attachment to this young man.'

'Mama, I could not because he had not spoken to me of his own feelings.'

'It is quite illogical, Eva. If I had known of your feelings for him we could have invited him over with Toby and Violet on some pretext or other.' She sighed with exasperation. 'However, it is done and if he is about to appear we must at least be ready for him. Speak to Mrs Tallant at once and I will go upstairs to speak to your father. But remember, Eva, please don't raise your hopes too high.'

*

Much to Christina's surprise and almost to her disappointment, she found herself liking Gerald Cottingham and the visit turned out to be pleasant for everyone concerned. He arrived while Christina and Henry were still discussing the question of Eva's engagement and she hurried down to greet him. She was at once charmed by his relaxed yet confident manner and his undeniable good looks. Gerald Cottingham was the kind of man most parents would wish their daughter to marry and he was well aware of this without being conceited. He came from a wealthy family and had always found the world a most agreeable place. Some of his ideas were rather unconventional, but he explained them in such an amusing way that it was difficult to argue with him and luncheon passed most agreeably in his company.

The Colonel was impressed with his expertise and his prospects and could not fault his background. Christina, in spite of earlier misgivings, was forced to agree his eligibility as Eva's future husband. In fact, she thought it unlikely she would find anyone more suitable. Gerald had brought with him a letter from his father in which he invited Eva and her parents to visit them at Heathleigh, their home in Devizes, explaining that he was a widower but his daughter managed the house and would make them comfortable and feed them well. Gerald was pressed to stay overnight and return home the following morning and he accepted willingly.

Later that evening, Gerald and Eva strolled in the garden together. They walked sedately down the path bordering the land whilst still in view of the house, but as soon as they turned the corner and were hidden by the tall cypress hedge, Gerald took Eva in his arms and for a while they clung together speechlessly, overjoyed at their good fortune. Then Eva turned her face up towards his and they kissed.

'At last I have got you to myself,' he said. 'I began to think that I would go to bed tonight without having the opportunity to talk to you. My dear Eva, I think we are going to be husband and wife!'

'My dear Gerry, I do believe we are,' she answered, breathless with excitement at the glittering prospect which awaited them.

'And yet at breakfast this morning,' Eva told him, 'when I spoke to Mama I was sure she was going to make trouble for us. She was so cold and as furious as you said she would be.'

'It was bound to be a shock, but I thought it better to tell them this way than give them time to work on their objections,' said Gerald.

Standing on tip-toe, Eva kissed him again.

'I dare say you are very pleased with yourself, Gerald Cottingham. Your little plan has worked perfectly and I for one am thankful for it. I can hardly believe they have given permission. I shall write to Julian tomorrow – no, better still, I shall telephone him at his rooms. He will be so pleased. Now tell me what you thought of Papa. Isn't he a splendid old man?'

'He is indeed.' He took her hand and they began to stroll along in the direction of the hop-gardens.

'And Mama?'

He shrugged. 'She was not the ogre you made her out to be. I was quite prepared to do battle with her but it proved unnecessary.'

'You charmed her, that's why,' said Eva. 'I thought she would find you attractive, but I feared she would be jealous.'

'Jealous?'

'Of me, Gerry. Or would protest that I was too young or too immature. That's her favourite word for me. I sometimes wonder how mature she was at my age.'

'I am sure you do her an injustice.'

'No, Gerry, I face facts. Remember, I know her better than you do, but let us not talk of her now. Let's talk of our life together and when we shall be wed and where we will live and all those wonderful things I have not dared to think about until now. Am I immature, do you think?'

'I would not say so but if you are, it is part of your charm.'

'But will I make you a good wife, Gerry? Are you sure I am the right woman for you?'

He laughed. 'You are fishing for compliments, Eva, but why shouldn't you? Of course you are the right woman for me. In my eyes there is no one to match you and I have never for a moment considered any other woman.'

'Oh Gerry!'

She clung to him again and he stroked her hair and kissed the top of her head gently. Suddenly she pulled back a little, her eyes gleaming with mischief.

'Isn't it terrible that at the most exciting moment of my life all I can do is to walk along this path in a ladylike fashion, when what I want to do is throw my hat in the air or turn a cartwheel or scream for joy.'

'Do all those things,' he laughed. 'I shall take great delight in watching you.'

It was Eva's turn to laugh. 'I dare not,' she said. 'It would be too, too immature!'

'Then I will do it for you,' said Gerald and before she knew what was happening, he had taken her hatpin and sent her hat spinning high into the air. Eva screamed indignantly.

'The hat and the scream,' he laughed. 'All that remains is the cartwheel.'

'Gerald Cottingham! Who is immature now?'

'It was your idea.'

'Then do you challenge me to turn a cartwheel? Perhaps you think I cannot.'

'I am sure you can, but why not prove it to me?'

By way of answer Eva picked up her skirts, took a few steps and then threw herself hand over hand to land unceremoniously beside a rhododendron bush. Her dark auburn hair, free of its hat, tumbled about her shoulders and her skirts billowed round her as she patted the ground beside her.

'Come and sit with me, you awful man, and stop smirking. If my hat was seen from the house I shall blame it on to your bad influence.'

He sprawled beside her on the grass, supporting himself on one elbow. 'I shall say that a gust of wind took your hat,' he said, 'and I was about to go after it when you pulled me to the ground.'

'A lie!' she protested. 'A wicked lie. You are not the man I thought you were, but I love you still. You might turn out to be a devil in disguise, but I fear you would still have my heart.'

The laughter had faded and she regarded him earnestly, her face radiant, her eyes tender and full of love. Gerald took her hand in his.

'My dear little Eva, I swear I will make you a good husband. I swear I will care for you and make you happy.'

Eva smiled. 'And I swear I will make you a good wife, the best wife any man ever had. At least I will try, and I will give you fine healthy sons and beautiful daughters. Oh, tell me it is not a dream. Tell me this is really happening!'

'It's not a dream, Eva. We will be married as soon as it can be arranged and for the rest of our lives you and I will be together.'

Gently and lovingly, he took her into his arms and as the twilight deepened and the air grew chill, they talked happily about their future.

*

At Foxearth the evening meal had been cleared away and the washing-up done. Now the staff sat round the big scrubbed table enjoying their own meal and exchanging jokes and snippets of news garnered during the day. Tim Bilton was in the middle of a story about a miserly Scotsman when the back door burst open and young Harry rushed in. Everyone turned to stare at him and Mrs Tallant regarded him severely. 'What are you doing back, young Harry?' she said. 'You have only just this minute left. I thought you had to be home early for—'

'It's Miss Eva,' he said, interrupting her in his eagerness to tell what he had overheard. 'It's Miss Eva and that young man of hers – they're engaged to be married.'

'Who says?' demanded Janet.

'I thought as much,' said Cook. 'When Miss Eva comes flying in here this morning to say lay an extra place for lunch, I thought to meself—'

'I tell you I heard it with me own ears,' young Harry told them. 'I was on my way to the stables when suddenly this hat flies up into the air—'

'Hat? What hat?'

'Why, Miss Eva's hat, spinning right up into the sky it was and then I heard her scream and then she laughed – they were both laughing – and he says to her what about the cartwheel and she says—'

'What are you *on* about, young Harry?' asked Edie.

She had grown slower with the years and found it impossible to grasp the significance of what he was telling them.

'Are you having us on, young Harry?' Mrs Tallant asked. 'Because if you are . . .'

'I'm not having you on, honest to God. Cross my heart and hope to die, if I'm telling you a lie.' He made a hasty crossing motion and Tim Bilton whistled expressively.

'Engaged, are they? Bit sudden, isn't it?'

'What do you mean?' Janet demanded, ever loyal to her young mistress. 'What do you mean by "a bit sudden"?'

'Nothing really,' said Tim hastily, 'but I mean, we've never heard nothing of this young fella.'

'Tim's right,' said Cook, 'we haven't. Mind you, *I* would say "Yes" if he asked me. He's a nice-looking man. Handsome, real handsome he is and that lovely wavy hair.'

'Who?' asked Edie.

'And those dark eyes.'

'Oh, you've had a good look at him then,' said Tim and then to Edie, 'Miss Eva's young man.'

'Has she got a young man, then?'

'So it seems,' said Janet. 'Go on, young Harry. What happened next?'

He shrugged. 'I don't know because I couldn't see, but there was a lot of laughing and then it all went quiet.'

'Ooh,' said Janet. 'How quiet? Very quiet?'

He nodded, and they all exchanged delighted grins.

'Did you hear any kissing noises?' asked Janet.

'Real kissing doesn't make noises,' said Cook.

'How do you know? I bet you've never been kissed.'

'Well, that's where you are wrong, 'cos I have. A long time ago, mind. But I have and I remember it as though it was yesterday.' They regarded her with doubtful eyes, for her present appearance defied the imagination.

'What, before you come here?' Janet asked.

Cook nodded. 'At my last place. Last and first place as you might say, when I was scullery maid. I was fourteen at the time but a big girl for my age.'

'You're a big girl now,' said Tim and ducked, grinning, as she took a swipe at him.

'He was the gardener's boy—'

'Don't look at me,' said young Harry.

'I wouldn't, not if you paid me,' said Cook calmly. 'Stanley, 'is name was. Stanley Morris, that was it. He had the same sort of hair as Miss Eva's young man. Wavy, just the same.'

But a reference to Miss Eva's young man brought them all back to the present and losing interest in her story, they turned once more to young Harry.

'Well,' said Mrs Tallant, 'is that all? Think you've told us everything, 'cos if so, you had better get off home. All that fuss about you mustn't be late.'

'I mustn't be late,' said young Harry. 'It's me Ma's birthday and I promised I would be there for the end of the jollifications.' He frowned. 'Is that all? Well, yes, I think that's all. Like I said, it all went quiet with them kissing and everything and I come back here to tell you.'

'I should think so too,' said Cook. 'I do hate to miss anything. Thanks, young Harry.'

'You had best be off, then,' said Mrs Tallant.

He hesitated a moment longer, racking his brains for any detail with which to hold their interest. Failing, he nodded 'Goodnight' and went out. Janet, her knife and fork poised to resume eating, laid them down suddenly. 'I wonder where they are now,' she said. 'If we were to look out from an upstairs window we might see them.'

'See who?' said Edie. 'Who are we going to see?'

'No one,' said Mrs Tallant sharply. 'Get on with your dinner, Edie.'

They continued their meal in silence. Then Janet said, 'I reckon we could see them from Cook's bedroom. If we were to creep up there one at a time—'

'You will do no such thing,' said Mrs Tallant. 'That's spying, that is. Pass the salt, please, Tim.'

Janet looked rebellious. 'No one would know,' she said. 'Not even them. I mean, no one could mind if no one knew.'

They all looked appealingly at Mrs Tallant, who hesitated. All except Cook, that is. 'Well, I'm not traipsing up all them stairs,' she said, 'just to stare at a courting couple.'

'Well, you could hold the fort, then,' said Janet. 'In case anyone comes into the kitchen. It would look a bit funny if none of us was here. I reckon they make a lovely couple, Miss Eva and that young man.'

She attacked her dinner with enthusiasm, as Mrs Tallant wavered. 'We-ell,' she said, 'I suppose if we are quiet and if Cook doesn't mind . . .'

Cook shook her head good-naturedly and there was a clatter of knives and forks as Tim, Mrs Tallant and Janet stood up.

'Just don't you touch anything,' Cook warned.

'We won't,' said Janet. 'Come on, Edie.'

'Where are we going?'

'Upstairs, you'll see.'

'Where's her ladyship?' asked Tim.

'She went into the Colonel's study,' said Janet. 'She won't hear us if we go up the back stairs.'

The housekeeper and Cook had a room each at the top of the house. Janet and Edie shared one. No one had ever been in Cook's room before, and they stared round curiously. In one corner there was an iron bedstead covered by a hand-made patchwork quilt and on the pillow a nightgown was neatly folded. A table held a wash-basin, water jug and soap holder which did not match; a flannel, folded into a neat square, lay on top of the soap. There was a small fireplace in which a few twigs had been arranged to soften the effect. A narrow mantelpiece jutted out above, on which was arranged a selection of photographs in a variety of frames. Several letters were tucked behind a small blue vase at one end. The bare floor was well-scrubbed and a striped jute rug had been placed in the centre. At the opposite end of the room to the bed was a small table and a chair; a game of patience on the table had obviously been abandoned half-way through. Placed in front of the dormer window was a small chest of drawers with a hand-worked runner draped across the top, on which stood a little china dog and two mugs celebrating Queen Victoria's Golden and Diamond Jubilees. From two hooks screwed into the wall hung Cook's Sunday uniform and her 'walking-out' clothes.

'You'd best move those bits of china off there before you go leaning out,' Mrs Tallant warned.

They did as they were bid and then Tim leaned across the chest of drawers to look out of the window.

'Can you see them?' asked Janet. 'Here, let me have a look. Move over a bit, Tim, you don't have to take up all the window.'

'What can you see?' asked Mrs Tallant, who was too short to see anything out of the window.

'I can't see a thing. There's nothing to see,' said Tim. 'I wonder if young Harry was having us on.'

'I don't think he was,' said Mrs Tallant, 'but maybe they've gone in. Oh, what a stupid place to put a chest of drawers. I'll never be able to see over that. Get me a chair, Tim, there's a love.'

Reluctantly Tim tore himself away from the window and

carried over the chair. Mrs Tallant climbed up and was thus able to lean out even further than the others.

'I see them!' she cried. 'They're coming in. You'll have to be quick. They're coming up to the house. He's got his arm around her. Oh, they do look lovely!'

'Oh, let me have a look,' cried Janet. 'I'm going to miss them. Move over, Mrs Tallant, will you? Let me get a foot on that chair. Oh, yes, I see them. Oh, look at the way she's smiling up at him. Doesn't she look lovely? He's a really lucky man.'

'How am I supposed to see,' cried Tim, 'with your two heads in the way? And Edie has not seen anything yet. Come on, Edie, make a bit of room for her, you two.'

Janet reluctantly stepped down and Edie took her place with one foot on the chair. Unfortunately, she was more heavily built than Janet and the frail chair creaked ominously.

'What am I looking at?' cried Edie. 'I can't see nothing.'

'Down there,' said Mrs Tallant. 'It's Miss Eva and her intended.'

'Can you still see them?' said Janet. 'Let me have another look before it's too late.'

'Oh!' cried Mrs Tallant. 'He's kissed her hand! That's so romantic.'

'He's kissed her hand?' cried Janet. 'Oh, I must see them. Edie, come down from there, you've had long enough. It must be my turn by now.'

She took hold of Edie's skirt and pulled it, but Edie slapped her hand irritably and refused to give up her privileged position.

'Where are they?' she yelled. 'I can't see them.'

'Well, if you can't see them, you might as well get down,' cried Janet and this time she gave the other girl's arm a tug. Edie jerked away from her, nearly knocking Mrs Tallant from her precarious position on the other half of the chair, which rocked precariously under the shift of weight.

'You'll have us all over!' cried Mrs Tallant but it was too late. As she and Edie fought to retain their balance, the chair suddenly gave way under the strain with a horrible rending sound. Edie managed to cling on to the chest of drawers, but Mrs Tallant fell backwards into Tim Bilton's arms with a muffled scream.

'Now look what you've done!' he cried.

'Don't blame me. It was her fault, she pushed me.'

'You shouldn't have—'

'What on earth is Cook going to say?'

'Who's going to tell her?'

'Not me,' said Janet, 'because I wasn't even *on* the chair when it broke.'

'But it was your fault we fell.'

Tim was examining the chair. The back legs had almost parted company with the seat and were splayed incongruously. Janet giggled nervously.

'Looks like a horse kicking up its back legs,' she said. 'Can you mend it, Tim?'

He looked at it doubtfully. 'I might be able to,' he said, 'but not before Cook comes up to bed. I'm not a magician.' Edie began to cry suddenly and Tim put his arm round her shoulders.

'Don't take on, Edie. No one is blaming you.'

'Well, I hope no one is blaming *me*,' said Janet.

'No one is blaming anybody,' said Mrs Tallant peaceably. 'We will just have to tell Cook how it happened and say we are sorry. Tim will mend it for her tomorrow.'

'I didn't say I would,' said Tim. 'I said I'd try.'

'You will,' said Mrs Tallant firmly. 'If you can't mend a bit of a broken chair, then it's a poor do, Tim Bilton.' She tugged at the legs of the chair, restoring it to something like its normal appearance.

'Now stop worrying, Edie,' she said, 'and let's get downstairs again or we will have the mistress up here, wondering what all the noise is about.'

This last threat was enough to send them hurrying downstairs, bickering in loudly hushed whispers as they went, as to who should break the bad news to Cook.

*

Later that same evening, just over a mile away, Rose lay wide awake beside her sleeping husband, staring unseeingly into the darkness around her. She had something to say to him and was at a loss how best to say it – and until she had perfected her little speech she was fearful of waking him. Finally, she turned towards him and pressed her face against his broad back.

'Tom,' she murmured. 'Tom, wake up.'

'Mmm?'

'Wake up, Tom.'

He stirred, muttering sleepily. Her courage almost failed her but she persisted.

'Tom wake up, I want to talk to you. It's most important.'

Slowly he came awake and turned over. 'What's the matter? What's wrong?'

He sat up, looking automatically towards the other room where the children all slept like sardines on the large mattress.

'It's not the children,' said Rose. 'It's something else I want to talk about. Are you properly awake, Tom?'

'Of course I'm awake.' He turned to look at her and she saw his profile silhouetted against the light of the window and swallowed hard.

'It's about Vinnie Harris,' she said. 'I want to ask you something, Tom, and I want you to tell me truthfully. I went to see Jarvis Tupp today.'

'Oh?'

'I asked him about Vinnie. About that day. I took a bible with me and I made him put his hand on it. Tom, he swore that Vinnie's baby isn't his.'

'Well, he would, wouldn't he?' She could hear the caution in his voice.

'I believe him, Tom.'

Slowly he slid back between the sheets. 'So,' he said, 'you woke me up at this hour to tell me that?'

'No, not only that Tom. I want to ask you something and I don't want you to be angry. At least I think you will be, but whether or not you are I must still ask it.'

'Look,' said Tom, 'Vinnie Harris is nothing to do with you or me. She has run away—'

'Isn't she, Tom? Isn't she anything to do with you? Would you put *your* hand on the bible and swear, like Jarvis Tupp did? Would you swear your soul away to eternal damnation if I ask you?' She propped herself on one elbow, staring at his face in the darkness.

'Do you know what they are saying, Tom? Some people are saying that if it is not Jarvis Tupp's baby, it must be yours. Is it yours, Tom?'

She heard him draw a deep breath.

'Tom, please tell me the truth. If it is, I'm not going to make a scene. I'm not even going to be angry, but I must know the truth. They say that when she left Jarvis Tupp, she came here. At least, that's what I heard; if she did, I wasn't here but you were and you have been so strange since that day. Not your old self at all. It is your baby, isn't it Tom?'

'It could be,' he admitted after a long silence.

'Oh, Tom!' The words sprang from her lips. She did not intend them.

'I only said it could be. Now don't take on. You *would* know and now you do. It could be, that's all I am saying.'

'You and Vinnie, Tom.'

'Look, Rose, I am not going to talk about it. You pressed me for an answer and now you've got it. Nothing has changed except that you know. It was just a sort of accident and she doesn't mean anything to me. It's done and can't be undone. The chances are the kid will die anyway.'

'Tom, how can you?' Rose was shocked. 'That child will be half yours.'

'I know, I know, but what chance does she have with no money and most likely no job?'

'But Tom, it's your baby. You can't just let it die.'

'What else can I do?'

'Tom! You're talking about a little girl like Bertha or Grace or a boy like Tommy. How can you just let it die? You must do something, Tom. You've got to go up there and find her and bring the baby back. We can adopt it, Tom. One more won't make any difference – but . . .' – her voice quivered – 'I don't want to see Vinnie Harris, Tom, not ever again. Oh, I wish it *was* Jarvis Tupp's child and she could wed him and likely it would all turn out for the best.'

'Well, it isn't Jarvis Tupp's,' said Tom, 'but the idea is quite mad. Even if I wanted to go to London, how could I take time off without giving a very good reason?'

Rose struggled into a sitting position. 'Then give a good reason, Tom. Go to Mrs Lawrence, and tell her the truth. Tell her I want to adopt the baby. Stand up to her, Tom, and make her listen.'

He did not answer and she went on, 'Oh, I know why you don't want to tell her. I know that too, Tom. I have always known. One woman isn't enough for you. I know that and I can live with it, Tom, because I love you. Folk may whisper about us but I don't care. I've got you and the children and that's all I want and I don't want any child of yours dying in the London gutter. So you've got to do something, Tom.'

Tom was taken aback by her directness. He had always congratulated himself on keeping his liaison secret but now it seemed she had always known and loved him in spite of it. He felt ashamed, although nothing would have induced him to say so. The thought of approaching Christina appalled him, but he had never known his wife in this mood and was afraid she might take matters into her own hands. As if to confirm this, she said, 'If you won't go and look for her, Tom, I will. I'll leave the kids with my mother and I'll go to London on the train.'

'Don't talk such nonsense,' Tom said angrily. 'You'll do no such thing, Rose.'

'I will, Tom, I swear I will. If *you* won't do something about Vinnie's baby, *I* will. If you are scared to face Mrs Lawrence, I'll go. I'm not scared of her. I'll tell her everything I know and I'll tell her that I love you and that—'

'You stay away from Christina,' cried Tom. 'If there's any telling to do, I will do it myself. I don't know what to say, Rose, and that's the truth. You'll have to let me think it over. You must give me time.'

'Then you will go? You will go to London and look for her?'

'Maybe, though what good it will do, I can't think. There's enough folks looking for her already. And if they can't find her, what makes you think I can?'

'Perhaps you will look harder,' Rose snapped suddenly, 'because it was you made her with child. Oh, Tom, please don't let's quarrel. I love you and you've hurt me very much, but I forgive you and I can't say fairer than that. You aren't a bad man, Tom, you work hard and you have a kind heart and you're a good father to the kids. But we must do something about that baby or I will never rest easy again.'

'I know, I know,' he said, 'and I'm sorry, Rose. I wish to God it had never happened. But it has and I suppose you're right. We must do something.'

'Promise me, Tom? You promise you will do something about it?'

'I promise, Rose. My poor little Rose, come here.' He took her into his arms.

'I'll think what's best to do, Rose. I swear it. I didn't mean to hurt you. I love you, you know that.' She nodded without answering and he held her close as her warm tears began to fall on his chest.

*

The Relieving Officer leaned forward over his desk, cradling his head in his hands. The former ached abominably and not for the first time he cursed his brother-in-law. Whenever he and his wife visited, they all ate and drank far too much and now as usual he was suffering for it. His stomach churned uneasily and he had been unable to eat any breakfast. The few words he had exchanged with his wife had not improved his temper and the prospect of his working day was not a cheerful one.

A naturally kind man, it depressed him to deal day after day with life's unfortunates, a dozen of whom were already waiting outside the door when he arrived. He was glad that his job was only to record their various predicaments, and that decisions as to what relief should be offered them would be taken by others. He took the watch from his waistcoat pocket and studied it blearily: two more minutes. Thankfully, he returned the large silver Hunter to his pocket and leaned back in the chair, his legs stretched out under the table and his left hand clutching his stomach. The first person would come into the office on the hour and not a minute earlier. Half-heartedly, he scratched at a stain on his jacket, but his efforts seemed to make matters worse, so he gave up and turned his attention to his desk. There was very little ink in the inkwell, but he decided it would be sufficient for the day; he would re-fill it tomorrow from the large bottle on the lowest shelf of the cupboard behind him. He opened the ledger, removed some tattered blotting-paper and took up a small wooden ruler. With this he marked off the previous day's entries and then wrote the date on the right-hand side two lines below. 'January 3rd 1898.' He underlined it with the ruler and blotted it carefully, pressing the blotting paper with the edge of a flabby hand. Then he laid down his pen, took another look at his watch and sighed. His name was George Hooper and he was nearing fifty.

'First!' he shouted and picked up his pen. An elderly woman shuffled in and he pointed to the narrow chair in front of his desk. She sat down and pulled her shawl close around her thin shoulders. Grey hair straggled untidily from her ancient bonnet.

'Name?' he said.

'Emily Reece.'

'Single or married?'

'Married but my husband—'

'Age?'

'Sixty-two, but my husband—'

'Occupation?'

'I was in service, sir for—'

'Home address?'

'I have nowhere, sir. I was—'

'Nowhere?'

'No, sir. I did have, sir. I lived with my daughter, but she's dead now. Died a week back. Dead and buried, sir.' He wrote slowly with a neat copperplate hand.

'I don't want to go in, sir,' she said. 'I just need a little money to tide me over.'

'Tide you over? Tide you over until when?' He looked at her curiously.

'Till better times, sir. I've never been in the Union, sir, and I don't want to. I just need a bit of money—'

'It isn't up to me,' he said quickly. 'I just take particulars, that's all.'

He finished writing, looked up and called 'Next!' in a loud voice.

'But, sir, I—'

'Your case will go before the Board,' he told her. 'Attend at the Union Workhouse a week tomorrow. Wait outside the Board room and you will get a decision.'

'But aren't you going to give me any money?'

'I don't have any money to give. I just take the particulars.'

The door opened and a young man hesitated in the opening. Mr Hooper beckoned him in and then, with the same hand, waved the woman outside. She, too, hesitated a moment but then shuffled out. The same finger which beckoned the man in now pointed him towards the chair, but he remained standing.

'Thomas Crump,' he said. 'Single, unemployed. Twenty-seven years of age—'

Mr Hooper did not even pick up his pen. 'You are wasting your time,' he said, 'and you are wasting mine. You got nothing last week and nothing the week before. Why do you do it, Mr Crump?'

'I'm entitled,' said Mr Crump defiantly. 'I know my rights and I'm entitled. I want out-relief. I have had out-relief for seven months and I am still entitled. Don't offer me the Union, because I'm not going in there. You have no right to keep back my money. I've a good mind to see a solicitor. If I don't get out-relief this week, I will do just that and then we'll see who's entitled.'

With the air of a patient man addressing an idiot, Mr Hooper said, 'Mr Crump, you are not entitled to anything. You were given out-relief when you were ill. You are no longer ill and there is no reason why you should not find yourself a job. If you are unable to find a job and are destitute, you will be offered a place in the Union Workhouse. Now, I have all your details already and need not detain you any longer.'

'You throwing me out? Is that it? Without hearing my case?'

'I am throwing you out, yes. I have heard your case many times over the past few weeks and I have all the relevant details on record. Now there are more deserving cases, Mr Crump. Please go away.'

'I'm entitled to my case being heard.'

'Your case will be heard. You may attend as usual at the Board room in the Union Workhouse a week from tomorrow, but you will get nothing. Next!'

Before the next person could enter, Mr Crump made his way out, slamming the door loudly behind him. Mr Hooper made a note in his ledger and looked up as the door opened once more to admit a young woman. She was very dirty and pitifully thin except for her swollen abdomen. Without waiting to be asked, she sank down on to the chair and stared dully at the floor. Mr Hooper coughed and she slowly raised her head to look at him. She looked exhausted and he hoped she would not faint while she was in his office. He was not a hard-hearted man, but he did not have unlimited funds at his disposal and was in no position to offer financial help, although occasionally he had parted with a few coppers to those he considered most deserving. He very much hoped this would not be one of them.

'Name?' he asked as briskly as he could.

'Vinnie Harris – no,' she corrected herself, 'not Harris, Crutchley.'

'Now, which is it to be, miss, Harris or Crutchley?'

'Crutchley.'

He shrugged and wrote.

'Single or married?'

'Married.'

'Occupation of husband?'

'Labourer, but he's dead now.'

They all told the same story, he thought and his depression increased. If they took her in she would get little sympathy and would doubtless discharge herself within a few days.

'How did he die?' he asked.

'In a fight and I don't know any more. He left me, you see, and when I went round to his parents' house they told me he was dead in a fight and that's all I can tell you – and it's not Vinnie, it's Winnie, short for Winifred.'

He drummed his fingers on the desk.

'May I remind you, miss, that it is an offence to give false information. Could we please start again and establish your real name.'

'I've told you, it's Winifred Crutchley. Mrs Winifred Crutchley.'

'You have decided, have you?'

'Yes.'

'I don't believe you,' he said, 'but have it your own way. Your husband, who was a labourer, left you and is now dead, leaving you apparently expecting his child?'

'Yes.'

Mr Hooper shrugged and made another note in his ledger. He looked at her again with narrowed eyes, then laid down his pen and began to turn the pages, running his finger down each one.

'Aha!' he said at last. 'I thought so. Vinnie Harris, age sixteen. Pregnant, without means of support. Refused to enter the Union. I am not quite as foolish as I look, you see. It is not policy to give out-relief to unmarried mothers. You will be offered a place in the Union Workhouse, where you can work in return for a bed and food.'

'I tell you, I'm married.'

'I see no wedding ring.'

'I pawned it.'

He shook his head. 'Good try, Miss Harris,' he said. 'Now I suggest you go back where you belong, confess to your mother and father and throw yourself on their mercy.'

'I have no one,' said Vinnie. 'I told you that before.'

'You told me your father left your mother. You told me your husband left you. Today you said your husband was dead. Last time you said your mother was dead, drowned in the river.'

'She was.'

'I am sorry. Your case will be heard a week tomorrow in the Union Board room. If you wish to attend, we will give you a decision at that time.'

He felt in his pocket and held out a threepenny bit. 'Buy yourself a bit of bread,' he said, 'and take my advice, don't come back. Send in the next one.'

'Thank you, sir.'

George Hooper's headache was growing worse. With a slight groan, he leaned forward and once more put his head in his hands. When he heard footsteps, he didn't look up.

'I'm not here for myself, so don't you think it.' The voice was loud, the tone aggressive. 'But there's no way I am going to bring up someone else's brat and that's the thanks you get. They die on you and leave you with the baby. Well, it's no concern of mine. If it's got no mother and no father, then the workhouse is the proper place for it. Asked me to take her in just for the night, then ups and disappears. Never come back. Now I ask you, what can I do? This here is her son, about two weeks old and if the Union won't accept him, my husband says he'll dump the brat on someone else's doorstep.'

George Hooper reached for his pen, then opened his eyes. He raised his left hand to his thumping head and said, 'Let's start again at the beginning, shall we?'

CHAPTER EIGHTEEN

The Chairman of the Workhouse Guardians, a Mr Frederick Sutton, was an ex-Sergeant Major with a reputation for harshness of which he was very proud. He made it a rule not to give money – or out-relief – as he believed this encouraged idleness and wasted public funds. If he offered a place in the Union Workhouse, most people would refuse and that way nothing need be done to help them. He strode into the Board room, sat down without a word and opened Mr Hooper's notebook which lay waiting on the desk. The rest of the committee eyed him nervously. He had a domineering manner and brooked no interference from his colleagues. Confronted by familiar names, he rattled through them at a great pace.

'. . . Harrison, Mary, idiot, Workhouse. Offham, George, unemployed, Workhouse. Reece, Emily, destitute, Workhouse. Crump, Thomas, unemployed, Workhouse. What's this?' He adjusted his spectacles and peered at Mr Hooper's neat handwriting.

'Vinnie Harris, alias Winifred Crutchley,' he read. 'Refused the House last time, is that right?'

'Yes, Mr Sutton,' said Mr Hooper from his seat on the Chairman's left side. 'This is her third appearance. She always gives a different name and always refuses the House.'

'How does she seem?'

'Honest enough, but claims that her husband is dead.'

The Chairman shrugged. 'They all do,' he said and there were nods of agreement from the other five Guardians.

'How does she look?' the Chairman asked.

'Very poorly. She could hardly stand. Hungry, I imagine.'

'Well, if they won't work, then they do go hungry. That's a

fact of life that no one can deny. If she hasn't learnt that yet, she never will.'

At the far end of the table a balding, elderly man said, 'They prey on our sympathy, these fallen women. They think a swollen belly makes them an object of pity.'

'An object of derision, more likely,' said another man.

'Fetch her in,' said the Chairman and Vinnie was called into the room. Despite her woebegone appearance and obvious weakness, she struggled to retain her natural dignity and held her head reasonably erect as she met the Chairman's disapproving stare.

'Who are you, then?' he barked. 'Vinnie Harris or Winifred Crutchley?'

'Winnie.'

'Hmm.'

He exchanged meaningful glances with the rest of the Guardians.

'So your husband is a Mr Crutchley?'

'Yes, sir. I mean, he was, sir.'

'And Mr Crutchley has conveniently disappeared, is that so?'

'He's dead.'

'Dead,' repeated the Chairman in obvious disbelief. 'The husbands of girls like you are always dead. Don't you think that a strange coincidence?'

Vinnie didn't answer.

'I say, doesn't that strike you as a strange coincidence?'

'I suppose it is, sir.'

He banged his fist on the table so that the ink pots jumped. 'You are damned right it is. I put it to you that you never had a husband and that the child you carry is the result of your own sin and will be born a bastard.'

Vinnie swallowed hard but made no answer and continued to stare at him without flinching. 'And when will this bastard child of yours be born? Do you know that?'

'The end of May, sir.'

'Oh, so you know when it happened.'

'Yes, sir.'

'When exactly did this so-called husband run off?'

Vinnie suspected a trap but fatigue made her slow-witted. He persisted. 'Last week? Last year?'

'I don't remember – a long time ago.'

'Try to remember. Would it be eight months ago, do you think?'

'It could be, yes.'

'Aha,' he said triumphantly. 'Then how did he give you the child due to be born at the end of May?'

Vinnie was aware of the amusement this interrogation was producing. For a moment she let her gaze travel from face to face and only George Hooper's eyes did not mock her.

'I must've got it wrong,' she muttered.

'Or else it is not your husband's child. Are you a street woman, Winnie?'

'No, sir. An honest girl.'

'Not honest enough, it seems.' There was a ripple of laughter.

'Now, Winnie,' the Chairman went on, warming to his task. 'Do you think it right that honest citizens should pay for girls like you? Immoral, lazy sluts like you? Do you think it reasonable that we should hand you money so that you can continue to live your dissolute life supported by charity? I am waiting for an answer.'

'Yes, sir, because I am not lazy or dissolute.' Finally, Vinnie had been goaded to defend herself. 'What happened only happened once and never will again and I would work if I could, but no one will give me a job.'

'The Union will find work for you, Winnie. We will offer you a bed to sleep on, food and drink, the company of like-minded girls and work for those idle hands of yours. Have you ever picked oakum?'

'No, I haven't,' said Vinnie. 'I don't mind picking oakum, sir, but I don't want my child to be born in the Workhouse.'

'Perhaps you have a better suggestion.'

She gave a slight shrug. 'If you could find me a job I would work really hard. I'm used to hard work.'

The elderly man at the end of the table said, 'If we give her out-relief she will be back on the street earning twice as much at her sordid trade.'

'I'm not a whore,' whispered Vinnie, 'I never was and I never will be.'

'Who is the father of that?' said Mr Sutton, pointing. 'If, as you say, it only happened the once, then you obviously know who the father is.'

'I can't tell you that, sir. There would be that much trouble, and folk would be hurt – folk that were good to me.'

'Your own father, was it?'

She shook her head, shocked by the question.

'An elder brother, an uncle, one of your family?' She shook her head again.

'A neighbour, perhaps?'

'No.'

'Your employer?'

'I'm sorry,' said Vinnie, 'but I can't say.'

Mr Sutton brought his fist down again.

'We will find a way of *making* you say,' he told her. 'Understand this, Winnie or Vinnie – whatever your name is. We don't give out-relief to women like you. Out-relief is for the deserving poor. I am offering you the House and you would be wise to accept. A few weeks there may loosen your tongue and perhaps then we shall know the true name of the child's father, who brought about this abuse upon your person. Charges can then be made and the matter dealt with in the proper way. He will be urged to make provision for you. You may come here week after week, month after month, but you will never be granted out-relief, so make up your mind to that. It is the House or nothing.'

Vinnie closed her eyes. She was faint from hunger and it had been an effort to drag herself through the streets this morning in order to attend the hearing of her case. Even if she had energy, she had nowhere to go. Her present humiliation depressed her immeasurably. The previous day she had stolen fruit from a barrow and knew that she would be forced to steal again or starve. If she was caught stealing, she would be sent to prison and presumably prison was worse than the Union

Workhouse. The choice was not a happy one, but Vinnie consoled herself with the thought that in a few weeks when she felt stronger she could discharge herself from the Workhouse and try once more to find work. The only other alternative was to make her way back to Teesbury and face further humiliation and disgrace there. To Vinnie that was quite intolerable and she did not seriously give it a moment's consideration. She closed her eyes and prayed, 'Dear God, help me.'

She looked up at George Hooper and he gave her an encouraging nod. 'I'll take the House,' she whispered.

*

There were seven admissions that day, but Vinnie was in no fit state to take an interest in her fellows as they followed the large grim-looking matron along an interminable corridor which led to the reception room. Of the seven admissions, five were men and they were led elsewhere by the workhouse master, a similar but no less grim version of his wife. The reception room was gaunt and bare and at one end a tub of water had been sunk into the floor. The matron handed them each a small piece of soap and told them to strip and wash themselves.

'Fold your clothes neatly and tie them with the piece of string you will find on the chair,' she chanted. 'Your clothes will be returned to you when you leave. Your uniform will be found on the table' – she pointed. 'Ten minutes is the time allowed, so make haste.'

While the two women did as they were ordered the matron transferred their personal details from one ledger to another. The water in the tub was cold, but under the woman's stern eye Vinnie washed herself as well as she could. Despite the chill temperature of the water, she was glad to have the opportunity, for she had gone several weeks without being able to wash and even the presence of a stranger sharing the bath with her was bearable.

The other woman nudged Vinnie and whispered, 'When's yours due?' but before Vinnie could answer, the matron barked 'No talking!' and they relapsed once more into silence.

The uniform was of a coarse grey material and there was a yellow stripe round one sleeve, but Vinnie could only guess at its significance. She was given a pair of ill-fitting shoes and while she laced them up she saw her own clothes being locked away in a large cupboard.

The matron was a large woman, with grey hair pulled back into a bun. She wore a high-necked dress with long sleeves in a striped material and this was partially covered by a large white apron. A bundle of keys hung at her waist and jangled disconcertingly whenever she moved.

'This way.'

They followed her along another corridor and out into a yard where a variety of women and girls wandered, apparently aimlessly. They wore expressions of hopelessness and talked in whispers.

'Exercise time,' explained the matron. 'They will be back at work in five minutes and you will join them.'

To Vinnie it all seemed like a nightmare, totally unreal. She knew the reputation of such places and had pitied the people incarcerated within. Now she herself was one of them. With this realisation came a trembling which started in her legs and spread to the rest of her body, so that by the time they reached the other side of the yard her teeth were chattering.

The young woman beside her, seeing her distress, nudged her and whispered, 'Cheer up!' but this brought a scowl from the sharp-eared matron and Vinnie found herself hoping that her companion would not provoke the woman further. Cold fear clutched at her stomach and a feeling of helpless dread swept through her as they left the yard and went in through a doorway. They were shown into a large dormitory with high brown walls and white ceiling. A dozen or more beds were ranged down each side and an upturned chamber-pot was visible beneath each one. The floorboards were bare and obviously newly scrubbed and a large black stove with a rail around it stood in the centre of the room. A few wisps of smoke escaping from the tall pipe proved that it *was* alight, but the room itself was very cold.

'Last two beds on the left,' said the matron. 'Your nightdress will be found under the pillow. The house rules are pinned to the wall there,' – she pointed – 'and failure to observe them will result in punishment. This may take the form of a caning, a reduction in food or an increase in the work load. Is that understood? Then follow me.'

They joined a short queue of people standing in the corridor waiting to see the medical officer. The queue was being supervised by a frail-looking woman in an identical grey dress to those which Vinnie and her companion were wearing, except that the coloured stripe round *her* sleeve was blue. The matron spoke to her: 'These two for the workroom afterwards.'

The woman gave a little nod and the matron marched away. As she turned the corner the woman smiled. 'Welcome to Paupers' Palace!' she said. 'Keep on the right side of her and you might survive. Cross her and she'll make your life hell.'

She looked at Vinnie. 'She'll probably cut that long hair of yours.' Vinnie was past caring.

A man came out of the doctor's office and another man went in. Two men in workhouse grey remained and at last it was Vinnie's turn. She wondered what the doctor would be like? Was there anyone within these walls with any compassion? It seemed improbable. The woman with the blue-striped sleeve seemed anxious to talk, although she kept her voice low.

'Keep clear of him, too,' she told them.

'Who?'

'Her husband. The master. He can't keep his mitts off any presentable female. It's touch, poke, prod. Ugh! He's a slimy toad he is! If he offers you a slice of cake or an extra mug of tea, take my advice and turn it down. He will be all over you and expecting favours and what can you say? It's your word against his. We had one girl, he got her in the family way.'

Vinnie was horrified. 'What happened?' she asked.

'He got her sent to prison. Accused her of stealing. We never saw her again.'

'That's terrible.'

The woman laughed shortly. 'That's nothing, that isn't. You wait. You will go out of here a lot wiser than you came in,

I can tell you. The things I've heard! You would hardly credit it, but I keep my mouth shut and say nothing. I've been here eight months now.'

'Aren't you ever going out?'

'Only in me coffin. I'm consumptive, you see. Last stages, the doctor says. I'm supposed to have beef broth every day but I never get it. I'm only telling you for your own good. There's only one way to survive in here and that's to say nothing and put up with whatever they dish out. You can't beat them, that's for sure.'

The doctor, to Vinnie's intense relief, was a kindly, well-meaning member of his profession. He spoke to her gently and promised her an extra glass of milk at breakfast time and two extra ounces of cheese at supper time.

'Must look after you and your little one, mustn't we?' he said and Vinnie nodded, her eyes blinded by unexpected tears.

'You have nothing to fear,' he told her. 'Do as you are told and cause no trouble and if the baby lives—'

'I want it to live,' said Vinnie, 'and then I'll take it away from this place.'

'Well, we shall see,' he said, sensing her agitation. 'We will talk about it later.'

He made several notes in his book and blotted them carefully.

'I shall see you again in a week's time,' he said. 'In the meantime, remember what I have said. Be a good girl and cause no trouble. Believe me, that's your best hope.'

He dismissed her with a smile and she returned to the corridor. While she waited for the other woman to join her, she learned a little more of the world she had so recently entered – that the blue stripe indicated sickness and that the insane wore a red stripe. Her informant's name was Sarah Gooding and because of her illness, she was excused the more strenuous work. When at last the doctor came out he went off to inspect the infirmary.

The two new admissions were taken to the workroom where the women sat on long benches, their heads bent over their work. They were unsupervised, but the amount of work each inmate was expected to complete kept them mainly silent, although a few heads were raised curiously when Vinnie and her companion entered. Vinnie's companion, who introduced herself as Pearl Holland, threw herself down on to an empty form and stared round her disconsolately.

'Every bloody time I get out of here I swear I will never come back,' she told Vinnie, 'and every bloody time I do!'

Vinnie sat down beside her. Sarah moved to a table at the end of the room on which stood a pair of scales. On the floor underneath this table was a large basketful of rope-ends, some tarred, some knotted. She weighed out an exact amount, which was in fact three pounds, and tipped it into Vinnie's lap. 'You had best make a start on that,' she said, 'before the old cow gets back.' She weighed out another amount for Pearl, who initiated Vinnie into the mysteries of oakum-picking.

'All you've got to do is unravel that lot,' she told her. 'Spread it out like this, see. Pull the strands apart with your fingers and drop them into a pile by your feet. It's tough going and your fingers will hurt like hell by the end of the day, but as the days go on the skin hardens up. Then it's not so bad. Don't sit there staring at it, Winnie, get on with it for God's sake – if you want any dinner, that is.'

Sarah began to cough, a thick rasping sound.

'Beat it, Sarah!' cried one of the other women. 'We don't want you pegging out in here. If you are on your last gasp, go somewhere else.'

'Leave her alone,' came another voice. 'Take no notice of her, Sarah. Who does she think she is, pushing everyone around!' Sarah hesitated but then departed.

'You are a hard bitch, Maude. She can't help being sick.'

'Well, I don't want to be sick like her. That's catching, that is, and I don't want to cough myself into an early grave, thank you very much.'

'Well, what you've got is catching, but we don't send you out of the room.'

'That's because you wouldn't dare.'

'Oh, stop squawking, you two.'

Vinnie whispered to Pearl, 'I'm to get extra milk and cheese. What about you?'

Pearl gave a derisive sniff. 'Oh yes, so am I. The doctor's generous enough. It's just that you never seem to see the bloody milk or the cheese. Last time I was here it was extra bread and margarine, but I didn't get that either.'

'Why not?'

'Because I didn't. How do you think matron gets to be so bloody fat?'

'She takes it, you mean?'

'Well, of course she does. She isn't going to let the likes of you and me have extra milk and cheese and what-have-you. They reckon if they make us too comfortable we'll want to come again. So they make it as hard as possible.'

'What did you come in for last time?' asked Vinnie.

'Same thing. In the family way.'

Vinnie was astonished. 'Where's your baby?'

'Dead. I had two. Both dead, one boy and one girl. But poor little brats, they're better off dead, that's what I say. I mean, fancy bringing up a kid in the bloody Workhouse. There are kids in here who have never set foot outside. Oh, you can look at me like that, but it's true. There's kids in here that was born here, seven, eight, nine years ago. Still bloody here! Sometimes the mothers die when they are born. Sometimes they take the babies outside and they die out there and the kids come back in again. Oh it's a funny old world, Winnie. Is that your real name?'

Vinnie hesitated, then shook her head and her companion laughed.

'Mine's not Pearl neither, but I don't tell anyone my real name otherwise I will be back in Holloway before I can wink.'

'Holloway?'

Pearl nodded. 'It's not much different to this place,' she said. 'But at least here you are allowed to walk out.'

'What did you—' Vinnie stopped in mid-sentence.

'What did I do to get put away? Can't you guess?'

Vinnie shook her head.

'They don't like the way I earn my living, see?'

'I think so.'

'What I say is, what other way is there? I mean, who wants to flog themselves to death as a bloody domestic for half the money? My Pa said to me, "You've no need to starve, girl, you're sitting on a gold mine", and he's right.'

'So, you're not married?'

'Married? No such luck. Are you?'

'Not really,' said Vinnie.

Pearl laughed. 'Well, cheer up, there's worse things happen at sea. Now, if you get half that bloody oakum picked by lunchtime, and I don't reckon you can, they'll give you some bread and cheese and a mug of water. You look as though you could do with it.'

Vinnie was about to agree with her new friend, but at that moment the frayed rope-end fell from her fingers as a blackness swept over her. She tried to cry out but instead slid, insensible, to the floor. The matron was duly called and as a great concession, because it was Vinnie's first day, she was allowed to go to the dormitory and lie on her bed. There was no more oakum-picking for Vinnie that day – but there was no food either.

CHAPTER NINETEEN

Mrs Agnes Bellweather was a great believer in the traditional Sunday dinner. Whenever Roland was invited to join them, he knew exactly what they would eat and on this particular occasion he was not disappointed. As usual, the cloth was white damask and the silver cutlery gleamed. The silver cruet set had also been polished with loving care and was obviously refilled regularly, for never had salt or pepper been known to fail. The wine glasses sparkled in the sunlight which filtered through the heavy lace curtains. The mustard was freshly mixed and freshly-grated horseradish had been used for the sauce. The St Emilion had been decanted into cut glass and the matching white damask table-napkins were ringed with white bone china to match the dinner service.

Agnes, Mary and Roland sat at the round table while Mrs Markham carried in the meal. Roland, as usual, was asked to pour the wine while Agnes began to carve the sirloin. The tureens contained baked potatoes, baked parsnips and brussels sprouts and the gravy boat stood on a matching white stand. Agnes cut three slices of beef for Roland and then passed the plate to him.

'Now, help yourself, dear,' she told him. 'Mary, make sure Roland has enough. He needs fattening up – there are plenty of potatoes and those brussels sprouts have come straight from my sister's garden in Esher, so they couldn't be fresher. Good heavens, that won't keep a flea alive, Roland! Do give him some more, Mary, he's much too modest in his portions.'

Mary and Roland exchanged amused glances while her mother continued to carve the joint: two slices of beef for Mary and one for herself. Later they would each be given another slice.

'It's so nice to have a man to cook for again and I do so enjoy Sunday lunch,' Agnes told them. 'It was your father's favourite meal of the week, Mary, and I always feel he is closer to us at these times. Almost as if he was in the room with us, watching with approval. Do you remember how your father used to enjoy his Sunday dinner? Don't you feel that he is here with us?'

'Perhaps, Mama.'

'Oh, there's no perhaps about it, dear,' her mother insisted. 'I feel the warmth of his presence. Do you suspect, Roland, that we are not alone?'

'It may be so,' he said. 'Yes, it very likely may be.'

'Gravy, Roland? Mary, you have given him no gravy. You are not looking after him properly. Roland will think I have not brought you up well.'

'Indeed I shall not,' said Roland. 'I think you have done an excellent job, Mrs Bellweather. Your daughter is a credit to you.' He winked slightly at Mary and an attractive flush tinged her cheeks with colour.

There had been a slight coolness between Mary and Roland after the sharp exchange over Vinnie Harris, since when the matter had not been discussed personally between them. However, Vinnie's plight had been raised at a meeting of the Brothers in Jesus and the £10 reward had been mentioned again – Roland urging that if one of *them* were fortunate enough to find her, they could keep the money which would augment their funds most satisfactorily. On that occasion Mary had said as little as possible and their relationship continued – on the surface at least – to be nearly as close as before. His flattering remarks, however, had taken Mary by surprise and her heart beat a little faster because of them. She served her mother with vegetables and then helped herself.

'A toast,' said Mrs Bellweather cheerfully, raising her glass. 'To all your good work!'

'I will second that,' said Roland and they each took a sip. Then Mrs Bellweather said, 'And another to our dear Queen

Victoria, God bless her. Your poor dear father always made that toast on Sunday, do you remember, Mary?' Mary nodded. 'He always remembered the Queen,' said Agnes, 'and he always maintained that a St Emilion was the best wine with which to toast Her Majesty.' She smiled at the recollection and set down her glass.

'Pepper and salt, Roland? A little mustard, perhaps, or horseradish sauce? My husband, you see, Roland, was a very loyal man. He adored the Queen and poor dear Albert. He drove to Chislehurst the year before we were married, I remember, especially to see the Queen, but it was dreadfully foggy. That horrid yellow fog – the Royal landau was closed and he could see nothing. Poor man, he wrote to me about his disappointment. Their Majesties had travelled from Windsor to visit St Mary's Church, where the remains of the French Emperor were laid to rest. Such a tragedy for poor Eugénie. I read an article in *The Times* and there were tears in my eyes. I couldn't help myself.' She sighed, speared some potatoes and meat with her fork and popped them into her mouth, chewing the mouthful ten times before swallowing it.

'Of course I have seen Their Majesties,' she said. 'Once when I was only a girl of ten. We were visiting friends in the north and the royal couple came up to Birmingham for the inauguration of Aston Park. It was desperately hot, but I can still remember that beautiful scene, banners and flowers everywhere, wreaths of flowers hanging in the streets and everyone shouting, "God bless the Queen – Victoria, Queen of Peace." They shouted for Albert, too, of course. I cannot recall ever seeing so many people. And then there was a spectacular procession through the streets to Aston Park itself. They were converting it you see, into a museum and park for the working classes. Such a generous notion. But it was so hot, I remember, and my father feared my mother would faint from the heat.'

'And did she?' asked Roland.

'No, thank heaven. She managed to retain her senses, poor dear soul, but it *was* so hot and such a press of people, as you can well imagine. These brussels sprouts are very good. I shall

write to my sister this evening and tell her so. Do you think the
parsnips a little over-cooked, Roland?'

'Not at all,' he said, 'they are quite delicious.'

'Mary, do you think them a little too crisp, perhaps?'

'No, Mama, they are very nice.'

'Ah! Then perhaps I am being too critical. I shall say nothing
to Mrs Markham if you assure me they are not overdone. But
listen to me, I do ramble on so! Forgive me, Roland. Here am I
talking about the old days, while you two young people live
very much in the present and no doubt have lots to talk about.
Mary keeps me well-informed, you know, about all your
plans. It really astonishes me how much can be achieved by
enthusiasm. Breakfasts for the poor! What a splendid idea and
proving very popular, Mary tells me.'

'Almost too popular,' Roland said with a smile. 'The
numbers attending each morning are gradually creeping up as
word goes round. And has Mary told you about our efforts on
behalf of one of our waifs?'

'One of your waifs? Why, no, Mary hasn't mentioned it,
have you dear?'

'Maybe not, Mama.'

'I don't think you have done. It all sounds very exciting.
What has happened to this waif exactly?'

Briefly Roland explained all that was known concerning
Vinnie's disappearance and Mrs Bellweather listened intently.
'And there is ten pounds reward, you say? Someone is very
eager to discover her whereabouts. Who has put up the
money?'

'Julian Lawrence, the Colonel's son. He is away in
Cambridge but is most concerned by the girl's disappearance.
He is quite determined that we shall find her again.'

'Aha!' Her tone was full of meaning. 'Do I smell romance in
the air?'

Mary said quickly, 'I was thinking the same thing myself.'
But at the same time Roland countered, 'Very unlikely, I
should think. Socially, they are miles apart.'

'She is with child, too,' said Mary, adding spitefully, 'but no
one is sure who the father is.'

'With child and barely sixteen?' Agnes threw up her hands in horror. 'What folly – to ruin her life before it's scarce begun. What sort of morals do these people have, I wonder? From what one hears, some of them are more like animals than human beings, but there,' she amended hastily, seeing the frozen look on her visitor's face, 'they are all God's creatures and we should treat them with compassion. After all, our Lord said of his enemies, "Father forgive them, they know not what they do." I hope you find your young woman, Roland.'

There was an awkward silence. 'She is not *Roland's* young woman,' said Mary with an attempt at a smile. 'Is she, Roland?'

There was no immediate answer and Mrs Bellweather became aware suddenly that all was not right.

'Of course she's not,' she said hastily. 'That was merely a figure of speech. Perhaps "protégée" would be more apt.'

There was still no comment from either of the young people and she looked from one to the other doubtfully. 'Well, let's hope that you find her,' she said cheerfully, 'and that the child's father can be persuaded to marry her. Even after such a sad start it may turn out quite happily. It often does in these cases. Some more wine, Roland? And you, Mary? I think we should refresh our glasses. Mmm, this beef *is* very tender, I shall tell Mrs Markham. I always think it is a good idea to compliment the cook whenever possible. It compensates for those times when we have to speak harshly to them. I have often told Mary that a good and loyal servant cannot be made by harshness and reprimand unless it is balanced by plenty of approval. I am sorry your father was unable to join us, Roland. He is most welcome and I do hope he will come another day.'

Roland began to explain for the second time that on Sundays his father frequently visited an old school friend who lived alone in Bayswater, but at that moment there was a knock on the door and the maid came in.

'Please, ma'am, there's a Mr Bryce asking for Mr Fry.'

'For me?' said Roland.

Agnes was obviously displeased by the interruption. 'Show him into the morning room, Alice, and offer him a glass of wine or a cup of tea,' she said. 'Tell him we are eating

our Sunday dinner but Mr Fry will be with him shortly.'
'Yes, ma'am.'

Roland hesitated. 'Perhaps I ought to see him now,' he began but Agnes dismissed the idea with a delicate wave of her hand. 'Nothing is more important than a good Sunday dinner,' she said firmly. 'You will ruin your digestion if you jump up and down in the middle of a meal. I am quite sure that whatever Mr Bryce has to say to you it will wait a little longer.'

Mary met Roland's anxious eyes. 'But, Mama,' she said, 'if it is urgent—'

'Mary, dear, nothing is that urgent. Whoever this Mr Bryce is—'

'He is from Teesbury, mother. He is a pole-puller at Foxearth.'

'Is he, dear, how very nice. Now do finish your sprouts before they get cold. Any more vegetables for you, Roland?'

He shook his head and hastily finished what remained on his plate. After that came the inevitable trifle: an exotic combination of fruit, custard and cream, richly decorated with toasted nuts and slivers of angelica. Ignoring the presence of Mr Bryce in the house, Mary's mother kept up a conversation on topics which ranged from the current price of coal to the latest news from India. Mary watched helplessly as Roland forced down mouthful after mouthful. The time came, however, when he laid down his spoon and fork and pushed back his chair.

'I do hope you will excuse me,' he said, 'but I really cannot keep Mr Bryce waiting any longer. Also, I am eager to hear what he has to say.'

He nodded to them both and without waiting for permission from his hostess, left the room.

'Well!' said Agnes, somewhat affronted by Roland's departure. 'What's so important about this Mr Bryce? What can he possibly have to say to Roland?'

'I dare say it's about Vinnie Harris,' said Mary, making an effort to speak lightly as though the matter was of no concern. Her mother, however, sensed her apprehension.

'What,' she said, 'is Vinnie Harris to Roland Fry? Surely not? He would never be so foolish.'

Mary made no answer but her appetite had disappeared and after toying with her food for a moment or two, she laid down spoon and fork, defeated.

In the morning room Tom Bryce put down his cup and saucer and stood up. The two men shook hands briefly.

'I am at a bit of a loss,' Tom said straightaway, 'to tell you the truth. I hardly know what I am about, but I hope you may be able to help me, if you will forgive me troubling you on a Sunday.'

'I will help you willingly,' said Roland. 'What can I do for you?'

'I don't know where to start. Everything is such a mess, and I am not proud of my part in it, but it is done and can't be undone. Now I must try to – and will – make amends, I suppose. I don't know how much you know, Mr Fry.'

'About what?'

'The Vinnie Harris business.'

'I know she has run away. I heard a rumour that she was with child and Jarvis Tupp's name was bandied around a lot. Apart from that, I know very little, except that Julian Lawrence has offered a ten-pound reward for anyone with information which leads to her discovery. I can't believe Julian Lawrence would seduce her, which only leaves Jarvis Tupp who denies it emphatically.'

'The child is mine,' said Tom. 'There is no doubt in my mind. She's a decent girl and I wish to God things were not the way they are, but they seem to be going from bad to worse and I don't know where to turn and that's the truth.'

He looked the picture of utter despair. Roland, whose mission in life was to help people, now prayed that whatever the difficulties were he would be able to contribute something.

'Sit down, Mr Bryce,' he said, 'and then go on. They say two heads are better than one. You tell me in your own time; I am entirely at your disposal.'

Tom gave a brief nod of acknowledgement. 'So much has happened,' he said. 'My wife, Rose, is a generous woman, Mr Fry. A very loyal and generous woman. I don't deserve her, but that's beside the point. She knows about Vinnie.'

'She knows that you are the father?'

Tom nodded. 'She guessed and she asked me. I could not lie to her, Mr Fry, although I wanted to save her pain. I simply could not lie to her. She was anxious about the baby, you see, afraid it would die neglected or unloved – or both. She wants us to find the child and bring it up as our own and I think maybe that's the best way out of the mess.'

'Poor Rose,' said Roland. 'As you say, she is a very loyal and generous person. She must love you very much.'

'Happily she does,' said Tom. 'Though God knows I don't deserve it. She persuaded me to ask the Colonel for a few days' leave to come up to London and look for Vinnie. I agreed and the Colonel was very understanding. He called me by a few harsh names, all well-deserved, and told me to count my blessings.' He smiled bitterly.

'But he gave you permission to come up here?'

'Yes. But then his wife found out and for reasons which I need not discuss, she was very angry. So angry that she has sacked me from Foxearth. I have a week in which to move my family and find another job.'

'My dear fellow, I am so sorry.'

Tom Bryce shrugged. 'Out of that week I have taken two days to look for Vinnie. To tell you the truth, I don't know where to start and so I came straight to you.'

'Did the Colonel give you a reference – for another job, I mean?'

'Yes. His wife was against it, but he insisted.'

Roland could imagine the scene and his timid heart quailed. 'Well,' he said, 'it's not easy to see a silver lining to this cloud, but I will help you all I can. If a letter from me will be of assistance when you apply elsewhere for work, I shall furnish it gladly, but you only have two days in which to search. I will be honest with you, Mr Bryce, Vinnie Harris doesn't want to be found and I don't think we shall find her. It is very easy to change your name and disappear in London, but at least I can bring you up to date with all our efforts and then maybe we shall be blessed with sudden inspiration. Would you mind if I ask Mary Bellweather to join us? There's no need to tell her all the background, only that you are here to search for Vinnie.'

Tom nodded and Roland went in search of her, but Alice the maid told him that Mary and her mother had gone to the park for a little fresh air and to 'shake their dinner down'.

It was therefore decided that the two men would go to Roland's house and when Mary and her mother returned half an hour later, they had left. A note from Roland promised that he would telephone her at a later date.

*

Christina's first instinct as she read Julian's letter was to tear it into shreds. The expression on her face changed from incredulity to anger and then to dark fury. She crumpled it suddenly in her hands, whispering, 'Dear God, I don't believe it! Don't let this be happening to me.' But it was true and it was happening. She ran up the stairs and flung open the door of the Colonel's room, where Janet was settling the breakfast tray across the old man's bed.

'Outside, Janet!' Christina cried.

'But—'

'Get out and don't argue with me! Look at this!' She waved the crumpled letter. 'I can't believe it. I can't believe the young fool has so lost his wits.' She turned suddenly to see Janet staring at her from the doorway. 'Get out and close the door behind you,' she shouted, 'and find something useful to do. Read this!'

She thrust the crumpled letter into the Colonel's wrinkled hands.

'My spectacles . . .' he began.

'Oh, for God's sake, give it to me.' She snatched it back and, striding up and down the bedroom, began to read in a voice that quivered with rage.

' "Dear mother. I don't know how to tell you this without causing you distress and yet you must know it. It will, I know, be a shock and I fear for its effect upon father. I am therefore writing—'

'What the hell is he babbling about?' cried the Colonel. 'Get to the point, woman!'

She spun round to face her husband. 'Don't take that tone with me, Henry Lawrence,' she said. 'You will hear soon enough what the boy is babbling about, as you put it.' She read on, '"I am therefore writing this letter directly to you in the hope that you will decide how best to break the news to father."'

By this time the Colonel had found his glasses on the bedside table and now held out a hand for the letter. 'Give it to me. Let me read it for myself.'

Christina ignored him and continued to read. '"I intend to marry Vinnie Harris."' She clenched her hands, crumpling the letter once more and made a gesture of despair. 'Vinnie Harris, Vinnie Harris!' she cried. 'If I hear that name once more I shall go out of my mind. That wretched girl is determined to haunt me to my grave.'

'Marry Vinnie Harris? Julian means to marry Vinnie Harris? Is that what the little fool is saying?'

'Yes, of course it is. Your precious son, it appears is determined to make an utter fool of himself over a twopenny-halfpenny trollop who seems determined to ruin us all. I don't think I can take any more of this, Henry. My health is going to give way with the strain. The whole world has gone mad and Vinnie Harris's name echoes from every corner of it. Such utter base ingratitude after all these years. I cannot believe it, Henry. I cannot believe it. What have we ever done to that child except rescue her from poverty and a life of shame and this is how she repays us. Not content with ruining everything else she has somehow bewitched Julian! My only son is so besotted with the miserable creature he wants to commit the ultimate folly and marry the girl. Henry, we must do something! We must stop this madness before it goes any further. Oh, I could weep tears of blood. If I could lay my hands on that miserable little bitch, I swear I would strangle her. I would hang for it but, dear God, it would be worth it!'

'Give me the letter,' the old man repeated. He was leaning back on the pillow and his rate of breathing had increased noticeably. He held one hand to his chest and was obviously suffering some discomfort.

'Take it, read it,' she cried, 'and then for God's sake tell me what to do. I will not surrender my only son to that wicked little harlot.'

She moved to the window, drumming her hands helplessly against the shutters and uttering inarticulate sounds of passionate resentment and loathing. Suddenly she spun round. 'Do you realise what this would mean?' she demanded hysterically. 'That if the child is a boy, Tom Bryce's bastard would stand to inherit Foxearth? He must never marry that girl, Henry. We must stop it. We must do everything in our power to stop it.'

'The boy will soon be of age, Christina. He is now nearly twenty.'

'I don't care if he is one hundred and twenty. I tell you, he will marry Vinnie Harris over my dead body and I don't make that threat lightly.'

She slammed herself down into an armchair. 'What has possessed the boy?' she said. 'He has always been so sensible. I still cannot believe that he is proposing such a monstrous thing. Oh, why did we ever take that child in all those years ago? If only she had drowned with her damned mother we would be well rid of her evil influence.'

The Colonel raised his eyebrows. 'She is hardly evil, my dear,' he protested. 'More sinned against than sinning, I would say.'

'I am not interested in what you would say, Henry. I might have known you would take the girl's part just because she reads to you and listens to your boring old stories, no doubt thinking what an old fool you are, but flattering you none the less. They say there's no fool like an old fool, Henry Lawrence, and you are the perfect example of it. Has the wretched girl bewitched you too? My son, my husband, my—' she broke off and closed her eyes.

'Your lover?'

Her eyes snapped open and she looked at her husband.

'Perhaps you thought I didn't know, Chrissie,' he said. 'That was foolish of you. I have known for a long time. Probably since it started. You talk about your son and the

wretched girl from the gutters. What about my wife and one of
the hired hands? Do you think that gives me a comfortable
feeling, my dear? You have looked to your inferiors for *your*
satisfaction. You of all people should understand your son's
behaviour.'

Christina flew out of the chair and across the room, her fist
raised to strike him, but he only smiled. 'Are you going to kill
me?' he asked. 'You have sent Tom Bryce away and you will
kill your husband. Soon you will have no one. Don't bother to
strike me, Christina. Your look alone could kill, but I don't
advise it. It is not in your best interests to have me dead.'

She stared at him and he saw her expression change from
anger to suspicion and then to fear. 'Not in my best interests?'
she echoed. 'What do you mean?'

'What I say. That you are better off while I live.'

'Henry, you don't mean—'

'I mean just what I say, my dear, that you would do well to
look after my health and keep me alive as long as you can.' All
the colour had left her face and her eyes darkened.

'The will,' she whispered. 'You have altered the will, is that
it? Is that what you have done?'

There was a look in his eyes which she could not interpret,
but he nodded slowly.

'No, Henry, I don't believe it,' she gulped painfully and put
up a hand to her throat. 'No, Henry, you would not do that.
You would not dare. No, Henry, no.' She began to shake her
head. 'You can't do this to me, Henry.'

'But I have already done it, my dear. It's signed and properly
witnessed and is in safe keeping. When I die all my property
and *every penny* of my money passes to Julian – and that's
rather ironic.'

'Ironic?'

'Yes. You see, I anticipated that after my death you would
find a way to marry Tom Bryce. Now it looks as though
Vinnie Harris will be the one to—'

'Never!' she shouted. This time she raised both fists, only
with a supreme effort refraining from bringing them down on
her husband's defenceless head. Instead, she snatched up the

breakfast tray and hurled it from the bed, scattering the contents across the room. Then she turned and ran to the door. She seized the handle and swung the door open, then stood for a moment in the doorway with head bowed and shoulders sagging. Her life was ruined and the world was crumbling about her. The old man turned his head and watched her without pity. She gave a choked cry, turned back to look at her husband with wild eyes, and then the door slammed behind her.

CHAPTER TWENTY

The first snow of the winter fell on the seventeenth day of the New Year, from a leaden sky overhung with clouds. Large flakes dropped through the still, dark air in the early hours of the morning, covering the Weald of Kent with a thick white mantle which, with the coming of daylight, would flatter the slopes of the valley through which the river Medway wound its way like a dark serpent, silent, almost menacing. Above the fallen snow the hop-poles reached up, acre upon acre, row on row. Bare and grey, like a petrified forest, they waited for spring when the hops would stir into life once more and the first tentative shoots would thrust themselves out of the soil and cling to the wooden poles. Now the plants lay dormant, while winter prepared to ravage the land above them. The hop-poles wore only a few tattered ends of string from the previous season's hop-tying, with here and there a cluster of shrivelled brown leaves which had somehow escaped the pole-puller's eagle eyes. The trees bordering the gardens were bare also, their gaunt branches outstretched to receive the snow-flakes which would clothe and beautify them, enabling them to play their part in the transformation which was taking place.

As the hours passed, the snow-covered valley was revealed to the waking eyes of the inhabitants of the villages – with delight by the children and dismay by their elders. Gradually, the still air began to move as a wind blew in from the east, chapping the faces and hands of all who ventured outside their homes. The wind continued to rise, occasionally gusting so that the snow accumulated on the trees was shaken free and spattered onto the snow beneath.

The chestnut tree in the courtyard of the 'Horse and Cart'

was no exception. The proprietor, Ted Hunter, cursed when he was caught by a particularly heavy fall as he manhandled a barrel towards his cellar and went inside, grumbling as he brushed the snow from his clothes. The 'Horse and Cart' public house had been run by the Hunter family for as long as anyone in Teesbury could remember, which was unfortunate.

It meant that the wind of change rarely blew through it and it continued from one generation to the next as a seedy run-down 'hostelry', offering little in the way of creature comforts to the regulars and only token accommodation to weary travellers hoping to be accommodated there for a night or two.

In fact, two small upstairs rooms were allotted for the purpose of bed-and-breakfast guests, but there was so rarely any demand for them that they were sadly neglected – so much effort being required to prepare them for unexpected visitors that it was generally considered by successive owners as hardly worthwhile.

Downstairs, the accommodation was a little better, but even so it was hardly inviting. The floor was covered by a worn, almost threadbare carpet of an indeterminate colour and the small wooden tables and rickety high-backed chairs gave it a bleak appearance which even the occasional vase of flowers did little to improve. The place was run by Ted and his wife Maisie, who could afford to be lazy and neglectful for the 'Horse and Cart' was the only remaining pub in the village since the 'Blue Fox' had been burnt down seven years earlier.

Ted Hunter was a giant of a man, bald-headed but with huge white side-whiskers; his wife, Maisie, was almost as large. However, she was shapelier than her husband, for she always appeared in public tightly corseted and with the bodice of her dress well-filled by her ample bosom. She, too, was grey-haired and wore her hair piled on top of her head in the extravagant fashion of her youth – which latter, she fondly believed, had never really deserted her although she was nearing sixty.

It was Friday night, but the parlour was more crowded than usual, which was entirely due to a heavy fall of snow during the morning. Penny-conscious visitors were aware that it was cheaper to make their way to the 'Horse and Cart' to take advantage of *their* fire, rather than waste logs and coal on their own. Sometimes, too, Friday evenings were graced by the appearance of local talent, although the pianola had ceased to function several months ago and had not yet been put back in working order; the singers would have to perform unaccompanied or provide an instrument of their own. It must be said that the fire provided was a generous one of logs piled on top of coal, but either the wood was damp or the chimney needed sweeping because thick clouds of smoke issued from it at intervals and no one dared to sit too close.

Steven Pitt was there with his wife, Ellen, and John Burrows shared a bench with them. Linda and Len Hudson sat at a nearby table, with Linda's mother and younger sister Grace. Further over Tim Bilton and young Harry from Foxearth were playing dominoes with Will and Jarvis Tupp – the latter being reinstated in the good books of the village since recent disclosures regarding 'that Thursday'. The door opened and old Robbie came in, dusting snow from his coat. A groan went up from some of those nearest the door and one wag held his nose: 'Hey, Robbie, you are supposed to leave the fish outside. I reckon his pockets are stuffed full of bloaters. Pooh, what a smell!' There was loud laughter at this sally, but Robbie joined in good-humouredly.

'If I had any bloaters, I would be at home cooking them,' he replied, 'but with all the roads snowbound, I shan't get much fish for the next few days.'

'Or weeks,' someone suggested.

Robbie's expression changed to one of exaggerated dismay.

'Don't!' he begged. 'It's coming down fast now and there's a bit of a wind getting up.'

'He's right. Once it starts drifting . . .'

Robbie made towards the counter, nodding to various acquaintances on the way.

'Maisie, my love,' he said, 'a pint of my usual as quick as you like.' He put twopence-halfpenny down on the counter top and said, 'Evening, Ted.'

'Evening, Robbie,' said Ted, who was busy drying beer mugs with a flimsy cloth. 'D'you reckon it'll set in then?'

'I hope not, but I'd not be surprised.' There were groans at this.

'Old Andy not in yet?' asked Robbie, looking around.

'Andy?' said Maisie. 'Haven't you heard?'

'Heard what?'

Andy was the village blacksmith.

'He's laid up. Can't work. Dropped a hammer on his toe and crushed it.'

'Never!'

'He did. Isn't that right, Ted?'

'That's right,' said Ted, 'and right in the middle of doing them wrought-iron gates for her ladyship.'

'She won't be very pleased, then,' said Robbie.

'Andy's wife's not very pleased, either,' said Linda. 'You know what she's like. Can't bear to see a man resting, so she's got him up already and hobbling round.'

There was more laughter. 'He wants to play his cards right,' said Len, with a wicked gleam in his eye. He was a slim man with bright red hair. 'With Tom Bryce out of the way, I should think there's an opening there for a willing lad, begging your pardon, Tim.'

He glanced across at Tim Bilton, who grinned. 'Leave me out of it,' he said. But now several heads were turning in his direction.

'He's right,' said Ted. 'I mean, Andy's a lusty-looking lad, and her ladyship must be missing it something cruel.'

'Poor old Tom!' said Will Tupp. 'But he had a fair old crack of the whip. Lord knows how long that was going on before he got rumbled.'

'A long time,' said his wife.

'Have you seen her ladyship since?' asked Robbie.

'She was in the shop a few days ago,' said Jarvis, 'and real sharp-tempered, she was. Never the world's sweetest woman, but now she's real frosty. I shouldn't like to cross her.'

'But how about *being* across her?' cried Robbie, at which there was laughter and shrieks of approval. He went on, 'I reckon old Andy's in with a chance there. She obviously likes a well-set-up man.'

Maisie said, 'You don't want to let her hear you talking like that.'

'Why not?' Robbie demanded. 'It's a free country, isn't it? She's not my landlady, so she can't send me packing with a flea in my ear, like poor old Tom.'

'Does anyone know where they've gone?' asked Linda.

Tom Bryce, Rose, Mrs Bryce and the children had vanished from Teesbury at dead of night soon after Tom's unsuccessful visit to London. The large waggon carrying their worldly possessions had creaked and rattled its way along the road, announcing their departure to all the light sleepers who rushed to their windows to pull back the curtains and watch them go.

'Well, I think it's a crying shame,' said Ellen Pitt. 'After all, he only did what he was invited to do. If anyone should have given him his marching orders, it was poor little Rose and she stood by him.'

'More fool her,' said Linda.

Rashly, Ellen rose to the bait. 'Oh, she's a fool, is she? Then what would you have done, Linda Hudson? How would you have managed without a husband with all those kids of hers? Money don't grow on trees, you know. It's all very well being high-minded, but it isn't happening to you, is it, and you haven't got six mouths to feed.'

'Ladies, ladies!' said Maisie, for Linda was still childless, much to her despair. 'Put another log on, Mr Pitt, will you?' she called in an attempt to change the subject.

Several people coughed as the rising wind outside blew more smoke down the chimney and into the room. At that moment the door opened again and Joan Little came in. Trying to keep a shawl over her shoulders, she let go of the door-handle and the door swung open with the force of the wind, letting in a blast of air and swirling snowflakes. There were cries of protest from those nearest and Ted gave the door a kick to close it.

'Here she is, Jarvis!' cried John Burrows. 'Oh, look at him! Jarvis is blushing.'

Since Vinnie's disappearance, Jarvis Tupp had turned his attention to Joan Little, a widow ten years older than himself – an attractive woman with dark curls, rosy cheeks and a ready smile. Sheepishly, Jarvis stood up and she made her way towards him.

'Look at him blush,' cried John Burrows.

'He's only jealous,' cried Maisie. 'Take no notice of him!'

'I don't,' said Joan, giving Jarvis a quick kiss. 'Any more cheek from him and I shan't tell you my news.'

The various conversations going on around her died suddenly.

'News?'

'What news?'

'She's kidding. She hasn't got any news.'

'News about what?'

Joan looked around her, triumphantly. 'About the Bryces,' she said. 'I know where they've gone!'

'You don't, do you?' said Jarvis, but she nodded. There was an instant clamour and a buzz of speculation.

'Tell us, then, Joan.'

'Cough it up, love.'

'Where are they, then?'

'Well, my cousin who works for Whitbreads in Maidstone, said that one of their drivers saw a new family moving into a cottage in Laddingford and the wife called the husband Tom.'

There was another clamour of excited voices.

'Could be Tom anybody.'

'Tom who?'

'Was there kids and a mother?'

She nodded. 'The driver asked another mate of his and he reckons Tom's the new pole-puller for Westerns. He could be right, because their man died of his lungs a few weeks ago and they say this new man's come with a very good reference.'

Tim Bilton said, 'That's right, the Colonel gave him a reference. Sent it to him by Janet, so her ladyship would not know.'

'He never did!'

'Really? Poor old Colonel. He's a good old boy.'

'He is that,' said Tim.

Jarvis brought Joan a port and lemon and she settled herself at the table beside him.

'And what d'you think on old Josh, then?' asked Ted. 'Setting his cap at that young Warren girl and her barely seventeen.'

'And a bit daft at that, poor kid,' put in one of his listeners.

'She'd have to be daft to take up with Joshua Parsloe,' said Maisie, 'after what happened to his poor wife.'

'She's got a funny look in her eyes, that Warren girl. Well, they all have, come to that.'

'How funny?'

Ted tapped his head and there were murmurs of agreement.

'Still, the Warrens are as poor as church-mice,' said Ted, 'and Josh has got a tidy bit tucked away. Women'll put up with a lot for a bit of security.'

For a while the conversation continued desultorily and half an hour passed punctuated by bursts of laughter, the clinking of glasses and a great deal of coughing as the smoke continued to billow out into the room.

'You want to get that swept,' said Steven at last, as he dabbed his streaming eyes. 'There's such a thing as a chimney-sweep, you know, love. They have black faces and long poles with a brush at the end and they shove them up the chimney!'

A roar of laughter greeted his remarks and encouraged by this and the amount of drink he had swallowed, he went on, 'What happens is that the brush goes up the chimney and pushes the soot out of the top of it. It's quite simple, really.'

'I do know what a chimney-sweep is,' said Maisie, her tone at once scornful and haughty, 'and when I need your advice, I'll ask for it. You stick to drying hops, Mr Pitt, and leave us to run the pub.'

'He's right, though,' said Robbie. 'My eyes are stinging.'

'It's the logs,' said Ted, but he was shouted down.

'It's the chimney,' Robbie insisted.

Ted looked at his wife. It was obvious that as the evening wore on, people would drink more and consequently speak more freely and the subject of the smoking chimney threatened to become an issue.

'Well, fair enough,' said Ted. 'I meant to get it seen to before now. I'll get it done over the weekend. Now, how about a sing-song, ladies and gentlemen? We've had no music yet tonight. Who is going to be the first brave soul? Linda?'

Joan said 'What about Ellen?' Ellen said 'I'm not going to be first.'

'One of the men, then,' said Ted.

'Oh, very well, then,' said Ellen and she rose from her seat looking as reluctant as possible, to loud applause. 'But I'm only going to sing one,' she said, 'so don't go getting on to me for an encore.'

No one was deceived for a moment. She cleared her throat, but Jarvis Tupp shouted, 'Get up on the chair, love,' and she allowed herself to be elevated to a position where everyone could see her. Her husband watched proudly as she smoothed her dress, patted her hair and straightened her flower-decked hat. All eyes turned towards her as she began to sing. 'I'm Only a Bird in a Gilded Cage' and for the next five minutes the smoking fire went unnoticed. By way of encore, she sang 'A Bicycle Made for Two' and then sat down to applause.

Joan was then persuaded to sing 'After the Ball was Over', on condition that Len Hudson recited a well-loved monologue about a shepherd and his faithful dog. Then Robbie insisted on playing several popular melodies on a variety of bottles and glass mugs. Jarvis had his arm round Joan and their heads were close together. Ted, afraid of incurring more complaints about the smoke, let the fire go down.

A few latecomers arrived and were served and duly acquainted with the news of Tom Bryce and his family. Will Tupp then organised a general sing-song which included many of the hopping songs the Londoners had brought down with them the previous autumn. The evening followed its normal course until at five-past ten the local policeman put his head in at the door to say the snow was coming down thick and fast and that anyone with any distance to go would be well advised not to leave it too late. This announcement effectively broke up the evening's entertainment, and within a quarter of an hour the parlour was empty.

Ted collected up glasses and mugs and put them on the counter, while Maisie washed them. He then emptied the ashtrays into a metal wastepaper bin and raked out the remaining coals. For a while, neither of them spoke. Ted straightened the chairs and tables perfunctorily and dried the glasses.

'That Ellen Pitt,' said Maisie at last. 'Whatever makes her think she can sing?'

'Don't ask me!'

'And did you see Joan and Jarvis? Talk about wandering hands.' Her husband nodded without comment.

'Still,' said Maisie, 'it's good news about the Bryces, if what she said was true.'

He nodded and, folding the cloth, laid it on the counter. His wife picked it up, pointedly unfolding it and hanging it from the counter so that it would dry overnight.

'Leave the empties until tomorrow,' she said. 'I can hardly keep my eyes open.'

'Nor me,' he agreed.

With a last look round the parlour, they went out and made their way upstairs to bed. The matter of the smoking chimney was not mentioned again.

*

The winter was a hard one. Although the snow had come late, it fell heavily and successive showers froze. For a few days, Teesbury was cut off except by river. By the middle of February it was thawing and flooding added to the general misery. In London the white snow was soon changed to a dirty-brown slush and many destitute people who normally slept in the streets were driven to take shelter in the Workhouses and common lodging-houses of which there were plenty.

The enterprising Harry Samm realised that there would not

be a better time to find Vinnie Harris if he was ever to claim the £10 reward which Julian Lawrence had promised. He therefore redeemed his only respectable suit of clothes and with a black curly-brimmed bowler to complete the picture, began an intensive search during which he presented himself as Vinnie's anxious uncle. His story was that Vinnie, his niece, finding herself in a certain shameful condition, had run away rather than break her father's heart. That father was now dead, he said, and with his last breath had asked Harry Samm to find his daughter.

Most workhouse masters were only too glad to get rid of one of their inmates, but at the first five Harry Samm drew a blank. The sixth, however, proved more hopeful. The description of Winnie Crutchley fitted Vinnie's and the matron allowed him to have a look at her while she walked in the Workhouse exercise yard. Harry Samm was convinced that, in spite of her dreadfully changed appearance, it *was* Vinnie Harris. But he was a cautious man and did not wish to alarm her or alert her to the realisation that she had been discovered. Therefore, he arranged with the matron that he would return with Roland Fry. Promptly at nine o'clock the following day, the two men were shown into the reception area.

'Wait here,' said the matron, 'and I will bring her to you.' Five pounds of the reward lay snugly in Harry Samm's pocket, the other five would be paid over when Roland Fry was convinced that it was in fact the girl they had been looking for. If it wasn't her, the money would be returned to Roland.

After a few moments, they heard footsteps in the corridor and at last Vinnie was pushed into the room. For a moment Roland stared at her, unable to believe that the pitiable sight meeting his eyes was the girl he had danced with at the hopping supper not six months earlier. She shuffled because her shoes did not fit; her hair was cropped short and she stared listlessly at the floor. She did not know why she had been brought to this room and was too weary to care. The shapeless dress did not disguise her pregnancy and her shoulders were bent as though under a great burden, but the worst thing was her expression of utter hopelessness.

'Straighten yourself up, Crutchley!' snapped the matron. 'You have two visitors. Say good morning.'

Slowly Vinnie raised her head and looked at Harry Samm and then at Roland Fry. Her mouth opened and closed and she swayed slightly.

'Say good morning, Crutchley.'

'Good morning.' It was only a whisper, but Roland felt his heart contract at the familiar voice.

'Vinnie,' he said gently, 'I have come to take you away from here.'

Vinnie heard the words, but they made no sense. Leave the Workhouse? The idea was almost frightening. The weeks she had spent there seemed an eternity and she could hardly remember the outside world; already the harsh pattern of everyday life there had imprinted itself indelibly on her mind.

'Vinnie, do you hear me? I want you to come back with me.'

'But *you* are not her uncle,' said the matron sharply.

'That's true,' said Harry Samm, 'but this gentleman is a friend of mine who has been sufficiently kind and generous-hearted to offer the girl a position in his home.'

'Do you hear that, Crutchley? Answer the gentleman. Thank him for his generosity.'

'Thank you, sir,' said Vinnie, and she gave a polite bob in Roland's direction but kept her eyes downcast, unable to bear the shock which showed so plainly in his eyes.

'She has been no trouble,' said the matron. 'But she is not very robust. No stamina. She does not work as well as the others and has barely earned her keep. But there you are, some of them can and some of them can't. I always maintain that it is mind over matter. If you put your mind to something you can do it, whatever it is. Winnie seems unable to do that. No doubt if we had kept her longer we might have seen a marked improvement. However, if she is leaving, there are a few formalities and your signature is required, Mr Samm. She lies, though,' she told them. 'Your name is Samm, isn't it, girl? Not Crutchley?'

Vinnie watched dully as she saw an entry being made in the book and it dawned on her slowly that she *was* leaving. She looked beseechingly at Roland and he smiled encouragingly. 'We are going to take care of you, Vinnie,' he said. 'Don't be afraid. You have nothing to fear now. Nothing at all, I promise you.'

Matron selected a key from her belt and unfastened the cupboard. She tossed Vinnie's bundle of clothes behind the screen in the corner and said, 'Get changed and don't dawdle. I have plenty to do and I don't want to hang about here.'

With trembling fingers, Vinnie tugged off the hated workhouse garment and pulled on her own. They had not been laundered, but had somehow acquired the strong smell of disinfectant that pervaded the room. She smoothed her hair down and rubbed feebly at her face to bring a little colour back into her cheeks. For the first time in months she cared what she looked like and it was a strange feeling. Finally, she put on her own shoes. They were worn and down-at-heel, but at least they fitted her. She pulled her shawl over her shoulders, picked up the neatly folded pile of workhouse clothes and stepped out from behind the screen.

'Why, Vinnie, that's better!' said Roland.

Harry Samm was signing the book and took no further interest in her.

'Well, thank you, matron,' he said. 'We are very grateful to you for all you have done and I am sure Vinnie is. Vinnie,' he called and she turned, 'I am telling matron you are very grateful for all they have done for you here.'

'Yes, ma'am,' said Vinnie.

'Well, I am sure we do our best,' said matron, 'with the limited means at our disposal. I hope we shan't see you back here again, Winnie.'

'Oh, you won't, madam' said Harry. Then the two men left the Workhouse taking Vinnie with them.

Once outside, Harry Samm demanded the rest of his reward and Roland paid it to him as quickly as he could, longing to be rid of the man. Within seconds Harry had melted into the crowd and Roland and Vinnie were left alone. Roland took her arm and led her unprotesting through the streets. Suddenly she stopped.

'My hair,' she said, putting a hand up to her head.

'It will grow again, Vinnie,' Roland told her. 'In no time at all it will grow, I promise you. It will be as beautiful as before, so don't give it another thought.'

'But where are we going?'

'To my home, for the moment,' said Roland. 'To think that you were so near all this time, only a few miles away from my own home. Dear Vinnie! It's so good to see you. We have all prayed for you. Oh Vinnie, say you are pleased to see me.'

'I am. Yes, I am.'

He smiled, reassured, and took her arm once more. Gradually they left the poor area and walked where the road was wider and lined with trees. Eventually they went up some steps, where Roland took a key from his waistcoat pocket and opened the door.

'Father, I am home!' he called. 'I have found her. Mrs Swayne, we are home. She is here, Vinnie is here!'

A tall man appeared on the top of the stairs and made his way down, his hand outstretched in greeting. He smiled warmly at Vinnie as he shook her hand. 'Welcome, my dear,' he said. 'I am so pleased my son has found you again. We have all been most concerned for your safety.'

From the far end of the passage the housekeeper, a small motherly-looking woman, bustled into view.

'Oh, Master Roland,' she cried. 'You have found the young lady!'

'Yes, I have found her. This is Mrs Swayne, Vinnie. Since my mother died, she has looked after us both.'

Mrs Swayne swept Vinnie into her arms and hugged her, then suddenly stepped back with a little laugh. 'Oh dear, mustn't squeeze the baby, must we?' she said cheerfully.

Vinnie felt close to tears, her courage undermined by so much kindness.

'I'm sorry,' she whispered. 'I'm sorry.'

'Bless me, there's nothing to be sorry about,' said Mrs Swayne. 'Supposing I take her with me,' she said to Roland,

'and give her a nice warm drink and something to eat. Then she will want a nice warm bath and a soft bed. How does that sound to you, my love?'

'It sounds like a dream,' said Vinnie with a faint smile. Mrs Swayne looked up at Roland. 'I don't think this poor young thing feels like talking just now, sir. Will you leave her with me for a while? Let her come to herself, like?' Roland, having just found her, was reluctant to relinquish her again but he nodded – the housekeeper was right and Vinnie must have time to adjust to the situation.

'That's a splendid idea,' he agreed. 'Will that suit you, Vinnie? Will you talk to us later this evening, or tomorrow, or whenever you feel rested?'

'Yes, I will,' said Vinnie, 'and thank you. I can hardly believe I'm here.'

'It's a wonderful surprise for all of us,' said Roland's father. 'Well, you go along, young lady, and I shall look forward to seeing you when you are quite recovered.'

The housekeeper put an arm round Vinnie's thin shoulders and led her down the passage towards the kitchen. 'Suppose I scramble you a few eggs,' she said, 'and pop them on a nice slice of buttered toast? That would go down a treat, I'm sure, and a nice cup of cocoa with lots of milk? We'll see, shall we?' The two men watched them disappear round the corner.

'She is home,' said Roland and his father nodded. He knew how much it meant to his son to have found Vinnie, and also half-guessed at the deeper feelings which motivated him: feelings which Roland had never admitted even to himself. He put a hand on his son's shoulders. 'It is a very good beginning,' he said, 'but you must not rush things, Roland. The secret is to take one step at a time.'

CHAPTER TWENTY-ONE

Ten days later Vinnie was almost unrecognisable as the pathetic creature Roland had rescued from the Union Workhouse. Her skin positively gleamed from the application of soap and water and perfumed creams. Her hair, treated to remove the lice, had been trimmed by Mrs Swayne and once more framed her face with a glow of dull gold. Nourishing food had done its work: her face had begun to lose its haggard lines and her arms and legs were less stick-like. The cowed, despairing expression had faded from her face and she began to smile again, blossoming in the warmth of the kindness which now surrounded her.

As each morning dawned, Roland made up his mind that he would telephone Julian with news of his success, but as each day passed he found an excuse not to do so. He would wait until she was a little more presentable, he argued, or he thought Vinnie herself was not yet willing. He even told himself that Mrs Swayne had befriended the girl and would miss her if she returned to Teesbury. The strongest argument, of course, was that no one knew what would happen to her when she did go back to Teesbury. Roland was able to convince himself that while she remained at his home she was secure and happy, and that time was needed for her to build herself up and prepare for yet another change in her life. All these arguments seemed entirely relevant to him, but not to Mary Bellweather who viewed each passing day with deepening suspicion and resentment. She held her tongue, however, and waited, hoping that the matter would resolve itself in some way without her intervention.

*

The meeting of the Brothers in Jesus had been planned for Friday night, and seven o'clock found Roland standing behind his favourite lectern facing five rows of members. Mary Bellweather sat in the front row, with Vinnie beside her.

'Ladies and gentlemen,' Roland began as he positively beamed upon them all. 'Tonight, as you know, we have a stranger among us – at least, she is a stranger to most of you. Lydia, Mary, Gareth and I have all met her before, but in very different circumstances. You are, of course, already aware of all the background, so I will not waste time. I will come straight to the point and tell you this: this is the happiest night of my whole life. Tonight is the crowning point of my ambition – the ambition which I shared with you more than two years ago when our little group was formed and we held our first meeting under this very roof. I said on that occasion that our duty lay with the unfortunate people who shared the streets around us, and I suggested that we turn all our endeavours towards making their lives more comfortable. I hoped that by our own example we might succeed in turning them away from sin. My very words were that if we could save one soul, all our efforts would be worthwhile. Tonight I have pleasure in telling you that we have done just that!'

Vinnie almost squirmed in her seat as he went on, aware of curious looks cast in her direction. She felt like an insect under a magnifying glass, as the list of her misfortunes was revealed one by one by the earnest man to whom she owed so much. The fact that everything he said was true made it no easier to bear, and there were moments when she wished that the ground would open and swallow her up. She was well aware, too, that the girl beside her did not share Roland's enthusiasm for her dramatic change of fortune. Not that Mary wished her any harm, but her jealousy was evident and Vinnie was uncertain how to deal with it.

'What we have been able to do for Vinnie Harris, we can do for others,' Roland was saying. 'We must not rest on our laurels. We must not be complacent over our success. When Vinnie is restored to her rightful place, wherever that might prove to be, we must renew our efforts on behalf of all the other wretched souls in need of salvation. Our aim continues to be the return of sinners to the path of God, and with this shining example before us, I believe we shall go from strength to strength. With each success, our experience and confidence must surely grow.'

He paused, obviously waiting for a round of applause, which was quickly forthcoming. Then he raised a hand to interrupt the clapping. 'And now for a surprise,' he said. 'I am going to ask Vinnie to speak to you. She is not expecting it and I am sure that if I had asked her previously, she would have declined, for she is as modest as she is good. So I have cheated a little and taken her unawares. Vinnie, will you come and talk to us for a few moments and tell us in your own words how it feels to be here tonight?'

Vinnie's heart almost stopped beating when she realised what was expected of her and instinctively she turned to Mary. 'I can't,' she whispered. 'Please . . .'

Mary hardened her heart. 'Do it to please Roland,' she urged and was instantly ashamed of herself. She reflected bitterly, not for the first time, that Vinnie Harris brought out the worst in her. Vinnie turned towards Roland, who was smiling and holding out his hands.

'Vinnie Harris!' he announced in ringing tones and there was no way out. Somehow her legs still functioned and she found herself walking out to join him. He took both her hands in his and squeezed them hard. 'There is nothing to be afraid of,' he said softly. 'You are among friends here. Talk to them, Vinnie.'

'But what shall I say? I don't know—'

'Say whatever comes into your heart.'

He turned to his audience, repeated, 'Vinnie Harris' in a quieter voice and then stepped back so that he was out of her line of vision. Suddenly she was very much alone; she put up a hand and took hold of the lectern to steady herself. A sea of faces seemed to swim before her and she coughed nervously to clear her throat, convinced that she would be unable to utter a single word.

'Ladies and gentlemen,' she began, and then stopped, her mind a complete blank. She made a great effort to pull her thoughts together and say something coherent.

'Roland has told you how it all happened,' she began, 'and nothing I say – no words of mine – can tell you how it was. All I can tell you – at least, all I can hope – is that none of you is unfortunate enough to find yourself in a Union Workhouse. It is not a happy place to be and no one chooses to go there. Someone told me that it is better than prison, but only just. I cannot imagine how anything could be worse.'

Her voice trembled and there was not a sound from the audience who all leaned forward in their seats listening intently. She swallowed nervously and continued, 'I once heard workhouse inmates referred to as the dregs of humanity – if that is so, then all I can say is that whatever you are when you go in there, that is what you become. The House is not a haven for unfortunate people who have nowhere else to go. It's a punishment – for poor, lonely sick people whose only crime *is* to be poor and sick and lonely.'

She glanced back towards Roland, hoping that she might stop at that point, but he made encouraging signs for her to continue. She went on, stammering in her nervousness, exposed and vulnerable with all eyes upon her. 'I'm one of the lucky ones, and if I were a good Christian I would pray daily for those I left behind me, but I will be honest and tell you I don't. That's because I'm a coward and I want to blot out the memory of the place and all the people in it – because . . .' her voice faltered '. . . because to remember them is to re-live the nightmare and I—'

She bowed her head and suddenly put both hands up to her face, sobbing helplessly. There was a murmur of shocked sympathy from the audience and Roland, stricken, stepped forward and took her in his arms, making clumsy attempts to comfort her and cursing himself for his foolishness in submitting her to what was obviously an ordeal. Embarrassed, the audience murmured amongst themselves while he

patted Vinnie's shoulder and whispered soothingly to her.
'You were splendid, Vinnie. Please don't cry. I didn't mean
to make you cry. It's all over now and we won't speak of it
again. I beg you not to cry.'

It was some time before she regained her self-control and
was able to check the flow of her tears with his large white
handkerchief. Finally, when Roland glanced for support to
Mary Bellweather, he found that she had left the hall.

*

Several nights later Vinnie, unable to sleep, came downstairs
just before midnight to pour herself a glass of milk and was
surprised, as she reached the bottom of the stairs, to hear voices
coming from the drawing-room – those of Roland and Mary.
The voices were slightly raised and Vinnie, not wishing to
eavesdrop, made to hurry past the door on her way to the
kitchen. However, she caught her own name and stopped
abruptly. Curiosity overcame her better judgement and
glancing around to see that she was not observed, she moved
closer to the door.

'. . . yes, besotted, Roland.' It was Mary's voice. 'You are
quite besotted with her and it is obvious to everyone. You are
making a fool of yourself, and I cannot let it go on any longer.'

'Mary, you are quite wrong. I simply take a delight in the
transformation we have brought about—'

'Stop fooling yourself, Roland! Your fondness for the girl is
written all over your face, for all to see. How do you think I
feel? Whenever her name is mentioned in my presence,
someone is tactful enough to change the subject, because they
know how hurt I am by your attitude towards her. No one else
will speak to you about it, so I must do so myself. I would like
you to think honestly about your relationship with Vinnie
Harris and then come back to me, Roland, and tell me one way
or the other.'

'How do you mean, tell you?'

'Tell me how your feelings for her affect the feeling that you
profess for me.'

'Mary! You surely cannot think—'

'That is exactly what I do think, Roland!' Her tone was hard and Vinnie could sense the bitterness. 'I think you are quite infatuated with her, to the exclusion of everything and everyone else. Surely you cannot deny that your feelings towards her have deepened over the last few weeks?'

He hesitated, uncomfortably aware of the truth of what she was saying, but still unwilling to face up to what was happening.

'Answer me this, Roland, and I beg you to answer it honestly. Why have you not contacted Julian Lawrence? It was his reward money that brought about her rescue and yet you have not told him. You are reluctant to do so because you know what will happen. He will come straightaway for her and take her back to Teesbury.'

Outside the door, Vinnie smothered an astonished gasp. The news that Julian was trying to find her came as a shock. But then he did not know of her child. Her momentary hope died – there was no way she could ever go back to him. Greatly agitated, she strained forward to catch every word.

'No,' Roland was saying, 'that may not be the best course for her. It may be better that—' He stopped abruptly.

'You see,' Mary said miserably. 'You cannot bear the thought that she will go away. You promised him that you would try to find her and yet he is still unaware that she is safe. All you have to do is to call him on the telephone. Ask yourself, Roland, why you have not done so and then I shall not need to say any more.'

There was a longer silence.

'Mary, I am sorry,' said Roland. 'There is some truth in what you say, I will confess it, but truly you are exaggerating.'

'Am I?'

'Yes, you are. I am fond of her, it is true, but I don't think that alters my feelings towards you.'

'You don't *think* it does? You are not sure?'

'I mean it doesn't,' he amended quickly. 'Of course it doesn't. I love and respect you, as I have told you many times. Vinnie Harris being here makes no difference to that.'

'Perhaps your reasons for keeping her here make a difference to *me*,' said Mary. 'Perhaps I find it intolerable to know that the two of you live under this roof.'

'Don't talk like that, Mary. I don't want anything to come between us.'

'But Vinnie already has,' cried Mary passionately. 'Don't you see that, Roland? Can't you see what is happening to us? You are so blind! All you can see is Vinnie Harris, your big triumph, your big success. Oh, don't misunderstand me, it's an achievement to have found her. I give you full credit for that, but I will not be humiliated by your continued attentions to her. I know why you have not told Julian. It is because you know he feels for her deeply, otherwise he would never have offered the reward.'

'Julian Lawrence and Vinnie Harris!' His voice rose slightly. 'Surely you don't suggest—'

'You are *jealous*, Roland. The idea troubles you.'

'No, it is you who are jealous. You quite surprise me, Mary. These last few weeks you have been different. The other night when you walked out of the meeting, how do you think I felt then?'

'How do you think *I* felt, sitting there listening to you talking about her as though she was some kind of saint, with that look on your face that made it clear as day where your heart really was – and then taking her in your arms in front of everyone!'

'That's nonsense, Mary. It was—'

'I have no wish to argue any longer. I didn't come here to quarrel with you, Roland, for I love you and make no pretence otherwise. I came to ask you to take a close look at your own feelings and to be honest with yourself and with me. You are going to have to choose between us, you know. If you persist in keeping her here, then I shall not call again.'

'Mary, you cannot mean that!'

'Oh, but I do. Later I may regret what I am doing, but I must do it for my own peace of mind. If, as you say, you still love me, then telephone Julian Lawrence and ask him to take Vinnie away, otherwise our relationship – happy though it was – is over.'

Before Vinnie realised what was happening, the door was flung open and Mary collided with her. She gave a startled cry and Vinnie saw the dark misery in her eyes.

'You!' gasped Mary and her eyes blazed furiously. She shouted back over her shoulder, 'Here's your precious Vinnie, listening at the door like the common little slut that she is. Take her and welcome!'

Vinnie put up a restraining hand, but Mary pushed her aside and all her anger and despair went into the thrust. Losing her balance, Vinnie stumbled and fell backwards against the door of the morning-room, while the front door slammed behind Mary with such force that the glass panel rattled. Roland came out of the drawing-room and found Vinnie struggling to her feet. He was appalled to know she had overheard their conversation and for a moment they regarded each other in dismay. Then, without a word, Vinnie moved past him and up the stairs.

Back in her bed, she lay awake all night in an agony of indecision. She felt humiliated, almost unclean and in no mood to face Julian, who would no doubt be contacted by Roland the next morning. Neither had she any desire to come between Mary and Roland, and the thought that she had done so genuinely grieved her. She had been so proud to count them both as friends and now it seemed she had unwittingly destroyed their relationship.

Dawn was breaking before she finally made up her mind. With a last look at the little room which had been home for the past two weeks, she crept out of bed and pulled on her clothes. If her old garments had been available, she would have put them on, but they had been burnt and new ones provided. She would have to wear them, for she had nothing else, but one day somehow she meant to pay for them. Vinnie left no note, but tip-toed downstairs as the nearby church clock struck quarter-past five and let herself quietly out of the house.

*

Eva sat in the tiny waiting-room watching all that remained of the inadequate fire provided for the travelling public. The coals shifted suddenly and rearranged themselves in a flurry of grey ash.

She wore a warm red coat with a fur collar and her hands were tucked into a matching muff, but in addition to this she had brought a red plaid rug from the carriage which was draped over her head and round her shoulders to provide extra warmth. The winter continued very cold and the March winds blew from the north-east, bringing the continued threat of more snow. There was no one else in the waiting-room, so she was able to give full rein to her thoughts and made no effort to hide her anxiety. She was, she reflected, betrothed to the dearest man in the world and should have been very happy. Several problems, however, loomed large on her horizon and cast a shadow over her happiness. One of these was the relationship between her parents, which had now broken down irretrievably.

Christina never entered her husband's bedroom and Janet spent more and more of her time attending to the old man. His wife moved through each day in a mood of suppressed fury and her temper was dangerously unpredictable. She was liable to fly into a rage at the slightest provocation and most of the servants had felt the lash of her tongue at some time or other over the past few weeks. Eva, too, had suffered her displeasure on more than one occasion. Robbed of the company of Tom Bryce, albeit by her own design, Christina seemed determined to ensure that no one else enjoyed the attentions of a lover. She had never taken up the invitation to visit the Cottingham family in Devizes and refused to invite Gerald to Foxearth, pretending that she was unable to cope with visitors, which to some extent was true. Her increasing hostility, barely suppressed, seemed to be affecting her mind. There were times when she seemed quite unable to make the simplest decision, and her memory occasionally failed her altogether. Eva was also becoming seriously alarmed by the steady deterioration of her mother's personality. Christina had never been an easy person to live with, but life with her at Foxearth was rapidly becoming intolerable. Mrs Tallant had already threatened to give in her notice after a particularly heated exchange

with her mistress, but Eva had persuaded her not to go.
Eva's other problem concerned Gerald, who had been
offered employment on the expanding railway system which
was opening up in India. He wanted them to marry much
earlier than planned, so that Eva could accompany him.
Christina had flatly refused to even consider such an idea, and
although Eva felt sure her father would give his consent, she
had shelved any final decision on the matter until Julian's
return for the Easter holidays. As it happened, however, Julian
had now learned from Roland of the fiasco of Vinnie's
discovery and subsequent disappearance and had immediately
made plans to return home. He was furious at the way the
situation had been handled and justifiably blamed Roland for
not telling him when Vinnie had first been found. He had
telephoned Foxearth earlier in the morning to say that he
would reach Wateringbury Station on the first train after
twelve. Wanting to talk to him privately, Eva had decided to
take the pony and trap and go to the station herself to meet him.
There was no doubt in her mind that her brother was
genuinely in love with Vinnie Harris, but she was also aware
of the unsuitability of the match and knew that Christina
would do everything in her power to prevent it.

Hearing the clang of the signal, she rose to her feet and made
her way out on to the platform. In the distance she could see the
smoke of the approaching train. She was looking forward to
seeing her brother, not only because there was a strong bond of
affection between them, but also because life was difficult and
she welcomed an ally.

'Good morning, Miss Lawrence.'

She turned and smiled at the station-master.

'It's a cold one,' she said.

'It has been a bad winter, one way and another.'

She nodded.

'First the snow and then the floods. I said to my wife, I will
be glad when spring comes. I don't enjoy the winters like I did
when I was a boy. Then, it was tobogganing and sliding on the
pond and throwing snowballs.' He laughed. 'Seems a long
time ago, those days. I am sorry for such a miserable bit of a

fire,' – he nodded towards the waiting-room. 'Waiting for a new delivery, we are, and I'm trying to eke it out. Wasn't really expecting anyone today, so I just put a few knobs on to show willing.'

'I am meeting my brother,' said Eva.

'Oh? Nothing wrong, is there?'

'No-o.' Her tone belied the word. 'At least, just a bit of a problem.'

'Life's full of those. Well, here she comes.'

He went back into his office and Eva waited as the engine, with its single coach, drew alongside in a rush of steam and squealing brakes. Julian jumped down and slammed the door behind him.

'You look like an eskimo,' he said, kissing her lightly, 'all bundled in that rug.'

'I feel like one.'

They both waved a farewell to the station-master and made their way out into the station yard. There they climbed into the trap and Julian took up the reins.

'Don't drive too fast,' said Eva. 'I want to talk to you before we go home. But first, Julian, I wanted you to know how sorry I am about Vinnie. I know how much it means to you to find her.'

Julian's pent-up anger exploded. 'That incompetent fool, Fry,' he said. 'It was fortunate for him that so many miles separated us, for I swear I would have thrashed him if I had been near enough. All that trouble to no avail, and doubtless she will see that we don't find her again. The baby must be due in a month or two, I just cannot bear to think of it.' He shook his head. 'They will both die, I am sure of it. I have this sense of foreboding that time is running out for her – now, just when it seemed that our luck had changed, that bungling idiot has to lose her again. Why he didn't tell me in time, I will never know!'

Eva had her own opinion on the subject, but decided this was not the time to speak of it.

'And Samm has run off with the reward, I suppose?' she said.

'But he is entitled to it, isn't he?' said Julian. 'He earned it. After all, he found her. However, the money doesn't matter, but I am so sick at heart. I can't pretend otherwise. I shall go up there myself and look for her; it is what I should have done all along.'

'Mama will not like it,' ventured Eva.

'To hell with Mama! From your letter, I gather she has problems of her own which she must deal with in her own way. Vinnie is *my* problem and that will require most of my energies over the next few weeks. But forgive me, I don't mean to scold *you*! Tell me more about Gerry's prospects in India. I confess, I should be sorry if you went so far away, but I would do nothing to stop you if that is what you really want. But you will have to marry him first!'

'There is nothing I want more,' she told him earnestly. 'But can you imagine how it will be if I defy Mama's wishes?'

'I see exactly how it will be,' said Julian grimly. 'You must resign yourself to the fact that she will oppose you in every way she can, but if you are sure Gerry *is* the man for you—'

'I am quite sure.'

'And do you really want to go to India?'

She gave him a sideways glance and laughed a trifle ruefully. 'I wouldn't say I want to go to India exactly,' she confessed, 'but I will say that wherever Gerry is I want to be with him and this is such a marvellous opportunity for him I could never try to persuade him not to accept it. But how can we wed from Foxearth? Mama will make it quite impossible. I dread to think what would happen. She would make a scene, I know it! I think I am becoming a little frightened of her, Julian.'

'We have both always been that,' said Julian.

'No, really frightened,' said Eva soberly. 'Not in awe of her, but physically afraid. Julian, do stop for a moment or walk the horse. We are nearly there and I have not told you the half of it.'

Julian slowed the horses to a walk and listened in alarm as his sister outlined the ways in which Christina had changed since Tom Bryce's departure. 'And since she learned about the will –

you know Papa has left everything to you—' He nodded and she continued, '– since she learned *that*, she has become strange in a way that I find difficult to explain. It is almost indefinable, yet I am aware of it. It is as though there are two sides to her nature now, good and evil, and the evil side seems to be gaining ground.'

Julian was frankly sceptical.

'But it is *true*,' she insisted. 'I knew you would laugh at me and I dare not say this to anyone else, but there is a kind of violence in her.'

He shook his head. 'Your imagination is running riot, Eva. You are letting it prey on your mind. I am sure it can be quite simply explained. She has suffered a number of setbacks over the past few months and is not used to being thwarted. She is angry and vindictive, nothing more.'

Eva sighed. 'I do hope you are right, but if she tries to prevent my marriage—'

He shrugged. 'Then you will have to obtain a special licence and marry quietly elsewhere. If necessary, speak to Gerald's father and arrange to marry in Wiltshire.'

'You make it sound very easy,' she grumbled.

'I don't mean to, I merely suggest it as a way out of the problem. Maybe the only way. One thing is quite certain – when she knows who *I* intend to marry, she will be twice as angry. I am prepared for that. If you are not, then I suggest you make arrangements to move to Devizes as soon as you can. For within a day or two I shall be in London and shall remain there for some considerable time – until I find Vinnie, in fact. I should not like to think of you at Foxearth facing Mother's wrath alone. If, as you believe, the problems of the last few weeks have unsettled her mind, which I hope to God they have not, then I fear she could prove an enemy to be reckoned with.'

He glanced at his sister's face and saw how pale she was. 'But let's not talk so gloomily,' he said, sensing her growing alarm. 'Everything may turn out better than we expect and we should not look on the black side. All families have their problems and life is never simple. We must do what we think is best in the circumstances and try not to hurt anyone else. What more *can* we do?'

Eva looked at him solemnly for a moment. 'We can pray,' she said, 'and I think we should.'

CHAPTER TWENTY-TWO

Janet tapped at the door of the Colonel's bedroom and, hearing no answer, went in. As she suspected, he was dozing and was quite unaware that his daughter had gone to the station to collect his son. She shook his shoulder gently: 'Sir, Colonel Lawrence, sir, wake up.'

He stirred sleepily. 'Is that you, Janet?'

'Yes, sir, I have got a bit of news for you, sir, if you can rouse yourself.'

'If I can rouse myself? Give me a hand, will you? Oh these confounded legs of mine! When a man can't even sit himself up in bed, it's a damned poor show.'

Janet put her arms round him and helped him into a sitting position. 'I would give my right arm,' he said, 'to regain the use of one of my legs.'

'Now I have told you not to talk like that, sir. It's not a nice thing to say.'

'Who says it isn't?'

Janet sighed. He was always a trifle irritable if she woke him from his afternoon sleep.

'So what is it?' he demanded. 'What is this news you have got for me?'

'Well, sir, it's Master Julian. He's coming home today. Any moment now.'

'What? Julian coming home? Where are we, Janet? It isn't Easter surely? I may be an old fool but I am not—'

'No, no, sir, it isn't Easter yet. I don't know why he's coming home, but Miss Eva has gone to fetch him in the trap and asked Cook to prepare him some refreshment. They'll be here shortly and I thought you'd want to be awake.'

'I most certainly do, Janet. Of course I want to be awake when my son comes to visit me.'

He thought for a moment, then said, 'Where is Christina? Does she know of his arrival?'

Janet hesitated. 'I don't know, sir. Tim says she has gone riding, sir.'

'Gone riding? But she has not ridden for years. Are you sure?'

'Yes, sir. Tim said –' she hesitated again.

'Tim said what?'

'That she seemed rather . . . well, rather odd, sir.'

'In what way?'

'She was talking to herself, sir. Sort of muttering – and she has taken Lancer.'

'*What?*'

'I know, sir. Tim knew you would be angry, but the mistress insisted. Tim said he had his orders and would not saddle him but—'

'Christina can't ride Lancer. Has the woman taken leave of her senses? Bilton had no right to let her take him.'

'Well, he tried to stop her but . . . well, the mistress stuck him.'

'*Struck* Bilton?'

'Yes, sir. With her riding-crop – and said if he interfered any more, she would give him a day's notice.'

'In God's name, what's got into the woman? Has something happened that I don't know about?'

'No, sir, not to my knowledge. But she is acting a bit strange lately – begging your pardon, but everyone notices it.'

He sighed heavily. 'I know, I know, Eva's spoken to me about it. She suggested that the doctor be called, but Christina would not hear of it. I really don't know, Janet.' He put a hand to his forehead. 'I feel so damned useless, stuck here in bed. I can't fool myself any longer, I am just a useless has-been. I never see my wife. My daughter wants to leave me. Did you know that, Janet? Eva wants to marry her Gerald—'

'Oh, don't say that, sir! It's not that she wants to leave you.

She's very fond of you, sir, but you know what a young girl is like when she is in love.'

'But she wants to go to *India* with him. That's a damned long way. It is not very likely I will ever see her again.' He beckoned her closer. 'Between you and me, Janet, she was always my favourite. Such a beautiful child and now she is a beautiful woman and wants to leave me.' He sighed. 'There is nothing I would not do for that girl, Janet, and I could not bring myself to refuse her, but it will break my heart if she goes.'

'Don't talk like that, sir. Miss Eva won't be going for ever, I'm sure, sir. She will come back and see you with her husband and family, write you letters – and maybe send photographs. It will be something to look forward to. Really it will, sir, and her young man is a very fine gentleman. He'll take good care of her, you'll see.'

'I should damned well hope so.'

'So no more sad thoughts, Colonel, because I won't have it.'

He smiled faintly. 'You are bullying me again, Janet.'

'Of course I am bullying you, sir. Somebody's got to bully you. Somebody's got to put an end to all these sad thoughts you are thinking. You have always been a very good master to me and I don't like to see you unhappy. Now, what about a clean nightshirt? That one's a bit crumpled, and you want to look your best when your son comes to see you.'

'Fuss, fuss, fuss,' he protested, but he was enjoying her ministrations. Quickly she found another nightshirt and then helped him out of the old and into the new.

'What happens to families, Janet?' he said suddenly. 'It bothers me, it really does. One minute you've got a family and the next it's gone. All gone, Janet, and all been for nothing. You won't understand that, will you?'

'Not really sir. I've never had any family. At least, you've been my family. You and the mistress, Master Julian and Miss Eva. I shall miss her, too, sir.'

'I know you will. You are a good girl.' He sighed heavily. 'When Eva was a little girl, she used to run to me, Janet, do you remember? She would race across the lawn holding out her arms and I would pick her up, swing her round and sit her on my shoulders.'

'Of course I remember, sir. She was a bonny little girl and they were good times. Do you remember, sir, when I first came? She was seven then. Remember how I taught her that little speech for your birthday? I can see her now, sir, standing in the morning-room reciting it to you.'

He laughed at the memory. 'I remember,' he said. 'Oh, Janet . . .' Unexpected tears sprang to his eyes and trickled slowly down his cheeks and he made no effort to wipe them away. Janet looked at him in consternation. 'Now there's no cause to upset yourself, sir. Those are happy memories. They were happy times.'

There were sounds of the door opening downstairs and footsteps in the hall.

'Oh, sir, they're here now! Don't let Master Julian see you so upset. Come on, sir.' Impulsively, she put her arm round the frail shoulders, gave him a hug and wiped his face with the corner of her apron. Then she stood back and surveyed him critically. 'I think you'll do, sir – you will pass muster, as they say in the Army.'

'What do you know about the Army?' he said, his voice shaking slightly.

'I know lots about it, sir, because you are always telling me. Oh, they are coming up, sir, I can hear them.'

She fussed with the pillows and tidied the bed-cover. There was a knock at the door and the Colonel cried, 'Come in!' and Julian and Eva came into the room.

'Thank you, Janet,' said Eva.

The maid gave a quick bob and smiled at Julian.

'Did you want some refreshment, Master Julian?' she asked, but he shook his head and Janet left them.

After the preliminary greetings father, son and daughter talked at some length about Christina's mental state, Eva's wedding and Julian's intention to go to London in search of Vinnie. They were still talking when there was a clatter of footsteps on the stairs and the door burst open to admit

Christina, still in her riding-habit. She was trembling with rage and for a moment no one spoke.

'What's this, then?' She looked at Julian. 'How dare you come sneaking home like this without a word to me? I am your mother, remember, and entitled to your respect and consideration. And you, Eva, you knew he was coming! You took the trap, I am told, and went to fetch him. Why? Why didn't you let Bilton go as usual? You are scheming, aren't you? The pair of you! You are all scheming against me and you thought I would not find out. That is the way of it, isn't it? You waited until I left the house.'

Eva's eyes flashed. 'I wanted time to talk to my brother, that's all. There is no crime in that, Mama.'

'Talk to him about what?'

'My wedding, Mama.'

'There will be no wedding,' cried Christina. She strode forward, the hunting-crop still held in her hand. In her agitation she beat it against the heavy fold of her skirt. She looked particularly handsome in the rich brown coat: she was still slim and the nipped-in waist with its small basque flattered her figure. She wore no hat and her fair hair fell to her shoulders in deep waves. Her eyes gleamed a little too brightly above the pale chiselled lines of her cheeks and but for the thin, hard mouth she would have been beautiful.

'Christina,' said the Colonel, 'there's no need to behave in this way. Please control yourself. There is no reason why the three of us should not be talking together.'

'There is every reason.' Her voice rose. 'Do you think I don't know what you are up to, Henry Lawrence? You mean to do me as much harm as possible. That you have proved already, but I will fight you, Henry, every inch of the way. I shall fight you, I shall fight Julian . . .' She struggled for composure.

'I rode out to be alone,' she told them. 'I needed time to think, away from it all. Away from the whole pack of you. I wanted to think out a plan of campaign and I have done just that. Tomorrow, Henry, I shall find myself a new solicitor, since Peacock obviously eats out of your hand. I shall find my own solicitor and I shall contest your will. Julian will not have Foxearth – *I* shall have it. It is my right! A man has no right to cut his wife out of his will.'

'You did not behave like a wife,' said the old man.

'Words!' said Christina. 'It is all you are capable of now – words. But words will get you nowhere, I promise you that, and as for you two—' She swung round to face Eva and Julian. 'You two deceive and defy me also. You side with your father, that is quite obvious, and you are all in league against me.'

Julian opened his mouth to intervene, but she raised her riding-crop threateningly. 'No, Julian. I *will* have my say. If I must fight you, I will do so. You, Eva, will not marry until you are twenty-one. If Mr Cottingham values you as much as he pretends, let him stay in England.'

'But Mama, his career—' Eva began.

'To hell with his career. I *won't* be defied, Eva. Try to understand what I am saying.'

'Please, Mama,' said Julian calmly. 'As Father says, there really is no need for you to distress yourself in this way.' She took a step towards him, her hands clenched by her sides.

'Distressed? I am not distressed, Julian. I am angry. Very angry! Why was I not told that you were coming home? Why have you left Cambridge in the middle of the term?'

'It is not the middle, Mama. The term is almost over and I have urgent business to attend to.'

'If by urgent business you mean that slut Vinnie Harris—'

It was Julian's turn to step forward now, his hand raised in anger.

'Go on,' she shouted. 'Strike me! I dare you to strike me! After all these years, you raise your hand to your own mother. What sort of son are you? I will tell you. A most unnatural son – Ah! You have thought better of it.'

Julian had lowered his hand, biting his lip and vexed that he had almost lost control.

'I beg your pardon, Mama,' he said. 'You have angered me, but I will not strike you. Nevertheless, I won't hear Vinnie spoken of in that way; she does not deserve it. She has not willingly done you any harm.'

'She has done me every harm,' cried Christina, 'the worst harm one woman can do to another. She has cheapened something – someone – I held most dear.'

'Don't talk of him!' cried Eva.

'Him? If you mean Tom Bryce, I shall most certainly speak of him if I wish to. Since when have you the right to tell me what I can and cannot speak of?'

'I only meant that you might regret—'

'I regret a lot of things,' replied Christina. 'Oh, yes, I regret a great many things. I regret that I ever gave birth to such ingrates. I regret my choice of a husband. I was a fool.' She turned towards her husband. 'I thought I had married a strong man – one whom I could respect – but I was misled most cruelly. It was the uniform, you see, which lent you a dignity and power that you did not possess. Without it and without the Army, you were nothing. Not at all a man I could respect. But I kept up the pretence as long as I could.'

'Don't talk like this, Mama,' begged Eva. 'I cannot bear it. You are saying things that should never be said.'

'I speak as I feel,' said Christina. 'I have given the best years of my life to this family and you have disappointed me, each one of you. Now you seek to destroy me. Oh, yes, you do. But I shall fight you and I shall win.'

An angry spot of colour burned in each cheek and her eyes were wild. She could not stand still, but brandished the crop jerkily. 'You think I have not noticed how you have all changed towards me during these last months?' she cried. 'But I am sharper than you think. The servants, too, they are all in this with you, plotting my downfall, maybe my death.'

'Stop it!' cried Julian. 'You don't know what you are saying. This is crazy, impossible talk.'

Christina moved over to the window and stared out. Then slowly and rhythmically she began to beat the curtains with a growing fury that was terrifying. While her back was towards them, Julian whispered to his father, 'She is deranged. We must fetch the doctor.'

The old man nodded, his eyes on his wife and Julian whispered to Eva, 'Run downstairs and send Bilton for Dr Mannering. Tell him it is urgent. Explain what has happened and don't come back without him.'

As Eva made to obey, Christina swung round with the crop upraised, barring her way.

'I hear you whispering,' she cried. 'What is it now? What new trick? Oh, I can see it all very clearly.'

Eva said quietly. 'Please let me pass, Mama.'

'Where are you going?'

Eva's hesitation was obvious.

'Please let her pass, Mama,' said Julian. 'There is no reason for you to detain her.'

'I shall be the best judge of that. You shall not pass, Eva, until I know where you are going.'

'I have asked her to go downstairs and speak to Mrs Tallant,' invented Julian hastily.

'You are lying!' cried Christina. 'You are all lying. You are all of you trying to cheat me. Every way I go, I am hounded by lies and whispers and deceit. But I am stronger than you think. I know what is going on. I have eyes to see and ears to hear. Even in the village I hear them whispering, I see the shifty look in their eyes. I am shown no respect, you know that? No respect.'

Slowly she lowered the crop, but as Eva stepped forward to pass her, she raised it again and then brought it down savagely across her shoulder so that Eva gave a cry of pain and stepped back, fearfully expecting another blow. There was a shout of anger from the Colonel and Julian stepped forward, his face white and tense. He took hold of the crop, but she did not relinquish it.

'That's enough, Mama!' he snapped. 'Don't ever do that again.' He caught Eva's eye and indicated the door. Christina tried to pull the crop from his hand; her hold on it was surprisingly strong and they almost wrestled.

'Quickly, Eva!' cried the Colonel, but Eva was transfixed with horror as she watched mother and son struggle together. Slowly she backed away towards the door, but before she

could reach it Julian had possession of the riding-crop and
Christina began to pummel him wildly with her fists. Then,
with a strangled cry, Christina turned suddenly and ran for the
door, thrusting the terrified Eva out of her way as she passed.
They heard her race downstairs and then the slam of the front
door. Eva ran to Julian's arms and the old man covered his face
with his hands. For a while nobody spoke, then the Colonel
drew a deep shuddering breath and raised his hand.

'We must forgive her,' he said. 'She truly is not herself. She
needs help. Eva, please tell Bilton to ride straightaway for the
doctor and ask Janet to fetch two of my pills. I feel most
unwell.'

Julian looked down at the riding-crop in his hand and then
hurled it into the nearest armchair as though it burned his
fingers.

'You are right, Father,' he said wearily. 'We must not blame
her. She is a sick woman.'

*

Once out of the house, Christina ran to the stables. She was
sobbing wildly and from time to time cursed vehemently.
Lancer, the Colonel's big bay, still stood saddled where she
had left him, his reins through a hook on the wall. His coat
glistened with sweat and there were flecks of foam around his
mouth. She had ridden him long and hard but Bilton, in the
kitchen, was not even aware that the horse was back. The
animal eyed Christina nervously: she had beaten him and his
flank still smarted.

'Come here, you brute!' she cried and snatching the reins
from the hook, scrambled once more into the saddle. This time
she had no crop, but she slapped him hard and he sprang
forward quivering in every muscle, for it was many months
since he had been ridden and he was no longer young. She
urged him to a canter and they swept out of the stable into the
lane. Then, jerking his head savagely, she turned him again so
that they passed through the hop-gardens. His hooves
slithered on the iron-hard ground between the bare poles,
where the field sloped steeply towards the river, but somehow

Christina kept her balance. Three women who were hoeing watched their erratic progress in astonishment, but Christina was not even aware of their existence.

At the bottom of the garden she changed direction again, and for a few moments they were within sight of the Colonel's bedroom window from which Julian was watching. Then they reached the level land alongside the river and here Christina forced the bay into a gallop, taking a delight in his flowing mane and the pounding of his hooves. A solitary fisherman glanced up in surprise as they thundered towards him, then realising who it was, he raised his hat but horse and rider were already gone. They passed the spot where Sue Harris had fallen into the river and galloped on past the weir. Then she turned Lancer across the wooden bridge and left again on to a narrow path leading through the woods.

This route had been a favourite of hers in the early days of her marriage, when she and the Colonel had ridden together, but it was years since anyone had used the track. The trees, undisturbed, had spread their branches lower with each passing year and the brambles had encroached on to the path. A few hundred yards ahead of her, two branches met and intertwined over the pathway and Christina rode straight into them. For a moment the force of her momentum carried her forward, forcing the branches to give way, but then they sprang back again, locking themselves around her neck so that she was suddenly torn from Lancer's back and hung in mid-air. Her neck was broken instantly and there was mercifully no time for pain nor for the awareness that her life was ending.

Julian, finally riding in pursuit, found her still swinging, her feet only inches from the ground, her arms hanging limply by her sides. Her face, with its staring eyes, was mercifully hidden by her tangled hair.

*

Christina was buried six days later in the family grave in the little church on the hill. Almost the entire village attended. The wind blew still, coming from the east now, but although there was no rain large clouds massed overhead – hiding the sun and adding a greyness to the already sombre scene. The Colonel, badly shaken by his wife's death, was not well enough to attend the funeral, so Eva and Julian followed the coffin and in turn were followed by the Foxearth staff.

In the far corner of the churchyard the remains of a bonfire still burned, the embers kept alive by the wind and the daily addition of a few new branches. Beside it the grave-digger warmed his hands, waiting for the ceremony to end. The wind blew directly from the bonfire across the courtyard to the huddled group beside the coffin, and Eva could never smell wood-smoke again without remembering that terrible week. When the last prayers had been uttered and the group of mourners had dispersed, the grave-digger took over. Once he, too, had deserted the graveside, a solitary figure made its way unobserved across the grass between the tombstones. It was Tom Bryce, who stood for a long time gazing down at the newly-turned earth and the delicate wreaths that hid from his sight Christina's body – the body which had been offered so generously and which he had taken so often with such delight. He tried to picture the long slim legs and the sweet contours, remembering the first time they had lain together. So much warmth and passion, he thought, but now she lay cold and still in her wooden coffin and no one would enjoy that sweetness again. The less pleasant events of the last few months had all fled from his mind and with them all hatred. He was left only with a sense of pity for the once proud woman. He had no wreath to give, but plucked a small spray from the evergreen tree behind him and put it to his lips. Then, kneeling, he laid it among the flowers.

'I'm sorry,' he whispered. 'Believe me, Christina, I'm truly sorry.'

Then he rose to his feet and without a backward glance, strode from the churchyard.

CHAPTER TWENTY-THREE

Eva left the following day for Wiltshire and she and Gerald were married three weeks later. A week after that they sailed from Southampton on the first part of their journey to India.

Julian, meanwhile, had gone up to London and found himself a room in the Clarence Hotel, an unpretentious but comfortable establishment. Relying entirely on his own endeavours, he began a protracted search for Vinnie, constantly frustrated by false leads that raised his hopes only to result in failure and disappointment. After several weeks he returned to Foxearth for three days to satisfy himself that all was well in his absence, then went back to London and continued his search. He knew that Vinnie's child was due towards the end of May and he desperately wanted to find her before that event. He was almost too late.

On the 29th of May he found himself in a seedy back alley in Clerkenwell. No. 19 was reached by a short flight of worn stone steps and a rusting rail. Several children played on the steps - their bodies gaunt, their voices shrill, their language blasphemous. Julian looked up at the house and saw the dirty tattered curtains hanging at the windows. With a sinking heart, he climbed the steps and knocked on the door. After he had knocked several times, it was opened by an elderly woman who stared at him suspiciously.

'I'm looking for a young woman,' said Julian. 'She is with child and I have reason to believe—'

'You're welcome to her,' said the woman.

'You mean—'

'I mean we have got a young woman here and we don't want

her. Turned up two days ago at dead of night, scared us half to
death.'

'May I see her?' Julian was afraid to hope.

'You can have her,' the woman told him and led the way up
the stairs. The house smelt damp and there were various
articles of ragged clothing strung across the passageway to
dry. The stairway lacked lighting and the stairs themselves
were filthy.

Out of the corner of his eye, Julian saw a cockroach and then
another. Paper peeled from the walls like the withered leaves of
a plant and the banister rail was sticky with the dirt and sweat
of countless hands. They passed several doors, one of which
stood open; two men stood watching him, their expressions
hostile.

'She'd started her labour,' the woman told him. 'Doubled
up, she was, and screaming fit to burst your eardrums.
Horrible it was, to hear her. Woke the whole house.' She
paused and turned to look at him. 'You a friend of hers?'

'I hope I am,' said Julian, 'if it's who I think it is.'

'She wouldn't give no name and they was all for turning her
out, but she begged so, I hadn't the heart. I'm soft like that.
Your kid, is it?'

Julian shook his head as they made their way up the second
flight of stairs; at the top, two toddlers sat staring apathetically
at them.

'What does the doctor say?' he asked anxiously.

'Doctor? What doctor?' she laughed. 'There's no money for
doctors here. Two days she was in labour – it was pitiful to see
her.'

'You mean she has *had* the child?'

The old woman continued up the next flight of stairs, only
pausing to put a hand to her side and gasp for breath.

'It was born about two hours ago. Dead, of course. But what
can you expect? She's got "workhouse" stamped all over her.
If you're a friend of hers, you can take her out of here.'

'Dead?' repeated Julian, his voice a whisper.

'Dead as a dormouse,' she assured him. 'Little boy, it was.
Shame, really.'

An indescribable stench came from the room. It was filthy in the extreme, but Julian was hardly aware of the smell as he followed the old woman across to the bed. Beside it, he saw a roughly wrapped parcel.

'That's the kid,' she said. 'I've no money for funerals, so it's to be hoped you've got a bob or two.'

Julian did not answer. Vinnie lay on the bed in a state of exhaustion, her eyes closed, her breathing irregular.

'What's the matter with her?' said Julian. 'She looks so ill.' In his panic he shook her roughly.

'Well, don't shake the life out of her, then!' cried the old woman. ''Course she's ill. On her last gasp, I should reckon, poor kid. Two days in labour and nothing to eat but a bit of bread. *You* wouldn't look so good either, in her shoes.'

'Vinnie, speak to me!' he pleaded. 'Please Vinnie, open your eyes. Can you hear me?' He shook her gently. 'It's Julian. I have come to take you home with me, Vinnie.'

There was no response and he raised his voice slightly: 'Vinnie, answer me, I say!'

'Don't shout at her like that,' the woman reproached him. 'Can't you see she's nearly gone? There's nothing you can do for her now.'

'Don't say that,' said Julian. 'Of course there's something we can do, there must be! We must get a doctor.'

He stared round him, trying to think clearly. 'Where is the nearest doctor?'

'Don't ask me.' She turned to one of the men from downstairs who now stood in the doorway, watching. 'He wants to know where the nearest doctor is. How do I know, I've told him. I've had nothing to do with doctors.'

'A cab, then,' said Julian.

He glanced up at the man in the doorway. 'How quickly can you get me a cab?'

'What's in it for me?'

'There's a guinea in it for you.'

The man straightened himself.

'Take it,' cried Julian and he drew out a coin from his pocket. 'If you can get a cab here within five minutes—'

'It won't get up the alley,' said the man.

'Then bring it to the end of the alley, to the top entrance. If you get one here in five minutes, I will give you another guinea.'

Hastily the man disappeared and Julian turned back to the girl on the bed and took hold of her hand.

'My dearest Vinnie,' he whispered, 'don't die. Please, don't die. I have come to take you back to Foxearth but first, I'm going to take you to a doctor. Vinnie, for God's sake, open your eyes.'

'It's no good,' the woman said, not unkindly. 'You had best make up your mind to it, young man. Whatever she is to you, she isn't going to last much longer.'

Julian had a terrible suspicion that she was right, but he also felt that once he admitted it there was no hope at all. He glanced down at the parcel. That is Vinnie's child, he thought – a little boy: born dead.

'Don't you want to look at it?' the old woman asked.

He hesitated. Perhaps Vinnie would wish it. With trembling hands he unwrapped the paper. The little boy was very small and grey, curled up as though he were asleep. He was quite naked. Julian touched one tight little fist with the tip of his finger.

'Wrap it in something else,' he told the woman. 'I'll pay for it. A sheet or a cloth, as clean as you can find.' He held out a handful of coins and she snatched them greedily and began to count them.

'Count them later,' he told her. 'Wrap the child up now. You must come with me as far as the cab – and hurry, woman.'

Gently he lifted Vinnie into his arms while the woman scuttled about behind him. She produced a threadbare tablecloth and wrapped the child hastily.

'Come with me,' said Julian. 'I'll carry Vinnie. You bring the child.'

She followed without demur. Vinnie weighed so little – Julian was horrified. Slowly they made their way downstairs, followed by curious stares from the other inhabitants of the house. Still Vinnie did not open her eyes. Her arms fell loosely and her head lolled uncontrollably. Please God, let me be in time. Please don't take her from me, Julian begged silently. To his great relief there was a cab waiting; he lifted Vinnie inside and laid her across the seat before stepping down again to take the child. He gave the man another guinea as he had promised and the woman three guineas.

'And my thanks to you for all you've done for her,' he said.

'Where to, guvnor?' called the driver.

'The nearest doctor,' said Julian, 'and for God's sake hurry!'

They rattled away, Julian sitting opposite Vinnie with the dead child in his arms.

Suddenly Vinnie's lips moved. 'Julian.' He stared in disbelief, her eyes were still closed. He set down the child and crouched beside her, holding her hand.

'I'm here, Vinnie, it's Julian. I'm here beside you. Everything will be fine, I promise.'

'The baby,' she whispered and for a moment her eyes fluttered open.

'The baby is with us,' he told her. That, at least, was no lie.

Her eyes rolled upwards and then the lids came down over them.

'Vinnie!' he cried.

'The baby,' she said again. 'Baby . . . the baby . . .'

As though the effort had exhausted her, her head fell limply to one side. Feverishly Julian felt for a pulse in the thin wrist – her heart was still beating. He began to pray again. It seemed for ever that they trundled, bouncing and bumping along the cobbled streets, but at last they pulled up and stopped and Julian realised that they had left the slums behind.

''Ere we are then, guv'nor, this is it,' said the cab driver. Julian told him to wait as long as was necessary and the man laid his whip across his knee and settled himself for a sleep.

The doctor's house was an imposing building with columns on either side of the door. Julian carried Vinnie up the steps and tugged at the bell. A young maid opened the door and her eyes at once took in Vinnie's bedraggled appearance. She closed the door a little and said, 'Do you have an appointment, sir?'

'I must see the doctor,' said Julian. 'It's a matter of life or death.'

'I'm sorry, sir, but the doctor doesn't see patients without an appointment.'

'He *must* see her.'

Pushing past her, he found himself in a broad but gloomy hall. 'Please tell the doctor I must see him *at once*. I have ample funds and he will be paid the proper sum, but only if he sees us immediately.'

The girl pursed her lips crossly. 'You have no right to push in here,' she protested. 'The doctor won't see you, I've already told you.'

'And I've told *you* that I will not leave until he does. For pity's sake, can't you see this girl is dying?'

Their raised voices brought an older woman to the top of the stairs. 'What is it, Natalie?'

'It's this gentleman, ma'am. He has no appointment but refuses to leave.'

The woman came a few steps further down and – seeing Julian with his burden – gave a gasp of alarm.

'I am the doctor's wife,' she told him as she hurried towards him. 'Thank you, Natalie. You were quite right, but now you can leave the matter in my hands.'

Sulkily, the maid departed.

The doctor's wife glanced at Vinnie with a practised eye.

'She gave birth to a child a few hours ago,' Julian told her, 'and is not recovering. I beg you to ask your husband to help her.'

'Indeed I will,' she said. 'Sit on the stairs a moment. He has a patient with him.'

She knocked on another door and went in – Julian heard her speaking and a man's voice answering. She returned almost immediately.

'Bring her into the waiting-room,' she said. 'My husband will see her as soon as his patient has left.'

Vinnie was laid down and the doctor's wife felt for her pulse.

'It's very faint,' she told Julian. 'I'm afraid there is very little hope but my husband, I know, will do what he can. Where did you find her?'

Briefly he explained, saying only that she was known to him and had run away from home. She shook her head sadly. 'It looks as though you have found her too late,' she said. 'Ah, that sounds like my husband now.'

She turned back into the hall, where Julian saw the doctor making his farewells to a young man.

'Bring her in at once,' he called and once more Julian lifted the frail body into his arms and carried Vinnie into the surgery. He hovered anxiously as Vinnie was examined. He made no comment until he had finished; when he turned to them his expression was bleak.

'I'm sorry,' he said to Julian. 'I think she has only hours to live. There is nothing I can do for her. She has obviously been starving for a long time and the birth of the child has weakened her immeasurably.' He turned to his wife. 'Fetch the Reverend Sowerby,' he said. 'Give him my regards and ask him to come at once for the matter is quite urgent.'

'But there must be *something* you can do,' Julian stammered as soon as the doctor's wife had left the room. 'Something we can give her? Nourishment or a restorative, perhaps?'

The doctor shook his head. 'Not while she is in this state, I'm afraid. She is barely conscious and she would choke.'

'But we must try,' cried Julian. 'If I can rouse her in any way – can you give her something? Anything?'

He shrugged. 'If we can bring her back to consciousness, we can try her with a little warm milk and brandy.'

'Then will you prepare it and I will see what I can do?'

The doctor gave another shrug and left the room while Julian pulled up a chair beside Vinnie's. He cradled her head in his arms and began to talk to her, patting her face and hands and shaking her gently in an effort to raise her from her stupor.

Vinnie felt his fingers like the flutterings of a moth against her skin, very faint and delicate. She heard his voice from a long way off, but one which she no longer recognised. She felt without substance, as though floating in a vast darkness. Dimly she was aware that there were words she wanted to utter, but her lips refused to form them. She remembered a long pain that had mercifully ended and she made no effort to recall it, content that she no longer heard her own screams. The word 'baby' echoed occasionally in the furthermost recesses of her mind and she waited for it to cry. It seemed an eternity since the small body had been thrust from her own, yet still it did not cry out. She could no longer measure time and only knew that she waited for a sound from her child. 'A little boy.' She was certain she had heard those words, they drifted in and out of her consciousness.

Her body felt light and she fancied that she moved effortlessly. There was no pain, no fear, no misery and this was good. Fleetingly, she felt herself shaken; for a moment her new-found peace was disturbed and she frowned slightly at this interruption. The shaking came again and this time she heard a voice. She was vaguely aware of light and sound and tried once more to open her eyes. She heard the name 'Vinnie' and knew that it was her own. With a supreme effort, she opened her eyes and the bright light dazzled her, painfully.

'Vinnie!' She heard the voice more distinctly. Her head seemed to roll and there were blurred faces around her but how many she could not tell. She struggled to understand what was happening to her, then heard the name 'Julian' and a slight smile touched her lips. A bell jangled in the distance, then there were several voices and a door closing.

'Vinnie, listen to me, my dearest girl. You have some words to say. You must say them. Do you understand me, Vinnie?'

She moaned slightly, then there was a hard edge against her lips and a fiery liquid trickling down her throat, which made her splutter.

'I, Lavinia Harris—' A voice persisted.

She nodded.

'No, Vinnie, you must say the words. To please me, Vinnie.' It was Julian's voice, she knew, and for Julian she would attempt the impossible.

'I, Vinnie—'

'No. Say Lavinia Harris.'

Someone said, 'That will suffice. Do take thee—'

There was a familiar ring to the words but their exact significance eluded her.

'Say it, Vinnie. Repeat the words, *please.*'

She tried again. 'Do take thee—' Her voice sounded hoarse and insubstantial.

'Do take thee, Julian Lawrence.'

'Do. . .' Her eyes closed.

'Vinnie!'

'Julian,' she whispered. 'I love you.' If only they would leave her in peace, she thought. If only they would allow her to sleep, but the voice continued relentlessly.

'—my lawful wedded husband. Say it, Vinnie.'

'Lawful . . . husband . . .'

Fleetingly, her vision cleared and she saw Julian very distinctly. The word 'beautiful' floated in her mind and she saw the clear grey eyes under the well-shaped brows, the fine nose and gentle mouth and above them the fair hair that was as fine as silk. Julian Lawrence was as beautiful as he was gentle – two attributes which Vinnie most admired.

'Husband—' she said again and smiled at him.

Then he was holding her hand, fumbling with the fingers of her left hand but her moment's clarity had faded and it meant nothing. Julian's arms were round her as she slipped into a long darkness.

*

The next thing Vinnie heard clearly was the swish of curtains and she opened her eyes to find herself in a strange bed in a strange room. Wonderingly, she stared around, her gaze travelling over the elegant furniture and soft furnishings and up to the embossed ceiling and broad high windows. A maid at the centre window half-turned and took a step towards the third window, where the curtains were still closed, but a movement caught her eye and she looked towards the bed. The two women stared at each other: Vinnie in amazement, Janet in delight.

'Miss Vinnie, you are awake – I mean Mrs Lawrence, I should say.'

Uncomprehending, Vinnie continued to stare at her, searching for words.

'I'll tell the master,' said Janet eagerly, but Vinnie raised her hand weakly to delay her. 'I'm sorry,' she stammered. 'I don't understand – where . . .'

'You're at Foxearth. Don't you remember? I'm Janet.' Vinnie put a hand to her head. 'Foxearth?'

'Of course. Where you belong,' she added mysteriously.

'Foxearth?' Vinnie repeated.

'That's right. Master Julian brought you home nearly a week ago, but you were feverish and talking a lot of nonsense. We all thought you were going to die, but Master Julian was wonderful. He refused to give up, he simply refused to let you die.'

'To die?' said Vinnie. 'Have I been so ill?'

'Very ill.' After a slight pause she said gently, 'Don't you remember anything?'

Slowly Vinnie shook her head. Janet, seeing Vinnie's expression change to one of anxiety, remembered that her instructions had been to say nothing when at last Vinnie recovered her senses. Already, then, she had said too much.

'I'd best go and find Master Julian,' she said hastily.

'No, please!' cried Vinnie. 'I don't understand what has happened.'

'It is not for me to say, ma'am.'

This time Vinnie responded. 'Why do you call me ma'am?' she asked, but Janet was hurrying towards the door. 'I am not allowed to say,' she said again. 'Master Julian wants to tell you himself but . . .' she turned, her hand on the door, 'but I am so pleased you are recovered, ma'am. We have been that worried about you.'

'Janet!' cried Vinnie weakly, but the door had closed and she heard the maid runing along the corridor and down the stairs calling for Julian. Vinnie closed her eyes, trying to create some order from the confusion in her mind, but she was still very weak and the effort exhausted her. She let her head fall back against the pillows, thinking, 'I am at Foxearth', and knew that whatever had happened for the moment she was safe.

There were more footsteps on the stairs, then the door swung open and in three strides Julian was standing beside the bed.

'Vinnie!' he cried. Dropping to his knees, he took her hand and kissed it fiercely. 'My sweet Vinnie, I can hardly believe it. They said you would never survive. They gave you only a few hours to live and then the fever set in. Dearest Vinnie, I can't tell you how much it means to me, to see you lying there so much yourself again.'

'Julian . . .' she began helplessly, 'I am trying so hard to remember what has happened.'

'*This* has happened,' said Julian and he held up her left hand. She gasped in astonishment to see a ring on her third finger – it looked vaguely familiar.

'Have you given it to me?' she asked, bewildered.

He sat beside her on the bed. 'Vinnie, I have a confession to make,' he said. 'I don't want to shock you or make you angry, but that is your wedding ring.'

Vinnie's eyes widened with shock and he quickly continued, 'They told me that you would certainly die, but I will tell you about that in a moment. All I could think of was that we loved each other and I wanted you to be my wife.'

He stood up.

'You mean – I'm your *wife?*' Vinnie stared at him. Her chaotic thoughts were beginning to fall into place. She remembered a long pain and her eyes darkened as she glanced round the room. Julian nodded.

'Julian . . .' she began hesitantly, 'there is something else. My little boy . . .'

He sat on the edge of the bed. The moment he had dreaded had arrived. 'Yes, Vinnie,' he said softly, 'You had a little boy.'

She made an effort to sit up and her eyes were anguished as memories flooded back. 'The old woman,' she whispered. 'She said I had a son. Where—'

'I am so sorry, Vinnie,' he whispered. 'Your little boy was born dead.' He saw that painful recollections were crowding in on her and, as her lips trembled, he quickly put his arms round her.

'I didn't hear him cry,' she said. 'I waited such a long time to hear his first cry.'

'He never did cry, Vinnie.'

To his dismay, scalding tears sprang to her eyes and began to stream down her cheeks.

'That terrible place,' she sobbed. 'I did not want him to be born in that dreadful place but—'

'Don't cry,' he said. 'Please don't cry, Vinnie. Your little son never saw that dreadful place. I saw him, Vinnie. His eyes were tight-closed.'

'You saw him?' She stopped crying abruptly and looked up at him. 'What was he like?' she whispered.

Julian dared not hesitate, although in fact his glimpse of the baby had been very brief and he remembered almost nothing.

'He was very small,' he told her. 'Curled up as though he was asleep. He looked very peaceful.'

'And his hair? Did he have any hair?'

'His hair was gold like yours. Very fine.'

'Like mine.' She seemed slightly comforted.

'I brought him home to Foxearth, Vinnie, and he is buried in the Lawrences' grave. I knew you would prefer that. So your little boy is at peace. He knew no unhappiness – and we buried him gently.'

Some of the horror faded from her face. She thought for a moment longer and then asked, 'Did you give him a name?'

Julian nodded. 'I called him Bertram, after your brother. I thought you would like that.'

'Bertie. That's nice. Yes, I like that.'

He sat back a little, holding her hands. 'I suddenly remembered you standing in the hop-garden all those years ago.' He mimicked her, 'I am Lavinia Harris and my brother is Bertram Harris and my sister is Emmeline Harris.'

Vinnie laughed shakily. 'I don't remember that.'

Julian smiled. 'But I do,' he told her, 'I remember everything about you from the moment I first saw you.'

'I am Lavinia Harris,' she repeated. 'My brother is Bertram Harris,' her voice broke, but she went on, 'and my sister is Emmeline Harris.'

'But now it's "Lavinia Lawrence",' he said. 'And your husband is Julian Lawrence.'

She put up a hand to touch his face. 'Poor Lavinia Lawrence,' she said, 'she can't even remember her wedding day.'

'We will be married again,' he promised. 'In church. But before that, when you are stronger, I will take you to your little boy's grave. And Vinnie, we'll have another son one day and a daughter – and then another son! Oh, Vinnie, the bad times are past, I swear it!' For a moment he held her at arms' length, then gently pulling her towards him, he kissed each tear-stained eye, and the poor trembling mouth.

'I'll make you so happy,' he said, 'there will be no time for grieving.'